THE RETURN

Volkov bent down to the driver. 'You'll have to circle round and come back; we want to keep the route clear. I'll go with you.'

He hurried round to the other side of the car, opened the passenger door and got inside. He gestured impatiently ahead. 'Go on, drive on!' The chauffeur only hesitated for a moment; the habit of obedience to authority was so strong that he had started the engine and moved off within a few seconds.

'Go round,' Volkov ordered; they swept forward and round the curve of the square. The man felt something suddenly ram into his side; he swerved slightly in alarm, and then he saw it was a gun. 'Keep going,' Volkov said, 'Do anything funny and I'll blow your guts out. Turn down here – now!'

Also in Arrow by Evelyn Anthony

Arrow Books Limited
62 – 65 Chandos Place, London WC2N 4NW

An imprint of Century Hutchinson Limited

London Melbourne Sydney Auckland
Johannesburg and agencies throughout
the world

First published by Hutchinson 1978
Arrow edition 1979
Reprinted 1985 and 1987

Printed and bound in Great Britain by
Anchor Brendon Ltd,
Tiptree, Essex

ISBN 0 09 920340 5

EVELYN ANTHONY

The Return

ARROW BOOKS

To my son Ewan
and to Ralph and Despina Sassoon
with my love

I

The traffic at six o'clock was dense and slow moving; it was the worst part of the rush hour which nightly frayed the nerves of anyone travelling through the centre of Paris in a car.

By Friday afternoon, the rush to the country for the weekend had begun; it was strange how avidly the conservative French had adopted the English custom, left over from a more gracious age, when the exit to green fields and fresh air was smooth and unhurried. Now the fugitive from the noise and pollution of the city arrived exhausted and unnerved. It was a long time since Anna Campbell Martin had spent a weekend in Paris. She had woken up that Friday morning with a feeling of disquiet which was quite untypical. She was not, and she had spent her life proving it, a temperamental person.

She hadn't quarrelled with Nicholas. He had taken her out to dinner and they had spent the night in her apartment as usual. He had bought her flowers, great bunches of sweet-smelling white narcissi; the scent was strong in the flat when they awoke.

He was a very affectionate lover, always touching her with tenderness, telling her how beautiful she was and how much she meant to him. It was as if he knew exactly how deeply her marriage had undermined her self-confidence. It had done more; it had left her without any faith in the fidelity of anyone who said they loved her. And this was the fourth time in six weeks that he had changed their plans without a really satis-factory explanation. He had told her the night before, after they had made love, and she noted this unhappily, that he couldn't go down to Rambouillet with her that afternoon. 'But why, darling? We always go down together . . .'

She had tried to hide the disappointment from him. They had spent every weekend at the Auberge St-Julien since they met and became lovers. Twice he had cancelled going on Friday, making the excuse that he had business. This time she waited for the explanation. He had very blue eyes and they were clear and innocent of deceit when he answered.

'I have a very difficult author, darling. I promised to go through the typescript and let her have my suggestions by Monday. I can't possibly work if I'm with you. I shall spend Friday in the office and we can drive down on Saturday morning. Please, don't be angry with me. If you knew the lady and her books, you wouldn't think it was from choice!' He was difficult to argue with, difficult to blame when he smiled at her, and held her hand to his lips, kissing it gently. A very sensuous man, of whose passion she was still a little afraid. Sex hadn't brought her any happiness until she met Nicholas. Six months ago, at a publishing party where she had known very few people and everybody else appeared to know each other, he had come over to her, when she found herself alone for a few moments brought her a drink and quietly taken her by the arm as though she had always belonged to him. That was the beginning.

There was a curiously old-fashioned quality about his court-ship; the word was the only apt description of the way their relationship developed. He was always gentle with her, as if he understood that she was vulnerable, even before she told him the dismal story of squalid adulteries and disillusion which characterized her marriage. He was very much a man of the present day, and yet there was a quality about him which did not quite belong. She supposed it was because he was a Russian. And then, at the beginning of the month, he had asked her to marry him. It had been a proposal quite unlike any other, and there had been other serious contenders for her, before the one when she finally said, 'Yes, yes, I'll marry you' – eight long years ago. . . .

'I've wanted to ask you for a long time,' he had said, looking into her eyes in the intent way that he had. 'But I wanted to be sure you were ready. I wanted you to know I loved you.

You do know that, don't you?' Anna had nodded, close to silly tears.

'I haven't any money,' he said. 'But I earn quite enough to keep you comfortably. I want you to belong to me, as completely as I shall belong to you. Will you trust me to make you happy?' She had clung to him and cried, and she had seen the blazing happiness on his face as he kissed her. But still the doubts niggled, the habit of insecurity was too ingrained to disappear. Why had he decided to work on the author's typescript that Friday, so throwing their weekend out of gear? Why not the day before – it was always a Friday when he changed their arrangements and the excuse was usually the same. Work on this or that manuscript. The mocking shade of her first husband grinned cynically at her from the subconscious. She hadn't been enough for *him*; why should Nicholas be satisfied . . . of course he loved her but then wasn't she very, very rich . . .?

They were murmurs, angrily suppressed, but strong enough to make her insist that they should meet at the Auberge St-Julien late on Friday night. There was no reason to wait till Saturday. She hated Paris at the weekend; it was such a joy to get out into the country, to take their long walks, to enjoy the homely comfort of the Auberge itself. She hadn't quarrelled or argued, but it had been made an issue, and she felt instinctively that she was in the wrong. He had agreed to drive down when his work were finished, and meet her there. She spent the morning restless and reproachful of herself, and then determined to go down early anyway, just to get away from the apartment.

When the telephone rang she thought it was Nicholas and she ran to pick it up. But it wasn't Nicholas. It was a voice she hadn't heard for a long time, and in spite of everything, the colour rushed into her face and then receded. She hadn't driven down to Rambouillet; she had stayed in Paris and it was now after six o'clock and she was on her way to keep an appointment that she had made in spite of herself, and only because Nicholas's name was mentioned.

She didn't take her car; she lived in a flat in the Avenue

Gabriel. It was the most expensive and exclusive residential pocket in the city, a superb eighteenth-century *hôtel particulier* which had been beautifully converted. That was one of the very few advantages of being Sheila Campbell's daughter; money was not a problem. Anna walked down the Rue St-Honoré to the Ritz, pausing to look in the shop windows, not because she wanted to buy anything, but because subconsciously she was delaying her arrival. Several men turned to look after her; despite ten years spent in Paris, five of them married to a Frenchman, she looked a foreigner.

Too tall for a Parisienne, her blonde hair worn casually to her shoulders, with a swinging walk, she wore the casual clothes that did not date. No ethnic look, no fashion extravagances; just the cool, thrown-together effect that is only achieved by spending a fortune.

It was exactly six-thirty as she turned into the Place Vendôme and crossed over to the Ritz. He was waiting for her in the bar; she saw him sitting at a banquette, a glass of whisky in front of him, and a cigarette hanging from the side of his mouth. He was reading *Le Figaro*.

A thin, slight man, with dark hair growing back from a wide forehead. Very dark eyes under heavy lids; a face usually described by women as sexy. She had been married to him for five years, and divorced from him for three. He looked up as she came towards him. He dropped the paper on the seat beside him, deposited the cigarette into an ashtray, and stood up. They shook hands; he wasn't the sort of Frenchman who kissed a woman's hand. An individualist, Paul Martin, a brilliant journalist with one of the big French left-wing political magazines, not by any stretch of the word a gentleman. A lover of good living, good conversation, and above all, of women. There had been so many women during Anna's marriage that she had lost count. Yet he had always insisted that he loved her.

'Anna – you're looking marvellous! Sit down. What will you drink, still Scotch?'

'No, thanks,' Anna said. 'Vodka. On the rocks.'

The dark eyes mocked her. 'A sign of the times, eh?'

She ignored the remark. He offered her a cigarette: she shook her head. 'Not for a moment, Paul. How are you?'

He shrugged. 'Busy, but otherwise the same. You know, it's a year or more since I've seen you – you look more attractive as you get older.'

'Thanks,' Anna said. 'I've still got my own teeth.' He burst out laughing.

'Darling,' he said. 'I never could say the right thing, could I – never mind. Here's your vodka. It was nice of you to come and meet me.'

'You made it sound so interesting I couldn't refuse,' Anna said. She looked at him. 'You said it was very important, Paul. I changed my arrangements for the weekend just to see you. What is it? And why all the secrecy – why did we have to come here instead of meeting at my flat?'

He leaned a little forward, his hands drooping between his knees; he was a man who moved loosely, and seemed totally relaxed when he was still. He had an animal quality about him, and she could see it quite dispassionately now. When they first met she had been blindly in love with him.

'Neutral ground,' he said slowly. 'If you're being followed. Nobody can listen to us here.'

Anna stared at him. 'What nonsense! What on earth would anyone want to follow me for – you can't be serious!'

'I'm perfectly serious,' he said. 'You have been living with Nicholas Yurovsky since January, haven't you – yes, well, if the KGB haven't got on to you, then you can be sure that the SDECE have. Perhaps the CIA. They're so clumsy you'd have noticed, so it's probably the other two. I know you don't like criticism of the Americans, darling, but they are the worst intelligence service in the world.'

'Would you stop calling me darling,' she said angrily. 'This isn't funny.'

'No, it isn't,' he said. He looked at her for a moment; she had changed colour. There was a flush under the tan.

'How much do you know about Yurovsky? I'm not playing the jealous ex-husband,' he said quietly. 'I'm really acting as your friend. Believe that.' He reached out and held her hand for a moment. Anna drew hers away.

'Nicholas has asked me to marry him and I've said I will. He works for Wedermans. We met at a party after Christmas.'

'I see,' Paul Martin said. 'Wedermans is a very good publisher, prestige books, high-class artwork – it's noted for its bright young men. Tell me, has he ever talked politics to you?'

'No,' Anna said. 'Never. He's not in the least interested. Paul, why can't you get to the point of all this? What are you trying to say – ?'

He didn't answer; he signalled the waiter, and ordered them both another drink, ignoring Anna's protest that she didn't want one.

'Nicholas Yurovsky is exactly what you say,' he said at last. 'The son of a White Russian army officer, born in France, educated here. Very intelligent, with a lot of charm. One of the brightest editors at Wedermans. No political affiliations at all. Except one.' He paused, there was a serious look in the dark eyes, and the full mouth, usually twisted in a mocking smile, was set and grim.

'He's a leading anti-Soviet activist. There's a group of them. They didn't cause any trouble till he joined. There's a lot of money involved suddenly: the word is out, Anna, that the money is coming from you. Is it?'

She squared herself to face him. He had always found her money an embarrassment. It was one of the main causes of friction between them. He had never understood that she couldn't help being Sheila Campbell's daughter.

'I've never given Nicholas a centime. I've never heard anything so crazy in my life.'

He watched her for a moment. He lit another cigarette. 'They've always been a pain in the neck, these Russians. They got what was coming to them in 1917, and they were damned lucky to get out alive. They've made trouble ever since. During the war, plenty of trouble. You're probably being watched because you're mixed up with Yurovsky. You're a very rich woman and they think you're giving him money. You're getting into something very nasty; something dangerous.'

'I see,' Anna said quietly. 'So "they", whoever they are, have sent you to talk me out of whatever I'm supposed to be doing – is that it? Frighten me away from Nicholas. Who are "they", Paul? Your left-wing friends, or just the thugs in the SDECE?'

'You're right,' he said. 'They are thugs. I should remember that. Anna, please listen to me. I hear a lot of things, and I have contacts. Nobody put me on to you – I decided to talk to you myself. For old times' sake, if you like. I loved you very much, though you wouldn't believe it. I don't want anything to happen to you.'

'And if I marry Nicholas something might?'

'Being the wife of a leading anti-Soviet political activist could be extremely dangerous,' he said and his voice was low. 'And not just from the Russians. Anna, I can't make you understand. The big boys are beginning to look at Yurovsky and that's bad news. All right, you love him. He hasn't told you the truth about himself. That ought to make you hesitate. That's all I'm suggesting. Hesitate. Don't rush into anything.'

'I don't know why I should believe you,' Anna said slowly.

'Because you know I never lied to you,' he said.

Anna stood up and they faced each other. There was something in his eyes she didn't want to see. Some depth reminding her of how he used to look at her, so many years ago. Before her family's attitude and his resentment of their social differences had started to turn their love to friction. His revenge had been terribly damaging; it had needed someone like Nicholas Yurovsky to restore the shattered self-confidence which was Paul Martin's legacy. The first affair began within a year of her marriage. He had needed to be unfaithful in order to keep his self-respect for having married an American socialite with a fortune, the daughter of a famous right-wing publisher Sheila Campbell, in defiance of his own background and political convictions. He had betrayed himself and his remedy was to betray her. She didn't hold out her hand. She felt the same old feeling of sick uncertainty, as if suddenly the clock hands had spun backwards, and she was still involved with him. Nicholas, Nicholas, her mind cried out the name – this is just a memory.

'I don't believe you,' she said. 'I shall tell Nicholas exactly what you've told me.'

'He'll deny it,' Paul Martin said. 'But it's true. He's bringing you into danger. Real danger, and he'll use you too.'

She turned and walked away. He spoke to her back.

'Goodbye, Anna. Take care of yourself.'

She didn't answer; she walked out into the foyer of the hotel, ignoring the reception clerk who smiled at her. She was well known there; her mother took a suite whenever she came to Paris. One of her former husbands had been a French duke.

She began to hurry back along the Rue St-Honoré, brushing against people in her haste. It was seven-thirty and the traffic was less concentrated. If she drove down immediately she would get to Rambouillet and the Auberge St-Julien around nine o'clock. Nicholas wasn't expecting her until late.

She went up to her first-floor apartment and hurried through to the bedroom. For a woman whose taste in clothes was casual, even austere, the decoration of the flat was surprisingly feminine. Soft pastel colours, a mixture of beautiful Louis Seize furniture and elegant modern sofas, Constable watercolours, and a glowing Van Ostade still life in the dining room. As a person, Anna had perfected an image which was in direct contrast to the ultra female represented by her mother. Crisp, almost boyish, the side of her personality which was deliberately thwarted was expressed in her bedroom. There was a *Directoire* bed, swathed in green silk, an Aubusson carpet, Boucher drawings of erotic subjects, extravagant flowering plants.

She had supervised every detail herself, just before her marriage to Paul Martin came to an end. It was almost a compensation for the endless infidelities to spend so much money on such a superbly sensual room. Paul had laughed at her; sitting on the bed, smoking as always, he had bounced gently up and down.

'It's hard, sweetheart and for two people it's not going to be very comfortable.' She hadn't intended to do what she did. It seemed to happen, as if everything in her life at that moment slotted into place.

'It isn't for two people,' she said. 'It's for one. I'm going to divorce you. Please get up; you're creasing the cover.'

He had left the apartment that night. It was the only time she felt that she had come out best in a situation since she married him.

The night Nicholas Yurovsky became her lover he had looked round the bedroom, taking time to appreciate everything, and then turned to her. 'It is beautiful,' he said. 'Like you.'

By the morning, Paul and his secretaries and colleagues' wives and girlfriends, might never have existed. Anna looked quickly at herself in the mirror. She had packed what she needed for the quiet country weekend that was her joy with Nicholas, and she looked at herself anxiously. He said he loved her face; he would run his fingers over it, touching her eyelids, tracing her mouth, making love to her with every movement. She had shadows under the eyes, a tense expression that made her look older. She brushed her hair, powdered the fine skin, lightly tanned from the previous weekend in the country, put on some lipstick because her mouth seemed too pale, and then rubbed it off again. Her hand shook, and this made her angry. Nicholas hated her to make up obviously; she had never set out to please any man until she met him. Now everything she did was geared to keeping him in love with her.

'Dangerous.' That was the word Paul had used about her position as Nicholas's wife. The wife of a leading anti-Soviet activist. It didn't make sense. Nothing he had said related to the Nicholas Yurovsky that she knew.

He had never mentioned politics; he never talked about his origins or his family, or showed any interest in the past. He didn't use his title. She had met several groups of his friends, mostly in the literary or artistic world, and there hadn't been a single Russian among them. And yet there had been anxiety in Paul Martin's eyes, and with all his glaring faults as a husband, lying or exaggeration was not among them. She stood staring at herself, not seeing the reflection. He's bringing you into danger, real danger. Paul had talked of others besides Nicholas – an influx of money that was presumed to come from her. . . . It was all quite crazy. Paul had always been mixed up in politics, it was his profession to know people and to hear things denied to the outside world.

She couldn't believe it. She couldn't believe Nicholas was involved in something dangerous and subversive. 'He'll use you –' Paul knew how to probe a weakness. Her money, her family connections, the doubt instilled into her since childhood that she couldn't take friendships or even love at face value. Remember who you are. . . . That was the best aspect of marriage to Paul in the beginning. He not only didn't want her money, he actively hated it. Anti-Soviet activity. The very idea of a group of White Russians, descendants of the old émigrés who had fled with their lives after the Revolution, pitting themselves against the Soviet Union, was pathetic; not dangerous. But she couldn't discount Paul's fear, and the menace of that remark, 'The big boys are beginning to look at Yurovsky –'

Anna had lived long enough in Paul's world to know what that would mean. It seldom happened that the rival intelligence services combined against a common objective, but if they did, the consequences were merciless. Accidents, beating-up, unsolved murders. Prison sentences procured by deliberate framing of criminal cases – she had heard Paul talk about the methods, and viewed his complacency with horror. He had shrugged. Politics were dirty, intelligence was dirtier still. He had stopped talking to her about his work because she couldn't sympathize or accept his standards of judgement. But she hadn't forgotten. And this was threatening Nicholas. Nicholas, with his cultivated mind and gentle charm, his strength and integrity. She picked up her handcase, and was annoyed with herself for having to blink away tears. This was no time for emotionalism; she had to be calm and patient and wait till she could talk to him. Everything would become simple when they were together. It was the keynote of their relationship. They loved each other, and they lived for each other. She had no secrets from him. He would have none from her. They would discuss the problem together and she would help him come to the right decision. The only decision, if they were to marry and have children. Nicholas loved children; they had discussed this early on, and he had said that he wanted a family. It hadn't been an issue with Paul; she hadn't felt secure enough even to think of pregnancy. But she wanted to have Nicholas's children, to make a home.

She hurried out and down to her car. The worst of the rush hour was over and she was soon speeding on her way out of Paris, on the road to Rambouillet.

The Auberge St-Julien was famous for its provincial cooking; it could accommodate a dozen people, in old-fashioned, comfortable bedrooms and it was a favourite place for Sunday lunch. It was surrounded by the forest of Rambouillet, once the hunting ground of the French kings, and still the haunt of stags. Nicholas had taken Anna there soon after they met; it was very quiet and casual, a perfect place to relax after a week spent in the hectic city atmosphere. He liked the trees and the sounds of the forest; he took her for long walks down the shaded rides, cut for the hunt to follow during the season. The green-ness and silence was soothing; they walked with their arms around each other's waists, like very young people in love. Anna's head leaning against his shoulder; he was very tall.

The proprietor was a thin, bustling man, who spent most of his time in the kitchen, and waited personally on his guests. His wife, known as Elise, was fat and talkative, and lived behind the bar.

She was in her usual place when Anna walked in that night. 'Madame Martin! Monsieur said you wouldn't be down till late – we were going to wait up for you. Pierre! Take Madame's case upstairs!'

Anna hesitated. There was no separate dining room: lounge, bar and tables were all together. She couldn't see Nicholas.

'Where is M. Yurovsky? – I'll go to the room . . .'

'He's not there, Madame,' Elise said. 'He went out immediately after he'd had dinner. Come and have a drink. He won't be long.'

Anna nodded. 'I'll be down in a minute. He's probably gone for a walk. You know how he loves your woods.'

Elise watched her go upstairs. It wouldn't do to have a

lovers' quarrel. She had a large glass of Pernod below the level of the bar. She sipped it; from the time the first customers came for a drink until they closed up for the night, that glass was never empty. It was said to induce madness and death in the addict.

Elise had never been drunk in her life; she had inherited her father's immunity to alcohol. She could remember him in drinking sessions with some of his old friends, and he was always standing at the end. How her mother had disapproved. But then, being a little bourgeoise, she couldn't be expected to understand a man like Elise's father. Elise had seen the disappointment in the American girl's face. She decided to give her a drink on the house.

Anna changed her clothes in the double bedroom; she felt hot and crumpled after the drive. Nicholas had unpacked; his suit was hanging in the wardrobe, the shoes neatly arranged below. His comb and hairbrush were on the dressing table, and he had emptied his pockets of the clutter of urban life. His apartment keys, a little leather folder with credit cards and driver's licence, loose change, a gold pen which she had given him, two paper clips and an old-fashioned gold fob watch on a chain. Anna looked at it. She had never seen him wear it. She picked it up and turned it over. There was a crest engraved on the back, rubbed thin by years of handling. It was a shield with many quarterings, surmounted by a coronet. He never used the title of Count Yurovsky, or mentioned his family or their background in Tsarist Russia.

He was entirely a man of the present day, a successful editor in a prestige publishing house. He had never shown the least interest or involvement with the past. It was quite out of character to find this relic of a past age among his daily possessions. She must have held it tighter than she realized, pressing the top of the key winder, because the back half of it suddenly fell open. There was a photograph inside it, carefully covered with a tiny disc of glass. A man's head, showing a line of collar buttoned high and to the side; Anna looked at it under the lamp.

It was a handsome face, immediately familiar because of the

18

high cheekbones and the set of the eyes. Hair brushed back and worn very short, a mouth set in a slight smile. Nicholas, and yet not Nicholas. The print was faded with age. She closed the watch, and put it back on the dressing table. She felt ashamed for having looked at it, for having found something which he had never shown her.

It had never been left lying around when they were together at weekends or in her flat. The man in the tiny photograph could have been a grandfather, or his own father. There was no mistake about the likeness, or the Russian dress. She felt irritated with herself as well as guilty. There was no reason to suppose that he always carried it with him. No reason to suspect him of concealing it when he might easily have brought it out to show her.

She sat at the bar and drank a glass of wine with Elise, not listening to the flow of talk, watching the door for him to come. She saw by her watch that it was close to ten o'clock; the time she had said she would arrive. The tables were empty; people were not encouraged to stay too late at the St-Julien; two couples lingered over coffee on the sofas round the fire. Elise's nervy little husband was giving them the bill. Anna's back ached from sitting upright on the stool. She turned away from the door, and finished her wine.

'I think I'll go to bed,' she said to Elise, and then she saw the older woman smile, looking beyond her, and at that moment she felt his hands on her shoulders and his face bending down to her cheek.

'My darling, I'm sorry – have you been here long?' Anna turned to him, slipped off the stool and into his arms. The eyes were so blue, so full of love and concern for her; the overhead light shone on his hair which was as fair as her own. Suddenly she was happy, excited.

'I came down early,' she said. 'I've been talking to Elise and drinking lovely cold wine.' He took her arm and they went upstairs; the fat lady watched them and smiled. He was so full of charm: the girl hadn't even asked him where he'd been.

In the bedroom he undressed her; he was demanding without losing the tenderness that enhanced their erotic life.

He told her endlessly how beautiful and exciting she was, and encouraged her to express her own passion in a way which Paul Martin had never done. Anna had never thought of having sex with Nicholas. It was simply making love. She told him she'd had a drink with Paul and avoided giving any details. Tomorrow was time enough to face reality. She fell asleep at last, lying so close to him that their bodies were entwined, the expression of serenity and tenderness on her face making her really beautiful. Nicholas lit a cigarette; the Russian tobacco was strong. Her head was on his shoulder, the long hair like strands of yellow silk. He looked down at her.

There was a shining honesty about her which he had never found in a woman before. No feminine twists and turns to gain advantage, no petty vanity. She had given everything of herself with total generosity. She had been sad, when he met her, in a subdued way, without really knowing it. Not a woman to go from one man to the next, too sensitive to enjoy casual encounters. Proud, and inclined to stand aloof. But lonely. He had sensed all these things, and taken time to get to know her. Time to lead her to love rather than follow the current trend and pull back the bedclothes the first night. He was surprised in himself; he liked women but he had never been in love with any of them. Long before he became her lover, he had thought of marrying Anna.

Nothing less than a total commitment would satisfy him. He knew that whatever her ex-husband had said had upset her. He had felt the tension in her body, seen a look of uneasiness in her eyes. Martin had been jealous, of course. Trying to make trouble while pretending to be concerned for her. Nicholas could imagine what had been said. A White Russian without any money, hooking a rich American wife. The classic pattern, a tired old cliché in pre-war society. She knew nothing about him, she was making a fool of herself. He could hear it all. It wouldn't be too difficult to deal with. He would ridicule it, destroy it, convince her that Martin's motives weren't to be trusted. Mercifully, she had never equated her personal worth with money; she hated display, wore no jewellery or expensive furs. She was quite unspoiled; she didn't indulge herself in extravagances, or challenge a man to keep up with her standards. She wasn't the kind of woman, and Nicholas had known a few, to whom it was impossible to give a present because they already had everything.

He didn't want her money. He wanted her. He stubbed out the cigarette; gently he eased his arm free of Anna and pulled the covers over her to keep her warm. His mind left her and traced back to the house he had visited in the early part of the evening, thinking her still in Paris. It hadn't been an easy meeting. It had taken all his authority and persuasive power to hold the more violent in check.

Finally he slept too, his arm thrown protectively across her, he was restless, murmuring in his sleep. When Anna awoke he was already up and in the bathroom. She sat up in bed and stretched; he had pulled back the curtains and the sun was shining outside. A branch in full leaf waved across the window, heavy with wistaria blossom.

It was going to be a lovely day. She got up to brush her hair, inspect herself in the mirror so that she would look fresh when he came back.

The gold fob watch had gone from the dressing table.

It was a very warm day, and they ate their lunch on the terrace outside. He was in a very gay mood, teasing her for being silent. Suddenly he became serious. 'What's the matter, darling? You're not yourself. You haven't told me why Paul wanted to see you last night. Is that what's upset you? What happened?'

Anna hesitated. This was the moment she hadn't been able to bring about herself. The moment to tell him what Paul had said and hear him dismiss it as ridiculous. Which he would, of course. All she had to do was ask. . . .

'Would it be easier,' he said gently, 'if I told you what he wanted?' She stared at him, caught off balance.

'Do you know?'

'I think so,' he said. He smiled at her; his eyes were very blue in the bright sunlight. 'He wanted to warn you against marrying me. A Russian, with no money and some bogus title – I'm sure he mentioned that – he was only trying to protect you against some unscrupulous foreigner who was after your money. Am I right, darling?'

'No,' Anna said. 'Not quite . . . he didn't run you down.'

'Only by inference,' he said. 'He's a clever fellow, your ex-husband. Very sophisticated and *rusé*. He's right to be suspicious, of course. You're a very eligible woman, my darling. What a lovely day! Don't let it worry you – I'm not offended. Tell me, when is your mother coming over?'

'In three weeks,' Anna said. 'I got a letter on Thursday. She's not an easy woman, Niki. She was so hostile to Paul that he never got over it. I don't want her being high-handed with you.'

'She won't be,' he said. 'It was easy for a grand American lady to make someone like Paul Martin feel uncomfortable. She can't do the same to me. I want to meet her and I want her to approve. Our wedding is going to be a happy occasion for everybody, a day for both our families. I have some Russian cousins, the Vorontzovs – they all want to meet you. There's a cousin or two on my mother's side. I want to invite them all. What about your father – will he come over?'

'I don't know,' she said. 'My mother's quite friendly with him. She makes a point of keeping up with all her ex-husbands.'

'Don't be so bitter about her,' he said gently. 'You never mention her except to make some criticism. There's nothing stronger than the blood tie.'

'Not in my family,' Anna said. She didn't want to talk about her mother, or about their wedding. She couldn't dismiss Paul from her mind. The opportunity to ask Nicholas for an explanation was slipping away in comparative trivialities. She felt almost panicked into saying something before it was too late.

'Niki – tell me something. Are you involved in politics?' It came out so abruptly that she reddened. It sounded almost accusatory. He was drinking coffee; he paused and put the cup down. There was no change in his expression except for a flicker in the eyes which vanished so quickly she could well have imagined it.

'Politics? What sort of politics?'

'Anti-Soviet,' Anna said. 'That's what Paul wanted to see

me about. He said you were in great danger, and I could be because we were living together.' She stopped, wishing that he would look at her. He finished his coffee. His silence was so inhibiting that she found herself stumbling over the words.

'He called you an anti-Soviet activist. I told him the whole idea was crazy and I didn't believe a word of it. He even asked me if I was giving you money –' He looked up at her and smiled: it was a half smile, slightly crooked and it gave his face a look of sharp cynicism.

'You were able to put him right on that, at least.'

'Nicholas, please – he went on and on about you. Is this true?'

'I suppose it depends on what you mean by an anti-Soviet activist,' he said quietly. 'Let's have some brandy. Elise?'

She came waddling over and he ordered two Armagnacs.

'There are anti-Soviet activists in the Soviet Union,' he said; he swilled the brandy round in his glass. 'But they're all in prison or labour camps. There are deviants, of course. That word used to apply to sexual perverts, but it's used now to describe anyone who differs from the official party line. The West calls them dissidents.'

'You're not answering me,' Anna said.

'If you're asking me am I anti-Soviet,' he said, 'then the answer is yes. I am certainly anti the system that murdered my family and drove them out of Russia. If your ex-husband wants to make something sinister out of that, then I can't help it. Drink your brandy, darling. And stop looking so intense. Can't you see that he's just trying to make trouble?'

Anna shook her head. 'No,' she said slowly. 'I tried to convince myself it was just jealousy, but it's not. Paul isn't that sort of person. He said you were in great danger, that some of the top people in SDECE were interested in you. Probably the Russians too. I really believe he was worried for me, and that was his only motive.'

'Which is exactly what he wanted you to think,' Nicholas said. 'Tell me, was he always so honest, so unselfish? I didn't get that impression before from what you told me.'

Since they met at the beginning of the year they had spent

all their spare time together, they had gone for a ten-day skiing holiday in the Italian Alps and they spent every weekend alone. But the man sitting opposite to her had become a stranger. The face was a mask, in which the eyes were cold and secretive; his upper lip was white with anger. 'He's lied to you,' she could hear Paul's voice. 'He'll use you, too . . .'

'If you love me,' she said quietly, 'you'll stop being furious and you'll tell me the truth.'

'If I said it was a pack of lies, would you accept that? – no, you wouldn't, would you? – you are really asking me to say yes, I am doing whatever Paul Martin says I'm doing. Actually, I am going to bomb the Kremlin from a hot-air balloon next Thursday morning. He can run to his Secret Service friends with that. You know, darling, I could sue Martin for this story? What do you suppose Raoul Wederman would think if it got round that one of his senior editors was mixed up in some political mess!'

'Nicholas,' she said helplessly, 'Nicholas darling, you know you can trust me, please. Last night I found a gold watch in our room. I didn't mean to, but I opened it. There was a picture inside of a man. It was so like you I got quite a shock. I'd no idea you had such a thing, or carried it around. You've never talked about your family, you've never shown any sentiment about your background. Why did you put it away this morning?'

He looked at her. 'Because it's something very private,' he said quietly. 'Something I don't leave lying around. It was my father's watch and that's his picture inside it. It was given to me by a friend of my father's when I was eight years old. There's nothing sinister in a son carrying his father's watch.'

'No,' she admitted. 'But I don't see why you should keep it hidden. You've never even mentioned your father. You talked about Russian cousins today. I didn't know you had any family over here.'

'Oh yes,' Nicholas said. 'A number of the aristocracy escaped during the Revolution. They didn't succeed in killing us all.'

The sun was very hot; the air still. Anna closed her eyes for a moment. He was lying and she knew it. 'Us.' It was only a slip, that corporate description of the émigrés who fled to Europe when the Bolsheviks seized total power, but it jarred on her. The cold, set face, that curt voice, dismissing everything with a sneer, was not the same man as the lover who had held her with passion and tenderness the night before. He was not only angered, but frightened by what she had said.

'It's getting very hot,' she said. 'I think I'll go up and rest.'

'I should, Madame.' She turned quickly, startled, and found the fat woman, Elise, standing beside the table.

'More coffee, before you go?' She asked Nicholas the question.

'No,' he said. 'I'll have another Armagnac. Won't you have one too, darling? It'll help you sleep.'

She shook her head. She didn't want him to see the tears in her eyes. She felt sick and hurt, and underneath there was a current of fear. Paul hadn't lied. It was Nicholas who was lying to her.

'I'll go now,' she said. He reached out and caught her hand as she passed him. The expression on his face was familiar again, tender and a little anxious.

'You have a rest,' he said gently. 'And be a good girl. Forget all that nonsense. Journalists love making up dramas. Especially when they're still in love with their ex-wives. I'll come and wake you in an hour and we'll go for a walk. There's a new restaurant about six kilometres away – I think we might have dinner there.'

He brought her hand up to his mouth and kissed it. Anna released herself and hurried inside. Nicholas lit a cigarette; Elise came back with the brandy and busied herself collecting the coffee cups on a tray. She didn't look at him.

'I saw Madame Martin come inside just now; she looked upset. Is anything wrong between you?'

'No,' he said.

'It's not for me to say,' the fat woman muttered, 'but it's a pity you brought her here – just at this time.'

'I know it is.' Nicholas looked at her, and she glanced down quickly. 'But she knows nothing and she won't be told anything. And you're right, Elise, it's not for you to say.'

'Yes,' she said. 'Yes, Count. Forgive me.' She hurried away.

They dined at the restaurant Nicholas had found; it was a small, unpretentious place but though the menu wouldn't have disgraced Maxim's in Paris, Anna didn't feel like eating. They sat opposite each other, divided by a single candle, and she looked at him as he studied the wine list.

The resemblance to the man in the little photograph was more striking in the subdued light; he had hidden his father's watch; his excuse that it was very private didn't make sense. It was almost an insult to her. And that remark, about the aristocracy during the Revolution.

'They didn't succeed in killing us all.' 'Us.' Was that really how he saw himself, in the secret places of his mind, a man born in France with a French mother whose only link with Russia was an émigré grandmother who had died in a nursing home and the cousins he had suddenly mentioned. The man she loved had no connection with what was literally past history. He was cultivated, a charming Frenchman, whose circle of friends was wholly French and largely intellectual. And yet, as she watched him, the element of strangeness was still there, as if the mask were not completely fixed in place, and the Nicholas Yurovsky she had seen that afternoon still lurked behind it.

He'd lied to her, without actually lying in words. He hadn't denied Paul Martin's accusation, he had simply evaded it.

One of the reasons she fell in love with him was because he had a quality of absolute integrity. After the quicksands of her marriage, Anna had tried to persuade herself that at last she was on solid ground, safe in a relationship where there were neither lies nor savage truths. Being the daughter of Sheila Campbell, owner and editor of the ultra-right-wing political journal *Truth*, had initiated Anna very early into the travesties of its title. Wealth and power and ambition, the inability to trust or to be trusted were part of the air she breathed, and it had stifled her. Her mother, armoured with millions made in steel by a Scottish immigrant father, had proved herself as tough and ruthless in her pursuit of power as the old pioneer himself. Her aim was one of the major embassies; her marriage to a penniless French duke had been part of this particular campaign. When the Paris post went to someone else, Sheila had promptly divorced him. Anna's own father had been a shadowy figure, pleasant but ineffective – her mother over-shadowed and dominated everyone around her. Anna's life had been lived in the frantic aura of Sheila's ambition and success, and she hated everything about it. If she were honest, marriage to a Socialist radical like Paul Martin had been partly an act of defiance, a rejection of the standards, political and moral, of her mother.

There were no hang-ups in her love for Nicholas. He had rebuilt her damaged confidence, assumed a responsibility for her which Paul had ruthlessly avoided; there was a quiet authority about him which she found both sexually and emotionally attractive. For the first time in her life, Anna could visualize a life which was both passionate and serene. It had made marriage inevitable. Nicholas was not the type to embark upon a domesticated affair, leaving the door open to escape.

She was the first woman he had ever asked to marry him. Knowing him, Anna appreciated the totality of that commit-ment. But now, springing back out of the past like a pantomime demon through the trapdoor, Paul had brought the one element she found most destructive: doubt. Doubt of Nicholas's motives, of his actions, even of his love for her. 'He'll use you.' She couldn't get rid of that poisonous prediction. If Nicholas were in danger then she wanted to know; even if she were involved in risk because of him, she wouldn't have run away.

But the old bogey of her early background stood in the forefront of her mind, wagging a warning finger. She was so vulnerable because of her money and her connections. She had to be careful when she made friends, or went on dates, that she wasn't simply being used as a means to an end. She could remember, with real anguish, asking the boyfriend of her campus days the question that had such a special meaning for her: 'You do like me, don't you?' Me, for myself, not my mother's daughter, or the Campbell money, or the estate in Florida and the private jet . . . Like me . . . Love me.

She had fled to Europe as soon as she inherited her grandfather's legacy, hoping for anonymity, for a chance to find herself and for someone genuine to find her. But the cornerstone of love was trust. The trust Paul Martin had found impossible to keep, when he slipped in and out of bed with other women, and told her coolly that it didn't matter . . . he was still in love with her. . . .

'Anna –' He was reaching across the table to her. She gave him her hand and he held it firmly.

'What's the matter with you? You're not yourself.'

She shook her head. 'Nothing – there's nothing the matter.'

'Don't lie to me,' he said quietly. 'I've never seen you like this.'

'I'm not the one who's lying,' Anna said. The grip on her hand tightened for a second and then relaxed. He took his own away.

'It's still that business with Paul Martin? That's what is upsetting you, isn't it?'

'You know it is.' He lit a cigarette and passed it to her. He did the same for himself. The waiter brought wine and Nicholas tasted, before signalling to pour a glass for each of them. Anna had the same feeling as she had that afternoon; he let the silence lengthen, sipping the wine deliberately.

'Anna,' he said suddenly, 'Tell me something. Do you love me?'

'You know I do.'

'And do you believe that I love you?'

She nodded. 'Yes.'

'Then I want you to promise me something.' This was no stranger, but the man she loved, reaching out for her again across the table.

'I want you to forget everything Paul told you. Put it right out of your mind, now and forever. It has nothing to do with us.'

'I can't do that,' she said slowly. 'Of course it has something to do with us. You can't shut me out of a part of your life and

28

pretend it isn't there. Paul talked about danger, real danger. . . .'

'I know he did,' Nicholas said quietly. 'I've been thinking about that. Danger to you, he said, didn't he? . . .'

'That doesn't matter, I don't give a damn,' she began but he interrupted her.

'It matters to me,' he said. 'It matters very much.' There was silence between them then. He squeezed her hand hard. 'What did Paul tell you to do?' She wasn't prepared for the question.

'He told me not to rush into marrying you,' she said. 'He said being the wife of a leading anti-Soviet activist could be very dangerous for me. I didn't know what he was talking about.'

'No,' he said gently. 'Of course you wouldn't. He didn't suggest you took a trip?'

Anna stared at him. 'No – what sort of trip? Why should he –'

He lifted her hand and looked at it: it was slim and without rings.

'It might be an idea,' he said. 'Just for the next month. Go to the States, see your mother before she comes over. You could prepare the way for me to meet her. Then I'd join you. We could come back to Paris and be married in June or July – would you do that?'

'No, I wouldn't,' Anna said. 'Why should I? Because you're mixed up in something and you won't tell me what it is – what's going to happen in a month, Nicholas? Why is it dangerous for me to marry you in three weeks, and safe to do it in July?'

'The more I think of it,' he said, 'the more I feel you should go – just for the month. I should have thought of this before.'

'You should have told me the truth,' Anna said. 'Because I'm going to find it out. And I'm not going to go away and I'm not going to marry you until I do.' Their food came, and she pushed the plate away. 'Don't you understand,' she said, 'I love you – I want to be part of whatever it is, because it's part of you. I want to help. If you need money –' She hadn't intended to say it, and she felt herself redden.

He smiled at her, and shook his head. 'No, my darling, I

don't need money. That's one thing I shall never want from you. Eat your dinner; it's very good. We'll talk about this tomorrow. Let's enjoy ourselves tonight.'

It was late when they got back to the Auberge: Elise left a key for them hidden under a stone by the entrance and they let themselves in. They made love, and it seemed to Anna that he was more tender than she had ever known him. As she lay in his arms she had a feeling almost of finality, as if something had ended and she didn't know it. She woke and the bed was empty. The curtains were open and the morning sky was only faintly pink. She sat up and knew immediately that he had gone. The drawers were open, his belongings cleared from the dressing table. There was an air of departure in the room. The letter was standing wedged upright against the looking glass, where she had found the gold watch. She stood and ripped it open and read it by the window in the dawning light.

'My darling. Since last night I knew that you and I couldn't have our happiness. There is no place in my life for marriage and I have been selfish and a fool to pretend that there was. Paul Martin is right. I loved you. Never forget that. Nicholas.'

She went back to the bed, switched on the light and re-read it. He had tried to make her leave him the night before, with his suggestion of a trip to the States, and when she refused he had left her. It was as simple as that. As simple and as heart-breaking: 'I loved you.' In the past tense.

She didn't cry: the feeling of loss was too acute to find relief in tears. Whatever he was doing was more important than their future; faced with a choice he had rejected her. To protect her – to protect himself – or in reality to protect his activities, because she had declared her intention of finding them out. 'Since last night I knew we couldn't have our happiness.' He had left her with a memory of love that would take a long time to die. She knelt on the bed and shivered. She had lost everything: her hope for the future, the man she loved, her chance to find happiness with him. She threw her clothes into a bag, opened the window and looked out. Her car was parked in the yard. Nobody was stirring in the downstairs rooms. She didn't want to see Elise or her husband, to stay another moment in the place where she had been so happy. She was going back to Paris, back to her empty apartment and her empty life. As she drove out on to the main road, pallid and dry-eyed, she thought that there was more of her gritty Scots ancestors in her than she realized. She had indeed lost everything but she was going to find out why.

2

Anna stood and looked at her telephone. Two days and not a
word. They had been the most miserable two days she could
remember. Several times she had gone to call Nicholas and
then put back the receiver, even as his number rang. Nothing
had been resolved between them. The questions were all there,
unanswered. She picked up the telephone and dialled Paul's
number at the magazine. He arranged to come round to her
apartment that evening. He had, he said, someone who
wanted to meet her. Someone who could explain, better than
he, why Nicholas Yurovsky was dangerous to her and to
himself.

They arrived after seven, Paul slightly dishevelled, smoking
his usual cigarette; he always needed to shave twice, and that
evening his chin was very blue. Her mother, fastidious to the
point of obsession, had said that he looked dirty after four
o'clock.

The man with him, older, rather stout, and very soberly
dressed was introduced as Raoul Jumeaux. He kissed Anna's
hand. He had small bright brown eyes, and a neat moustache.
He could have been a doctor or a civil servant. Paul got them
all a drink, with the familiarity of someone who had once lived
in the apartment. He sat next to Anna, Jumeaux on the sofa
opposite.

He asked her permission and produced a pipe. There was an
extraordinarily awkward silence, which Anna didn't know
how to break. It was Paul who spoke first.

'My wife wants to know about Nicholas Yurovsky,' he said.

Jumeaux nodded. 'We all want to know about him,' he said.
'He's become quite a problem to us.'

Us. Anna stiffened. No doctor, no Paris bureaucrat. SDECE. She had called them thugs. Jumeaux spoke directly to her.

'Paul is an old friend,' he said. 'I warned him about Yurovsky when you came into it. He tells me you mentioned his conversation and Yurovsky denied it.'

'Yes,' Anna said. 'He did.'

'He was certain to deny it,' Jumeaux said.

'I don't see why,' Paul Martin interrupted. 'If he wants to use Anna's money, it was a perfect opportunity to talk her into helping them. He didn't, did he?' She might have known he would see through her – he used to laugh at her because he said she was so transparent. A clean-cut American kid. He had called her that once and it infuriated her.

'No,' she said, trying not to look at him. 'He certainly didn't. I told you; he denied everything.'

'He is in love with you, Madame Martin?' Jumeaux asked.

'Yes,' Anna admitted. 'Yes, I think he is.'

'Then he wouldn't want to mix you up in something as dangerous as this business. What you don't know can't be got out of you. It minimized your risk. But there certainly is a risk.'

He leaned forward and knocked ash out of his pipe. He glanced round him and then back at her.

'You have a beautiful apartment, Madame. As I was saying, these people, these fools who think they can throw stones at the KGB, not only bring trouble to themselves. Everyone connected with them becomes suspect. If you take my advice, Madame Martin – and I know it's what your husband would like you to do – you'd pack up and go on a long trip. Go to the States. Forget about Nicholas Yurovsky.'

'I can't do that,' she said. 'I can't just walk away. Paul said that you could explain what it was all about. Why should Nicholas care about Soviet Russia? He was born here!'

'Yes,' Jumeaux nodded. 'And his mother was a Frenchwoman. Has he ever talked to you about her? No. Understandable, perhaps. The Druets didn't behave very well – he was brought up by his grandmother, Countess Zia. So, in spite of being born and growing up in France, he was steeped in the legends. But the real trouble began with his father. Has he ever talked about him?'

She shook her head. 'No,' she said. 'But this weekend I found a gold watch, one of those old-fashioned fob watches. There was a picture of a Russian officer in the back of it. Nicholas said that was his father. That's all I know about him.'

'Well,' Raoul Jumeaux said. 'If you're not in a hurry, Madame, and Paul here would like to fill up my glass for me, I'll tell you about Count Michael Yurovsky and his friends. Ah, thank you, Paul.'

He settled a little into the sofa. 'Your health, Madame.' He raised his glass. 'Most of the White Russians stayed in Paris. Some had brought jewellery or had foreign bank accounts, most had nothing. They congregated together, they were received with sympathy in France to start with, and then with indifference. Their attempts at political intrigue were an embarrassment to our governments; they didn't integrate. There were men and women living in Paris in the twenties and thirties who acted and talked as if a counter-revolution would sweep the Reds away and they could all go home again. They preserved their language, their customs and their religion. Many of them starved. You won't remember the old movies – the taxi-driver turns out to be a prince –' He filled his pipe and lit it. 'If you want to understand Nicholas Yurovsky and the men and women like him,' Jumeaux said, 'then you have to go back, Madame. Not too far. But back to 1943. To the middle of the war, when France was occupied by the Nazis. I have a special interest in this case, you see. I knew Nicholas Yurovsky's father.'

Count Michael Vladimirovich Yurovsky met his wife when he had been working for her father for a year. Etienne Druet was a shrewd businessman who had made a fortune in textiles; he employed the Russian aristocrat with some misgivings. The émigrés had a reputation for being difficult to assimilate; there were sad stories of suicides among the older ones who found themselves unable to adjust to a life of near-penury and exile. But Michael Yurovsky was different; he worked hard, he showed no resentment at taking orders or performing the humblest duty. Etienne admired him; he had dignity and style, and he charmed everyone. There were rumours about him, of course; tales that he had been a Cossack officer in the counter-revolution, or, as some described it, the White Terror. He never mentioned the circumstances in which he left Russia. He had a mother living in Paris, in modest style, and two sisters had died in the influenza epidemic. Etienne introduced him to his family, and it was obvious to everyone that his daughter and heiress, Liliane, had fallen head over heels in love with the Russian. She was a pretty girl, and her father doted on her. In spite of her wealth, she couldn't hope to be accepted within the narrow confines of French society. When she became engaged to Michael Yurovsky, Etienne was delighted. He bought them a handsome house at Vermeuil in Normandy, promoted his son-in-law into a top job in Druet Textiles, and swelled with pride to think that his daughter was a countess.

Liliane was very happy, until the war broke out. Michael had horrified her by suggesting that he should enlist and fight for France. Etienne used all his influence to dissuade him, and by 1940 France was defeated and occupied by the German army. As far as Liliane was concerned, the war was over. Desperately in love with her husband, and with their son toddling in the nursery, patriotism never entered her head; she listened anxiously to her father and her husband as they discussed the future, and couldn't think of anything but the immediate safety of her own family and her home. France was defeated. There were German troops occupying the main towns, pouring into Paris, gathering for the final assault against England. By the end of the year the whole of Europe would be dominated, directly or through alliance, by Nazi Germany. Etienne Druet made his decision. He had spent his life building up a profitable business and a fortune. He had his daughter and his grandson to consider. The war was lost, and the old way of life would never return. Survival on the best terms possible was the only sensible course. He drove to the local headquarters of the

German army and offered to assist the occupying forces in any way he could. Within three months his factories were making uniforms for the *Wehrmacht*. German officers were entertained at his flat in Paris, and invited to Vermeuil where Liliane made them welcome. Etienne Druet, his daughter and son-in-law became known collaborators; they were criticized by a few but most of the people they knew were doing the same.

At Vermeuil itself, life continued with little alteration, and the war seemed to have detoured round them. There were no shortages of food or luxuries; Liliane became pregnant again; Michael Yurovsky travelled to Paris and back at the weekends, and petrol was always available. When Germany attacked Russia, the influence of Etienne Druet protected Michael. It was suggested that he could obtain French citizenship without any difficulty. Father and daughter were surprised at how vehemently he refused.

No one had troubled them. It was two years later and the little boy Nicholas had a sister. Michael Yurovsky had come down from Paris; petrol was short now; an old taxi, powered by a gas bag tied to the roof, had jogged along the road and brought him from the station. He couldn't find Liliane, so he went to the nursery, where a village girl was looking after the children, and took his son in his arms. The child was very blond, like his mother, but he had his father's tilted blue eyes; he hugged him round the neck and kissed him. The baby, as dark as Michael, cooed in her bassinette. It was a mild, sunny evening; the house was peaceful, the countryside breathed gently round them. The girl watched the Count playing with his son. He talked to him in Russian and was teaching him different words. The Countess didn't like this, because she said it confused the little boy. She liked the Countess, but there was something very aloof and withdrawn about the Count. Always polite, but very much the aristocrat. The girl grimaced at him when his back was turned. Who did he think he was, anyway – working for old M. Druet, marrying the daughter to get himself set up for life? Rubbing noses with the Germans, all of them.

People in Vermeuil were sensible enough; nobody wanted

trouble, but when you saw the perks some of them got – fresh butter, bottles of brandy, *she* even had silk stockings. Marie had worked for them since the little girl was born. She loved looking after the baby, but the boy Nicholas was self-willed and difficult. She didn't like the way his eyes tipped up at the corners. His father's were the same. It made them both look so foreign. Michael Yurovsky didn't notice her antagonism; his wife, who loved him better than anything or anybody in the world, sensed the same quality of reserve, and suffered silently because of it. He stood apart, a private person who had never revealed himself completely to her, a man whose past had been severed like a limb. He kissed his son, smoothing the child's fair hair, and murmured to him in Russian.

'Go to Marie now, I want to kiss Olga. Then I shall find your mama.'

Nicholas held on to him obstinately. 'No, Papa. Niki, kiss Niki. *Potsyelui myenya* –' he used the Russian words and the Count smiled. He bent over the baby's cot, lifted her and held her for a moment. Then he put her back, nodded politely to the girl, who was holding Nicholas, struggling against her knee. 'Goodnight,' he said. 'Goodnight, Niki. We'll go for a walk tomorrow morning; after breakfast Marie will bring you down stairs.'

He walked slowly down the corridor, past the pictures bought with his father-in-law's money, across the big hallway which had been furnished from the same source, out of the house which didn't belong to him, into the evening sunshine. He cast a tall shadow as he walked across the lawn, a slim man in his forty-fourth year, with a soldier's stride, his eyes narrowed against the still bright evening sunshine. His wife was in the garden, getting vegetables for their evening meal. She did the cooking now, because there was such a shortage of people active enough to work. The nursemaid and the old pensioner who kept the garden tidy and looked after the produce were all they had left.

Liliane had grumbled bitterly as she had to cope with more and more domestic work; Michael didn't comment. He was proof against the changes which upset his wife so much. Little could hurt him, or if he were truthful, animate him now. He paused to light a cigarette, fitting it into a holder. He had kept that with him. It was amber, with a gold band. His General used to smoke cigars, thin, black, vilely strong. Michael crossed to the edge of the lawn and turned down the path to the vegetable garden. He had seen his General only half-a-dozen times in the last twenty years. The last time he had brought him down to Vermeuil the visit had been a disaster. Liliane had burst into tears and begged Michael never to bring him there again. She hadn't understood: he didn't blame her. All she saw was a down-at-heel old man, sodden with vodka, spilling out tales of violence and bloodshed that horrified her. To Michael, it was his old commander, the man who had treated him as a son; the bravest, most feared of all the White generals, now living in a dirty room in the Quartier, doing odd jobs. He had lost his job as a circus rider for getting drunk.

Michael saw his wife coming towards him; she carried a basket over her arm, full of vegetables. She smiled, and hurried as she saw him.

He took the heavy basket from her and they walked back to the house, she linking her arm through his. There was no doubt about her love for him. He had been very lucky. He loved her too, in his way. He liked her father and accepted the life they offered him. But the core of him was cold. It had died long ago in his homeland. He went into the kitchen with her and poured her a glass of wine.

'Sweetheart,' he said, 'I've had a telephone call today. The General has asked to come and see me.' She was standing by the big wooden table, sipping the wine. She turned to him with a look of alarm and then disgust.

'That man! Oh, Michael, no – you promised me last time – I can't have him here again. He was so drunk – so, so horrible –' she stopped, seeing his face. She hated that cold look, it frightened her with its threat of withdrawal. Of course he loved her; he said so. But deep within her there was a quiver of doubt. He was angry with her. That dreadful old Russian meant so much to him, and she couldn't understand why. They'd been in the army together twenty years ago. But they had nothing in common. Nothing. She began to cut up the greens; there were tears in her eyes.

'You needn't worry,' Michael Yurovsky said. 'He's quite sober; we had a long talk this morning. He's only coming for an hour. It needn't disturb you.'

'What does he want?' she asked. 'Why don't you just send him some money if he's in a bad way . . .'

He turned at the door and looked at her. He shook his head, more at some inner thought than at her.

'You don't give charity to Alexander Shuvalov,' he said. He went out and closed the door. Liliane prepared the vegetable stew. If he didn't want money, why was he coming . . .? Why was he intruding on their lives again? She thought of the General and shuddered. He was sixty years old, the same age as her father. He had reminded her of a wild beast, crouched over their dining-room table with a glass of vodka in his hand, talking in Russian to her husband. He had a way of shouting with laughter and banging his fist into his cupped hand. She had understood some of it, when they spoke French out of courtesy to her. Tales of old battles, names of comrades, incidents which meant little to her. And then suddenly the old man had swung round to her, red-eyed and leering with drunken joy. 'You know, Madame – you know how many of those scum we killed in our Caucasian campaign – thirty thousand! Shot them, buried them, burned them – thirty thousand of the swine!'

She had stared in horror from him to Michael, and seen the smile of reminiscence on his face and heard him say in his quiet voice, 'No General – between thirty-five and forty, I should say.'

She had made every excuse to herself afterwards. Shuvalov's bedroom was a shambles; broken glass and cigar burns on the sheets, a stench of human sweat and vodka, a frightened maid who had complained that the Russian had lurched after her in the corridor on his way to bed. But the real reason why she never wanted him in the house again was that brief, terrifying glimpse of a Michael Yurovsky she had never known. She heard their two spaniels barking, and slipped out of the kitchen to the door into the hall. A car had come to a stop in front of the entrance. A car. Nobody had petrol now except the Germans. Michael had gone outside to meet him. She came to the window and looked out. It was a camouflaged army car, with a *Wehrmacht* corporal at the wheel. Her husband was shaking hands with the small, lean figure; for a moment the older man embraced him. They turned to come into the house and Liliane had a clear view of Alexander Shuvalov. He looked sunburned and fit, a furred cap pulled rakishly on one side. He was dressed in the uniform of a German general.

Alexander Shuvalov leaned against the sofa, one arm stretched along the back. His legs, encased in shining boots, were crossed, one foot swinging. He was smoking one of his thin cigars. Michael Yurovsky had gone down to his cellars and found their last bottle of vintage champagne. The General looked at him, and smiled. He had never married, never had a son that he could acknowledge. Michael Yurovsky had arrived at his headquarters one bitterly cold October day in 1918, with what was left of his men and horses, and demanded to fight with him. The boy had a look on his face that Shuvalov had seen before. Anguish, despair and hate. Something had touched him that night; some chord of compassion, of empathy with the young man standing shaking with cold and weariness, and hunger too, in the dark doorway of the room. He made him sit down and eat before he let him speak.

That was the beginning of their friendship; even his admirers described Alexander Shuvalov as a ferocious beast, living on vodka, loot and war, a throwback to his own wild tribal ancestors, that twentieth-century Russian society had completely failed to tame. But he loved Michael Yurovsky as if there had been a blood tie between them. He kept him close to him in action; taught him his own tricks of fighting a mounted war, how to ravage the enemy like a wolf and slip away like a fox; how to live off the land and the people without conscience, to punish collaboration with the Bolsheviks by means of total devastation. To take no prisoners; to commandeer horses, food, clothing and money in the name of the imprisoned Tsar. They had been great days; days which Shuvalov had shared so closely with the young man, now middle-aged, who was sitting opposite to him in his handsome French country house.

He leaned forward.

'Tell me, Michael. Before we go any further into this, tell me the truth. How happy have you been in the last twenty years?'

Michael Yurovsky hesitated. He had no expectation of happiness; that had vanished long ago when the Revolution erupted, and the world became a place of death and devastation. His only instinct, second to that of vengeance, had been to survive. To survive the Civil War when it was lost and to exist with some degree of dignity in exile. He had disapproved of the attitude of many of his fellow émigrés; he despised their self-pity and expectation that others should provide for them. He abandoned the old attitudes because they were irrelevant to his new status in an alien society, where goodwill was so important.

He loved his wife in a gentle way, but without the passion of heart and mind which she lavished upon him. He adored his children, but they were in a separate compartment of his inner life, reserved for his mother and his family and his past. Shuvalov had a place in it. His wife would never understand the bond between them, and he had never tried to explain it. Had he been happy in the last twenty years? It was not a question he had asked himself and he didn't know how to answer.

'I don't know,' he said. 'Compared to most of our people I've been very lucky. Liliane is a very good wife – I have Niki and Olga. I didn't expect to be happy. That was all over when my father died. I don't see the relevance of your question, General.'

'Like hell you don't,' Shuvalov said. 'I know you too well, my friend, to be taken in by all this . . .' He waved his hand at the room. 'You may deceive yourself, but you haven't fooled me. You're no fat cat, lapping up someone else's cream! You've got a nice little rich wife, two fine children, a father-in-law who's well in with the Germans, and nothing to worry about, eh? If you were happy with it, you wouldn't have had to think about it. Well, I'll tell you the truth. You're like a dead man. There's nothing in your belly – there's nothing here, either.' He tapped his own chest above the heart. 'You're empty inside. I was the same; yes, I didn't have your luck, I was broke and living like a dog for the past twenty years, scraping a few francs here and there, getting drunk and running away from the emptiness. But the sickness is the same for both of us. We're Russians; we can never belong anywhere else. We fought for our homeland and we lost; everything we had was taken from us, the people we loved were butchered. In the end we were running like rats to save our lives – remember?'

'Yes,' Michael Yurovsky said in a low voice. 'I remember. I remember it all.'

'We've been like dead men ever since,' Shuvalov said.

It was very quiet in the room; the evening sun was dipping behind the skyline, and the shadows lengthened. Soon it would be necessary to switch on the lamps.

'Forty thousand Cossacks have joined the German army,' Shuvalov said. 'Thousands of Ukrainians went over to them when they invaded. Exiles from all over Europe are joining the special Russian divisions under General Daslov – remember him? The old commanders of 1919 have come forward, and they're going back to fight the enemy. I need you, Michael. Alone, we are nothing. With the power of Germany behind us, we can help defeat the Reds and free our country.'

Michael Yurovsky didn't answer. He sipped the last of his champagne. There was a tightness in his throat and chest. It was insane; the General, in his German uniform with white flashes on his collar denoting this Cossack army, was saying things that should never be said; or listened to. Telling him to cast off his life for the past twenty years, to break the ring of habit that had protected him, and using the expression of his vanished youth, pull on his boots again. It was incredible, crazy.

'I have two children,' he said slowly.

'Yes,' Shuvalov said. 'Two children who will never see their homeland. They'll be exiles like their father; your son will be a Frenchman, with a great Russian name. You owe it to him to strike at the swine who butchered his grandfather and robbed his family of its inheritance!'

'It's all over,' Michael said slowly. 'You're talking about the past.'

'I'm talking about the German summer offensive,' Shuvalov said angrily. 'A million men are going to be launched against the Stalinists. And we're going to be among them. If Germany takes Moscow, Russia will be liberated. And I believe we're going to win; I believe that Russia will be a free country again, free for us to go home; think of it, Michael – think of going back at last . . .' He paused, watching the other man in the dimming light. He was pale, and his hands were gripping together.

'I've had enough,' the General said slowly. 'When I was called by General Daslov, I knew it was a sign from God. My life hasn't been worth living since we left Russia. I used to think of it. One bullet, that's all I needed to get out of it. No more shame, no more hunger; I've swept the streets! If I'm killed this time, I shall die decently, like a man and a Russian. It's my destiny now. I know it. It's your destiny too.'

'You shouldn't have come,' Michael Yurovsky said. 'I'd made my life. I'd shut the past away.' He got up and poured some champagne into Shuvalov's glass and then refilled his own. The bottle was empty.

'You're right, of course. If Germany defeats the Red armies, Russia will be freed from Communism. Do you really believe this offensive will succeed?'

'I know it will; Germany has to break the Reds this spring or she loses the war,' Shuvalov said. 'You're like my son to me. I want you back.'

There was a moment's silence then Shuvalov leaned back. He watched Michael Yurovsky quietly. It was the crisis point when his decision would be made, and the old Cossack had a deeply intuitive feeling for the younger man which warned him to say nothing more.

Suddenly Michael stood up; he fitted a cigarette into his holder, lit it with the gold lighter Liliane had given him for his last birthday.

'I've never really felt this was my home,' he said. 'Nothing belongs to me; Druet paid for everything. I took it, but I didn't admire myself. I married a rich girl because she was rich, and pretended to myself that I loved her enough to justify it. In a way, I've been kept as much as Kramov who moved down to Monte Carlo and slept with the old women. But I if go with you, General, I throw my security away.'

'If you don't,' Shuvalov answered, 'you've thrown yourself away. In the end a man needs to be among his own people. If we win you won't need Druet or his money. You'll be a Russian again.'

'I'm teaching my son to speak Russian,' Michael said. He smiled slightly. 'Liliane doesn't like it; she says it confuses the child. But he's learning. He can say quite a few words.'

'I want you on my personal staff,' the General said. 'With the rank of colonel. I have a special job for you, my son. Something you could do better than anyone else.'

He always called Michael his son in the old days. 'We will leave for Poland in the middle of next month.' He came and put his hands on Michael Yurovsky's shoulders. He still had a grip like iron.

'You're coming with me, aren't you?'

'Yes,' Yurovsky said. 'Yes, General, I've made up my mind. I'm coming with you.'

'Thank God,' the General said. 'Your son will be proud of you.'

He hated seeing Liliane cry. Her face puckered and her mouth turned down like a child's, and the tears seemed to gush rather than flow.

'Don't,' he said gently. 'Don't upset yourself, sweetheart. Listen to me – try to understand . . .'

'I can't,' she wept. 'I think you've gone mad.' They were in the drawing room, and the smell of the General's cigars was still in the air. Michael had his arm round her; she was slumped against him on the sofa, devastated by what he had told her.

'I've never talked to you about what happened,' he said slowly. 'That was wrong of me. I shut it out because I wanted to forget. And when the General came that time you seemed so upset by it all. Will you listen to me now?' He turned her face towards him; he felt more love for her at that moment than at any time in their life together. 'Wipe your eyes; don't cry any more.'

She gazed at him in despair; the last few minutes seemed like a nightmare. He was going to join a Russian division and fight with the Germans on the Eastern front. At first she had genuinely thought he was playing some kind of cruel joke on her. When she realized that he was serious, she became hysterical. Now, gazing at him, seeing the concern and the tenderness in his face, Liliane forced herself to be calm. It wasn't certain; he hadn't really made up his mind. . . . If she could make him feel sorry enough for her and the children. . . .

'My family were very rich,' Michael Yurovsky said. 'We owned vast estates, and my father was a friend of the Tsar Nicholas. You know that he sent my mother and my two sisters out of Russia before the Revolution because he could see what was coming. We had a wonderful childhood, a wonderful life, my sisters and my parents and I. My father was a man of culture and humanity; he lived to serve his country and his Tsar, and when the opportunity came to leave and save his life, he wouldn't take it. I was serving in his old regiment at the front, and he stayed behind. He stayed to look after his people and his home. Do you know how he died, Liliane?'

She shook her head. Little of what he was saying made any impression. What did all this matter now?

'He was taken out by the Bolsheviks, with my aunt who was an invalid, and some of the servants who'd been with us all their lives and wouldn't run away. They stood them all against the wall of my mother's conservatory, and opened fire on them. Then they killed them off with bayonets, and beat them with rifle butts if they were not quite dead.' He paused; his arm was no longer comforting around her. The grip was tight, and she tried to ease away from him. 'The same sort of thing happened to our friends and the rest of my family; only some of the Vorontzovs escaped. Murder, rape, looting, destruction. Nobody was spared. My uncles and aunts, my mother's parents who were in their eighties – the commissars used to have a special form of entertainment for their women. They called them cellar parties. They'd get drunk and have in the prisoners. . . . I had a beautiful cousin, Natalie Vorontzova. She was sixteen, and my mother used to talk about us marrying one day. She died in a cellar party. I didn't find that out until Shuvalov and I captured the town near the Vorontzovs' estate and I went looking for them. Do you know what we did that night? We rounded up every man and woman and brought them to the square. There were two prisoners left in the jail; they pointed out the Reds to us. We shot them all. The place was full of bodies. I picked my way through them, wondering if any of them had helped to kill Natalie. The local commissars and the members of the Soviet had got away. We only caught the scum.'

Liliane was sitting upright; she watched him in silence. He was very pale, and he looked strange. It was as if he had worn a mask for the seven years they had been married, and now she was seeing the real man.

'My country,' he said, 'was ravaged by Jews and Mongols, instruments of an international Marxist conspiracy to conquer the world. They killed millions, and they've gone on killing them. Not just people like us, the aristocrats, the officer class. That was easy. We were all wiped out. The Church was destroyed, its priests murdered or deported, our shrines were desecrated. The whole of Russia's history and culture was destroyed. In the name of freedom and humanity, Russia was chained in the worst tyranny she has ever known.'

Liliane turned to him. 'But what can you do about it? All right, it was terrible, your family were murdered, I'm sure you had a horrible time but it was all so long ago! Nothing's going to change it now – you've been living here since you were twenty: your home is here, your children are here – your responsibility is to us!'

He looked at her; her face was red and her eyes swollen: there was a look of obstinacy, impatience and fear in them. He realized that she hadn't listened to a word with understanding.

'You talk about going to fight with the German army,' she went on, not seeing her mistake. 'Don't you see what that makes you – putting on German uniform. My God, Michael, just supposing things go against them! Supposing they lose the war!'

'What will happen to your father – what will happen to all the people who have collaborated, most of all the Druet family? There's no shame in doing openly what we've done privately since they came here. If I wear their uniform it's because their enemies are my enemies. And the enemies of the whole civilized world. I have an opportunity to fight for the liberation of my country. There are hundreds of thousands of Russians, prisoners of war, civilians, émigrés, people from all over Russia, who've welcomed the German army and come over to fight with them against the Reds! Doesn't that show anything? Doesn't that explain to you, Liliane, that I can't stay back and refuse to join with them?'

'No,' she said. 'It doesn't. You've no right to leave your family and go and get yourself killed. It isn't your war, whatever you say – that's just a lot of crazy nonsense, talking about liberating Russia! It's that dreadful man, that Shuvalov, dragging you into his clutches again – let him go and fight the Communists and I hope they catch him and hang him!' She stared at him, tears coming again, a great sense of anger and betrayal growing in her.

'If you loved me or the children,' she accused, 'you wouldn't have even listened to him!'

Michael Yurovsky stood up. 'I'm sorry,' he said. 'I hoped you'd understand.' He took out his holder, and fitted a cigarette into it.

'I understand one thing,' his wife said. 'I'm going to my father, and we'll see what he thinks of all this. He'll have something to say to you, after all he's given you! Where would you be without him – without me?'

'I don't know,' he said quietly. 'But I shall soon find out.' He walked out of the room, closing the door quietly. He went outside into the garden; there was a half moon, and the evening was mild. Behind him, the house rose like a cliff, its windows blacked out to prevent any light from showing. Not that there had been any Allied air raids. They were miles away from any military target.

He felt a sense of anti-climax. It had been a sad, degrading scene with his wife; the most surprising thing was the way he had explained his own emotions, defined his duty. He knew now that the passion and eloquence were not for Liliane but for himself. Like the waters of a captive lake, they had gushed out and turned into a flood. He had ceased to hide from what he was and who he was – he had knocked the struts supporting him away, and for the first time he felt alive. And free. Shuvalov's words came back to him. 'Your son will be proud of you.' He would talk to the child tomorrow, prepare him. . . . When he grew up, if the worst happened and he was killed in Russia, Nicholas would understand.

He left Vermeuil two weeks later; a German staff car came to take him on the first stage of his journey to the headquarters in the East. Shuvalov had arranged everything; the driver was in German uniform, but he sported the same white flashes on his collar. He saluted and spoke to Michael Yurovsky in Russian. He couldn't have been more than twenty-five. His accent proclaimed him a Western Ukrainian – Michael knew that the territory had been annexed from Poland by the Soviet Union in 1939. The boy and his family had been introduced to the joys of Communism without any choice. He must have made his choice when the Germans invaded. He had a round fresh-complexioned face and little blue eyes; he wore his astrakhan cap pulled forward on his head. His name was Krosnevsky.

Michael gave him his luggage, and stood for a moment on the steps of his house. Not his home. The word didn't occur to him in connection with Vermeuil. Liliane had refused to come down and say goodbye. She was shut up in the nursery, preventing the children from coming to see him leave. There had been a painful scene with his father-in-law, in which Etienne had accused him of gross ingratitude and irresponsibility. Michael hadn't tried to defend himself. The Druets didn't understand. How could they, when they hadn't made any effort to resist the ravishers of their own country . . .? He had tried hard to comfort his wife, to persuade her that what he was doing was inevitable and that he couldn't respect himself if he declined his duty. He had tried, unwillingly, to arouse her greed by describing the estates which would be restored to him when the war was won. Nothing succeeded with Liliane; she had looked at him with red eyes and dismissed the idea as fantasy. He was bored with her and he didn't love his children; that was why he was abandoning them in order to consort with a lot of dirty traitors who were fighting with the Germans against their own people.

Her bitterest invective had been directed against Alexander Shuvalov. 'That disgusting brute! Talking about burning people and burying them alive! My God, if that's what all of you were like, it's a good thing Russia went Communist.'

Michael had turned and walked out of the room, leaving her shouting after him in the same vein. If he'd stayed, he would have hit her.

It was strange, but now that the decision was made, the days passed lightly, in spite of the atmosphere with his wife, and his father-in-law's refusal to speak to him after the final quarrel. He travelled to Paris, saw Shuvalov, who entertained him handsomely to lunch at the Ritz with a group of Russian officers, some of whom had names he knew, and others who were definitely Soviet fugitives. There was an atmosphere of festivity and excitement; one of the guests was a certain General von Bronsart, a German whose home in Poland had given him a command of Russian as well as Polish. Toasts were drunk to victory; Shuvalov, his eyes burning with vodka, flung his arm round Michael's shoulders and promised him a place in the first Free Russian column to enter Moscow after it fell to the German army. He had gone to be measured for his uniforms. It gave him a feeling of identity to be a soldier again. Field grey, with the white flashes on his collar, a Cossack cap, soft Russian-style cavalry boots. He stared at himself, and remembered Shuvalov's words that day at Vermeuil. 'It's my destiny. Yours too. If I die now, I'll die decently, like a man and a Russian.' Standing in the cubicle before a full-length mirror, with the fitter fidgeting over the cut of his jacket, Michael Yurovsky had seen himself as a complete entity for the first

time in twenty-four years. It was entirely possible, even prob-
able, that he would be killed in the spring offensive. There were
many worse ways to die. A creeping old age, a passive surrender
of life in the big bedroom at Vermeuil, never having known
what it meant to be himself again. His only anguish was for his
children. But his son Nicholas would not forget him. He had
taken the child on his knee and told him gently that he was
going away for a time. To fight, he said. To fight the enemies
of their country, which he hoped Nicholas would be able to see
one day. Holy Russia. He used the old phrase, and made the
little boy repeat it.

'Never forget this,' he said to the child, who was gazing up
at him, his mouth turned down ready to cry. 'You may live in
France but you are a Russian, just like me. And one day,
when our country is free, you will be able to go there. I shall
take you. It is the greatest country in the world. The most
beautiful. Take care of your mama, and be good while I'm
gone.' He had laid his hand on his son's head and blessed him
as his own father had done to him.

He walked down the steps and the driver sprang to the
door of the staff car and opened it. Michael glanced upwards
at the façade of the house. There was no one at the windows.
He got inside and drove away. His destination was a prisoner-
of-war camp near Nantes. His first duty was to recruit men for
Shuvalov from the thousands of Russians held there.

Anna had been sitting very still; Paul had given Jumeaux a
refill, she had refused anything. Pipe smoke hung in the air of
the elegant drawing room, and its smell was pungent. Jumeaux
paused and looked at her. 'This must sound an odd story to
you,' he said. 'Nobody realized how many of these people
fought on the German side. We were all brainwashed during
the war, Madame, about our gallant Russian allies. I say we,
because I was a member of the Free French forces, and of
course I was as subject to propaganda as anyone.'

'I've never heard of anything like it,' she said. 'I'd no idea
there was a Russian division or Cossacks fighting in Russia . . .'

'No,' he said, and grinned a rueful grin at Paul. 'It wouldn't have looked very good, would it, to let people know that there were nearly a million Russians who preferred to live under the Nazis instead of our great ally Stalin. We took good care not to let the secret out. Poor bastards.' He sucked at his pipe, fumbled for matches and re-lit it.

'Liliane Yurovsky was a stupid woman,' Jumeaux said. 'Not bad-hearted, but stupid. She'd never understood her husband and she couldn't forgive him. She took it as a personal rejection. But if she'd lived and things had gone differently, her son Nicholas wouldn't be mixed up in this mess today.'

'It's getting late,' Paul Martin said. 'And I'm hungry. Why don't we go out and get some dinner?'

Anna got up. 'I'll make something for us,' she said.

'I think we'd be better to go somewhere quiet and eat,' Jumeaux said. 'Paul, what about that place near the Madeleine – we had lunch there one day and it was very good . . .'

'Le Réduit,' Paul said. 'We'll go there. My car's outside.' Anna sat in the front beside him, Jumeaux in the back. They drove in silence through the crowded city, bright with lights, tourists wandering slowly down the broad streets, window shopping and idling, the pavement cafés crammed with people. She hadn't sat in a car with Paul for so long she'd forgotten how he drove. It was an uncomfortable experience; he was a fast, aggressive driver, always jerking and accelerating. The restaurant was in a side street quite close to the massive Madeleine Church, brooding at the top of its pyramid of steps. It was an unpretentious little place, with wooden tables and no concession to décor. Anna knew from long experience that in such places the best food in Paris was often to be found. Paul sat himself beside her; Jumeaux had disappeared into the back to wash.

'You look a bit harrowed,' he said. 'Don't get too emotional about it, because you haven't heard anything yet.'

'Why is he taking all this trouble,' she asked him. 'He must have a motive, besides being a friend of yours.'

'Oh, he has,' Paul admitted. 'Jumeaux's as tough as they come. He's wearing two hats at the moment, darling. One is the SDECE and the other is old Paul Martin's good friend. They just happen to coincide, that's all. But I want you to hear it through. You won't like it.'

'I don't have to listen,' she pointed out. There was something about his attitude that grated on her. He already knew the story, and had formed his own conclusions about the effect it would have on her. He had been wrong about her reactions before, and he could well be wrong again. It might be a pity that Jumeaux told the story with such conviction. She had a very clear mental picture of Count Michael Yurovsky in her mind. And of the child, with his fair hair and Russian eyes, embracing his father before he went away to the war.

'Ah,' Jumeaux said, when the meal was finished. 'That was good. I like this place. Trust Paul to know the best places to eat.' He ordered coffee.

'Tell me,' Anna said. 'What happened to Nicholas's father? Was he killed?' She saw him glance quickly at Paul and then his eyes came back to her.

'Yes,' he said slowly. 'He was certainly killed. But his first task when he joined Shuvalov was to persuade Soviet prisoners to fight for Germany. He was very effective. Let me tell you about it.'

The camp was a huge complex fifteen kilometres outside Nantes. Michael Yurovsky was entertained to lunch in the Commandant's quarters before he went to inspect and speak to the prisoners. The Commandant was a huge, bearish man, almost a caricature of the ugly German, bullet-headed and coarse; his fat body bulged in the black uniform of the SS. His name was Pfizer, and Yurovsky abhorred the type. He had seen its like in Russia, wearing the uniform of the Bolsheviks and the Whites in turn; a brutal, pitiless bully, delighting in oppressing the helpless. He managed to be polite; he was already dreading what he would find among his fellow-countrymen.

They were drawn up in ranks in the main square of the camp: row after row of men in their dirty, tattered khaki uniforms, their heads shaven to the skull, faces so gaunt with hunger that

Yurovsky felt as if he were looking at human skeletons. Few had anything but bloody rags bound round their feet. There was an indescribable stench even in the open air, and the atmosphere of wretched apathy was shot through with fear. Ranks of SS guards carrying whips, as if they were driving cattle, moved among the men. There was a total silence. Nobody dared to move. Yurovsky followed the Commandant to a small platform, about four feet above ground level. There was an empty socket about nine inches in diameter in the centre of it, and he glanced down. The outline of a trap door was clearly visible. He realized with horror that he was standing on a gallows. Pfizer had a junior officer with him, and this officer used a loudhailer to shout orders in Russian. The SS man spoke with a Polish accent. He told them that a Russian officer had come to address them; those who accepted his offer would be recruited into labour battalions, and not forced to take up arms. Yurovsky turned to the Commandant.

'What is this about labour battalions? I've come here for fighting troops!'

'These are Red Army men,' Pfizer said. 'They won't fight against their own. Once they're in a labour battalion it's up to you to arm them. They'll go along.' He laughed. 'Give 'em a taste of food and women and they'll fight all right. Scum!'

Yurovsky looked at him.

'I'm not tricking any man into joining us,' he said. 'Give me the loudhailer.'

The sun was beating down upon them; there were three thousand men, and the only food had been a bowl of cabbage soup and two ounces of black bread. They got the same ration at night, with the addition of one potato to the soup. They had been in the camp since the beginning of the year, and already a third of them had died of starvation and ill-treatment. They stared at the smartly dressed man in his odd uniform; German field grey, with a Cossack cap. He spoke to them in clear, cultivated Russian, with an accent that was unfamiliar. He explained the formation of a Russian division dedicated to fighting against the tyranny of the present Soviet government. Any man who felt in conscience that he could join this division would be released and treated as a member of the armed forces with full pay and privileges. He guaranteed that no force would be used to persuade them, and nobody would be penalized if they decided to stay where they were. Some of the men shuffled their feet, and muttered to each other.

A Red Army corporal who had been captured outside Kiev glared at Michael Yurovsky through eyelids crusted with sores from malnutrition. 'That bastard,' he hissed to his neighbour. 'That's one of the stinking swine from the old days – my father told me about them – standing up there trying to get us to turn traitor!'

'Be quiet,' his neighbour snarled. 'Watch your mouth . . .'

The corporal had fought desperately before he was captured; his home had been overrun by the advancing Germans and most of the villagers he had grown up with were shot for harbouring guerrillas. He was weak with dysentery and lack of food. He had been beaten and kicked by the troops when he was captured, and herded in a stinking cattle truck with hundreds of Russian prisoners, many of them badly wounded, on a nightmare trip across Europe to the camp at Nantes. Nothing but hatred for the Germans had kept his spirit intact. Now, looking at the elegant figure of Michael Yurovsky, symbol of the aristocracy he had been brought up to despise, recruiting for the very army which had ravaged his homeland and murdered his friends, something snapped inside him.

He pushed forward, stumbling; Michael saw him and for a moment imagined that he had his first volunteer. The corporal reached the front rank; he weaved a little with weakness, looking up at the figures on the platform. He summoned his breath and yelled.

'You stinking bastard! You won't find any traitors here – long live Stalin!'

He was seized so quickly that Michael Yurovsky heard the Commandant bellow something in German and the next moment there were three shots. The Russian lay on the ground, shot dead. He swung round on the German, aghast.

'That man was a prisoner-of-war! You'd no right to shoot him!'

Pfizer grimaced. 'Red swine – don't worry, Colonel. You'll get your volunteers after this.'

Even as Yurovsky turned back to the ranks of wretches lined up in front of him, there was a movement and men began to come forward. He stood helplessly, watching them gather in front of the platform. The dead corporal lay sprawled on the ground; prisoners stepped over his body.

Yurovsky turned to the commandant. 'I want to see all these men individually. I'd like an office put at my disposal.'

'It's not the normal practice,' Pfizer said. 'The last one of your people who came here didn't talk to them. He didn't mind a few of them getting shot. They weren't so hungry then and they were full of fight.'

'I'm not interested in my predecessor's methods,' Yurovsky said. He turned and stepped down from the platform. 'I want to see each man.'

They gave him one of the store-rooms; he had a table and a chair and the SS liaison officer who spoke Russian was with him.

It took a long time; the window showed a darkening sky by the time the last man stood before him. Yurovsky asked the same question as he had done with all the others; there must have been several hundred of them.

'Why do you want to join us? Don't be afraid to answer truthfully.'

All but a few told lies; he knew that. They couldn't give the real reason in case this odd sort of officer refused to take them. They were dying of hunger; their life expectancy from sheer mistreatment and hard labour was less than a few months. Once out of the camp, many thought they might escape. Others only wanted to survive, and saw no further than freedom and decent rations instead of a slow death.

But others were different. They had lost friends, parents, suffered imprisonment themselves. And not at the hands of the invading Germans. These were the victims of Soviet laws, where free speech, religious observance, or a lukewarm attitude to official directives was ferociously punished. These men, and there were a number of them, wanted to go back and fight.

By the end of that day Yurovsky was exhausted. He drove to Nantes, where he was the guest of the German district commander and for the first time in many years he went to bed too drunk to undress. He remembered the driver, Krosnevsky, taking off his boots. The scene in the camp haunted him; images of horror merged again and again in the contorted face of the man who had spat defiance at him and been shot down. 'Traitor.' It was an epithet that stung. 'The last one of your people who came here didn't talk to them . . . he didn't mind a few of them getting shot . . .' The gross face, its brutish eyes gleaming, swam in front of him, distorted by the effects of the alcohol. He could have walked away and refused to carry on. He could have left the camp and the men in it, and told Shuvalov to find someone else for this particular task. And they would have died of hunger; been shot, beaten to death, worked till they collapsed. The men who had signed up with him would live; whatever their motives he had saved their lives. He thought in confusion that it was as much a rescue operation as a recruiting drive for Shuvalov's division. And these were simple people, peasants, dragged across Europe away from their homes. They knew nothing of the outside world except brutality and suffering since their capture.

It was his responsibility, and that of his brother officers, to educate them and convert them to the cause of Russian freedom. By the time he joined Shuvalov in Poland, he had visited five major camps and personally recruited five thousand Russians for the German army. It was already March and the great spring offensive against the Red Army was planned for the second week in April. He had written to Liliane but received no reply. He had resigned himself to her attitude. He could only hope that if Germany was victorious and the Soviet defence collapsed, he might be alive to convince her that he had done the right thing. And see his children again.

3

They were the only customers left in Le Réduit; the proprietor was helping clear the tables, and he glanced at the little group of two men and a woman who remained in the corner, their coffee cups empty, a blue halo of cigarette smoke drifting above them. One of the men looked up and beckoned him.

'We'd like three brandies,' Paul Martin said. 'You don't mind keeping open for us?'

'Of course not,' the proprietor shrugged. 'There's no hurry. I have a fine cognac I can recommend. It would be a crime to hurry it.'

He thought the blonde girl looked very pale. It hadn't been a happy gathering: he hadn't heard anyone laugh.

'So,' Raoul Jumeaux said, cradling the brandy in both hands and sniffing it, 'that was how it ended. The German offensive was a failure, the German armies were broken, and the Russian counter-offensive began. Shuvalov and his Russians and the entire Russian auxiliary force fought for their German masters like devils; I think it was Winston Churchill who remarked on that when the question was being debated. But it failed. The crazy dream of driving out Stalin and the Communists was undoubtedly what motivated men like Yurovsky. The need to stay alive rather than starve and die in German prison camps was what drove thousands of Soviet prisoners to join in. As for those who welcomed the Germans in the Ukraine, Finland, Estonia and the other émigrés who came running to fight with them – they had their reasons. Stalin starved five million of them to death in the Ukraine alone, when they wouldn't cooperate with his agricultural dictatorship. To them the Germans were liberators. It sounds extraordinary to me to say that – less so to you, Madame Martin. Your generation has seen Soviet Russia for what it really is, a menace to the freedom of mankind. I can see Paul shaking his head. Well – we won't argue, you and your radical Socialism are no more acceptable to the Russians than capitalism. For these Russians there was only one course; when Germany was defeated, those that were left of them surrendered to the English and the Americans. They hadn't heard of the Yalta agreement.' He looked at Anna. 'They believed, in the most naïve way, that the Allies would understand and protect them.'

'I can't believe it,' Anna said. 'I can't believe that nobody knew, nobody tried to help them –'

'Oh, they did,' Paul Martin interjected. 'People like Raoul here, for instance. Some of the British officers and a lot of their troops protested. The Americans – always such a sentimental people, darling, made a terrible fuss. But the politicians had their way and the army carried out its orders. We couldn't risk offending Stalin. Also there were a large number of Allied prisoners who had been overtaken by the Russian advance. It's all part of the way the world is run that human beings are used as bargaining counters. And obviously, there wasn't any sympathy with people like Yurovsky in official quarters. They were regarded as traitors, getting exactly what they deserved. And nobody sympathized with the ex-prisoners-of-war who had found themselves drafted into the German army to fight when they'd been promised their freedom if they volunteered for road building. It's a dirty world, Anna; I used to try and make you see that, but you only accused me of being cynical.'

'That gold watch,' Anna said slowly. 'With the little photograph in the back. I keep seeing his face. So like Nicholas –'

'Yes,' Jumeaux said, 'Even as a child he looked very like his father. I gave him the watch, you know.'

She raised her head quickly. 'You? You gave it to Nicholas –'

'Yes,' he said again. 'I was at the camp at Baratina. Michael Yurovsky asked me to get it to his son. He gave me his own cigarette case as a memento. Finish your cognac, and I'll get the bill. Now that you know the background, you can see why

Nicholas Yurovsky lied to you. You can see that you are dealing with a total fanaticism based on revenge. And despair. He and his friends are the last of their kind. Your man is not a Frenchman, in spite of having a French mother. He is a Russian, with a score to settle. Yurovsky is a political maverick, dangerous now because he's got money, and he's been under cover for a long time. We don't know the source of that money and it's worrying. He is going to get himself killed in some crazy gesture which won't make any more difference to the Soviet Union than an ant trying to stamp on an elephant. All it will do is embarrass the Western powers and give the Russians an excuse to blame France. I *am* a Frenchman, Madame Martin, and my duty is to protect my country's interests. Some stupid act of anti-Soviet violence is against her interests at the moment. I am satisfied now that you are not involved in any of this. If you want to help Nicholas Yurovsky, then go back and tell him that the SDECE are aware of his activities and determined to thwart any nonsense. Tell him that. If he won't listen, then my strongest advice to you is to get out of the country and avoid being associated with him. Because if we don't move against Yurovsky within the next few weeks, then the KGB certainly will. I am speaking to you now as a friend of your husband.'

'My ex-husband,' Anna said quietly. 'We've been divorced for a long time. You've been very helpful, M. Jumeaux. I really didn't understand what was happening or why a man like Nicholas should mix himself up in something subversive. I understand it now. And why he lied to me.'

'What are you going to do?' Paul asked her. She had finished her brandy and pushed the glass away. It was a decisive gesture. She stood up.

'I'm going to deliver M. Jumeaux's message,' she said.

'And if he doesn't listen? Will you do what Raoul advises?'

'No,' Anna said. She turned to Jumeaux. 'Thank you for dinner,' she said. 'I'll take myself home. Goodnight.'

They watched her walk out of the restaurant. Paul Martin swung round to Jumeaux.

'Congratulations,' he said. 'You told the damned story so well she's going straight back to him!'

'To deliver my message,' Jumeaux said. He picked up his pipe and knocked the cold ash into an ashtray. 'That's what I wanted. She's a very determined young woman. She may well persuade him; and if she does, then "Return" will crumble to pieces. It is nothing without him. I always try persuasion first. Come on, it's nearly midnight. This poor fellow wants to close up.'

'Nicholas, sit down. It's very good to see you.' Anton Kruger was in his seventies, a short, thick-set man, with iron-grey hair and a rugged face; he moved like a much younger man, and everything about him, from his impeccably cut clothes to the Piaget watch and Hermès tie, bespoke money and power. They were alone in the study of his château outside Chartres; a telephone call had brought Nicholas down by car that evening, with an invitation to spend the night. He didn't like the Château Grandcour; it was not very large, because Anton Kruger was a practical man who insisted upon being comfortable, but it was dark and over-furnished, filled with a mass of priceless pictures, tapestry and furniture. Kruger's taste was oppressive. He liked size and splendour, and despised simplicity. The study was crammed with heavily gilded French furniture and every table was littered with objects. He looked at Nicholas and smiled.

'I'm sorry to drag you down here at such short notice,' he said. 'But I'm flying to Zürich tomorrow and I wanted a report before I go.'

'The delegation will be arriving in Paris on June 17th,' Nicholas said. 'Staying at the Embassy. There will be a reception at the Elysée, and a performance by the Comédie Française. They'll visit the usual places, Versailles, the Louvre; they're due to fly back five days later, after a lunch given by the Chamber of Deputies.'

'A very full programme,' Kruger said. 'I'm sure our friend will enjoy the theatre. He's become very culture conscious, I hear.'

'It must be a nice change from his usual entertainments,' Nicholas said quietly.

'You mustn't let personal feelings come into this,' Kruger said seriously. 'We've waited a long time for such an opportunity. You must act with absolute calculation, complete coldness. I know it isn't easy, especially for you, Nicholas, but it's the only way to make certain we succeed.'

He sat back, playing with an unlit cigar. Nicholas Yurovsky was exactly the right type to lead this particular enterprise. Courageous, cool-headed, determined, and with natural authority over the others. Kruger had been completely happy about him until now.

'Tell me,' he said gently, 'is it true that you're getting married?'

Nicholas looked up quickly. Elise must have told him about Anna.

'No,' he said, 'Not now.'

'An American lady,' Kruger said. 'Very rich, divorced. I don't wish to interfere in your private life, my friend, but was it wise to have personal entanglements at just this time? Is it possible that this girl knows anything about our enterprise?'

Nicholas didn't hesitate. 'No,' he said. 'She knows nothing.' Kruger had light-blue eyes; they were watching him with penetration. Nicholas knew more about him than the magazines and newspaper stories that were full of lies which Kruger had circulated about himself. He had made millions, he was involved in enterprises all over the world. He had a contracting business in France, had financed the building of a giant aluminium smelter in the Middle East. He arranged financial backing for overseas projects in return for a percentage of the profits; there were rumours that in his early years he had dealt in arms. He owned a block of shares in the Wedermans Publishing Corporation more as a hobby, because of an interest in the arts. He was the most ruthless operator in private that Nicholas could imagine. Only such a man could have taken up 'Return' and made it into an organization capable of striking a serious blow at the Soviet Union. Kruger was the financier, and on a massive scale.

'We broke up last weekend. I shan't be seeing her again.'

He faced Kruger boldly as he said it. The grim mouth smiled at him.

'It's sad, but just as well,' he said. 'I heard that you and she had quarrelled – I wondered what about, that was all.'

'Not about my work,' Nicholas said. There was a silence. Kruger found a box of matches and lit his cigar. He puffed for a moment or two.

'That's all right then,' he said. 'I've waited many years for this – we all have. No one and nothing must get in the way. Come, let's go and have dinner. My wife will be glad to see you. You know, you're quite a favourite of hers.'

Madame Kruger was an elegant Frenchwoman in her fifties; she had been married to him for thirty years and they were ideally happy. They had no children and seemed to be completely absorbed in each other. So far as the world knew, Anton Kruger kept no mistress and had no interests beyond his enormous business empire, his art collection and his wife. She was a beautiful woman with a gentle manner that Nicholas admired. Very feminine, very soft, yet he knew her capable of immense fortitude and courage. She would have given her life for Anton Kruger. Looking at her smiling across the table, seeming deceptively young in the candlelight, Nicholas remembered that she had almost done so. . . . Danger of that magnitude created a bond stronger than ordinary love between a man and a woman.

He thought of Anna, half-listening to the conversation which was concerned with a new play the Krugers had seen. If only she had agreed to go to the States, just for that month. Mentally he chided himself for being a selfish fool. Kruger was right; there was no place in his life for a woman, much less marriage. Not until their plan was carried out. He had loved Anna too much to admit that he was involving her in danger, until Paul Martin forced him to face reality. That nagged at him constantly; how did Martin know of his activities? How, when the security of 'Return' was so tight that no single member ever met or contacted another outside their organized meetings? He himself had kept a deliberately low profile ever since he met Kruger, avoiding any connection with fellow-Russians.

There was no way a journalist like Martin would know his political feelings were anti-Soviet or anything else, unless someone had talked. And that meant they were being watched. He hadn't told Kruger the truth, because he didn't want Anna involved and he was afraid that Kruger might suspect her, might believe that he had hinted to her that he wasn't what he seemed. He didn't rationalize his lie to Kruger; it had been instinctive. It made him uncomfortable, sitting with them.

'Poor Nicholas,' He started, as Madame Kruger spoke to him. 'How dull this is for you – two old people gossiping about a play you haven't even seen – have some more soufflé?'

He shook his head; she was smiling kindly at him. He liked and admired her more and more. So feminine and gentle, yet incredibly brave and strong. Without Régine, Anton Kruger often reminded him, I would have been dead, like all the others. . . .

'I'm not very hungry, thank you,' he said. She got up, and looked at her husband.

'We'll have coffee in the salon,' she said. 'Nicholas looks tired; you're not to keep him up all night talking.'

'We've had our talk,' her husband said. She paused and looked at both of them.

'Is it going well?' she asked quietly.

'Very well,' Nicholas said.

'Good.' Her beautiful smile showed again. 'I'm looking forward to seeing Feodor Gusev. I wonder if he'll recognize me?'

'Of course he will,' Anton Kruger slipped his arm around her as they went out of the room together. 'You were as beautiful then as you are now. He'll recognize us all.'

There was no reply from Nicholas's apartment: he lived in a first-floor flat in a crumbling, elegant eighteenth-century house in the Rue de l'Université, hidden away in one of the dark little courtyards that had survived Napoleon's planning of the city. It was a simple three-roomed flat, not luxuriously furnished, but comfortable and whenever Anna had been there, untidy. She had found it too dark and oppressive, preferring to have him stay with her. And then there was the escape to the forest at weekends, the warm and cosseting atmosphere of the Auberge St-Julien. But it was odd, Anna thought suddenly, that she had never liked the proprietress, Elise. She put the receiver down. It was one o'clock in the morning. He might be out, or away. The suspicion that he might be with another woman was quickly brushed aside. It was not the moment to be jealous, but she was surprised at how the idea had wounded her. Love, she thought, looking at the silent telephone. This was love, this agony, this determination, this ache above the heart. Never for Paul Martin, nor for any of the men she had known in the States. Only for Nicholas Yurovsky. The son of Count Michael Yurovsky, who had come to life for her that night, as she listened to Raoul Jumeaux. She could see him as clearly as if she had known him all those years ago. A tall, elegant man, unmistakably an aristocrat from a vanished world. Jumeaux had fleshed out the man in the tiny photograph in the back of his watch. She could see Vermeuil and Liliane Yurovsky, and her father, the collaborator, and the two children in the nursery. Nicholas had a sister, Olga. Jumeaux didn't say what had happened to her. . . . Anna couldn't sleep; she poured herself a brandy, and made coffee to go with it. Her kitchen was streamlined, super-fitted. She seldom cooked in it until she met Nicholas. Paul was not a husband who liked dinners at home. He was restless, always on the telephone, dashing out to meet someone, promising not to be long and coming back in the small hours. Life with him had been a nerve-racking existence, full of uncertainties. Full of shadowy figures who were contacts, instead of friends, restaurant meals and bars. Politics dominated the conversation and motivated his life. Even when he wasn't being aggressive, Paul managed to make her feel a criminal because she was rich and had a mother with extreme right-wing views and the power to advance them. He had used sex like a weapon, and made her feel inadequate there too. Now he was back in her life, playing a new role, the concerned ex-husband who was trying to protect her. The result of his interference was to precipitate a misunderstanding that had nearly parted her from Nicholas for good. She was grateful to Raoul Jumeaux for clearing her doubts; she was certain that hadn't been part of Paul's motive in introducing them. That part of his plan had definitely gone wrong. She could sense his reaction in the restaurant, watching her as she listened to Jumeaux.

It was not a story that aroused his sympathy. Jumeaux was more compassionate than he was, and Anna didn't consider him a type who indulged in sentimentality. Jumeaux had delivered the watch. She took her coffee and brandy into her bedroom, kicked off her shoes and lay down on the bed. The room was full of ghosts, flitting between her and the Boucher drawings, the silk walls, mocking the luxury which was her consolation to herself for not being loved. Men and women, and children too. The Cossack General Shuvalov glared at her with his fierce eyes, full of suffering and defiance; there was the sound of weeping and gunfire in her head. The coffee turned cold, as she forgot to drink it. She fell asleep with the lights on, and the last conscious image in her mind was Nicholas's father. The image changed as she began to dream. It was Nicholas she saw, bareheaded, gaunt, going to his death.

After the Allied invasion of Europe began, Liliane Yurovsky shut up the house at Vermeuil and moved in with her father. Nicholas was six and his little sister four; they didn't mind going to live with their grandfather; they regarded the big, ugly Château as a second home. Nicholas, albeit still segregated in the nursery with Marie, whom he hated because she showed such a preference for Olga, sensed that his mother was anxious and upset. She never smiled; he often saw her look as if she had been crying. She became extremely angry and punished him on the occasions when he asked when his father was coming back, until he learned not to speak about him. He was very sensitive to the atmosphere of alarm and confusion which was spreading through his family, and he couldn't understand why his mother and grandfather kept talking about losing the war.

The Germans were losing the war, not the French. Marie had explained that to him one day, and he couldn't see why she sounded so vindictive. The Germans were being driven out of France, she told him. And then a lot of people would have some explaining to do. . . . She left when they moved out of their house. He had been standing in the hall, holding Olga by her hand, pulling at her to make her stand upright, becaused she sagged at her fat little knees deliberately. His mother was there, looking white and unwell as usual, and there was a jaunty, impudent air about the girl Marie as she said goodbye.

'Goodbye, Madame Yurovsky. I hope it won't be too bad for you and M. Druet. I just feel so sorry for the children!' Then she had walked out of the hall and down the steps to the courtyard. Her father was waiting outside with a handcart filled with her luggage. Olga had begun to cry. 'Marie . . . Marie . . .' She had loved her nurse. Nicholas was so angry that he let go her hand and she tumbled on to her bottom. To his surprise his mother hadn't been cross. She had picked up the little girl and comforted her, and for a moment she stroked Nicholas's head.

'Don't cry,' she said. 'Don't cry, darlings – we'll be all right. Don't worry. We're going to grandfather's. We'll manage.'

The little boy had looked at her. 'I'm not crying, Mama. And don't *you* worry. I'll take care of you, till Papa comes back.' He never forgot that moment. His mother had looked at him, and he saw that in spite of his mistake, she wasn't angry. Her eyes filled with tears and overflowed.

'He won't be coming back,' she said. 'They'll get him too.' Later that afternoon his grandfather's car came over to fetch them; there was a big inflatable gas bag on the roof, because for a long time the Germans hadn't permitted civilian use of petrol. Not even to supporters like Etienne Druet. He hadn't asked his mother what she meant. There was a shocking finality in her words which was matched by her grief. For the first time she hadn't seemed to hate his father or be cross at hearing him mentioned. He cried himself to sleep that night. The time passed and like all healthy children he occupied himself playing in the Château gardens and hunting rabbits in the woods with his grandfather's terriers. Christmas came, a subdued Christmas with very little of the good things he remembered. There were no servants; his mother and grandfather seemed strangely lonely, as if everyone had left them. He saw some Germans come to the Château but he was always kept away from them. Six months later his grandfather was arrested. Among his story-books was a romance about the French Revolution, with some engravings of mob scenes and the guillotine. The way in which his grandfather was taken away reminded him of one of the illustrations. A crowd of people came to the Château. There were two cars and a lot of bicycles; men and women, most of them young, were carrying sub-machine guns and had belts full of rifle bullets slung round their chests. He recognized people he knew among them; the baker and the *charcutier*, the village schoolteacher and his young wife. He had never seen any of them with guns before. The village gendarme was with them, and there were strangers, wearing berets and combat boots with the trousers tucked into the tops.

They began to hammer on the door of the Château and shout. He watched from an upstairs window, and ran down to find his mother. He was suddenly very frightened. She was in the hall, holding on to his grandfather's arm; her face was contorted with weeping and fear. Grandfather Etienne had always been a solid figure in Nicholas's life, benign and confident, the purveyor of expensive presents, someone who spoiled them and took his father's place after he had gone away to fight for Russia. Nicholas had never forgotten that was where his father had gone. And why. To make Russia free again. They were safe till he came home because Grandfather Etienne was there. Now the old man was weak and trembling, his heavy face had sunk round the jowls and the mouth quivered. There was another heavy crash against the door and his mother screamed. He saw his grandfather pull free of her and go to open it; she flung herself after him, trying to drag him back. He heard his grandfather shout at her.

'Go away, Lili, for God's sake, they'll only take you too!

What about the children? Get out of the way! If they break down the door they'll run mad in here.'

He turned and seized Nicholas's mother and pushed her towards the stairs. Then they both saw Nicholas, and with a cry of anguish Liliane ran to him and gathered him to her. She was hysterical, he couldn't understand her because she was sobbing.

'Niki, Niki, oh, my God, my God save us, help us . . .'

He saw his grandfather open the front door; his mother was half carrying, half dragging him up the stairs on to the landing. She crouched down behind the balustrade, and they stayed hidden. She was gasping and crying, her tears wetting his face. He put his arms round her and wept with her, as the crowd caught hold of his grandfather. Somebody, he thought it was the schoolteacher, struck the old man in the face. Both his arms were seized, people were pushing him and hitting him with their fists. He had a moment's glimpse of his face as he was hustled through the door, and there was blood all over it, like a red mask.

He never saw his grandfather Etienne again.

His mother moved out of the Château. They had to walk to the station, he leading Olga by the hand, and his mother dragging their suitcases, because nobody would help them. When his mother went into the village for a few supplies women she had known all her life refused to serve her. Several times people spat in her face.

They moved into their grandfather's flat in Paris. It had been shut up for a year; he remembered the smell of must and stale air when they opened the door. He had never visited it, and he thought it very bright, full of gilt furniture and pretty ornaments which Olga was always trying to touch. But there was nowhere to play, he hadn't been able to bring many toys, and he saw no other children. His mother had few visitors, but among them was his father's mother, Grandmother Zia. She hadn't visited them very often. He didn't know why. When she came now, the atmosphere was stiff. He sensed that she and his mother didn't like each other, although they were always polite. His grandmother seemed to be sorry for his mother. He heard her say once, 'My deepest sympathy, Liliane – but it is a blessing. He couldn't have survived such a sentence.' His mother was wearing a black dress, and he thought with great fear that his father had died. He learned later, when his mother told him, that his grandfather Etienne had had a heart attack. He couldn't see why, in his grandmother's words, this should be a blessing. The world was an unsafe, crumbling place, constantly changing and always in a frightening way. He felt sorry for his mother who was getting very thin and seemed too tired to cry or be cross. He felt it his duty to protect her, and he tried hard to put up with Olga, who was infuriating and never did what she was told. He had to help his mother and hold on until his father came home. He had heard his grandmother mention that too.

'Of course he'll come back,' she said to his mother one day. They always talked in low voices when the children were near.

'He isn't a Soviet citizen. He's a prisoner-of-war. The Allies would never . . .' He didn't hear the rest. He went on waiting for his father to come home.

Nicholas woke with a start. His body was cold with sweat; he had been dreaming the same nightmare again, going back through his subconscious to his childhood. Re-living, albeit through the distortion of sleep, the traumas of the time when the war ended. His grandfather had died in prison; it was less than a year, and it seemed shorter, till his mother caught scarlet fever, and gave it to him and to Olga. They were in the same hospital, but there were screens round Olga's cot, and his mother was in a separate room. His grandmother, Countess Zia, came to take him home when he was better; Olga had died, and they had told him very gently that his mother had gone too. He was eight years old. He reached out for the light by his bedside. There were cigarettes there and a lighter. He sat up and lit a cigarette.

Nightmares about the past were a part of his life; he accepted them and recognized the necessity for the injured psyche to express itself. Otherwise he showed no visible scar. He had learned very early to suppress his feelings, to discipline his mind and toughen his body. His Russian grandmother had taught him that weakness was unforgivable in a Yurovsky. He had gone back to her small apartment in a house in the Rue Fourcray in the 17th *arrondissement*.

It was let to Russian émigrés like herself. They lived in a tight community, speaking Russian and observing the customs and even the protocol of their long-forgotten world. There was a weekly dinner given by each family, and the grey-haired man who presided at the head of the table worked as a tally clerk in a local factory. But he was always addressed as Prince, and Nicholas had to bow to him. A mad world in a way, Nicholas thought, watching his cigarette smoke drift into the column of light cast by the bedside lamp. But no madder than the one in which he and the Krugers were living. Anton Kruger, with his millions, a new identity established after thirty years, was as bound by this past as the sad little émigrés in the Rue Fourcray had been by theirs. As Nicholas was himself. The call of blood was too strong, the cry for retribution too clear, in spite of the years. They were Russians, all of them, and they had never integrated except on the surface. Kruger least of all. It was exactly three years since Nicholas got the letter inviting him to what was described as a reunion.

It was a dinner party, given in a private room of the Ritz Hotel. Anton Kruger was the host. Some of them had known each other; Nicholas knew none of them, except Volkov, whose parents had been friends of Countess Zia and her group. He had never liked Volkov even when they were children. He had been a wild, unstable boy, inclined to solve everything with his fists. A compensation, Nicholas had once said to himself, for being so stupid. Nicholas had cut loose from all his childhood contacts when his grandmother died. He was nineteen and studying Literature and History of Art at the Sorbonne. Countess Zia had been better off than he supposed. She had left Russia with enough jewellery and some outside investments which had survived the vicissitudes of the French stock markets. He was independent although not by any standards well off. He sold her pearls and a diamond cross she always wore, with the exception of one piece she had asked in her will should never leave the family. He had been going to give it to Anna as a wedding present.

He had accepted Kruger's invitation against his better judgement; he was curious in spite of himself. They had met in the private room and eaten a magnificent Russian meal, presided over by the famous financier and his French wife, and nothing had been said until the table was cleared and waiters came in with a portable screen and a 16mm projector. The lights went down and one of the waiters stayed behind and began showing them films. There was no sound: Kruger gave the commentary. Nicholas would never forget the atmosphere in the dark room, pierced by the long beam of the projector and the flickering figures on the screen. There were twenty people sitting round the long table, turned towards that screen, watching in total silence, while Anton Kruger talked. There was suddenly a shattering cry from a woman seated not too far away from him; a fat, middle-aged woman who had told him she kept a hotel. 'My father! My father!' She had broken down and begun to weep. And then he heard his own name mentioned. 'Yurovsky.' He could hear Kruger saying it now. 'Count Michael Yurovsky.' It was a very brief glimpse, a face turned momentarily towards him from the grave, sunken and unshaven, a look of total despair in the eyes. When the show was over there was a stricken silence. Even the fat woman had stopped crying.

It was nearly dawn before they began to disperse, and when they did 'Return' had come into being. Kruger's brainchild, Kruger's proposal for a corporate vengeance which would shock the world. And strip away the lies and the hypocrisy which had hidden the truth from the West. Feodor Gusev. He had appeared in the movie too; there were several shots of him. Nicholas had almost smoked his cigarette down to its filter; Gusev. He was called Grigor Malenkov now, his past identity carefully obscured. A respectable elder statesman with a popular image in the free world. A jolly figure, fond of vodka and folksy jokes. A Khrushchev type, now that Khrushchev himself was dead, and the Soviet needed a link man for *détente*. Someone more human than the austere Chairman of the Central Committee and President of the USSR.

They couldn't be too bad if Malenkov was an example of the top rank. Possibly even the ultimate leader. . . . Cartoonists liked him; that was always indicative of success.

Nicholas stubbed out the inch of cigarette. He was not to be killed. Kruger was adamant about that. People like Volkov wanted to rip him to pieces. Elise too. She had been fourteen when her father was captured. His memory was indelibly fixed in her mind. When she spoke of him at their meetings, her eyes filled with tears. A big, laughing man, with immense vitality for life. A marvellous horseman, a total hero figure to his daughter. Elise certainly couldn't be trusted. There were times when he wondered if, face to face with Gusev, he could trust himself. He lit a second cigarette, helped himself to the Vichy water which was by the bedside. Kruger liked the old-fashioned embellishments when he had guests. There were cigarettes, mineral water and a little glass and silver jar of biscuits in every bedroom, and, regardless of the time of year, a hot-water bottle to take the chill off the sheets.

In many ways it was a pre-war house; there was a sense of the thirties about the way in which Régine Kruger entertained. The attention to detail was extraordinary. He enjoyed staying there; he had hoped to introduce Anna to them; he was sure the Krugers would have liked her and she approve of them. He had been trying not to think of Anna, occupying his mind with the preparations for Kruger's plan, keeping the pain at a distance. Now, in the empty hours of the night, he had no defence. It was finished; Kruger was right, when he said it should never have begun. But then neither should *his* love affair with Régine, all those years ago . . . he had forgotten the power of the heart when he rebuked Nicholas. He tortured himself, imagining her reaction when she found the letter. She had been badly hurt in life already. Now he had inflicted another wound, and he couldn't forgive himself. But he knew he had no other choice. Marrying her, with what was ahead of him, would immediately endanger her. He had deluded himself that it would be possible because he loved her, and needed her so much that he wouldn't face the truth. And it might well be that he and others would be killed. Certainly if they failed, there would be no survivors.

He had no right to lie to Kruger; three long years of patient planning were at stake, the objective was coming closer every day, and he had denied Kruger the truth. And the truth couldn't be avoided. His cover was partly blown. It was useless to pretend that Paul Martin had made an inspired guess, hoping to influence Anna against him. That explanation was too glib; he had rejected it immediately Anna told him of their meeting in the Ritz. Martin knew something, not much but enough to put the security of the whole group at risk. Anxiety for Anna had overridden everything when he wrote that letter and walked out of her life. Now his first duty was to Kruger and his comrades, to men and women like Zepirov whose entire family had been destroyed, to the orphaned Maximova, von Bronsart with a judicial murder to avenge, to stupid, stormy Volkov, whose mother had committed suicide. . . .

Above all to Anton Kruger. It would have been easy for him to forget, to enjoy his money and his old age, without concern for the injustices of the past. The bond between him and Nicholas was of a very special kind, more personal than anything he shared with the other members of 'Return'. He owed his job in Wedermans to Kruger; he hadn't discovered that until later. Kruger knew he was his father's son. . . . He threw back the bedclothes and got up. He needed to get out of the confines of the room, to breathe fresh air and think.

The Château was in darkness; a tall window lit the landing and he groped his way down the stairs. He switched on the light in the hall, unbolted the big front door, and walked out into the cool spring night. The garden was full of scents from flowering shrubs; a three-quarter moon lit the sky. He walked slowly round the path to the side of the house; there was a rose garden and a swimming pool, shimmering in the silver moonlight. All the members of 'Return' were bound by the same circumstances of betrayal and death. Yet their existence was known. The idea froze him. He stopped, hands clenched in his dressing-gown pocket.

He had to tell Kruger immediately. If there was a leak, it had to be stopped. He wouldn't let himself think what it meant if the SDECE were watching them seriously. He turned and walked back to the house. There were lights in the hall and he remembered switching them off; Anton Kruger was waiting for him.

He wore a blue dressing gown, with his initials on the pocket, and he was smoking calmly. He put his arm round Nicholas's shoulder.

'I've known there was something wrong since you came down. Let's go into the library and have a drink. You'd better tell me all about it.'

'Madame Martin?'

Anna had never heard the voice before. 'Yes, speaking. Who is that?' It was a foreign accent, definitely not French; holding the telephone she felt herself stiffen. It was early in the morning; she felt drained and uneasy, and the unexpected caller worried her. 'Who is that?' she repeated.

'You don't know me, Madame,' the voice said. 'My name is Anton Kruger. I am a friend of Nicholas.'

'Oh, is anything wrong? Is he all right?'

'Of course,' the man sounded soothing. 'Of course. He's very well. But I wondered whether you would meet me. I would like to talk to you about him. Privately.'

'He's never spoken about you,' Anna said.

'I'm on the Board of Wedermans,' he said. 'We've known each other a long time. I do hope you will meet me. Could I take you to lunch today?'

She hesitated. Wedermans; the name Kruger was familiar, but she couldn't think why. Perhaps Nicholas had mentioned him and she'd forgotten. If he wanted to talk about Nicholas, then she was certainly going to meet him.

'Where is Nicholas?' she said. 'I've been trying to call him – he's been away . . .'

'Staying with me,' he said. 'Please, don't telephone him until you've talked to me. Could you come to the Tour d'Argent at one o'clock? I would send a car for you, but I think it's better if you meet me at the restaurant.'

'I'll be there,' Anna said.

'Excellent,' the voice said. 'I shall look forward to meeting you.'

When she arrived at the Tour d'Argent, the head waiter came towards her. It was one of the smartest restaurants in Paris, filled with a fashionable clientele, who came to be seen as well as to eat some of the best food in the world. 'I'm meeting M. Kruger,' she said.

'This way, Madame. He is waiting for you.' She didn't notice people looking after her as she passed – in a room thronged with elegant women, superbly dressed and presented, Anna's natural colouring and beauty attracted the attention of both sexes. The manager, preceding her, was aware of the looks and the interest. He had served Anton Kruger for many years. It was the first time he had ever entertained a young woman. Someone very different from the hothouse Parisiennes all around them, lunching with rich men.

He had a genius for slotting his clients into the proper social niche. The American lady was also of consequence in her own right. He brought Anna to Kruger's table, summoned a waiter with an imperious snap of his fingers, pulled out her chair himself. The man who rose to kiss her hand was older than she had expected: very heavy set, with broad shoulders and a large head, thatched with white hair. It was a broad face, with bright deep-set blue eyes. Even before he spoke she knew he was a Slav. His hands were thick and powerful, coarse, the right wrist fringed with grey hairs and encircled by a platinum Piaget watch.

'I am delighted you came,' he said. 'It's very good of you.' He had an attractive voice, deep toned, very male. She was immediately aware of an abnormally strong personality. Magnetism was not too strong a description of Anton Kruger's aura. He smiled at her, and his face became very soft.

'No wonder my Nicholas fell in love with you. You're very beautiful!'

My Nicholas.

'I expect you know he's left me,' Anna said.

75

He nodded. 'Yes, he told me so. Let us order first, and then we'll talk. Are you in the mood for fish? The *sole Colbert* is very good . . .'

She chose without taking any trouble; she felt no desire for food. When the dishes came, she picked at them. Kruger ate sparingly but with a gourmet's appreciation. He had ordered a fine Chablis which he spent some moments discussing with the wine waiter. Anna watched him, and as she did so, felt that she was seeing a performance, sensitively given, for her benefit. He was playing the rich dilettante, the connoisseur of food and wine; he had said he was on the Board of Wedermans' publishing house, and this was surprising. There was nothing of the intellectual about him; he radiated power, and the coarse hands and features were at odds with his superbly cut clothes and accessories.

He was what he had made himself, not what he was born. She didn't wait for him to begin.

'You're Russian, M. Kruger?'

He pleased her by showing surprise. 'Yes. I was born in the Ukraine. You have a sensitive ear.'

'I wasn't sure at first. Your French is so good.'

'I've lived here a very long time. Longer than you've been alive, I think. I had the good luck to marry a Frenchwoman. She helped with my grammar, but she couldn't do much about my accent.' He laughed.

'Tell me,' Anna said. 'Why did you ask to see me? What do you want to tell me about Nicholas?'

'He's very much in love with you,' Kruger said. 'Do you feel as strongly about him?'

'Yes,' she answered. 'I do.'

'We had a long talk last night,' he said. 'He told me about you; he told me about the conversation you had with your ex-husband. That was very disturbing.'

'It disturbed me,' Anna said quietly.

'Your husband was telling the truth,' Kruger said. 'Nicholas is engaged in very dangerous work. The reason I said it was disturbing is because I had no idea that anyone knew about it. This has put Nicholas at risk. And more than Nicholas. How did Paul Martin come to hear about his political activities? Did he tell you?'

'I know how he heard it,' Anna said quietly. 'Let me understand this, M. Kruger, are you involved in this too?'

He didn't answer.

'Please, Madame Martin, tell me who told your husband.'

'A friend of his in the SDECE, a man called Raoul Jumeaux.' She saw his expression change; the little eyes flickered like a camera shutter. 'I had dinner with both of them last night. Jumeaux told me what happened to Nicholas's father. To all those thousands of people.'

She paused, not seeing him for a moment. 'I couldn't believe it. Jumeaux was there, acting as liaison for the Free French. He was the last person on our side to see Nicholas's father. He told me the whole terrible story, and he warned me that Nicholas was getting himself mixed up in some mad anti-Russian scheme. He told me to go back and tell Nicholas that the SDECE were watching him and probably so were the KGB.'

She looked at Kruger. 'Whatever you're planning,' she said quietly, 'they know about it. You'll never get away with it. Nicholas will just be killed.'

'And that was Raoul Jumeaux's message,' Kruger said; he spoke as if to himself. 'Now that I know how your husband found out, how did Jumeaux find out? – that's the next question we've got to answer.'

'I don't see it matters,' Anna said. 'I spent most of last night thinking about it. You can't hurt the Soviet Union, whatever you do! You won't even be allowed to make the gesture – the French will simply crush you.'

Kruger smiled at her. 'Jumeaux was very convincing, wasn't he? He thoroughly frightened you, so that you would come back and frighten Nicholas. Yes, and perhaps you could persuade him to back out. Isn't that right, Madame Martin?'

'Yes,' Anna admitted. 'I'm sure that's why he told me. But you know, I felt he sympathized. Not that it would make any difference, but he obviously understood how Nicholas felt. And you must feel too. Did you lose someone?'

The old man knotted his hands together and leaned his chin upon them. His head seemed disembodied, dominated by the bright sharp eyes.

'I lost my comrades,' he said slowly. 'Men I'd fought with and shared some of the worst battles of the war. Their wives and children too. And my officer; I'd been with him from the beginning. We went through everything together, him and me. Right to the end. Raoul Jumeaux told you about the end, didn't he, Madame? About the political dilemma of the Western powers, about the agreement made at Yalta that condemned us all? Well, I will tell you about what happened after that. I was there, you see. I'm a big man now, my dear lady, very important, very rich. But I was born Antonyii Krosnevsky in a little village in the Western Ukraine. My father had a small farm, not much, just a few acres, and we all worked on it. I was twelve when the Soviets annexed it. They shot my father, and our land became part of the big collective farm. I joined the Germans when they invaded us. We told them where our local commissar was hiding and they hanged him. We all stood round and watched. I joined the Russian Free Division, and I ended up as Colonel Count Yurovsky's driver.'

He leaned back suddenly; the wine waiter was beside them, inquiring if there was anything they wanted. The restaurant was filled with people; the chatter of conversation was like an accompaniment to the tinkle and murmur of food and wine being expertly served.

'Would you like a liqueur?' Anton Kruger asked her. The waiter hovered by his chair. She shook her head. He turned to the man and smiled. 'Yellow Chartreuse for me, and a cigar. My usual. Thank you.'

'We were all taken to Baratina Camp,' he said. 'Separated from our officers, of course. We had our Orthodox priests with us; nearly all of the men and their families were Cossacks. I was there because I was taken with the Colonel. He wouldn't let them send me to the Ukrainian camp. It was too near the Yugoslavian border. He said he needed me, and they let us stay together for the first part. We were being guarded by the

English. They were civilized. We were all full of optimism. All except the Count. He used to talk to me. He knew all along what was going to happen. There were some Free French liaising with the English, and some French nurses helping to look after the sick. My wife was one of them.'

He paused, taking the pierced cigar from the wine waiter, drawing on it gently. He sipped the Chartreuse. 'Thank you,' he said. The waiter left them. 'I am going to tell you exactly what happened and why,' Anton Kruger said. 'Then I am going to ask you to make a decision; a very important one for us all. And especially for the man you love, Madame Martin. Will you listen to me – it will take some time and it won't be pleasant.'

'Please tell me,' Anna said quietly. 'I want to know everything.'

One of the terms of the Yalta agreement was the Western Allies' promise to repatriate all Soviet citizens who had been captured by the Germans and any who had fought for them. Stalin had already announced that any Russian guilty of surrender to the Germans was counted as dead; it was inconceivable that Russia should admit that a million of its citizens had actually joined the German army and fought alongside them. Churchill and Roosevelt's decision to accept this agreement was due to the desire to maintain good relations with the Soviet Union. Her armies were established in Europe and constituted a threat to peace, and a bargaining point was the return of thousands of British prisoners-of-war whose camps had been overrun by the Russian advance. The extent of the forcible repatriation was not completely realized, until the numbers of Russians involved became evident. Soviet liaison officers were sent to the camps throughout Europe, Britain and the United States, where Russians captured in German uniform were held. One of the largest of these camps, where the Cossack division had surrendered, was at Baratina on the Austro-Hungarian border. Baratina had been a minor concentration camp, and the accommodation housed all the Russian prisoners and their families. Conditions were good; Yurovsky found himself on friendly terms with the British officers and the officer commanding, an austere Scotsman, was scrupulously fair. There was an air of unreality about Baratina; he used to walk round the compound, smoking, and talking to Shuvalov, who had brought his troops to the nearest British column and surrendered. He had no intention of being surprised by the advancing Soviet forces and taken alive. His people would be safe with the Allies. Yurovsky hadn't tried to argue. The war was lost and so were they. All they could hope for was mercy and understanding from the democracies, who must certainly be menaced now by Soviet armies in the heart of Europe. Shuvalov and he took their daily exercise in the compound. Beyond the officers' quarters the Cossacks, with their families and their horses, encamped in a huge complex, loosely guarded, expecting to be absorbed into the Allied forces.

The air of hope was sustained by innocence and desperation. Nobody wanted to consider an alternative. It was incredible to Michael Yurovsky that a seasoned soldier like Alexander Shuvalov, should cling to the same illusion as his simple Cossacks.

'You're gloomy,' Shuvalov accused him. 'What's the matter with you?' They had been at Baratina for a month. Nothing was happening, but there were always rumours. Rumours of release, of being broken into units and sent to different camps, rumours even that war between America and Britain on one side and the Soviet Union on the other had already broken out. Michael heard most of them from Antonyii, his driver, who was allowed in to help him and perform orderly duties. There was nothing simple or optimistic about the Ukrainian. He was full of dread, and he talked of escaping and running off into the mountains. Yurovsky knew that only his devotion to him had so far prevented him from doing so. He looked sideways at Shuvalov before he answered. The General had shrunk; his hair was now completely white. He had led his men through some of the most savage fighting on the Eastern front, retreating in a rearguard action against advancing Soviet forces which had cost terrible casualties. None of his wounded had been left alive to be captured; on their side no prisoners were taken. No quarter, but a fight to the death. And defeat at the end, the ruin of the dream which had brought him and others like him back into soldiering, and given their persecuted people hope. Russia had not been freed; the Communist enemy was victorious, and their only thought was to escape that enemy's revenge.

'Colonel Macdonald has called us to a meeting tonight,' Michael Yurovsky said.

'I know, I know,' Shuvalov interrupted. 'He wants to explain to us what the Allies have in mind. Why should that make you suspicious, Michael – you're always suspecting them of cheating us, and they haven't done a single dishonourable thing so far. I trust these British. They're soldiers, men of their word. If Macdonald says we're going to be resettled somewhere while they think what is best to do for us, then I believe him!'

'It's not Macdonald I suspect,' Yurovsky said. 'It's the politicians. He'll carry out his orders. Whatever happens, it won't be his fault. But I don't believe we're going to escape, that's all.'

'You'll see tonight,' Shuvalov said. 'I hear the senior officers and myself are going to be sent to England.'

'I heard it was Lünnen,' Michael Yurovsky said. 'Somebody else will tell you, we're going to be moved to Rumania, and handed over to the Soviets . . .'

'I'd cut my throat now,' Shuvalov said, 'if I thought they'd do that! They can't give us up to them, Michael – we're not Soviet citizens – we left Russia before 1920! I'm going to face Colonel Macdonald with this talk about Rumania tonight. He'll have to answer me.'

Colonel James Alastair Macdonald had fought through the worst of the Italian campaign, and right up into Europe. His regiment were among the toughest troops in the British army. He sat in his office with a bottle of whisky on the table in front of him, and faced two men sitting opposite to him. The Englishman of the two was a bland, rather effeminate civil servant, the kind of pedantic civilian for whom the Colonel had nothing but contempt. He had a pale face, long, adorned with horn-rimmed spectacles, and thin receding hair; he was muffled in a British army coat, without insignia, and this affectation also irritated Macdonald. The other man, his camouflage jacket removed, wore the olive grey uniform of the Soviet army. He was short and round faced, his head so close cropped that he looked bald. His age was difficult to judge; Macdonald guessed him to be in his twenties. He had said nothing so far, and Macdonald assumed that he couldn't speak English. The odious civilian was on hand to act as an interpreter as well. The letters of authority he gave the Colonel were signed by the General commanding the area.

His name was Redway.

'You have to appreciate the position, Colonel,' he said. 'It has been agreed at the highest level that these people must be repatriated to account for their crimes. It isn't the ethic we're discussing, and I must point out that this is not really your concern. It is the practical method of separating the officers from the rest. Without provoking a riot. I've explained all this to Major Gusev. And I must ask you to hand over to him your list of those officers so that they can be checked against Soviet records.'

Macdonald looked at him. He felt the Russian watching him.

'There are between thirty and forty thousand people under guard here,' he said. 'I haven't sufficient troops to cope with a serious attempt either at resistance or escape. You're asking me to gather these officers together, tell them a pack of lies, and get them on a train which will deliver them into Soviet territory. One rumour that they're being forcibly repatriated, and this whole camp will explode like a bomb. I won't be responsible for that. If Major Gusev wants these people, then he'd better bring in a detachment of Russian troops and do the dirty work himself!' He took an aggressive swallow of his whisky. Shuvalov, Yurovsky, the German General von Bronsart had been his mess guests. The thought of deceiving them revolted him.

'The lists, if you please, Colonel. We can start with that.' It was Major Gusev who spoke, in perfect English. Macdonald nearly swallowed his drink the wrong way. The round black eyes were expressionless as glass.

'The General has authorized you to hand them over,' Redway reminded him. Macdonald stood up. He went to a metal filing cabinet and jerked open the top drawer. He took a folder out and threw it on the desk. He spoke to the Russian.

'There you are,' he said. 'Some of them won't concern you. They're not Soviet citizens.'

'They're Russians,' Major Gusev said. 'We want them all.'

Antonyii Krosnevsky was in the dispensary. He had queued for two hours, with men, women and children, suffering from minor ailments. He had been suffering from eczema on the backs of his hands; they were raw and itched intolerably. Régine Bourand was the nurse in charge. Antonyii had been struck by her gentleness and sympathy with the sick Cossacks none of whom could speak a word of French. Whenever he came for treatment, he acted as interpreter. Living as the Colonel's driver servant, he had picked up a little of the language. She was an attractive girl, soft spoken and compassionate, with large brown eyes that he never tired of looking into when he got the chance. He was motivated by three things during his weeks in Baratina. The desire to escape, his anxiety for Colonel Yurovsky, and his love for the nurse Régine.

It was an odd courtship; he continued to queue long after the skin infection had improved, and she continued to treat him. He stayed during the clinics and interpreted. It was Régine who whispered to him that she had seen an army car drive up and a man that she was certain was a Soviet officer go into Colonel Macdonald's office.

Antonyii was due to go into the officers' compound that evening. He left the clinic, warning Régine to say nothing to anyone, and tried to decide what to do. The rumours that their officers were going to be resettled were already sweeping through the Cossack camp. It was thought to be a good sign. All round him, fires were being kindled and the evening meal prepared by families from rations given to them by the British army. The Cossacks maintained their customs even as prisoners. The women cared for their men and their children and the men looked after their horses. The atmosphere with the British soldiers was increasingly friendly; since there was little communication possible, sign language served as well. Soldiers were generous to the Cossack children. Goodwill and the futility of trying to escape made life in the camp deceptively carefree. Religious services were held in the main compound; Orthodox priests led the singing of hymns and preached sermons exhorting their people never to return to atheist Russia.

Antonyii wandered miserably from one hut to the next; he talked to everyone, trying to decide upon the general mood. If their officers were taken, would they revolt? If he spread the word that there was a Soviet officer already in the camp, would the reaction be panic, outrage, or the hopeless apathy which had at times permeated the whole compound? . . . He couldn't make up his mind. Gradually the decision became clear. He would warn his Colonel, and let the General and the senior officers decide what action to take. One thing was certain. The officers must not be persuaded to go anywhere. Without them, the Cossacks would be leaderless. When he went to the entrance to the officers' compound, a sentry barred his way with a rifle. No one was allowed into the officers' quarters that night. They were all at a meeting. In hopeless despair, Antonyii argued and pleaded, trying to make himself understood, not understanding the explanation given to him. All he knew was the rifle with its bayonet at the end, jabbing towards him as he tried to pass.

'Get back!' the sentry shouted. 'Get back or I'll stick you!' The Russian turned and stumbled away. Régine had not been mistaken. The Soviets were in the camp, and already the officers were being isolated prior to being moved away. He went behind one of the huts and leaning his head against the wooden wall he wept.

He couldn't warn Colonel Yurovsky. But perhaps Régine Bourand could. He ran off to the dispensary; it was closed and the Red Cross staff had returned to their own quarters. He spent the next few hours hanging round the perimeter of the wire that separated him from Michael Yurovsky, hoping to see him walk across the compound. When it was too dark to see, Antonyii gave up. He dragged himself back to his hut and crawled into his bunk. A group of men playing dice called him to join them. He mumbled an excuse and turned away.

They were doomed, all of them. He most of all, because he was a citizen of the Soviet Union and had fought in the German army. He was still in uniform, with the flashes of the Cossack army on his collar. Doomed. He would be shot as soon as he was handed over. Or sent to the dreaded labour camps in the north. Better to die than be starved and worked to death. . . . Better still to escape, and take his chance in the mountains. Security at the camp was still slack. It was easy to slip away now. Tomorrow, after he had tried once more to see his Colonel. Perhaps in the morning they would let him through to the officers' compound. If they did, he might still be in time.

The air above the ranks of seated Russian officers was dense and blue with smoke. Colonel Macdonald was addressing them. Redway sat on a chair behind him, his adjutant was on the left.

Alexander Shuvalov, accompanied by Michael Yurovsky and a dozen senior officers, was seated in the front rank.

'As I told you, gentlemen, the trucks will arrive at 1100 hours tomorrow morning and you will be escorted to the station and entrained for Lünnen. There you will be temporarily housed while further discussions about your future take place.'

Michael Yurovsky watched him quietly. The Colonel was sweating; there was a sheen on his forehead and a thick frown between his bushy brows.

He had cleared his throat several times while speaking, and he hurried his words as if he were anxious to finish with them. A man thoroughly ill at ease, doing something he detested. A man of honour who was lying to men who trusted him, men who had given their promise not to escape, precisely because of that trust.

Yurovsky saw Shuvalov get to his feet, and the British Colonel paused. Shuvalov asked his question in French; he looked round for Michael to translate.

'There are rumours that we are being sent into Soviet-held territory, where we will be handed over to the Red Army. I must ask you, Colonel Macdonald, to deny that this is true.'

Michael Yurovsky saw the British officer turn for a fraction and glare at the civilian who was seated near him. He gave a loud, angry sounding cough.

'You have my assurance, gentlemen. You are going to Lünnen.'

'Thank you,' Shuvalov said in French. He bowed to the Colonel and sat down. There was a moment when Macdonald and Michael Yurovsky looked at each other. There was shame and real distress in the eyes of the British Colonel. Yurovsky took his seat again and spared him, by glancing away. They were going to be handed over. He had always expected it, and now the miserable charade being played out convinced him. Not just the deserters from the Red Army, like the two officers on his left, or the prisoners-of-war who had saved their lives by joining up, but others who had never even lived under Soviet rule.

Men like himself and Alexander Shuvalov. Old enemies who would not be permitted to escape a second time. He could so easily have been killed fighting. An honourable death rather than the firing squad. Poor Shuvalov, suddenly gullible as a child. The heart had gone out of him, although he didn't realize it. They had all gambled, Yurovsky thought, and they had lost. He needn't have joined Shuvalov. He could have stayed in safety with Liliane and his children. There hadn't been any word from them since he left Vermeuil. His letters were returned, with Liliane's writing scrawled across them: 'Not known. Return to sender.' She had never forgiven him. It would go hard with old Druet because of his collaboration. Hard with his family, too. But there was nothing he could do for them. No way he could send a word to his wife, asking her forgiveness, or to his son, in the hope that he would not forget him.

When the meeting was over they filed back to their quarters. Michael took Shuvalov aside. He lit the General's cigarette and noticed that the old man's hand was trembling.

'He's lying,' Michael Yurovsky said quietly. 'I saw it in his face. We're not going to Lünnen. It's a trick!'

Shuvalov looked up at him; his eyes were red-rimmed, but his mouth was set in anger.

'He gave his word! You've got this idea into your head and nothing will move it! We're not going to be handed over, I tell you! We can't be – don't you understand? No man can be returned to a country when he isn't a citizen of that country! Out of the whole lot of us, only about twenty officers were even *born* in the Soviet Union – we're stateless persons, some of us took out French citizenship – damnation, Michael, you're determined to cause a panic . . .' He swung away from Yurovsky, stubbing out the cigarette. 'I order you not to spread this nonsense; you'll seriously damage morale!'

'You won't face the truth,' Michael Yurovsky said. 'The British have had their orders – we're going to be separated from our people, because without leadership they'll be easier to manage. I know Colonel Macdonald; he's a decent man and a bad liar. But he was lying tonight and he knew that I knew it.'

'All right,' Shuvalov snarled at him. 'All right, he was lying. We're going to be handed over to the Reds . . . so what do you suggest we do, eh? We've no weapons. We've got nowhere to go –'

Yurovsky laid his hand on the General's shoulder. 'We're going to be betrayed, and all our people with us. Call a meeting of the officers, tell them what we suspect. Refuse to go tomorrow, and call for a mass escape. They can't stop us, General, don't you see that? They haven't enough troops – we can simply march out and away, and if they open fire it'll be murder, killing unarmed men with their women and children. Good God, man we have twenty-odd thousand horses here, enough to take an army into the mountains!'

Shuvalov reached up and pushed his hand away.

'This is fantasy,' he said. 'We have nowhere to go. I told you this morning I'm not going into the mountains to be hunted down like a dog and take my Cossacks with me – to what? To die of cold and hunger, to be shot down by anyone who sees us? And why, because you have convinced yourself that the British are in league with the Red Army?' He shook his head, and some of the anger faded. 'No,' he said. 'I don't believe it. I trust Macdonald. I trust the British. I asked him tonight, and he gave me his word as a soldier. You can escape if you like, my son, but I am going to Lünnen tomorrow with the others.' He walked away from Michael Yurovsky and lowered himself into a chair, alongside two other officers who were playing cards. He looked old and shrunken, and he didn't speak to them.

Michael Yurovsky went to his bunk and sat down. Shuvalov was a broken old man; the tiger had died in that last retreat, the fierce spirit was finally quenched; all he could do was to hope for the best against his better judgement. He stayed alone for a long time, grieving for his General.

Raoul Jumeaux found him there; it was quite late and he had come over, bringing a bottle of wine. He was acting as liaison officer between the British and the Free French forces, and he had formed a friendship with the Count as soon as they met. He was a young man, but of the same quiet, civilized turn of mind; they talked about books and stamp collecting, which had been Yurovsky's hobby as a boy, discovered a mutual delight in the French classical theatre, and enjoyed each other's company. Jumeaux had come to understand and admire the Russian; he recognized a steadfastness of spirit which distinguished certain men from their fellows. He had no sympathy with the pre-war Russian émigrés on principle; his political leanings were to the intellectual left, but Yurovsky had impressed him as an example of what was the best in a vanished caste. He had also, in spite of himself, conceived a liking for the Russians as a whole. Listening to the singing in the camp stirred emotions he didn't suspect in himself – the sight of so many thousands worshipping with their priests in the open compounds aroused his compassion and his disquiet. It was a sensation that was growing, as he heard of the officers' removal to Lünnen.

He and Michael drank to each other; he thought the Russian looked suddenly drawn and much older.

'I hear you're being moved out tomorrow,' he said. 'I came to say goodbye and wish you luck.'

'Thank you,' Count Yurovsky said. 'We're going, but not to Lünnen.'

Jumeaux stared at him. 'What do you mean – I was told this evening.'

'I think,' Michael said quietly, 'that we are going to be handed over to the Soviet army. I'm very glad you came to see me, *Capitaine;* you could perhaps do me a favour?'

'But this is nonsense,' Jumeaux protested. 'You can't believe a thing like that? I heard it specifically from Colonel Macdonald's adjutant. You're all going to Lünnen to be resettled.'

'I hope you're right,' Yurovsky said. 'But I don't believe it. I tried to convince my General, but he won't listen. Nobody will listen. They all trust Colonel Macdonald and are happily packing their bags.'

'Then why the hell don't you run for it?' Jumeaux couldn't contain himself. 'Look, Colonel, we're friends, you and I. You can walk out of the camp with me and disappear! I shan't say anything – My God, if this is true I've never heard of anything so monstrous!' The young Frenchman had turned quite pale. He had got up and was standing beside the Count, his fists clenched with anger.

'I'll help you to get away,' he said. 'Don't you realize what will happen to people like you if you're given up to the Red Army? It's unthinkable – surely international law forbids forcible repatriation . . . it must do. . . .'

Michael Yurovsky shook his head.

'You're a good friend,' he said gently. 'But I can't do what you offer.'

'Why not?' Jumeaux demanded. 'Are you just going to stay and be handed back?'

'I've been with General Shuvalov from the beginning,' the Count said. 'We're comrades from a long way back. From 1919 we fought together; he was like a second father to me when I lost everyone. He needs me now. I can't leave him.'

Jumeaux stared at him; Yurovsky went on calmly. 'Try to understand. When a man dies it's sad enough; when his spirit dies and he still lives, that is the worst of all. I never thought to see Alexander Shuvalov surrender; but he has. His heart has broken. He'll need me after tomorrow. If I had been the one to die inside, he would have stayed with me. I shall go with him.

After all, you may be right. We may find ourselves in Lünnen after all.' He smiled, and standing, took something out of his pocket.

'In case I am right,' he said. 'Would you give this to my son Nicholas – as and when you can? It's all I've got to give him. It was my father's gift to me.' Jumeaux took the flat gold fob watch. 'My wife lived at Vermeuil, in Normandy; God knows where they are by now, but if you could try and find them, and give this to my son . . . Kiss him for me, and tell him that I loved him and send him my blessing. Tell him that I died for the freedom of our country.'

Jumeaux took the watch, 'I don't believe it,' he said. 'I can't.'

'And this,' the Count said. 'Give this to my orderly, Krosnevsky. He's a good fellow. Would you do me another favour?'

Jumeaux nodded. He was not an emotional man but there was a tightness in his throat.

'Accept this,' Yurovsky said. 'Keep it and think of me sometimes.' It was an old-fashioned silver cigarette case, with a monogram in gold. Impractical because it held only half a dozen cigarettes. He had seen such things in junk shops, priced at a few francs. Nobody used them any more. He put it in his pocket with the watch and the little amber cigarette holder for Antonyii Krosnevsky.

'I am going straight to Colonel Macdonald,' he said harshly, 'And demand that he tells me the truth. As liaison for the French forces, I have a right to be told!'

He turned and rushed out into the darkness of the officers' compound. His last memory of Michael Yurovsky showed him standing by the bunk, with his glass raised, sipping the wine Jumeaux had brought him. He reached the British officers' mess in a state of agitation and mounting rage. It was unthinkable that such a despicable trick should be played on men who had given and honoured their own word not to escape. Unthinkable and quite out of character with the upright commander of the British forces. When he found Colonel Macdonald, he was sitting at a corner table, with the civilian

Redway, drinking whisky. Jumeaux stood very still; there was another man, also drinking, sitting beside Redway. He wore the uniform and insignia of a major in the Soviet army. Colonel Macdonald looked up, gestured to Jumeaux to come and join them. He seemed acutely embarrassed and uncomfortable. Jumeaux didn't speak. He looked at each of them in turn, and then walked away and out of the mess.

The trucks arrived promptly at ten o'clock and the officers began loading into them with their luggage. Antonyii Krosnevsky had not been allowed to attend his officer that morning. Large crowds were gathered on the other side of the wire, watching the General and his officers leave. There was a deep silence, almost a numbness as the Cossacks watched. But it couldn't be a bad sign, because their officers were leaving quite voluntarily and didn't seem downcast. Many of them, especially the General, seemed in very good spirits.

Antonyii fought to the front of the wire, pushing and cursing to make his way. There he saw Michael Yurovsky walking towards a large covered truck, carrying his bag. He shouted to him, and Yurovsky turned. He hesitated, seeing Antonyii, and then walked over to the wire. Antonyii was crying, reaching his hand through the barbed strands, begging him not to go, that it was all a trick, the Reds were in the camp. . . . For a moment their hands touched; blood ran down Antonyii's bare arm where the barbed wire had ripped him. Yurovsky looked into the distraught face of the young man, and shook his head.

'It's no good, my poor friend. I know, I know . . . be calm now, don't cause a panic. Make sure you get away. And God go with you. Remember me in your prayers.'

Anton Kruger paused. He did a strange thing; he passed his hand quickly across his eyes. 'That was the last I saw of him,' he said. 'They were all driven away. The train waiting for them was a series of cattle trucks. They were bolted in and driven to Judenburg, where the Red Army took them over.

When they opened the trucks, blood was streaming through the cracks in the doors. Many had killed themselves with their own razors, others were hanging from the roof. Nicholas's father did not commit suicide. Films were taken by Soviet cameramen of that scene and many others like it. He walked out quite calmly, and went up to the Red Army officer who took possession from their British guards. He saluted him. It was a man called Feodor Gusev. He had travelled from Baratina to be there. He tried to be at every reception point. He picked out the first two hundred from his list and they were taken outside the railway station and shot. But they kept Nicholas's father and the other Tsarist ex-officers. They sent them to Moscow.'

It seemed to Anna as if the noise around them had receded. She was hardly aware of the hum of other conversations; it was as if she and Anton Kruger were isolated from their surroundings.

She felt physically chilled.

'He gave Captain Jumeaux his gold watch before he left Baratina,' the old man said. 'And a memento for me.' He felt in his pocket, held out his hand to Anna. A small amber cigarette holder with a gold band lay in the palm. 'I kept it with me,' he said. 'I wouldn't part with it even to Nicholas.'

'How did you get away?' Anna said slowly. She found it difficult to speak. Her throat was constricted.

'Through Régine,' he said. 'Immediately security was tightened round the camp; the Cossacks were forbidden to wander off into the country. Hundreds of them escaped before they could make the place completely secure. I was caught.' He put the little holder away.

'I was given detention as a punishment, and by the time I was released, Baratina was ringed with troops and wire. We all knew what to expect when Feodor Gusev returned, and men were brought before him in batches. He had the lists in front of him, lists given voluntarily by our officers when we surrendered. He spent a month at Baratina, looking for specific persons on that list. My name was not on it, Madame Martin, because I was a Ukrainian, and Colonel Yurovsky hadn't given any details of my background. He had tried to protect me, you see. But hundreds of others were singled out and sent back by force in small groups. It was a clever technique. Those that Gusev wanted were not returned to the main camp after their interviews. They were kept in a special compound where the troops could manhandle them into transports the following day. All these were marked for death. As for the rest – quite soon the suicides began. Men murdered their wives and children and then killed themselves rather than go back to Russia. Colonel Macdonald and his troops had to be replaced; they were threatening to mutiny. They were tough fighting men, Madame Martin, but they didn't like using bayonets and clubs on helpless people to beat them into the trucks taking them to the cattle trains. They didn't like unlocking the huts in the mornings and finding bodies hanging from the roof.

'When Gusev had finished selecting his victims, the order came to clear the camp. And that was when the Cossacks staged a last resistance. When the transports came to take them away they barricaded themselves into the camp, with the women and children and their priests, and they refused to move. I will spare you the details of how that attempt was broken. But I'll tell you this. I saw women and children being dragged to those trucks, by soldiers who were weeping as they carried out their orders. My arm was broken by a rifle butt; they picked me up and threw me into the back of a truck. It was full of crying, screaming people, and of unconscious men, bleeding from the beatings they'd been given. And then I saw Régine. Régine with her hair all pulled down, struggling and shouting at the soldiers guarding that truck. She was crying, and they couldn't understand her. But she was in French uniform and they didn't dare to mishandle her. One of the officers came up.

'She began to argue with him – I heard her telling him that I had no business being taken away. "He's Polish," she was saying. "He's one of my orderlies in the clinic . . ."'

'"I'm sorry," the officer said. "He was in with all the others. I can't let him go. He can see the officer in charge at the depot. They've got some Polish workers there. If he's a Pole he won't go on the train." Do you know what she did, Madame Martin, my wife? She climbed up into that truck and travelled with me.'

There were tears in Anna's eyes. She tried to blink them back but Kruger saw them.

'When we got to the station she tried to argue for me. The officer had red hair, I remember that. He was very young and he looked sick and nervous.

'"I'll call someone over," he said to her. "They'll identify him. Some of these poor devils say they're Polish just to stay behind." I heard him call out, and I knew it was hopeless. The truck was empty now – there was only Régine and a soldier guarding me. I'll remember her beautiful face as long as I live. She came up to me and pushed me; she'd bound up my arm.

'" Run," she whispered. "Run now! Go on, for God's sake, run!" I didn't stop to think, I just did as she said. I ran, Madame. I heard the sentry yell at me and I heard a shot. I turned round and saw Régine – she had thrown herself at the rifle as he fired. That's how I got away. They were too busy driving the poor wretches on to the train to bother looking for one man. I owe her my life. Not one of those men, women and children who were sent back survived. Those who weren't shot on arrival died in the labour camps.'

The restaurant was almost empty; the head waiter made a gesture to his staff. M. Kruger was deep in conversation. He was not to be disturbed.

'And Nicholas's father,' Anna asked. 'And the General . . . they died, didn't they? – '

'Yes,' Anton Kruger said. 'It took a long time to find out exactly what happened to them. But I did it. Money can buy anything in the end. It bought me those documentary films and it bought me the details of Michael Yurovsky's death. After many, many years.'

He had been in the semi-darkness for so long that the bright corridor lights were agony to his eyes. Time had long ceased to have any relevance – night and day were the same in the windowless gloom. He hadn't been interrogated for a long time; he sometimes dreamed of his questioners, and the round, flat face of the officer who had received him at the railway station was always floating in his subconscious.

He had enjoyed his work. Once, Yurovsky had seen General Shuvalov coming out of that room just before he went in. He had looked distraught and mad, like an old broken doll being dragged along. He blinked in the bright lights, walking with slow steps down the white-painted passage, his eyes watering. His hands were strapped behind him. It had come at last, and he was thankful. He was going to die at last. They had got tired of tormenting him. He mumbled a prayer to himself. He had forgotten about his family, his children. His mind was floating, disorientated, capable of periods of lucid thought but not for long.

Death. He welcomed it. The bullet would be quick, a soldier's end.

They stopped in front of a door, and when it opened, he was led inside. His eyes cleared and he looked round him. Shuvalov and the German General von Bronsart were already there, so was the seventy-year-old Tsarist General Daslov. He thought it must be them because there was an odd familiarity about the figures in their prison grey. He looked about him for the firing squad. There was none. Then he saw the gallows.

'Good afternoon, M. Kruger – I hope everything was satisfactory?'

The head waiter held open the door for them.

'Thank you,' Anton Kruger said. 'An excellent lunch.' He took Anna's arm and they walked down to the street.

'My car is over there,' he said. A big Mercedes began to slide away from the pavement and come towards them. The driver wore a dark blue livery; he handed Kruger and Anna into the back. Kruger pressed a button and the glass partition came up, sealing them off.

'You are quite sure you want to do this?' he asked her. She turned and looked at him. She was very pale, but there was a look of determination that owed a lot to the grandfather who had founded Campbell Steel.

'Nothing in the world would stop me,' Anna said. 'I'm with you, and everything I've got is with you too.'

'I'm glad,' Kruger said simply. 'I gambled on you, even before we met. I thought you might reach this decision.'

'There couldn't be any other,' Anna said. 'Last night I would have done my best to dissuade Nicholas. And you. But not now. Now I'd kill that man myself.'

'He isn't going to die,' Kruger said quietly. 'That would be too easy for him. He's just going to tell the world the truth.'

'Nicholas won't like this,' she told him. 'He won't want me to get involved.'

'You became involved the moment your ex-husband talked to you,' Kruger said. 'Nicholas will accept it when he knows you won't be in any personal danger.'

'I don't mind if I am,' she said. She put out her hand and touched his arm. 'I'm going into this with all my heart.'

Kruger took her hand and kissed it.

'I know you are,' he said. 'And it's a brave and generous heart. You remind me of Régine. Nicholas is very lucky.' The car had turned on to the A13 leaving the suburbs of Paris behind. It began to pick up speed as it took the road to Chartres, and the Château Grandcour, where Nicholas was waiting for them.

4

'It's very touching to see them,' Régine Kruger said. She slipped her hand through her husband's arm. 'It's good to see people in love like that. It makes me feel young.'

'You are young,' he said. 'You never change, sweetheart. He's chosen very well; she's a rare woman.'

'I hope nothing goes wrong,' his wife said quietly. 'I wouldn't want anything to happen to him. Or to her.'

'It won't,' Anton said. 'If everything goes as we plan, there is no danger after the first phase. And I've planned that to the smallest detail; you know that. There is no danger after we take him. And finding Anna Campbell Martin involved in it is a pure gift from God. She is going to make the most difficult part the easiest.'

His wife looked at him. 'How – what do you mean?'

'Because she is who she is,' he said. 'And her mother is coming over to Paris to meet Nicholas.'

'You have some scheme,' Régine said. 'Some trick to play you haven't told me about. Anton, what is it? You're not to hurt these two young people. I won't let you!'

'Don't worry,' he said. 'Nicholas means as much to me as a son; and I like the girl. The one I'm going to hurt is Gusev. Let's go and walk in the garden. I shall tell you my little plan.'

Nicholas took her to his room; they didn't wait for explanations, the need to make love overwhelmed them. Almost without words they touched and came together; their reunion, their reconciliation was an intrinsic part of the sexuality, which was stronger than it had ever been.

'It's never been like this before,' he whispered to her.

'No,' she said. 'I love you so much, I can't believe it. More than ever, my darling, now that I know what you suffered.'

He raised himself and turned on his back, his arm holding her close.

'They say it's very important for a son to love his father. Even though I was so small when he left, his memory remained as clear to me as if I'd seen him only the day before. He taught me my first words of Russian; I can see his face now, and remember how he used to lift me in his arms and kiss me. He was a very affectionate man, very tender.' He turned his head to look at her. 'My mother kept saying he'd deserted us. I didn't believe her. I knew he'd gone to fight for Russia. Do you know, my darling, that it took them nearly the whole year to break his spirit? They used everything; starvation, brutal beatings, sensory deprivation – sleep, light, continuous noise. They knew the psychological tricks that can send a prisoner mad, and they used them long before we in the West had any knowledge of such methods. In the end they had to destroy his will with drugs. He wrote a confession for them; Anton showed me a photocopy of it. He admitted being a criminal, guilty of crimes against the State and he asked to be punished by death. There were marks on the paper; they looked like tears.' Nicholas wasn't looking at her; he was staring upwards, his voice very low.

'They weren't satisfied to kill him; they wanted to break him as a human being, to bring a shuffling zombie to the gallows. They did the same with the others. They drove Shuvalov completely mad . . .' Anna felt him crying, although he lay perfectly still. She reached up and caught him in her arms.

'Don't, don't, my love – don't distress yourself – they didn't break your father, or the others. Nobody could stand against that sort of treatment. Think of him as he was, as you remember him –'

'You shouldn't be here,' he said at last. 'Kruger had no right to mix you up in this. My darling, I left you because I couldn't bring you into danger!' He kissed her gently, first on the lips, then the eyelids and the lips again; the kiss lingered, 'But I couldn't do without you now. I couldn't lose you a second time.'

She twisted her arms round his neck. 'From now on,' she said, 'we're together in this. I love you with all my heart, and what happened to your father and your family feels as if it happened to me. I'm part of everything to do with you. I'll never forget what Anton told me, and even then I had no idea the ending was so dreadful for them.' She paused a moment, and he felt her shiver. 'There are some things that just can't go unpunished, and what happened to your father and all those helpless people who were sent back, has got to be accounted for. If life means anything at all, then you've got to stand against real evil. That's what you're doing, my darling, and I want to help. I want to get married to you very quickly. No fuss, no relatives, just ourselves. And the Krugers. What an incredible story –'

'It's been the love of a lifetime between them,' Nicholas said.

'It'll be the same with us,' Anna said. 'He's going to introduce me to the other members. I've got to be part of "Return". I want to be a part of it.'

'No,' he said. 'That isn't necessary. Telling you the facts was enough.'

'No it wasn't,' Anna insisted. 'I'm the link with Jumeaux and the SDECE. That makes me very important; I've got to convince him that "Return" is falling apart, that I've persuaded you to leave it. He may tell me more, if he thinks I'm on his side.'

Nicholas held her close to him; her enthusiasm frightened him. Kruger had awoken a crusading spirit which he didn't know she possessed. He had touched her heart and her sense of justice, and she couldn't be deflected. When she talked of his father there were tears in her eyes.

He had never loved her more, but there was a part of him which was angry with Anton Kruger and uneasy for her. Very uneasy. The idea of her deliberately misleading a senior member of the French secret intelligence service disturbed him deeply. He didn't argue with her; the initiative had suddenly been taken away from him. Now she wanted marriage without even waiting till her mother met him; her commitment was not just to him now, but to the ideal behind 'Return', to Kruger's inflexible quest for justice in the name of the dead.

He had never doubted her courage and generosity; it was the degree of her determination that surprised him. He hoped the matching mood of recklessness would pass.

'Are you really prepared to marry me, without even waiting for your mother?'

'My mother,' Anna said, 'never treated me as anything but a kind of extension of herself. If people were nice to me it was because they were hoping to get something out of her – if a man wanted me, it was really because I was going to inherit all her money. She can come and she can meet you, but by that time we'll be married. If she doesn't like it, I don't give a damn.'

He rolled over on his back.

'The Orthodox service is very beautiful; my grandmother used to worship at the Cathedral of St Vladimir. She used to take me there when I was a child.'

'Then that's where we'll be married.' Anna said. She kissed him. 'I'm going to make you very happy,' she said softly. 'When I think what you suffered as a little boy it breaks my heart. Your mother and little sister dying like that – your father! When this is all over, we're going to have a wonderful life together.'

She felt his arms tighten around her; tenderness gave place to passion. She met and matched his desire, and they slept in each other's arms.

Below them Anton and Régine Kruger strolled in the garden, arm in arm. Régine looked up at her husband.

'You're a genius, my love,' she said. 'It was always the most difficult and dangerous part of our plan. Now, thanks to this girl it will be the simplest. And the most deadly.'

'Better than all the bloodthirsty suggestions of fools like Volkov and Elise,' Kruger said. 'In this way, Gusev will execute himself.'

'It's very kind of you to entertain me again, Madame Martin,'

Raoul Jumeaux said. He glanced round Anna's drawing room; he sighed with pleasure. 'You know, I do admire your taste; I love beautiful things.'

'Thank you,' Anna said. She handed him a drink and sat down. 'Paul never liked this flat; it was one of the things we used to argue about. He said it was over-furnished and decadent.'

Jumeaux smiled. 'He's very Spartan, isn't he – very radical Socialist? Every yard of fitted carpet is an affront to the poor, I know the sort of thing. Ever since I met you, I wondered why you ever married. You've really nothing in common.'

'I've often wondered that myself,' Anna admitted. 'I suppose I married him to spite my mother – it was a sort of gesture of independence. God knows why he married me.'

'I think he genuinely loved you,' Jumeaux said. 'He always talks as if he did. I think he's jealous of Nicholas Yurovsky. I imagine you gave him my message?'

She nodded. 'Yes, I did. I wanted to tell you exactly what happened.'

Jumeaux settled more easily into his armchair. His brown eyes were mild and interested. He began to fill his pipe.

'I told Nicholas exactly what you told me,' Anna said. 'I asked him about his father, and his own political activities and he admitted that he'd been getting together with a group of other Russians, children of émigrés like himself.'

'He did?' Jumeaux's eyebrows lifted. 'I'm surprised – please go on.'

'It wasn't easy,' she said quietly. 'He denied everything at first, but in the end he had to admit it. Your knowing about it was the crucial point. He couldn't go on lying then. I said exactly what you told me – that he was being watched by the French secret service, and that he would be caught between you and the Russians if he didn't give up whatever he was doing.'

'Ah,' Jumeaux said. He puffed hard on his pipe. 'And did he say what this thing was – this activity?'

Kruger had primed her for this question. She was carefully prepared for it. For someone who found lying difficult, she felt she was carrying it off extremely well.

'Not for a long time,' she admitted. 'I threatened to leave him for good; I said I wouldn't accept his promise to give up unless I knew what it was he was doing. It was such a stupid, hopeless gesture – I don't know how he could have been such a fool as to think it would make any difference.'

'And what was it, this gesture?'

'There's a Russian delegation coming over soon,' she said. 'Apparently there's a gala performance at the Comédie Française in their honour. Nicholas planned to infiltrate the audience; they were going to forge invitations. Then they were going to rush the stage and he was going to make a speech denouncing the Soviet Union and bringing up the Human Rights agreement at Helsinki. I told him I thought it was the most ridiculous idea. People like that don't care about a few demonstrators. They'd just laugh at them.'

'No,' Jumeaux said slowly, 'I disagree. I don't think they would find it very funny. I think it could have been a very ugly diplomatic incident and caused a great deal of trouble. This delegation is coming over with one of the most senior members of the Soviet Praesidium as its head. A man called Malenkov, Grigor Malenkov. He could be the next President of the Soviet Union. A demonstration in public like that, before an important audience, could have damaged the principle of *détente* between France and Russia for years. Not at all a stupid gesture, Madame. Our goodwill would have been questioned, our security blamed. Even our connivance suspected, in some quarters. It gives me a *frisson* to think of it!' He tapped his pipe against the ashtray and sparks glittered. He was visibly upset.

'Well, it's not going to happen now,' she said firmly. 'I told him I would tell you. He really got into a state then, but he couldn't stop me. That really decided him to drop the idea. It was very distressing; he actually cried.'

'Did he?' Jumeaux said. 'Very emotional people, the Russians. Did he mention who else was going to take part in this, who the other "infiltrators" were . . . he may find it difficult to dissuade them from some act of criminal stupidity!'

'He didn't say,' Anna shook her head. 'He just said it was all ruined, and he would have to tell them. I got the feeling, M. Jumeaux, that in one way that Nicholas himself was rather relieved. I felt he'd got in deep and couldn't get out. Anyway, we're getting married in a week's time. There won't be any more nonsense, I can assure you.'

'I'm very relieved to hear it,' Jumeaux said. He appeared to have relaxed again. 'Did he mention anyone called Volkov, by any chance? He's a White Russian, he works for an advertising firm and he's got very anti-Soviet views. Rather a hothead and a nuisance. Is he a friend of Nicholas, do you think – part of this group – what do they call themselves – "Revenge", "Return" . . . something like that . . .?'

She saw the trap just in time. She shook her head again.

'I don't know,' she said. 'He never mentioned anyone called Volkov and I never heard anything about a name for any of them. I think they were just a few people daydreaming about doing something to hurt the Russians. Much as I love Nicholas, he's not a very realistic man, you know. He's a great romantic.' She made herself smile, struggling hard to gain his trust and make him believe her. That attempt to get the name of 'Return' confirmed had warned her that he hadn't been gulled completely. 'I think he liked the secrecy and the cloak-and-dagger stuff. He wasn't too happy when I mentioned the SDECE though.'

'Then he is more realistic than you think,' Jumeaux said, 'which is just as well. If you're getting married, where will you spend your honeymoon?'

Another trap had opened; fear for Nicholas made her exceptionally acute. 'Venice,' she said. 'And then I think we may go to the States. Nicholas hasn't met my mother yet. And it'll help to break off from all this Russian nonsense. That's my intention, anyway.'

'I congratulate you, Madame,' Jumeaux said. 'You've acted with great good sense; I hoped you might be able to put a stop to this affair. I am sorry for these Russians; I can understand how Nicholas Yurovsky feels because I was involved myself, and it was a horrible experience, even for an outsider. But it would be sheer disaster for him or anyone else to try and make a gesture which could disturb Soviet–French relations at this time.' He looked at her and shrugged; he gave the impression of being genuinely relaxed.

'What's so strange, is that in different circumstances, we would have encouraged someone like Nicholas to show up Malenkov and cause trouble. Now it doesn't suit our policy. There's no guiding ethic in politics, or intelligence work, except expediency. Today's enemies can be tomorrow's friends. But I've got used to it. I live by the day.'

'You like your work,' Anna said. 'Just as Paul loves his; he used to say the same sort of thing, how rotten everything was and how cynical, but he wouldn't have given it up for the world. I don't think you would either.'

'No,' Jumeaux smiled. 'I'm hooked too. But I'm always happy when a problem works out as well as this one.' He got up, banged his pipe free of ash and slipped it into his pocket. He took Anna's hand and kissed it.

'Thank you, Madame Martin,' he said. 'You've been a great help to us, and I promise you, you've probably saved Yurovsky's life. I wish you a very happy marriage, and be sure to take a long trip for your honeymoon. Malenkov and his delegation leave by June 22nd. Goodbye.'

She went to the apartment door and watched him down the stairs; standing behind the window curtain she saw him cross the street, dodging the busy traffic, and disappear down the Rue St-Honoré.

The door to her bedroom opened and Nicholas came out. He took her in his arms. 'You were wonderful,' he said. 'I heard every word. He never caught you out once.'

'Do you think he believed me?'

'I think so; difficult to be sure without seeing his face. But when he said goodbye, I felt certain he'd accepted it.'

'I thought so too,' Anna said. 'You know, darling, I'm just beginning to shake slightly now – isn't that silly?'

'No,' Yurovsky said. He kissed her. 'Men like Jumeaux can be very dangerous. I didn't know we were going to America for our honeymoon. You might have consulted me,' he teased her gently. He didn't like the look of strain in her eyes.

'I wasn't thinking.' Anna said seriously. 'Don't joke, darling, please. I just said the first thing that came into my head.'

'You couldn't have said better,' Nicholas told her. 'Anton will be delighted with the way this has gone.'

Jumeaux went back to his office. He called for the file on 'Return' and studied it, smoking and making little marginal notes. Volkov, Zepirov, Natalie Maximova, Nicholas Yurovsky. Little ineffective people, poor and unsupported until the emergence of Yurovsky. He didn't believe Anna when she denied giving him money; she was a very rich woman and the suggestion made by Paul had embarrassed her. She had almost certainly given her lover large sums, as was quite usual, and he had channelled them into 'Return'. The quality of the anti-Soviet literature had rapidly improved; Zepirov and Maximova had been able to travel to London to liaise with the Ukrainian association, which was another nuisance group, mercifully located in Britain. Some startlingly anti-Russian articles had been planted in some of the intellectual newspapers and monthly magazines. This too was Nicholas Yurovsky's doing.

The campaign had suddenly increased and this in itself had caught the attention of the security services. But if he thought Anna was lying about giving Nicholas Yurovsky money, he was sure she had told him the truth when she said she had persuaded him to abandon the group. He knew the rich, and wild quixotic gestures weren't their style at all. She was a charming young woman, but sensible and accustomed to having her own way; he had seen the independence of her attitude when they first met.

And Nicholas, faced with the prospect of losing her and all that she represented in terms of security, had made his choice. Without him, and without Anna's funds, the little group would sink back into its ineffective obscurity. The danger that might have loomed hadn't materialized after all. He phoned through and gave orders to drop the continual surveillance on the known members of 'Return', but to make spot checks. Nicholas and Anna were to be watched closely until they had left the country. Arrangements must be made for a discreet surveillance in Venice until such time as they were known to have embarked for the United States. He closed the file and made a little satisfied doodle on his pad.

Kruger gave a reception for them at the Ritz Hotel. The Board of Wedermans' publishing house were there with their wives; there were over two hundred people invited. Anna had given Régine Kruger a list, and as the social columns reported the next day, it was a representative gathering of French intellectuals and the wealthy smart set.

The American Ambassador, by no means a friend of her mother who had angled for his post, graced the party and was charming to Anna and complimentary about Nicholas. He asked with false enthusiasm when Sheila Campbell could be expected, and hoped that she would be his guest at the Embassy. The party was a tremendous success; they posed for photographs, and it was while she was standing raising a glass with Nicholas for the photographer that Anna suddenly saw the face of Elise from the Auberge St-Julien in the crowd. She spilled champagne on the carpet. She took Nicholas by the arm and whispered to him. He nodded, 'I know. They're all here, mixing with the guests. You're going to be introduced to them afterwards. This is the perfect cover for us. Trust Anton.' He squeezed her hand, and they were engulfed by people wanting to talk to them. The rooms were very hot, stifling, and thick with cigarette smoke. By the time it was over the massive flower decorations were past their first freshness. She had shaken hands with so many people that her wrist ached. Anton and Régine came over to them. The old man smiled at her, his eyes very bright. His wife looked the personification of elegance in dark green velvet with a massive antique emerald brooch on her collar. She took Anna's arm.

'This way, my dear,' she said softly. 'They are all waiting to meet you.'

It was a small suite on the second floor, taken by Anton for that week. Régine needed to do some shopping and the party given to celebrate his protégé Nicholas's engagement was a good excuse to spend a few days in Paris. One by one the members of 'Return' had gathered there, waiting. There was a table loaded with drinks in one corner; as always the furniture was traditional but comfortable, and a large basket of formally arranged flowers stood on the table, with the compliments of the manager. Anton was in the centre of the group. There were about twelve people in the room, with a preponderance of men. Anna recognized Elise, and nodded to her. She felt suddenly awkward and ill at ease. Nicholas took her by the arm and led her forward.

'I want every one of you to meet my future wife. We will be married in five days' time, at St Vladimir's Cathedral.

'As a Yurovsky, she will be a member of "Return". She has already helped us a great deal.' He looked around the circle of faces. Some of them were hostile. 'In fact, my friends, if it weren't for her, our plan wouldn't be able to go forward. Tonight could have seen the disbandment of the organization. We owe her a great debt, and I am sure you will welcome her.' There was a moment when nobody moved. Anton and Régine Kruger hadn't spoken. Nicholas and Anna stood alone. Then a woman moved; not Elise who knew her, but a slim, dark woman in her forties, with a pale face and intense brown eyes, her hair cut simply with a straight fringe. She was beautiful in a stark way. She came to Anna and held out her hand.

'Welcome to "Return",' she said. 'My name is Natalie Maximova. My father fought with General Shuvalov; he and my mother were both shot.' Her clasp was firm; the look in her eyes was friendly. A tall, thin man, shabbily dressed, came and took her hand.

'Zepirov; my parents were part of the Ukrainian army. They killed themselves and my sister before they could be handed back. I ran away. Welcome.'

Another man, whose name made her start, with a crushing handshake. 'Volkov. My father and eldest brother were with Shuvalov. Both went back to Russia from prison camp in England. They were never seen again. My mother cut her throat.' He had eyes that burned when he looked at her; he turned and hurried back to his place. There was a violence in his movements and expression that frightened her. She remembered Jumeaux's description. 'A hothead, nuisance . . .' More than that, surely. A very dangerous man.

And then Elise, lumbering her heavy body towards Anna. 'We know each other,' she said. She smiled, and it was the same smile as when she welcomed her to the Auberge. Nothing had changed in her attitude to the American girl. She announced herself as all the others had done. 'My name was Rodzinskaya, my father fought with General Denislov. It took three men to get him on to the transport. I saw it with my own eyes. My mother was French – she wouldn't go with him.' A look of hate crossed her face. 'I don't know how he died. I hope they shot him quickly. Welcome.' She didn't take Anna's hand, she turned and went back and stood by the bar table.

Others followed her, a grey-haired woman with a motherly face and spectacles, a man not much younger than Anton Kruger, who had escaped death by running off into the mountains in Austria and was hidden by an Austrian girl who later married him. Somebody gave Anna a glass. It was vodka. It was Anton Kruger who proposed the toast to her. 'To Anna,' he said. 'Soon to be Countess Yurovskaya. God keep you and may the years bring happiness and children.'

She felt the dark eyes of the woman Maximova; their message was friendly, the red gaze of Volkov, whose dreadful history had been contained in those few sentences, the stare of the others, including one tall blond young man, whose grandfather had been the German General von Bronsart, hanged with the select few.

Fritz von Bronsart was studying law at the Sorbonne; he had lived in Paris for the past two years, made a circle of friends among the more serious students and was unofficially engaged to a girl he had known from childhood in Germany. It was understood by both families that they would marry when he was in a position to support a wife. They were from the same Junker background, members of what their parents bitterly described as the new poor, their estates confiscated in the Communist East German Democratic Republic, sustained by the determination and hardiness of their race and caste.

Fritz watched Nicholas and his wife; she was a very attractive woman, and she seemed rather shy and ill at ease. He understood her feelings because in many ways he shared them. He was part of the organization almost by an accident of injustice. His grandfather had been seconded to the Russians because he spoke Russian.

His delivery to the Soviet forces had been an act totally without legality or precedence; his execution as a war criminal was merely a judicial murder. Fritz had nothing in common with men like Volkov and Zepirov who were so much older, or the pale, fanatical Natalie Maximova, except the bond of the infamy inflicted upon their dead. He felt young and, in spite of his education and intelligence, ill at ease with all of them, except Count Nicholas. Nicholas had a binding charm; he neither patronized someone so much younger, nor ignored him. He was rather in awe of Anton Kruger; he hated him too, drinking the vodka which was being pressed on him, remembering how astonished he had been when he opened Kruger's invitation to that dinner which was followed by the silent film show. Fritz had seen his grandfather in several shots. He had looked very thin, his uniform ill-fitting because of it, with a look of stoic dignity that overcame the jostling and insults of the Red Army soldiers who took him in charge from the British at the train. Fritz hadn't known then which he hated most – the hereditary enemy, acting as always from the best possible motives in support of murder and injustice, or the Russians themselves, seizing their victims like wolves.

The vodka was taking its effect; he felt a little drunk, his emotions, normally well in hand, were not quite under his control. He had an urge to greet the Count's new bride and say something welcoming to her. He began to edge towards them.

Anna felt Nicholas slide his hand through her arm; the pressure of his body was strong against her side. He raised his glass to her and drank it down in one. Then he threw it into the marble grate. It shattered. 'No one else shall drink from that glass,' he said. 'No other toast will ever be drunk from it but the one to you. My love.' He took her hand and kissed it.

Anton Kruger began to clap. Soon the room was full of the sound of quiet applause. Then they were surrounded. Zepirov threw his arm round Nicholas's shoulder, the grey-haired woman kissed Anna, Maximova pushed towards them, her grave face alight with a lovely smile. The same word was repeated to her. Welcome. Welcome. We are so happy to have you. Glad you are one of us. Nicholas was referred to constantly as the Count. It sounded archaic, strange. More vodka was pressed on her. The blond young German came and sat himself beside her.

'Nicholas is so lucky,' he said. 'I could never involve my girl in this – she won't listen to the past. Wants to forget everything that happened, whitewash it all. My father was only a boy during the war – my grandfather was a German officer who never did anything dishonourable. Those bastards took our estates, ruined us, drove my grandmother out to beg . . . but my Ilse doesn't give a damn. She doesn't want to know about the old Germany . . . she's ashamed of the war . . . '

The woman Maximova came and pulled on his hand. 'Come away, Fritz, vodka doesn't agree with you – it makes you talk too much. It's my turn to talk to our new member. Go and get us a drink.'

She turned to Anna with the same gentle smile.

'Don't let us overwhelm you,' she said. 'We're a mixed little group. Some of us not too sane, perhaps. All we have is one thing in common. The blood of the innocent. And I know what you have, besides loving Count Nicholas. You have a conscience. I can see it in your eyes. The mirror of the soul, Madame. You love justice. Thank God for you.'

'Thank you,' Anna said. She felt a sudden prick of tears. The atmosphere of highly charged emotion was contagious; she wasn't proof against it. And yet, a part of her tried to insist, it's alien to you, alien to your sensible twentieth-century upbringing, your free-thinking American tradition. The use of titles was absurd, but it was outweighed by the natural courtesy and warmth of the people she was criticizing. They clung to the past, as young Fritz von Bronsart clung to his, holding fast to the traditions of the Germany which war and defeat had swept away for ever. She looked at Nicholas, talking and laughing,

Anton Kruger near him, and her heart ached with love for him and with the need, suddenly so urgent, to accomplish what he had sworn to do, and then, please God, if there was a God listening to her appeal, bury the dead once and for all, and get on with living.

'Darling,' she heard his voice beside her, 'I'm going to take you home.'

'All right,' she said. 'I'm beginning to feel the vodka.'

He laughed. 'I'm not surprised, it's not that stuff you buy over here calling itself vodka. It's the real thing. Russian – 80° proof – we'll say goodbye to Anton and Régine. Take my arm, darling.'

They walked out of the lift and down through the luxurious foyer. The last time had been when she met Paul; when they sat in the bar and he told her a story she hadn't wanted to believe. A story about anti-Soviet activists, and the danger she was in because of Nicholas. Because of her love for Nicholas. Now she was part of what he had warned her against. Committed to it, accepted by it. Within five days she would be married, her name changed to the unfamiliar Russian one. Within the circle of 'Return' she would be Countess Nicholas Yurovskaya. . . . They called a taxi and drove back to her apartment. He made her sit down in the splendid drawing room, where she had told Jumeaux all those effective lies, and she lit a cigarette and waited. Her mind was surprisingly clear, as if the vodka that made walking difficult had sharpened her perceptions. After their marriage they were going to Venice. Anton Kruger owned a *palazzo* on the Grand Canal, and he had offered it to them as a wedding present. Their public plans were to go on to America. She had explained all this in great detail to everyone she met at the reception, including the American Ambassador. Her mother would come back to Paris with them for a brief stay. The cover for Nicholas was being established. Jumeaux and his colleagues had to be convinced that he had left 'Return', and the group was disintegrating. There would be no demonstration at the Comédie Française, no embarrassing diplomatic incident to mar the visit of the murderous Malenkov, who had once, thirty years ago, called himself Feodor Gusev and ordered the deaths of thousands of men, women and children . . .

The Comédie Française. Anna found herself laughing. If only Jumeaux knew what they were really going to do – he'd settle for a few banners waving on a stage before a select audience, and think it was a blessing.

'Food, darling,' Nicholas said. 'Come on, I've made something for us. It's a surprise.'

He had bought it and prepared it before the party. She looked at the kitchen, spread with caviar and dishes of chopped onions and egg yolks, black Russian bread and gleaming yellow butter. There were dishes of pickled gherkins and beetroot, of smoked sausages and a bowl of sour cream. He put his arms round her and she leaned against him. He kissed her.

'It's been a long evening for you,' he said gently. 'I know that. My beautiful cool American lady has been through a thoroughly Russian emotional experience. Even this is the same. But we can't help it, sweetheart. We are a people who need drama in order to live. Or to feel alive. I've had enough vodka too. This is our own private feast. If I were one of my own ancestors I would get very drunk and ravish you. But I'm a civilized man. Sit down, I shall serve you dinner, and then ravish you.'

They both began to laugh, like children. There were tears on both their faces. He kissed her wildly, 'I love you, I adore you. We daren't drink any more vodka, my darling, but we can eat and open the wine. Before I serve you, tell me something – do you still love me?'

'Still?' she questioned. 'Why still – what could have changed me?' And then she saw that he was very sober, the joke of a moment before was just a play.

'Meeting my friends,' he said. 'Seeing the reality. Maybe regretting what you've done . . .'

Anna reached up and touched his face; she let her hand rest on his cheek.

'I've been thinking,' she said slowly. 'It's marvellous how vodka clears the head. I've spent most of my life trying not to get involved, I kept out of my mother's political life, I dodged my stepfathers'. I ran away from America and settled in Paris and pretended it was to find myself. It wasn't. It was just avoiding taking part in the world I was born in. I didn't feel adequate. Oh God, darling, there are always excuses for being selfish or a coward. Even when I married Paul I couldn't become part of his world either. I needed something like the story of your father and those poor murdered people to make me into a human being. To make me really feel for something outside of myself. When Anton took me to lunch that day I felt as if someone had smashed a glass wall that I'd been hiding behind all my life. I was so angry, darling, so upset, so damned emotionally moved – and for the first time, I wasn't the centre point of my own feelings. Other people were: dead people, people I couldn't possibly relate to myself except through you. Don't ever ask me if I regret meeting a woman like Natalie Maximova or the Krugers. I'm truly committed now, and it's a wonderful feeling. We're together in this, whatever happens. And I'll be a better wife for you because of it.'

He didn't answer for a moment. He held her very close.

'As for still loving you,' Anna said. 'You're just my whole life, that's all.'

They were married at four o'clock on the Friday afternoon. The civil ceremony took place that morning. But for Anna and Nicholas it was the Orthodox wedding that bound them. The Orthodox Cathedral of St Vladimir in the Rue Daru was a lofty domed building; the roof was an arc of gleaming gold mosaic, with a massive Christ in Majesty above the altar: there were tall candelabra and arching sprays of flowers, and the figures of the priests in their robes of cloth-of-gold, thickly embroidered and set with coloured stones, glittered in the candlelight. A superb Russian choir sang the anthems, as the Mass proceeded, and incense rose in fragrant drifts from the swinging censers of the acolytes.

To Anna it was a scene from history, a step backwards from the pragmatic present into the past of centuries ago. Anton Kruger stood witness for Nicholas; she had asked that Natalie Maximova should perform the office for her.

Two gilt crowns were held above their heads after they had

exchanged the solemn vows and wedding rings, and proceeded to the central table for prayers. The choir began the triumphal final anthem, and Nicholas turned her to him and gently kissed her on the forehead. She wore a long dress of cream silk, with a small flowered cap on the back of her hair. His wedding present gleamed and glittered on her breast. It was a brooch, made of a crystal heart, surrounded by diamonds and surmounted by the diamond-studded double-headed eagle of the Romanovs. It was the piece of jewellery Countess Zia Yurovskaya had stipulated should never be sold out of the family. It was the gift of the last Empress of Russia to the Countess on her wedding day. No one besides the Krugers and Maximova had been invited. A few worshippers stayed for the ceremony and the Mass; she and Nicholas walked out into blazing sunshine, and stood for photographs. Publicity of that kind was what they needed. The second marriage of Sheila Campbell's only daughter to a Russian in Paris would make the world press. It would please Jumeaux. At the steps, Maximova came up and kissed them.

'I have to get back to work,' she said softly. 'It's been a joy to be with you both. God bless you, and keep you.' She slipped away.

They lunched in the Krugers' suite at the Ritz; they seemed as happy as if Nicholas and Anna were their own children. Anton drank a toast to them, and there were tears in Régine Kruger's eyes when they left for their honeymoon flight to Venice.

'Have a happy time,' she said, holding Anna by the hand. 'I think you'll like the little *palazzo*. Anton and I have had some of our happiest times there.'

'We will,' Anna said. 'It's a wonderful wedding present. You've been so sweet to us —' She clung for a moment to Régine's hand. Anton Kruger put an arm round Nicholas.

'You'd better go, or you'll miss your flight. You have everything booked for the journey back?'

'Yes,' Nicholas said very quietly. He glanced at Anna, still talking to Régine. 'Back to Paris in transit for New York on the 18th.'

'Good,' Anton said. 'I think you may be watched in Venice. Don't let it disturb you.'

'I shan't,' Nicholas said. 'If they're checking on us, they won't be thinking about you. We'll drive straight down to the Château on the 18th.'

'If God wills,' Anton Kruger said in Russian. 'Goodbye, my dear boy.' He kissed Anna, and they came to the lift with them.

Régine Kruger plunged her hand into her bag and surprised them with a handful of rose petals. 'For luck,' she called out. The elevator doors closed and they were borne down to the street level.

Kruger put his arm round his wife's shoulders. They walked down the corridor back to their suite. He poured her a glass of champagne.

Now, my love,' he said. 'Our work begins in earnest. We have two weeks to get ready for our friend Gusev.'

'I'm seeing the builder tomorrow after lunch,' his wife said. She smiled. 'That little room will be easy to soundproof.'

Sheila Campbell was in bed when Anna's cable arrived with her morning mail. She had bought a charming small house in Georgetown as an adjunct to her apartment in New York and a mansion in Palm Beach, had it done over by a Washington decorator, emphasizing that she wanted everything functional rather than fancy. There were two big intercommunicating rooms for entertaining, a bedroom with a fine view and an office and a room for her secretary. She made a rule of being in her office by eight o'clock every morning, but she had developed a cold, and she was as adamant about spreading germs and neglecting her health as she was about every other aspect of her life. That morning she was staying in bed, fortified by vitamins, and her secretary brought in the mail as soon as her breakfast tray was removed. Sheila had dieted all her life; she weighed 150 pounds, exercised every day and never touched spirits. Sitting up in a cream bedjacket, her spectacles pushed up on her forehead, she looked a handsome woman in her early forties. She was nearer sixty than she would ever admit. She had her father's fiery red hair, suitably toned down by age and artifice into a rich gold, cut short and curly and she wore her favourite pearl necklace in bed because she believed that pearls gained lustre from contact with the skin. She took the cable from her secretary; she was a young, politically ambitious girl from the East coast, efficient as gloss paint, and she had worked for Sheila for five years. They had no secrets; Ruth Paterson reminded Sheila of herself as a young woman. The same drive, ruthless attention to detail and ambition. But without the money which had made Sheila's achievements that much easier. Ruth would have to do it the hard way.

She was having an affair with the nephew of one of Washington's most powerful Republican Senators, himself a successful lawyer and politician. She chose her lovers with the same motive as Sheila had picked husbands. Love or even sexual need had never played a part in the selection.

'Good morning, Mrs Campbell. You'd better see this cable first. There are some news items in the press and the *Post* has run a photograph and a piece in the gossip column.'

Sheila took the cable and read it. She looked up at Ruth Paterson, and said a single inelegant word.

'Give me the *Post*. Jesus, what a fool she's made of herself again.' She looked at the picture taken of Anna and Nicholas outside the Russian church, her lips moving as she scanned through the news item. She threw the newspaper down.

'A Russian count this time,' she said to her secretary. 'A White Russian count. Last time it was a common little left-wing journalist – she must be out of her mind! No wonder she didn't tell me a word about it – '

'But she wrote you there was somebody,' Ruth reminded her.

'Yes,' Sheila brushed that aside. 'But I haven't got time to read between the lines. She wanted me to come over and visit and it just coincided with our plans to go to Europe. No wonder she married him first. She did the same with the other one – trotted him out over here and expected me to welcome him with open arms! She's never had any sense, that girl. You never saw Paul Martin, did you? No, well, I can tell you he was the sort of person you wouldn't let in except through the tradesmen's entrance! One of those social chip-on-the-shoulder types, self-styled intellectuals, you can imagine how he went down in New York! I simply wouldn't introduce him to anyone and they left. Now she does this – a phoney Russian count!' She rammed the spectacles up on her forehead again.

'It's the money he's after, of course,' she said. 'You'd think my daughter had enough sense to realize it. Pass me the box of tissues, Ruth, please.'

Ruth Paterson picked up the newspaper, opened it out and studied the photograph.

'He's a good-looking man,' she said.

'Well, he would be, wouldn't he?' Sheila snapped. 'You'd better call Fredericks. Tell him to get through to Paris and find out everything he can about this Yurovsky. I haven't the slightest doubt he'll have to be paid off.'

'Don't let it worry you,' Ruth said. 'It'll make your cold worse. Maybe he's genuine?'

'Ruth,' Sheila Campbell said, 'are you being serious?'

She shook her head; her hair was dark and sleek, caught back behind small pale ears.

'I guess not,' she said. 'I'll go and call Fredericks. The rest of the mail is just routine. Buzz when you want me to take your letters. Senator Hathaway sent flowers this morning, and Mrs Hughes sent a fruit basket. Shall I have them sent up?'

'Just the fruit,' Sheila said. 'Flowers take up oxygen when you're sick.' She leaned back and closed her eyes for a moment; she heard the bedroom door close quietly as Ruth Paterson went out. She had never been tolerant of noisy people; she moved with economy herself, without fidgeting or banging around a room, and she wouldn't have tolerated clumsiness in anyone who worked for her. She liked Ruth, as much as she was capable of liking a subordinate, and it amused her to help the girl. She had introduced her to influential people and then sat back and watched her seize her opportunities. When she married, it would be to a man of substance and importance, where she would play the political role on which she'd set her heart. Working for Sheila had fostered that ambition. The understanding between them was unspoken. She would work for Sheila with absolute loyalty and devotion until her own opportunity came. And when it did, she would leave without a qualm, no matter what the circumstances.

There would be no fortune-hunting Russian phoney for her. How people in Washington would snigger! Sheila scowled, her eyes coming open quickly at the thought.

The fool. Always messing up her life; even as a child, she had two left feet, tongue-tied with people, backing off from situations. And behind it all, the silent criticism which Sheila sensed every time they came in contact. Anna hadn't approved of what her mother was doing or the way in which it was being done.

She had no personal ambition, no drive; in Sheila's eyes she was a negative personality. The perennial poor little million-airess, crying out that she wanted to be like everybody else. . . . Sheila had lost patience with her and interest in her at an early age. She would have preferred her only child to be a son. Had he been like Anna in temperament, it would have aggravated and disappointed her even more. She had neither the time nor the inclination to try a second time. Her life was too full, her involvement with men too superficial. She had enjoyed her sex life. She was different from the cool little cat who had just gone out; Sheila married, rather than took lovers, because she was careful about her image.

But her growing journalistic empire and her political aspirations claimed her time and energy. She hadn't remarried after the last one, a charming industrialist in his fifties, who was as rich as she was and equally obsessed with outside interests. She sighed irritably, and put her daughter out of her mind.

She was due to go to Paris on behalf of her own magazine. She would deal with Count Nicholas Yurovsky then.

Venice in early June. The sun glittering along the canals, the streets and squares not yet thronged with too many people, the gondolas and waterbuses plying along the Grand Canal, passing under the windows of Anton Kruger's *palazzo*. The bedroom suite was on the first floor, its windows opened out on to the

Canal itself, with the smooth, white symmetry of the Church of Santa Maria della Salute almost opposite on the other bank. The days of their honeymoon ran into one another in dreamlike sequence; they made love, they wandered round the city, finding new treasures of architecture to enjoy, the delights of small restaurants hidden in medieval side streets, with the dark waters of the little canals lapping gently at their feet. The *palazzo* itself was dark and furnished with the rich Italian furniture and hangings of the seventeenth century. It was a silent, rather secretive house, with an atmosphere too old and steeped in its own history to bear any imprint of the Krugers.

The bedroom was dominated by a huge seventeenth-century Italian tester bed, its faded velvet hangings cascading from a massive gilded canopy, surmounted by the arms of the Strozzi. It was a room made for sensual pleasure, with Venetian mirrors reflecting the shadowy arabesques of love; a Correggio nude smiled voluptuously down from above the marble chimney, her pearly flesh glowing in the candlelight, for there was no electricity in the room. Every evening two gilt candelabra were lit, and on cool nights a fire burned in the open grate. Nicholas loved to move the candlelight so that it showed him Anna, naked and beautiful, nestled in the bed like a pearl. His passion for her body was only matched by the surpassing tenderness with which he guided her down new and varied avenues of love. He taught her to admire her own beauty, to enjoy her own sensual capacity instead of being ashamed of it and holding back. It was as if the spirits of the long dead Venetians who had lived and loved in the same room and used the magnificent bed as a vehicle for their desires, were permeating the atmosphere and watching with approval from the shadows.

He told her he loved her in many ways; in words, with unexpected presents, chosen with sensitivity and taste, by laying a flower between her breasts in tribute to their perfect symmetry. And Anna bloomed; if his love was dominant, protective, hers was enhanced now by a total mental and spiritual commitment. Never before had she understood the words incorporated in the Christian act of marriage 'With my body I thee worship.' He said them to her one morning, as the bright sunshine flooded the room, reflected by the mirrors and the sparkling waters of the Grand Canal. And Anna repeated them, softly to him, and opened her arms again.

The days and nights ran into each other, sublimely happy, completely private; they lived for each day and each other; nothing was mentioned of what lay ahead.

To Anna it was a supreme experience, a final emergence into self-realization and the womanhood which her past had suppressed and distorted into insecurity and doubt.

There was a moment when they wandered through the vast Square of St Mark's, one couple among a throng of tourists, and she thought suddenly that if she were to die that moment she had known all the happiness possible in life. He had squeezed her hand and asked her what was making her smile. She had just shaken her head and gone on smiling, holding his hand in hers and walking through the golden evening.

The housekeeper, bribed by Jumeaux's agent, had nothing to report. Nicholas's luggage, expertly searched, revealed their tickets booked to New York at the end of the fortnight. Jumeaux gathered the evidence together, and assured his chief in Paris that they could discount Nicholas Yurovsky in any attempt to embarrass the visiting Russian delegation. And without him, the few known troublemakers like Volkov and Zepirov, who printed anti-Soviet pamphlets, presented no threat to anyone. Jumeaux was congratulated, the word was passed through to Moscow that while extra security would be maintained to protect Grigor Malenkov and his colleagues French intelligence services did not anticipate any trouble.

The probability of a Zionist demonstration in favour of Soviet Jews was regarded as routine and of no consequence.

Jumeaux took Paul Martin out to lunch. They were old friends, dependent upon each other for information mutually exchanged, and they enjoyed talking politics.

Martin looked a little more dishevelled than usual; there was a look of dissipation which Raoul Jumeaux recognized as the sign of another of his short-lived affairs being in full spate.

'Well, the honeymooners are enjoying themselves,' Jumeaux

said. 'She's a remarkable woman, your ex-wife. I didn't think Yurovsky would be that easy to tame.'

Paul Martin looked at him, and raised one eyebrow.

'You're very confident, aren't you – they're doing all the right things and you're so relieved you can't wait to believe them. I'd like to point out that Anna never changed me. Why should a man like Nicholas Yurovsky suddenly turn into a pet poodle, doing exactly what his new wife says?'

'Because he isn't you,' Jumeaux said. 'You shouldn't be married to anyone. You're just a maverick, jumping from bed to bed.' He poured some wine into Martin's glass.

'Yurovsky's a Russian; they're not the most stable or reliable people. She said she felt he was relieved to back out of it. When I think of them taking over the stage at the Comédie Française – '

'All right,' Martin said, 'So Anna has talked him round. But what about the others. What about Volkov? – you've had your eye on him for some time. You really think this organization will wither and die without Yurovsky?'

'I know it has,' Jumeaux said. 'We've kept one or two under surveillance – not full time, but enough to know what they're up to. No meetings, no contacts, nothing. And the word is that "Return" has disintegrated; when Yurovsky backed down, they lost heart. And leadership. It's all over, my friend. My chief has been able to reassure Moscow.'

Inevitably, since the meal was finished, his pipe came out. Martin grimaced.

'You'll give yourself cancer of the throat with that,' he said.

'And you'll get cancer of the lungs from cigarettes,' Jumeaux retorted.

'You'll lose your balls if you're wrong about this,' Martin said quietly.

'I'm not wrong,' Jumeaux said. 'You don't want to admit that your wife has so much character, and intelligence. It offends you, Paul. And you're jealous because she's married again. I can't see why you two ever got married, but I do think you underestimated her, and you don't like to be proved wrong.'

'We were in love with each other,' Paul said. 'She believed

that she could change me, make me respectable, faithful – you know the sort of ideas women get when they marry. She couldn't. She couldn't make me into a gentleman, or stop me wanting to sleep with pretty girls. I couldn't make a mature woman out of her. She was still the rich little American heiress pretending she wasn't different. And her mother – ' He laughed, but it was unpleasant. 'A real member of the dollar aristocracy, that one. She treated me as if I smelled bad. She patronized me and hid me from her friends, and I heard her giving Anna hell for marrying a vulgar little beggar like me. I tell you, I went out and screwed the first girl I could pick up after that. It didn't stop me loving Anna, and I don't think I would have left her – she threw me out in the end. Maybe that's what I wanted her to do – ' He shrugged. 'Not that it matters now. She's a countess; her mother will be pleased about that. I've been thinking. I might write an article about her and her filthy right-wing reactionary magazine. You know she got elected to Congress? I think I might write it now . . .'

'It's one way of getting back at your wife,' Jumeaux said.

'My ex-wife,' Martin reminded him.

Jumeaux allowed himself to smile. 'That isn't how you see her,' he said. 'You know, Paul, I think she's the only woman who's ever got under your skin?'

'Go to hell,' Paul Martin said. 'For that, you can pay the bill.'

Grigor Malenkov celebrated his sixty-first birthday the day before he left Moscow for France. Being a senior member of the Praesidium he lived in a handsome second- and third-floor flat in a prestige modern block on the Lenin Hills with a magnificent view over Moscow. It was reserved for important members of the Politburo, and he also had a *dacha* some sixty *versts* outside the city. His wife, to whom he had been married for nearly twenty-eight years, and his son and daughter, Nadia and Vladimir, were gathered round the shining mahogany table in the dining room, eating a celebration dinner, which had been specially prepared by the Malenkovs' cook. Grigor's taste in food was simple – he preferred the homely Russian dishes of his native province near Kiev.

He had never developed the penchant for champagne or foreign dishes which some of his colleagues displayed. He and his wife and children lived in simple comfort, wanting for nothing, but despising ostentation. Olga Malenkov had been a schoolteacher when he married her; her background was similar to his own peasant origins which had progressed in two generations to urban intellectual status. Her father was a minor administrator in Kiev itself; Grigor's father had been a political commissar in the Red Army, and his mother a doctor. They were married in 1950; their son was born three years later, and their daughter four years after that. Two children were considered the socially accepted maximum, although there were theories that because of Russia's massive casualties in the war, larger families should be encouraged. But this did not apply to the élite like themselves. Olga planned and spaced her pregnancies, and went on working as a teacher in the Faculty of Journalism and Law at Moscow University. The children of their friends and colleagues, scientists, senior civil servants, politicians and professional parents, studied there. Olga loved her work. She was a pretty, dark-haired girl when they married; there was a photograph of them on their wedding day, taken in the Wedding Palace, Grigor smiling and handsome in his uniform, herself in a plain blue suit and white shirt, with a little hat on one side of her head. His name had been Feodor Gusev in those days. She was grey-haired now, but as slim and neat as she had been all those years ago, a woman with a firm, handsome face, a dedicated, hyper-intelligent mind, and an unwavering love for her husband.

He had changed, of course; his body had thickened, the broad shoulders were stooped, and the hair was thin now, showing a sheen of scalp. He looked at her and smiled. There had been other women, but only at intervals, when he was on a tour of duty abroad; none of them had meant anything to him. He had only loved Olga, and he still did. He was proud of his son, Vladimir, who was following in his steps in the Military Intelligence section of the Soviet army, and fond of his daughter Nadia. Unfortunately she was not a clever girl; however hard she worked she only managed to keep on the lower level of her studies. She lacked the seriousness of his son. He and her mother recognized that there wouldn't be a place for her in the hierarchy where they moved. But she was sweet-natured and affectionate, and very proud of him. He was a happy man; fortunate in his family, in excellent physical and mental health and just coming to the final ascent of that long ladder of power and ambition which ended at the central place in the podium above Lenin's tomb. For thirty years he had worked and schemed and struggled, rising in the war through ruthless dedication and skill to the front rank of intelligence officers.

Stalin himself had commended him for the operation of repatriating traitors which had brought him to prominence. He would never forget that meeting with the ruler of Russia, the architect of Soviet victory. However he was vilified after he was safely dead, Feodor Gusev remembered his immense personal magnetism and the aura of terror which surrounded him. A great leader had indeed to be a Man of Steel. Merciless, implacable, immovable in his service to his people and his country. When he decorated Gusev with the Order of the Red Banner Feodor felt as his own ancestors would have done in the presence of the Tsar.

His motives and attitudes were forged in the heat of a war of annihilation, a war when the old principles of international Communism, which had been the mainspring of people like his father, simply disappeared. A furious, fanatical Russian nationalist replaced them, headed by the father of his people, Josef Stalin.

Feodor Gusev, the brilliant young student at Moscow University, the dedicated NKVD operator whose activities had been charted from time to time in the Western world and then lost under aliases and translation to the political arena in Russia, had remodelled himself. He had cultivated a friendly, common-sense image, stealing a little from the folksy *persona* of the disgraced Khrushchev, because he had seen at close quarters how eagerly the Western powers responded to it, set out to present himself as a man of moderation whose own record protected him from any accusation of being weak. He deliberately shed the skin of the tight-lipped intellectual, which was his natural character, made himself expansive, good-humoured, grew fat, and plotted every word and gesture with the ultimate goal in mind. His name had been changed so many times that he had effectively forgotten his real one. He had been Grigor Malenkov for the last fifteen years, a member of the Praesidium of the Supreme Soviet, an intimate of the glum Brezhnev, whose tenure of power was threatened by ill health.

One of Russia's rulers. Only Zemenov, head of the KGB, resented his power. Zemenov was an enemy. . . . He raised his glass to his wife. She and his children responded.

'Happy birthday, darling,' Olga said. 'We shall miss you.'

'I shan't be away for long,' he said. 'A week from tomorrow and I'll be home again.'

His daughter looked across at him, her chin leaning on her hands. There was a wistful expression in her eyes.

'I wish I could go to Paris one day,' she said. 'You've been there before, haven't you, Papa?'

'After the war,' he said. 'I went to our Embassy for a short tour. It's a lovely city. The art galleries and the architecture are magnificent.'

'But not as well laid out as Leningrad,' his son remarked; Malenkov smiled. He understood the insularity. At Vladimir's age, nothing anywhere could compare with Russia. 'And surely they've nothing to compare with the Hermitage!'

'No,' he agreed. 'But don't underestimate the effect of French culture on world civilization. It is a living organism, unlike the culture of Italy, which is a preservation of the past. France has a genius which is alive and progressing. It would do you good to go there, my son. When you're dealing with the world, you have to have experience of it.'

'Our leaders don't travel,' Nadia pointed out. Her parents glanced quickly at each other. Even a remark as innocent as that could be interpreted as criticism.

'They don't need to,' Olga said quickly. Unlike her husband, she found the girl's stupidity irritating. 'Your father was talking about general administration.'

'That was the great weakness of Hitler,' Malenkov said. 'He was a middle-class bourgeois himself who knew nothing of Europe or the outside world, and he surrounded himself with men of similar background and ignorance. They made no attempt to widen their experience or to assimilate culture, to study history. . . . Policies were influenced by the views of someone like Himmler or Hess who wouldn't rise above the rank of minor provincial civil servant anywhere else. There is a very good saying, and it isn't Russian. Know thine enemy. And the same applies to your friends. France is anxious to preserve *détente*; so is America. Their invitation to me to lead a delegation for talks with the President is perfectly timed. We want the good offices of France at the moment. We want to present a compatible image of the Soviet Union which can undermine Eurocommunism. I am going to fall in love with France and let the whole world know it.'

He got up from the table, took his wife by the arm. 'It's late,' he said. 'I have to be fresh for tomorrow. Goodnight, Vladimir, Nadia. Thank you for my birthday. Take care of your mother while I'm away.'

Alone in their bedroom Olga put her arms around him.

'You're quite sure it's safe now?' she said. 'I didn't want to say anything in front of the children. Especially Nadia.'

'We've had complete clearance from the French,' he answered. He stroked her grey hair. 'They've worked very closely with our own people. It was a demonstration at the theatre, apparently. Nothing to worry about.'

'Have they arrested these people?' she demanded. 'They must do that while you're there.'

'They will,' he soothed. He shook his head and smiled at her; she looked very anxious.

'They're scum,' he said softly. 'Rubbish. Little crawling creatures with banners and slogans. Jews at the root of it, as usual. If I could, I'd banish every one of them to Israel and clean them out of the country.'

'Take care,' she begged. 'You know how Zemenov hates you – he'd love the visit to fail –' He kissed her lightly on the cheek.

'I have the best security in the world to guard me,' he reminded her. 'Both ours and theirs. Now come to bed, and stop worrying.'

At eight the following morning, Feodor Gusev who had become Grigor Malenkov, contender for the Chairmanship of the Supreme Soviet, left with a delegation of nine officials, from the Trade Ministry, and some eight KGB men, with a senior officer in charge of security. They arrived in Paris after an uneventful flight to be met at Charles de Gaulle airport by the President of the Chamber of Deputies.

At dawn that morning, the addresses of Volkov, Zepirov and Natalie Maximova were raided by the SDECE, including half a dozen well-known Zionist supporters. It had suited Raoul Jumeaux to dismiss 'Return' as a spent force to Paul Martin; he didn't want that acute journalist to start making an issue of possible hostility to the Russians, but he and his department were not taking any chances. The Zionists were taken into custody, suitably warned about behaving themselves, and by the following morning their lawyers had got them released.

The three members of 'Return' had disappeared and the investigations by SDECE revealed nothing overtly suspicious. Volkov had told the *concierge* in the seedy building where he lived that he expected the police to pick him up and was going into the country until the Russians had left France. The *concierge* said that he appeared to be drunk and truculent, cursing and swearing about the visit and the injustice he anticipated at the hands of the gendarmerie. It was not the first time that Volkov had taken off, announcing his intention of doing so.

Zepirov had gone on a trip to Lausanne, according to his wife. His insurance office confirmed this. Natalie Maximova had had a row with her employer in a dress shop in the Quartier, and lost her job. The woman she shared a flat with said she had been very upset and suffering from depression; two days before the police arrived, she had gone away to stay with friends. Her flat-mate suggested that she was probably going off with a man.

Jumeaux had to accept the situation. If it wasn't coincidence, then he had something to worry about, but with Nicholas Yurovsky out of the country, it was probably safe to accept the explanation. His agents in Venice had confirmed that the Yurovskys were still there. They were due to fly to the United States the following day.

Anna and Nicholas were packed, the private motor boat was moored outside the *palazzo* landing stage, waiting to take them to Marco Polo airport. Nicholas turned her to him and took her in his arms.

'My darling,' he said. 'I wish you'd stay here.'

Anna shook her head. 'I want to go back,' she said. The Italian papers carried reports of Malenkov's arrival, and there was a photograph of him waving to crowds at the airport. They had looked at them together, and suddenly Nicholas had crumpled the paper up and thrown it aside.

'I'm not afraid either,' she said. 'I feel quite calm.'

'That's good,' he said. 'But it will be different when we're there. I don't want you with me, Anna. I don't want to think of you being in any danger.'

'I won't be,' she said gently. 'I shall be waiting at the Château for you. There's no danger to me. You're the one who'll be risking your life.'

'And the others,' he reminded her. 'If anything goes wrong, Anton will be right in the front . . . he's an old man, he shouldn't have exposed himself. But he wouldn't listen to me.'

'Of course he wouldn't,' she said. 'Without him, the plan wouldn't have a hope. He has to be part of it. Darling, we'd better go.'

'I know,' he said. He kissed her. 'This has been the happiest time of my life. You're everything in the world to me. Do you really know that?'

'Yes,' she said. 'It's the same for me. Whatever happens we've had this. I'll remember Venice and this house as long as I live.'

They went downstairs and out into the morning sunshine;

it was very warm and a soft haze rose from the canal waters. He helped her into the boat, waved goodbye to the housekeeper who had been spying on them for Jumeaux, and the boat opened its engine and began to skid through the water, leaving the *palazzo* and the white dome of Santa Maria della Salute receding in the distance.

Anna turned and looked back. She had a sudden, frightening premonition that she would never see any of it again, that Venice and the idyllic two weeks of being Nicholas's wife were as lost and ephemeral as the heat mist which was covering them like a veil. She shivered. She hadn't been afraid in the *palazzo*, but a sensation of panic overcame her as they sped on their way out of the city. She found Nicholas's hand and held it; her own was cold. Malenkov was in Paris. The children of his victims, and the one who had escaped him, were gathered, waiting. Within a few hours they would have joined them.

5

The aircraft touched down at Charles de Gaulle only ten minutes late; the flight was uneventful, and they sat together reading, seldom speaking. Anna wore a hat, which helped to conceal her distinctive blonde hair and shadowed her face, Nicholas pulled on a cap as they prepared to disembark.

'Just walk straight through,' he whispered to her. 'Go to the front and wait for me. We'll be picked up. Keep just ahead of me.'

At the turning marked transit passengers, Anna veered to the left, leaving the stream of passengers booked through to New York to go ahead to the transit lounge. She walked on, carrying a small overnight Alitalia bag. Their luggage had been loaded on to the plane. There was no question of collecting it at Paris; Kruger had assured them they would get it back in due time. Anna wore the Romanov crystal brooch under her scarf. She pulled the hat a little down, and hurried forward to the passport control. There was a passport in her bag, a French passport, with her photograph inside it, made out in the name of Madeleine Duplessis, given to Nicholas by Anton when they left for Venice. She handed in her boarding card, walked into the customs hall and through the green area, not turning to see where Nicholas was, and out into the main airport reception hall, following the exit signs. The automatic doors slid back for her and closed behind her; she was outside in the sunshine, waiting. A man came up to her. He wore sunglasses, a sweat-shirt and jeans.

'Taxis this way,' he said. He didn't wait for her to answer, he just took the little bag out of her hand and walked away. Anna followed him to a car parked in the general car park.

Then she did turn and, to her relief, saw Nicholas threading his way through the cars towards them. The man opened the rear door for her, and climbed into the driving seat. He took off his glasses and she saw that it was Volkov.

'Where's the Count, Madame?'

'He's coming. I saw him a minute ago. Here he is now –' she reached for the car door and swung it open for Nicholas to climb in beside her. He squeezed her hand, and spoke to Volkov.

'No problems, Vladimir. We weren't checked coming in. Everything went exactly right.'

'Good,' Volkov said. 'I hope you and Madame Yurovskaya enjoyed your trip, Nicholas. I've never been to Venice.'

'It was beautiful,' Nicholas answered. He clasped her hand between his. 'You should go there yourself one day.'

'Old buildings don't interest me,' Volkov said. 'The traffic is like soup; have you seen the papers?'

'Yes,' Nicholas said. 'We've seen them.'

'He's going to the Comédie Française tonight,' Volkov muttered. He had swung out on to the main road, and was absorbed into a stream of cars.

He said something in Russian which sounded ugly to Anna. 'That face,' he broke into French again. 'Photographs of him, grinning and waving like an ape. The television every night – do you know he was clapped for five minutes when he appeared in the visitors' gallery in the Chamber of Deputies? They're calling him the new Khrushchev; the soft-line Russian. Jesus Christ!'

He accelerated suddenly, savagely cutting in front of a large green van which hooted furiously at him. He didn't seem to hear it. In the driving mirror his face was flushed a dull red; though the eyes were masked once more by the sunglasses his mouth was drawn back into an animal-like snarl.

'Calm yourself,' Nicholas spoke sharply. 'And watch your driving. What does it matter what they call him – he's got another two days to go – he'll be called something else when we've finished with him! How is Anton?'

'He seems well,' Volkov said. 'Those pigs of police came looking for me; and for Maximova and Zepirov. He'd got us

131

all away in plenty of time, though. Look at this hold-up – typical, with one police hog standing in the middle doing nothing – we'll never get to the Château by seven o'clock!'

Anna turned to Nicholas.

'I thought we were going to the Auberge St-Julien,' she said.

'So did I,' Nicholas answered. 'Why the Château, Vladimir?'

'Anton changed the plan,' he answered. 'You'll both be better hidden there. Someone could recognize you at Elise's place.'

'Where are Natalie and Zepirov?'

'At the Auberge,' Volkov said. 'I'm at the Château too. There's a meeting called for tomorrow. And a last-minute dress rehearsal.'

'Nicholas?' Anna turned to question him. He shook his head, and then leaned forward to kiss her gently.

'Anton will explain it,' he said. 'He'll tell us everything when we arrive.'

The Krugers were waiting for them in the Château library. It was full of roses from Régine's favourite garden, and the smell was almost overpowering. She came forward, slim and elegant in country clothes, and kissed Anna warmly, reaching up to be embraced by Nicholas. Anton Kruger greeted them both and beamed, looking at them for a moment.

'Ah,' he said. 'Such happiness! I can feel it, like an aura – How did you like our little retreat from modern life? Isn't it peaceful and beautiful? Just made for lovers.' He had his arm around his wife. 'Isn't it, my darling?'

'Now, Anton, don't remind me how old we are! My dears, come upstairs and you'll find fresh clothes. I'm afraid we took a liberty, Anna, and went into your apartment one night to get some things for you. And some mail.'

'Yes,' Anton Kruger said. 'Especially the mail. There was a notice of an undelivered cable from America. I had it collected for you. That is upstairs too.'

Anna felt herself change colour. 'My mother,' she said. 'If it's a cable it has to be from her!'

'I'm sure it is,' Kruger said quietly. 'So please open it and tell us what she says.'

'Damn her,' Anna said. 'Damn her . . .'

Nicholas had his arms around her. They were alone in the bedroom and the cable had fluttered down to the floor at their feet.

'Don't worry,' he said. 'It's only what you expected. I don't mind what she says.'

'Oh, of course I expected it,' Anna said. The tears had come so suddenly she had no defence against them. Tears of hot rage and bitter hurt. The childhood wounds burst open again, the insecurity and lack of self-confidence came rushing back, the awful void of having neither love nor support from the primary source. And then, furious with herself, she fought it down and anger won.

It was a disgraceful cable, curt and cruel.

'Your letter received, plus cable giving news of your marriage. Am confounded by your ability to make a fool of yourself for second time. Inquiries being made at this end into credentials of undoubted charlatan. Arriving Ritz evening of 22nd. Will call you. Mother.'

'Of course I expected it,' she said again, 'But I just hoped for once she might have shown some spark of human feeling or understanding, or love – I wrote her a long letter, Nicholas, I told her all about you and how much I loved you. I really thought that this time she might behave like any normal mother! I'm so sorry, darling. I never meant you to see it. I was just so upset when I read it first.'

He calmed her gently. The contents were no surprise to him. Her reaction was exactly what he had expected it would be. His anger was for the hurt she had inflicted upon Anna. And he would make her pay for that, he said to himself.

If he couldn't deal with a bully like Sheila Campbell then he was not a Yurovsky with a thousand years of lineage behind him. He didn't question his own feelings; they bore no relation to the attitude to his French mother, who would have been devastated by a woman like the formidable American politician. It was the arrogance of his grandmother, Countess Zia, the intimate of the Tsarina, the upright, rigidly aristocratic moulder of his early youth who influenced him from the grave. She would have annihilated such a woman with a glance.

'My love,' he said. 'Forget what she says. The only important thing is the date of her arrival. We'll have to consult Anton. She'll expect to see us and it is the day after our plan is carried out. That is what matters. Her timing and the plan.'

'I'm sorry,' Anna said. 'Sorry to have such a dreadful mother-in-law for you. But she won't interfere, I can promise you that. She did it once with Paul and me, but never again. As for seeing me or meeting you, she can go to hell. It was my fault for getting sentimental and writing her that silly letter. Some people never learn. You go downstairs, darling. I'll tidy my face and come in a minute. God, why couldn't Régine Kruger have had children, instead of someone like Sheila!'

They had dinner with the Krugers and Volkov. He had changed into a suit, and he looked stiff and uncomfortable. Nicholas told Anna that his grandfather had been a landowner and a member of the minor nobility with estates near St Petersburg. His father too had been a Tsarist officer who had left Russia in 1918. He said very little; unlike Nicholas and Anton, he was dour and without animation except when he showed anger. And anger smouldered in him, a furious suppressed rage that gleamed and glittered at odd moments when his guard was lowered, exactly like the fire of which Anna was reminded as she watched him.

Anton had heard the date of her mother's arrival and made no comment. She had a feeling that he was satisfied, and couldn't think why. She felt also that his wife was not quite at her ease. After the emotion of her welcome, she seemed a little forced, as if she were making conversation. Several times Anna caught her watching Anton anxiously, and glancing quickly away to Nicholas and back. She herself didn't feel hungry; she drank some of the excellent wine and listened to Nicholas and Anton talking, drawn in to describe some incident in Venice as if by design. She felt strongly that she was playing a part in a charade, of which the scene in the dining room was a planned interlude. As soon as the coffee was served, not in the library but at the table, which was customary in French houses, Anton rose with Régine, and wished Volkov goodnight.

It was done with courtesy but firmness. The big Russian

kissed Régine's hand, did the same to Anna, who disliked being touched by him, and went upstairs.

There was a thin pretence that Anton and Nicholas and she were also going to bed, which took them into the hall, and ended in the library, with its powerful scent of roses.

'Now,' Anton Kruger said. 'Now we must talk seriously. Get us some brandy, Nicholas, if you please. Crême de menthe for you, my love?'

Régine shook her head. 'Brandy tonight,' she said. 'I feel I shall need it.'

'To celebrate,' Nicholas said. 'Not to calm the nerves. To drink a toast to our success the day after tomorrow.'

Anton Kruger smiled at him, and then at the two women.

'Here is the man for the enterprise,' he said. 'It's a pity poor Volkov couldn't drink with us, but the less he knows beyond his own role, the better. He can't help being such a fool.'

'None of that family had any brains,' Nicholas said. He laughed. It seemed to Anna that he was in a strangely euphoric mood. 'My grandmother used to say that his father and grandfather were the two stupidest men in Russia. But he has his good points. There's nothing he wouldn't risk; he doesn't know the meaning of fear.'

'Thank God for that,' Régine Kruger said.

Anton handed a glass of brandy to Anna. He looked down at her and his face was grave. 'To our new member,' he said. 'Who is also brave but not at all stupid. I think the moment has come when you should be told everything, my dear. And the special part that you can play in it; if you will help us.'

The following morning two cars left the Château Grandcour, Kruger's big silver-grey Mercedes, driven by Volkov, with Anton and Régine in the rear, and a small Citroën with Nicholas driving and Anna beside him. They left separately, with an interval of fifteen minutes between them. The big car shot past them on the road, driven at Volkov's usual hectic speed. Nicholas parked in the centre of Chartres; it was a Friday morning, and the town was full of visitors and people shopping for the weekend. The great grey stone cathedral rose above them; the towers at the west end so different in design pierced the bright blue sky; the glorious stonework delicate as lace. Nicholas took Anna's arm as they walked up the steps together. It was a building of breathtaking beauty, a monument to the genius and religious faith of medieval man.

Built to dominate the twelfth century and to act as a focal point in the life of the community, forever reminding them of the majesty of God and the glory due to Him, it served the same purpose still, presiding over the bustle and traffic of modern Chartres, immutable in its own splendour, a great choral symphony of Divine praise in stone and jewel-coloured glass.

The interior was dim, the light diffused into rich reds and blues from the magnificent windows. Anna paused, looking upwards. The Rose Window, one of the wonders of medieval architecture, glowed and glimmered in its stone tracery, unearthly in its height and symmetry, the unique colouring of the stained glass richer than precious stones.

'He'll come in through the main door,' Nicholas whispered. 'Walk down the central aisle, turn and stand almost where we are now. It's the best place to see the west windows. Then he'll be conducted through the cathedral, up to the high altar and round the choir cloister. He'll be shown the statue of Notre-Dame de Pilier, the Chapelle Ste-Mort and then back down the aisle here and out again. That's when he'll be given his bouquet. Just before he gets into the car.'

'Supposing he throws the flowers out of the window?' Anna said. 'I kept worrying about that last night.'

'He won't,' Nicholas said. 'It would cause offence if that bouquet was thrown away; he'll hold it and keep it with him till they're well outside Chartres. There's Anton and Régine. Don't stop, there are probably police here already, keeping an eye out. The church will be crawling with them tomorrow. Just walk on and we'll look round the cathedral, with the other tourists.'

They passed the pews where Anton Kruger and his wife were kneeling in prayer, their heads bent over folded hands. A group of Americans with a guide were making a slow progress up the central aisle. A man was trying to photograph the Rose Window.

'Why did he choose Chartres,' Anna murmured. 'Of all the great cathedrals, why this one?'

'It was suggested by the French Foreign Office,' Nicholas said. 'And it's near Paris. I suspect Anton has a friend there. He just had to see the great Rose Window, or he would have missed a unique cultural experience. And he's a great man for culture. He's bent over backwards to admire everything French since he arrived. Flowers and Russian caviar to the cast at the theatre last night, a banquet at the Russian Embassy tonight – he's playing to the crowd as if he was Chairman of the Supreme Soviet on a state visit. Once he thought the French wanted to show him Chartres, of course he was going to put it on his itinerary. The Tomb of the Unknown Soldier was going to be his last piece of stage management before he flew home. But he'll never get the chance to lay a wreath on that grave. He'll be thinking about the other graves, all half a million of them, where he helped to bury his own people, and my father. . . . Do you want to see any more?'

'No,' Anna said. 'Let's go back. Now that I've seen it I'm getting frightened. Frightened to death for you, and the others. Where's Volkov?'

'Going through his part with Zepirov. They're all in position, getting everything worked out to the split second. They'll be coming to the Château afterwards.'

They walked back down the centre aisle.

Outside the sunshine struck at them, blinding after the rosy dimness of the cathedral. Nicholas walked her round to the main entrance, and there he paused. There was a cobbled square surrounding the cathedral, with crowded streets leading through into the city. Mentally he noted where the Russian car would stop; he narrowed his eyes against the strong light, visualizing Feodor Gusev walking down the steps and stopping to take the posy of flowers that a small girl would run forward and present to him. A small girl who would disappear into the anonymity of the crowd, where her aunt, Natalie Maximova, would be waiting to vanish with her.

'I can't believe it,' he said suddenly to Anna. 'I can't believe it's really going to happen. Tomorrow, at exactly this time. I shall be face to face with him at last.'

He put his arm round her, guiding her back to the little Citroën in its berth the other side of the square. 'And I shan't kill him, or let the others hurt him. I'll do exactly as Anton has planned. If I hadn't got you, my darling, I don't think I could do it.'

'You must,' Anna said. 'As Anton said last night, this way he'll destroy himself.'

'Yes,' Nicholas said slowly. He switched on the engine, but for a moment he held the car immobile. 'Then our dead can rest in peace.'

Nicholas slept soundly that night; Anna lay awake beside him, listening to the chimes of the massive clock in the Château hall as it struck the quarter, the half, and then the quarter and the hour itself. Sleep was impossible. The scene that night wouldn't leave her mind. They had come to the Château one by one; Maximova, with a little girl, who had been fussed over and then sent to bed, Zepirov, looking down-at-heel and anxious, Elise, huge and imperturbable, without her little husband. He was looking after the Auberge. He knew nothing about her other commitment. There was something menacing about Elise; her expression never altered, she was always friendly and cheerful, enclosed behind a wall of secrecy that concealed something that frightened Anna. And Fritz von Bronsart, looking painfully young and nervous. He had gravitated towards Anna as if seeking reassurance. He was a handsome young man, blond and blue eyed; forty years ago he would have typified the Aryan ideal of Hitler's Germany.

These were the people who stood out, because of the roles they were to play the next morning, or like Elise, because of the force of their personalities. The young German was in a special category. Anna felt that he had no place in the group, that his wrong was too far off in relation to himself. He had given an uncompromising answer to that suggestion.

'My family's honour is at stake, Countess. My grandfather has been branded as a war criminal, a man who was given to the Communists because he had committed inhuman crimes. That is a lie. He wasn't tried for anything, he was just handed over and murdered. It's my duty to clear his name. Nobody else cares enough to do it except me.' He had looked at her with a mixture of pride and courage that she found infinitely touching, because it was allied with the anxiety of his youth. 'I shall have an important role to play later on,' he announced. 'Tomorrow I shall just have to wait here.'

'We'll wait together,' Anna said.

They had eaten a cold supper, left for them by the house-keeper, whom Régine had sent off for the weekend. There was very little drinking and no heroics. Anton and Nicholas set the tone. It was serious, cold-blooded, devoid of the Russian emotionalism which Anna detected just beneath the surface with the others. One spark of rhetoric, one extravagant gesture, and they would all have been alight.

Everyone dispersed to their rooms, saying goodnight quietly. Nicholas and Anton Kruger stayed behind; Anna took the hint when Régine left them, and she too went upstairs. When he joined her, they lay in each other's arms but he didn't make love. She felt him drift into sleep, and was glad. She hadn't wanted him to sense how afraid she was for him, and for all of them.

The next morning they gathered in the library. Nicholas stood beside Anton. He wore a plain navy serge suit, with a white shirt and a black tie; he carried a peaked chauffeur's cap under his arm. And something else stuffed into the soft headpiece of the cap. Zepirov wore faded denim jeans, a cord jacket and sweat shirt. He was unshaven, and his appearance had been altered by a pair of metal-rimmed glasses. Anna knew, because they had discussed the plans last night, that Zepirov was to drive the container lorry. Volkov was smoking, slouched in a chair; he was wearing the uniform of a colonel of gendarmes, with white gloves. There was nothing different about Maximova; she seemed her usual neat self, unobtrusively dressed, with a scarf over her dark hair. She was pale, but her fine eyes were shining. The motherly, grey-haired woman whom

Anna had met at the reception before her wedding, and whose name was Olga Jellnik, had arrived that morning. She looked exactly like any other middle-aged, middle-class Frenchwoman who would be driving her car through Chartres on a Saturday morning.

Natalie had spent the previous two days at the Auberge with Elise and Olga Jellnik. They hadn't discussed what was to happen that day; they had chatted about trivialities, commented upon the sweater Olga was knitting, played the roles of normality for their own benefit. Natalie spent a long time praying before she went to bed. Her mother, whom she remembered very clearly, had brought her up to be devout. Both parents had fled Russia after the Counter Revolution failed, and lived meagrely in Paris, her father eking out a living by giving riding lessons at a school in the Bois de Boulogne; her mother, who was an exquisite needlewoman, helped by dressmaking. They were a close-knit family, who confined themselves exclusively to other Russian émigrés for company, disdaining the hospitality of French friends from old days of opulence, because they couldn't return it in kind. Her father, a former cavalry officer, was fiercely proud. He never ceased to believe that the Soviets would be overthrown and that they and their friends would one day return to Russia. Natalie, although she went to a convent school close to their two-roomed flat, was brought up to speak Russian and to maintain the old religious and cultural traditions. When her father was captured her mother took her down to Baratina and they stayed together, confident in their belief that the Western Allies would either absorb them into their own forces or resettle them together. Natalie Maximova was seven years old, and her memories of the camp in the early days were happy ones. People were cheerful and kind, there were other children to play with, the soldiers gave her sweets and her parents seemed full of hope. And then the day came when her mother explained very gently to her, and without any tears, that she was going back to Russia with her father, and that she, Natalie, was to stay with their friends the Rasumovskys. Natalie hadn't understood; she had cried, and she had never forgotten her mother chiding her gently. It was her duty to be brave and to live with the Rasumovskys, because it was her mother's duty to go and care for her father.

Madame Rasumovsky had taken her that night, and the following week they left the camp. Natalie didn't understand that either, but it had something to do with being Polish citizens . . . Years later, when she was working in Paris, she learned through the sensitive grapevine of her fellow Russians, that both her parents had been shot on arrival inside Soviet lines. Natalie had never married; she worked for her living, practised her Orthodox faith, and remained within the circle of her own people united by common ties of language, tradition and tragedy. Olga Jellnik was another of the circle; she had married a fellow Russian who worked in the accounting department in a branch of Galeries Lafayette. He had died of cancer four years earlier, and Olga lived alone. They had no children. Olga was quiet and homely, and passionately fond of knitting; she talked of her dead husband with affection, but there was a portrait of her father and her elder brother which was never without flowers in her sitting room. To her, as to Natalie, the horror of the past was more potent than the life they lived in the present. To Natalie, membership of 'Return' was a crusade, with a fervour that was almost religious. To pleasant, placid Olga Jellnik, it was a deep and burning wish for vengeance, which discounted any scruple and shrugged off personal risk.

Elise lurked near the window, her big body a dark mass against the light. She too was remaining at the Château with Anna and Fritz von Bronsart. The Krugers were both smartly dressed: Régine wore a wide-brimmed hat and a spring coat, Anton was soberly dressed as if he were going to Paris. He looked at his watch.

'It is exactly ten o'clock,' he said. He spoke to the grey-haired Madame Jellnik. 'You set off now with Zepirov. The lorry is waiting at the service station. You have the keys?'

'Yes,' Zepirov said. He held them up between finger and thumb, and then dropped them into his jacket pocket. 'Then go, and good luck,' Anton said. 'You know exactly what to do and when to do it. Both of you.'

'Don't worry,' the older woman said; she smiled a strained little smile. 'I'll come out the moment I see the car headlights flash.'

'Right, Natalie, get your niece and set off. Buy her an ice cream, walk round the square. Keep those flowers hidden until the last moment. And don't wait to see *anything* after she's presented them; above all, be careful nobody photographs you, keep your face hidden.'

'God go with you,' she said softly. 'Wherever they are, I believe my mother and father are with us today.' She left the room, and they heard her calling to her niece. 'Janine? Come on, sweetheart – we're going shopping and to see the big church . . .'

'Well,' Anton looked round at them and smiled at Anna before he turned to Nicholas. 'If our driver is ready, I think we'll leave now. Elise, check that everything is prepared for our guest. Anna, you and Fritz listen to the radio in case there is a news flash. Pray there isn't one, otherwise we will have failed. And if we haven't returned by one o'clock at the latest, then take the Renault and drive to Paris. Leave it in the garage near my office block, and disappear. Vanish and stay hidden. Don't wait here or come to Chartres or try to find out what has happened. You'll hear soon enough.'

Anna went to him and Régine and kissed them both. She saw Elise and Fritz come and shake hands. She threw her arms round Nicholas and held him close.

'Be careful,' she whispered. 'My darling, for God's sake be careful.' She felt his embrace tighten round her quickly, the words murmured in her ear.

'I love you. But if we don't come back by one, you're to go. You promise me?'

'I promise,' she whispered, knowing that nothing in the world would make her leave the Château without waiting for him. Then they were gone, and through the window Anna saw Nicholas open the rear door of the big Mercedes limousine, help Régine in, close the door upon Anton, and take the driver's seat himself. He wore the chauffeur's cap pulled down. The car moved sedately away from the forecourt and down the short drive to the main road.

'Well,' Elise said behind her. 'This is the day we've waited for. It feels quite odd. But they always say the anticipation is the best part. I'm going upstairs to look at the "guest room".' She gave a throaty fat woman's laugh. 'If you haven't seen it, come up. I want to make sure he's comfortable.'

They followed her out into the hall, and back through the rear passages, until they reached a little low door, which opened on to a stone stairway that climbed upwards in a spiral. Anna knew they were climbing one of the short towers at the north-east corner of the main building. It wasn't very high, but the space was constricting and it was not possible to go up quickly. More difficult still to come down, except a few steps at a time. There was another door at the top of the steps. There was a massive bolt on the outside; it had been recently oiled. The room was lit by two windows, high up in the thick stone wall; it was carpeted and furnished with a bed, a small table, an armchair, an anglepoise lamp; the ceiling had been lowered by a false one, and behind the heavy outer door there was a second door, that fitted flush to the wall. The little windows were securely double glazed, and in the second door there was a seeing eye.

'So,' Elise said. 'It's been well done, don't you think? Madame Kruger has a nephew coming to stay who's a drummer with a pop group. Her builder soundproofed the room so she and his uncle wouldn't go mad when he was practising – very neat, eh? He can scream his fucking head off in here, and nobody will ever hear him. I'm looking after him, you know.'

The sudden obscenity was so unexpected that it shocked Anna; the expression on Elise's face was far more shocking than the crude expletive. She moved over to the bed; it was an old-fashioned variety with a brass rail at the head and foot. Elise dug under the single pillow and brought out something metal that glinted as it swung from her hand. It was a pair of hand-cuffs. She opened one of them with a key, and locked it round the bedrail.

'If I'd had my way,' she said, 'I'd have kept the bastard chained up naked in the cellars. But M. Kruger is a humane man. He doesn't want him hurt.'

'Let's go down,' Anna said. She felt sickened and disturbed by the woman and the manacle, swinging a little on its own weight. 'We should listen to the radio.' She turned and pushed past Fritz von Bronsart. She sensed his discomfort as he came down behind her. Elise stayed on in the room. Anna thrust the word 'gloating' out of her mind. She went back to the library and switched on the radio part of a sophisticated record player and cassette recorder that stood near Anton Kruger's chair. He was passionately fond of classical music, and had a huge collection of records and tapes. Music murmured through from the radio station, punctuated by announcements from the disc jockey, and advertisements. Anna sat down, with the young German pacing up and down.

'I make it eleven,' he said suddenly. His voice sounded tense. 'What does your watch say?' As if to answer them the big clock in the hall began to chime exactly the same hour.

'He was due to arrive now,' Anna said. She forgot about the tower room and the look of sadistic expectation on Elise's face. All she could think of was the cathedral at Chartres, the square crowded with sightseers, police everywhere, and Feodor Gusev walking up the steps into the interior of the church.

Grigor Malenkov agreed with the French Foreign Ministry's suggestion that he should visit Chartres privately; he had no time to waste on being lunched by the mayor of the city. He left the Russian Residence in the Rue de Grenelle with one of the Trade secretaries, followed by a very fast Zim carrying four members of his own security force who had travelled with him. French intelligence were responsible for his safety inside the cathedral and in the city itself. The visit had not been publicized; he was looking forward to spending some time wandering round the cathedral. His companion had brought a camera; Malenkov was a student of medieval architecture and an authority on Moscow's early churches. Even as a young man he had cherished his country's cultural history. Every building became precious in view of the destruction and desolation resulting from the scorched earth policy during the war.

Russia had lost much of her ancient heritage; he had seen enough rubble and smoking ruins to appreciate beauty and want to preserve it. Its origins, sometimes a source of disapproval to the purists, didn't concern him. If man had created magnificence in honour of the Christian myth, then it was human genius which it commemorated.

He relaxed in the car, not talking to the rather awed younger man sitting beside him, clutching his camera. The visit was going well; the reaction from the French press and television had been friendly, and the world coverage had been very satisfying. He had projected exactly the image he thought most acceptable; a man of simple honesty allied to intellectual shrewdness, a lover of French culture and with a quality usually lacking in Russian leaders, a quick sense of humour. Comparisons had been made between him and Khrushchev, and Grigor Malenkov was judged the better politician from a Western standpoint. There would be jealousy at home; he accepted that, but he knew his enemies and there were none who frightened him. He had the friendship and the trust of the Chairman, who had blessed the visit and agreed the line it should follow. He had nothing to fear from his own success.

They drove into Chartres, and there were suddenly police directing traffic to make a route for his car, and they swung round into the square facing the cathedral. It was crowded with groups of people, all kept at a discreet distance from the entrance. The sun was hot; he got out when the car stopped, followed by the Trade man, who wasn't interested in church architecture, his secret service entourage emerging from the second car and discreetly gathering around him. He waved them back, and stood looking up at the enormous façade. It was a pity that the town itself had encroached so close to the church. One needed to appreciate it from a distance. He was met by the Prefect of Chartres; he shook several people by the hand, smiled warmly at them and spoke in perfect French. Then, eagerly, he began to walk up the steps to the cathedral and disappeared inside the great west door.

The Russian Embassy Mercedes waited in the square. The square was rapidly filling up as news spread of the arrival of the

Russian statesman. The driver saw a French policeman approaching him and lowered the electric window. The man was a senior officer; he saw the rank of colonel on his uniform. A big man with a typical policeman's look of belligerence about him.

Volkov bent down to the driver. 'You'll have to circle round and come back; we want to keep the route clear. I'll go with you.'

He hurried round to the other side of the car, opened the passenger door and got inside. He gestured impatiently ahead. 'Go on, drive on!' The chauffeur only hesitated for a moment; the habit of obedience to authority was so strong that he had started the engine and moved off within a few seconds.

'Go round,' Volkov ordered; they swept forward and round the curve of the square. The man felt something suddenly ram into his side; he swerved slightly in alarm, and then he saw it was a gun. 'Keep going,' Volkov said, 'Do anything funny and I'll blow your guts out. Turn down here – now!'

The muzzle of the gun jabbed at him viciously – there was murder on the face of the gendarme colonel, and the driver did as he was told. They turned down a busy street full of shoppers and slow-moving cars. For a second the driver's hand crept to the door handle; a snarl from Volkov brought it back. 'Left here, and then right!'

Another street, narrower than the one they had left, and a right turn which ended in a cul-de-sac. A big warehouse with the name Kruger Enterprises was on the left. Its massive doors were open. The gun thudded into him for emphasis. 'In here.'

Semi-darkness swallowed them as the Mercedes slid into the huge shed. The driver half turned to Volkov, terror on his face, but he never asked the question.

The gun butt smashed across his throat, shattering the windpipe. He fell backwards choking to death. Volkov got out, put the gun back in his holster, went to the driver's seat and dragged the dead man out on to the ground. From the shadows of the warehouse, Nicholas Yurovsky walked towards him. He looked down at the corpse and then at Volkov. 'He's dead! You fool, Anton said you weren't to hurt him . . .'

'I hit him too hard,' Volkov said. 'Never mind him, I'll put him somewhere. Take the car back, and hurry!' He checked his watch. 'It took five minutes to get here.' Nicholas bent down to the dead man. Blood and froth were seeping out of his mouth. Kruger had said the man was to be knocked out. Volkov had murdered him. The first mistake had been made. He jumped into the car, started it up and reversed out into the side street. 'Good luck,' Volkov called after him. Nicholas didn't answer. He turned back the way they had come, weaving the big car expertly through the traffic, punching his horn imperiously to clear a way. He drove round to the north door of the cathedral and came to a halt in three minutes. Malenkov's car had been absent for exactly eight minutes. Inside the church itself, Malenkov, standing a little apart from the Prefect of Chartres and his own entourage, stood in the middle of the central aisle, his back to the high altar, lost in contemplation of the stained-glass windows at the western end installed about 1150. In the centre, rising nearly forty feet, was the great window representing the childhood of Christ, each scene in alternating tones of blue and red. The window surmounted by the Virgin in Majesty was flanked by two windows on a lesser scale, but themselves rising nearly thirty feet – and above the incomparable circular Rose Window nearly forty-five feet in diameter and rising to the roof itself. The ancient art of staining glass to produce that density and shade had long been lost. No modern process could compare with it.

To those watching, Grigor Malenkov's expression was rapt. The total effect was dark and cold, 'Chartres blue', broken by shafts of sunlight which bathed him in a sombre spotlight. There was no service at that hour; the visit had been carefully timed to avoid confrontation with the cathedral clergy, who were purposely absent. A few sightseers and worshippers were herded into the side aisles by the police, and a bevy of SDECE in civilian clothes, watching suspiciously. Anton and Régine Kruger were among them, she kneeling beside him, he sitting, turning to watch the Russians.

'Like an actor on the stage,' he murmured to her. 'With the

lights playing on him. He's very changed; the thin murderer has become the fat uncle . . .'

Régine rose from her knees. Anton was an atheist but she had been praying.

'Nicholas should be outside,' she said. 'It's nearly eleven-fifteen.'

'We'll go and see in a minute,' Anton said. 'That is, if we're allowed to leave before he does. Look, he's moving on. We'll go out now.'

He took her arm and they walked back, away from the party of Russians; a gendarme with his accompanying secret service man directed them to the side door. They came out into blinding sunshine, two elderly, wealthy French people, carefully negotiating the steps down to the square. They walked round to the west door, where they were shepherded into the crowd. The black Mercedes was waiting in front of the main entrance. The chauffeur, his face hidden by a cap, sat stiffly in the front seat. Kruger pressed his wife's arm.

'It's Nicholas,' he said. 'And I can see Maximova in the crowd. She has the bouquet.'

'Would you mind if I asked you something?'

Anna turned to Fritz von Bronsart. 'Of course not.'

He was sitting opposite to her, leaning a little forward, his hands clasped between his knees. 'Why are you mixed up with us? Is it because you love Nicholas?'

She hesitated. The easy answer wouldn't do; it was an occasion for truth, a moment when self-knowledge was an essential part of what was happening to them all.

'No,' she said. 'It's more than that. I loved Nicholas before I knew anything about his father or his background. At first I didn't want to believe it; I didn't want him to be involved, much less do anything about it myself. I had no personal motive at all.'

'What changed you?' the young German asked.

'Anton,' she answered. 'He told me what happened to Nicholas's father and to all the others. He made me see and feel as if I was there. It was extraordinary; it altered everything for me. I suppose I'd resented a lot of things in my life and rebelled in a pretty futile way against them, but I'd never hated before. I hated Feodor Gusev; I wanted those poor people to be revenged. He showed me feelings I didn't know I had. A sort of thirst for justice. It must sound very melodramatic.'

'Not at all,' Fritz said. 'It was like that for me. My family broke up after the war; my mother divorced my father, we lost our estates, our money, my poor grandmother died. . . . I was ashamed of being German, ashamed of my father's war service, the grandson of an executed war criminal. I didn't know who I was or where I belonged. This must sound very silly to you,' he glanced at her anxiously. She shook her head. 'When you are a von Bronsart,' he said simply, 'you have to be proud of it. You can't wipe out generations of family tradition and put nothing in its place. Anton Kruger gave me my identity back. He told me the truth, and he gave me the chance to get rid of the lies and the shame. I told you I had a girlfriend.

'Her family were Junkers too, but her father was in the SS. She won't have anything to do with him, or her mother. He was only nineteen, but she feels so bitter about it. I can't make her understand that it wasn't all concentration camps and horror on our side. What we're going to do will show her . . .' He lit a cigarette and offered one to her. They smoked quietly for a few moments; the radio sang and chattered in the background.

'The most important thing,' he said suddenly, 'is that nobody's going to be killed. Anton and Nicholas assured us all of that. I know some of the others wouldn't mind – but I'm a pacifist. I believe in the sanctity of human life. So does Ilse, my girl.'

'I'm worried about Elise,' Anna said. 'She shouldn't be left alone with him. There was a look on her face up in that room – '

'I know,' he said unhappily. 'We'll have to warn Anton and Nicholas. My God, it's nearly a quarter to twelve! They must be at the rendezvous point by now – '

Anna got up and walked to the window. She knew the place; the turn-off on the N10 road out of Chartres, where Zepirov and Madame Jellnik would be waiting. Waiting for the car with Malenkov in it, driven by Nicholas Yurovsky, with a car full of the KGB security men close behind them.

The library door opened, and Elise stood framed in it. She looked at them and smiled.

'It won't be long now,' she said. 'And we'll have him. Come on Countess Yurovskaya, Herr Fritz – don't look so worried. It's going well, I feel it in my bones! I'll get us all a little drink to pass the time. Oh, it'll be a great moment, I can tell you – when they bring him here and give him to me . . .'

'Elise,' Anna spoke sharply, and the smile faded on the big woman's face. 'He's an old man and you're not to touch him. Those were Anton's instructions and the Count's; if he's hurt or anything happens to him, the whole plan will go wrong!'

'I know that,' Elise said. 'I shall do what I'm told. I won't wring his neck or pull his hair out.' She glared at them, her eyes blazing. 'I'll wet-nurse the bastard, feed him his meals, empty his chamber pot, plump up his pillow for the night. That's understood, Countess, you don't have to remind me. But if he does *anything*, if anything goes wrong for us – I'll kill him. And Anton Kruger knows that. That's why he's given me the charge of him. I'll go and get us our drinks. Excuse me.'

Volkov had changed out of the gendarme's uniform. There was a cardboard box in a corner of the shed; it contained a dark suit and a peaked cap, similar to the one Nicholas had worn. He rolled up the uniform. The sliding door was tightly shut; he had switched on a single light above the door leading to a flight of stairs and the upper offices. It showed the Krugers' Mercedes in the far corner. Volkov walked over to it, opened the door and climbed in behind the wheel. He turned the key and the engine started in a gentle hum. He backed the car slowly up to the entrance, taking care to avoid the dead body crumpled on the ground. He got out, opened the boot and stowed the uniform in it. Then he bent down and lifted the dead Russian under the arms; he was immensely strong, but it was a dead weight, and he grunted. He heaved and pushed until he got the trunk over the edge of the boot, doubling the legs up. The man's cap lay on the floor, and there were marks in the dust. A small pool of bloody saliva gleamed in the mean little yellow light. Volkov was concentrating; nothing must be left behind. He couldn't come back to put anything right, it had all to be done at once, and time was short. He found a heap of old paper in one corner, and blotted up the little puddle, standing on it till everything was absorbed. He made a fan shape out of more paper and swept the dusty floor area until there were no marks left to show that he had dragged the body. But the patch of wet worried him. He had a vague idea of analysis showing human blood and, cursing, began to search round the inside. The warehouse was a dropping point for some of the big container lorries that operated for the company, exporting furniture from one of the Kruger factories. Volkov was looking for water, but instead he found something else. A can of motor oil. He stood and dribbled a little of it on to the spot where the dead man had spewed out his life. The oil spread, gleaming. It looked natural. It would be splotched and streaked when the shed was next used. Nobody would think it covered traces of anything else. He nodded to himself, satisfied. He threw the cap and the soiled papers into the boot, slammed the lid down and locked it: he switched off the light, slid the door open and backed the car out. There was time to spare after all. He got out, closed the doors, and drove away. He parked the car at the entrance to the cathedral square, and as he did so, he saw Anton and Régine Kruger coming through the crowd towards him. Grigor Malenkov had just appeared in the west door and was shaking hands with the Prefect again, before going down the steps to his car.

'Aunt Natalie – why do I give the man the flowers?'

Maximova's little niece pulled at her aunt's hand. She wanted to hold the bouquet, but her aunt wouldn't give them to her. They were a little home-made arrangement of flowers, picked from a garden and tied with red ribbon.

'Because he's a good man,' Maximova answered, mindful of people listening, 'and a friend of France.' A small group of Communists had gathered and she had managed to get close to them; they began to clap politely as the Soviet party came down the steps. The KGB security men formed a screen around Malenkov, and Maximova's heart thudded. There was no way the child could get to him. The Krugers, who she knew were in the crowd, must see that it was impossible. And without the flowers, it would all fail. . . . Nicholas Yurovsky sitting motionless in the seat of the Embassy car, Volkov, who had abducted the real driver, Zepirov in his truck and Olga in the little Citroën. . . . Without the flowers it would end in a terrible disaster. Her mouth and throat was suddenly dry. He had almost reached the car, and one of the security men was about to open the rear door. Maximova acted instinctively because there was nothing else she could do. She thrust the bouquet into her niece's hands and pushed her forward.

'Now, sweetheart – run and give them to him now . . .'

It was Malenkov, with his eye for effect, who saw the little girl, clutching her home-made posy. He waved his screen of men aside and stepped forward, bending down to take them from her. She looked up at him, confused and shy. He patted her head, smiled; he held the flowers in his left hand. He showed them to the crowd and waved. He turned and stepped into the Mercedes, followed by the Trade secretary. The door was closed, his security men sprinted into their own car, and the little cavalcade moved off. A photographer had caught the incident; it would make a nice exclusive for the local press. Maximova had nearly fainted in those few moments. She rushed out from the crowd, caught her niece by the hand and hurried quickly away. There was no time for anyone to notice her. She disappeared, carrying Janine who couldn't run quickly enough. In the back of his Mercedes, Anton Kruger picked up his car telephone. He gave a call sign, and on the other side of the city, on the road which led on to the Paris autoroute, Olga Jellnik answered.

'They're on their way,' he said. 'All goes well.'

There was an excited little laugh in the parked Citroën, which nobody else heard. She pressed her own control button, and said, 'Good. We'll be ready.'

Her next call was received by Zepirov in the cabin of the container van.

Zepirov was sweating; he wiped his face with his bare arm, and a smudge of grease streaked across it. The spectacles, filled with plain glass, irritated him. He had found driving the massive lorry very tiring. He had picked it up at the petrol station as Kruger had arranged and driven it slowly, to the infuriated hoots of other drivers, until he reached the intersection on the right-hand side of the N10 road. He had pulled onto the verge and pretended to be asleep. His nerves were so taut that when the telephone hidden in the glove compartment buzzed, he physically jumped upright in his seat.

'They're on their way,' Olga Jellnik's voice sounded tinny. 'Everything goes well. I'll be driving up and stopping just in front of you in a few minutes. The minute I see them I'll move out and you be ready to pass me.'

'Understood,' Zepirov said. His hands were as sweaty as his face; he wiped them on his trousers and took a preparatory grip of the wheel. So far so good. The driver had been exchanged for Nicholas, Volkov had got away and was taking the Krugers out of the city, and Maximova's niece had given the flowers. It was too good to be true. Zepirov, who had no reason to regard himself as lucky, didn't believe it could go on without some disaster overtaking them. He had gone to Lausanne on the instructions of his firm, a firm with a connection to the Kruger empire, which was why he had a job at all, and then called in sick the day before.

When it was over he would fly back and report for work next morning. His alibi was safe. If he ever got to the airport. . . . He thrust the pessimistic thought away.

This time, just once, and because men like Kruger and Yurovsky were in command, fate wouldn't turn and spit in his eye. He had no faith in his own stars, but he did believe in theirs. He kept his eyes on the driving mirror, and then he saw the little green Citroën coming up behind him. He switched on his engine. The Citroën pulled up in front of him, its nose out on to the main road. He could see Olga leaning forward in her seat, watching that road. It was ridiculous to think of a woman of her age taking part in an operation of such danger and where nerve was so important. She should have been at home with her grandchildren. There was no room in her life for anything but the past and the people connected with it. He had never known a woman so fierce in her desire for vengeance. Except Elise Rodzinskaya.

In the Citroën, Olga Jellnik glanced briefly at the lorry behind her. She had left him plenty of room to swing out. He was sitting alert in his seat. When the moment came, there wouldn't be much time.

'Comrade Malenkov, shall I throw those away?' Malenkov glanced round at the secretary. He was holding the posy, its red ribbon partly untied, with a look of distaste on his face. His expression and the political insensitivity it betrayed annoyed Malenkov. What a clumsy idiot, to suggest throwing the little girl's flowers out of the window. If such an incident were seen and reported, it would provide ammunition for the opponents of his visit. 'Child's gift rejected.' He could just see the right-wing press seizing on it, trumpeting about insults. He gave the young man a glare. He had just spolit his chances of promotion. Malenkov never forgot or forgave a political mis-judgement, however trifling.

'Certainly not,' he snapped. 'Put them on the seat.'

'There's some weed in them, Comrade,' he explained. 'They have a nasty smell.'

'Then put them in front with the driver,' Malenkov said irritably.

Nicholas had heard every word, and as the limp little cluster of cottage flowers dropped over on to the seat beside him, he went cold. There was no partition in the car; he had expected that. The secretary was right; there was a faint smell coming from the posy. Faint now but not for much longer. In less than twenty seconds the pin mechanism activated by Natalie Maxi-mova would have pierced completely through the little plastic capsule and released the Niacyn gas. It was timed for exactly fifteen minutes after activation. After those twenty seconds, he and the two Russians in the back would be unconscious. They were out of sight of the city now, cruising steadily at sixty kilometres down the old road to Paris.

The intersection where Zepirov and Olga Jellnik were waiting was only six kilometres away. He jabbed the electric button and closed his window, and in the same movement he pushed his cap up from his forehead and pulled down the rubber gas mask hidden beneath it. He saw in the driving mirror that his action had been seen, and that Malenkov's face was frozen in horror, the mouth opening, and that the young man beside him was diving into his coat at the shoulder for a gun. Nicholas threw the flowers back over the front seat, and as he did so, Malenkov began to collapse. He fell back against the seat, his eyes rolling up, and the secretary lolled against him, the gun falling out of his slack hand. Nicholas began to increase speed. He didn't want a car passing him and seeing the mask over his face. Behind him the passengers were unconscious, and would remain so for at least half an hour after the gas had dispersed. At that moment the Mercedes was full of it, imprisoning it.

His wing mirror showed the Zim with Malenkov's bodyguard speeding up behind him, keeping two cars' length away and closing up instantly if anything tried to intervene.

God only knew how little Olga Jellnik would have the nerve. He kept a steady speed, watching the Zim; nothing would be apparent to the car following.

A kilometre ahead, he saw the intersection, and poking out of it, the green snout of the Citroën. He slowed down, dropping speed, and forcing the Zim to do the same. As he approached within half a kilometre of the intersection, he flashed his headlights twice. As he came to the turning itself, he flattened his foot on the accelerator and the Mercedes leaped forward to 120 kilometres an hour.

Kruger's Mercedes was taking the back roads, speeding recklessly along the narrow lanes, Volkov hunched low in the driver's seat. Régine put her hand through her husband's arm to steady herself as she swayed at the corners.

'Does he have to drive like this?'

'We can't risk being even a minute behind the time,' Anton said. He looked at his watch; his expression was grim. 'Just pray Olga's nerve doesn't crack; I should have got someone younger to do it, but an elderly woman looks more convincing.'

'She'll be all right,' Régine said. 'She's as tough as nails; she'd ram them if she had to – Oh, my God, look!'

A farm lorry, loaded with straw, was turning out into the lane ahead of them.

She heard Anton swear fiercely, and at once Volkov's hand was blasting the horn at it. The lorry, far from coming in to the side to let them pass, moved further into the middle of the road, completely blocking the way. Volkov looked over his shoulder; his face was contorted. 'The swine is doing it deliberately – I can't possibly overtake!'

'Give me the map,' Anton snapped. 'Wait, we're here –' his finger ran along the maze of country roads; there was no turn-off for another four kilometres. And if they were forced to detour, more precious time would be lost. 'Stop hooting, you fool!' he shouted at Volkov. 'You're just making it worse. Drop back, so he can see you in the mirror –'

'We won't get there,' Régine said. 'They'll stop and we won't be there –' He didn't seem to hear her. He was leaning forward, every muscle tensed, watching the lorry bump and sway in its leisurely way, shedding wisps of straw on the way.

He looked at his watch again. 'We will be late,' he said. 'They'll just have to wait for us.'

At the moment when Nicholas suddenly accelerated, the driver of the Zim had unconsciously relaxed at the lower speed. He was less aware of the gap that opened so quickly between them than he should have been, and before he could react to close it, a green Citroën drove straight on to the roadway in his path, and stopped.

There was a shout from the men behind him, and he braked, swerving to the right to avoid a collision; as he did so a huge blue and silver container lorry came out of the same turning as the Citroën and took the road. The Embassy Mercedes was completely hidden from their view. There was a woman in the Citroën, a grey-haired woman, wrenching at the wheel, turning the car quickly to follow the lorry. The Russian leaned out of the window and yelled abuse at her; if he hadn't been going so slowly there would have been an accident. He signalled, indicator flashing, and swung out to overtake the Citroën and the lorry; the little green car immediately did the same, hugging the lane way, hovering by the side of the container and swinging back in indecision, making it impossible for the Zim to get past either of them.

The driver was hooting at her, becoming frantic; she gestured angrily at him in her driving mirror. Their orders were never to let the Mercedes out of view, and it was impossible to overtake the little car and the container at the same time because of oncoming traffic. The senior security officer sitting in the back leaned forward.

'Call through to the police. This could be trouble . . . and the next time that old —— drops back, go out, and if we hit her, too bad!'

Nicholas saw Zepirov loom up behind him in the lorry; he glanced once into the back. The two men were deeply unconscious. The next right-hand turn-off was coming up; it was only a few kilometres from the one where he had escaped from the Zim. He slowed down, and for a second, the lorry flashed its lights. Olga was holding them up in the rear. Her instruction was to keep them blocked in for another three kilometres. It was unlikely they'd notice the right-hand turning so quickly after the one where they had lost sight of the Mercedes; they would be concentrating on getting past. He swung the car off into the side road, screened by the bulk of Zepirov's lorry, and sped away. It was exactly twelve o'clock. He knew the route by heart. It was a quiet area, with a few houses scattered in the countryside. The rendezvous point was at a crossroads, deep in agricultural land. He saw nobody and there were no other cars. When he came to the crossroads there was no sign of Kruger's grey Mercedes. Nicholas pulled into the side of the road. He got out of the car, ripping off the gas mask; his face was sticky with sweat. He wiped it with a handkerchief; he wore leather gloves and they made it awkward to find a cigarette and light it. He stood by the side of the car and inhaled deeply.

By now, the duel between Olga and the Zim would be over. At the given distance she would drop well back behind the container and allow them to pass. When they did so, they would find no trace of the Mercedes and no turn-off for twenty kilometres.

The police would have been called in by now, and their patrol cars would be converging on the route. Olga would pull into a service station, fill up with petrol, and delay as long as possible in the hope that the pursuit would have long gone ahead of her. If she was stopped, she carried a driving licence in a false name, with an address in Paris. She was to be flustered and tearful, complaining bitterly of the fright she had been given by a strange car trying to pass her on the road without due regard to safety. Zepirov was driving back to Chartres, to park the container in the factory warehouse where Volkov had killed the Russian chauffeur, and then make his way back to Paris and then to Orly and a plane to Switzerland.

Everything had gone as planned. Except that Kruger hadn't reached the rendezvous, and by now the hunt for the Mercedes must be in full cry. He looked at his watch. Twelve-ten. He heard a car coming down the narrow road behind him, and knew it wasn't Kruger because of the direction. He couldn't get into the Mercedes because of the gas, he dared not pretend to be in trouble and hide his face under the bonnet in case the motorist decided to stop and offer help. He threw the cigarette into the hedge, and ran to the rear of the Mercedes. When the little Peugeot 204 with its family of mother, father and three children passed on their way to a visit with their grandmother in the next village, they hardly noticed the chauffeur fumbling about in the boot of the big black car by the side of the road.

Nicholas came back and stood by the side of the car; he checked his watch again. In God's name, where were the Krugers? He dared not stay too long, because although the place was isolated every street and lane would be searched once it was established that Malenkov had vanished. He went a few yards up the left-hand arm of the crossroads, listening, hoping to hear the car. And then he saw it.

Volkov was driving like a madman, the grey Mercedes hurtled towards Nicholas, and he turned and ran back to the Russian car. The Mercedes stopped with an ugly screech of tyres, just behind it. Kruger and Volkov leaped out; Nicholas had a glimpse of Régine, white-faced in the back.

'We got held up – ' Anton was already at the rear window, looking in on Malenkov and his companion. He turned to Nicholas.

'They look dead . . . it worked all right.'

'Perfectly,' Nicholas answered. 'I almost gave up on you – you're ten minutes behind the time!'

'I know, I know, we couldn't help it. Open the back door, Nicholas. We can't touch them till we let the gas out.'

Nicholas swung the door open, and also the door to the driver's seat. He pulled on the gas mask.

'I'll pull him out, you be ready to get him into your car. The stuff disperses very quickly in the air. It'll be safe in a few seconds.'

He reached in and grabbed Malenkov, catching him under the arms; he sagged against him, and his hat fell off. Nicholas heaved and the dead weight of his body slid off the seat. He began to pull him out of the car and on to the roadway. Volkov came to help him; together they manhandled him into a semi-upright position and Volkov lifted him bodily off the ground. They got him to the grey Mercedes and Régine stepped out, holding the door wide. They set him down on the floor, his legs doubled under him, and Nicholas threw a travelling rug on top. He went back, picked up the hat, and found the posy of flowers, wilted and dead, lying on the seat near the Trade secretary. He put them and the hat under the rug.

He pulled off the mask and stuffed it into his pocket.

'Right,' he said, 'Let's get back to Grandcour!' Kruger had been staring into the Russian car. 'Is it safe now?'

'Yes,' Nicholas said. 'I'll leave the rear window open. There won't be a trace of anything when they find it. Anton, hurry!'

He saw Kruger lean inside the car; when he came out he had the secretary's gun in his gloved hand. He didn't say anything. He walked to his own car, and pulled the rug off Malenkov. He crouched down, and clasped the gun in Malenkov's right hand for a moment. Then he straightened. Nicholas moved towards him, but he had sidestepped and was leaning into the Embassy car. Nicholas came up behind him as he pressed the gun to the Trade secretary's temple and shot him through the head. He dropped it on the floor, slammed the door and turned round to face Nicholas.

'Don't look so shocked,' he said calmly. 'It had to be done. Now no one will know what happened. Our explanation will be believed. You drive; Volkov terrifies Régine.' He went back, climbed in over Malenkov's body, seating himself beside his wife and Volkov. Nicholas got behind the wheel and started the car.

'Drive normally,' Anton Kruger's voice said. 'Remember you're chauffeuring an elderly lady and gentleman and their friend. And if we're stopped, I'll give the explanations.'

'We have our feet on the swine,' Volkov said. 'Isn't that appropriate?'

Nicholas didn't answer. The cold-blooded killing of a human being had numbed him with shock. No killing. No bloodshed. That had been Kruger's promise, the theme of justification which had run through their preparations. Now two men were dead.

Volkov had murdered the driver, and Kruger had killed the secretary. With a gun carrying Malenkov's fingerprints. He took the back roads, driving in silence. He heard a snatch of laughter from the back, and a quick glimpse showed him Anton Kruger smoking a cigarette and smiling. They turned in at the gates of the Château Grandcour at exactly twelve-forty. No one had stopped them on the way.

Raoul Jumeaux was in his office when the news reached him on the telex. He had been busy with desk work, sucking on his pipe, his mind tuned to extra alertness because of Malenkov's presence in France, but with no premeditation of disaster. Security was satisfactory and there had been no incidents. A small group of Zionists protesting about the persecution of Soviet Jewry outside the Comédie Française had been hustled away long before the Russians arrived. Thinking of the protest which had been averted by his own foresight and the defection of Nicholas Yurovsky from his friends, Jumeaux had congratulated himself all through the performance. The trip to Chartres cathedral had presented no special problems. It was not publicized, Malenkov's own bodyguard were in attendance and the route was straightforward. His departure from the Russian Residence had been covered by Jumeaux's own men, and the car had left at their suggestion by the back entrance. It had carried no Soviet pennant or diplomatic plates. If Malenkov wanted to absorb French medieval culture, then Jumeaux was not worried. His wreath-laying ceremony at the tomb of the Unknown Soldier was causing all the anxiety, and the Russian was insisting upon it. Every rooftop and building overlooking the route and the Arc de Triomphe would be thick with police and marksmen. The car carrying him was bullet-proofed and armoured, courtesy of the French government. An escort of motorcycle outriders would cluster round it like flies on a honeycomb, providing a human screen. That was the occasion when some fanatic might try to make his gesture, and Jumeaux focused all his attention and precautions on it.

The visit had been a great success so far. The Russian had presented himself in a favourable light to the press and the public, as a man of moderation with liberal leanings, and government circles were impressed with his sincerity. He desired friendship with France, closer economic and trade links between the two countries, and the usual cultural exchanges to promote goodwill. *Détente* was sounding a sweet word, and the traditional French love of baiting the mighty Americans was allowed full play.

When his secretary came in with the telex sheet, he was deep in his papers and not pleased at the interruption. One glance at her face and he was on his feet, grabbing the paper from her.

'Malenkov car disappeared on way back to Paris. Separated

from escort on route N10 from Chartres. Car vanished without trace. All forces alerted.'

'Jesus Christ alive!' Jumeaux actually yelled aloud. 'Oh my Christ . . .'

At that moment his telephone began to ring, and then the second phone, until the office was a cacophony of noise. The Minister of the Interior. The Russian Embassy. The President himself. And then another message, brought by a frantic man from the outer office. Jumeaux, purple in the face, was stuttering down the telephone.

'They've found the car,' the officer hissed at him. 'Secretary Sashevsky's been shot dead, the driver's vanished and Malenkov's gone!'

Jumeaux put his hand over the receiver and groaned. The President of France repeated his furious question on the line and for a few seconds there was no answer. Jumeaux sank down on to his chair.

'I have to tell you,' his voice was choked, 'I have to tell you, M. le President, that it is the worst possible news. Comrade Malenkov has been kidnapped. It is a total disaster.'

Anna and Nicholas were alone. He was holding her in his arms, very closely without speaking. They had left the Krugers, with Volkov, Olga Jellnik and Natalie Maximova celebrating, with Fritz and Elise. Kruger had opened champagne and they had all stood together and drunk a toast; it was mid-afternoon and the sun was very hot outside. Upstairs in the tower room, where Malenkov, who had been Feodor Gusev, lay handcuffed to his bed, it was stifling hot. Anna had seen Nicholas signal, and they had slipped away and gone upstairs. She had cried with relief that he was safe, and he had simply held her, stroking her hair.

'I can't believe it,' she said. 'I can't believe you've done it, that he's actually *here* – all through the morning I was sick with fright imagining what could go wrong. And nothing did, except Anton being late because of a farm lorry – it's almost a miracle!'

They had recounted every detail of the story downstairs,

congratulating each other, highlighting their own particular dramas. Volkov hadn't mentioned the murder of the driver, and Kruger said nothing about the passenger in Gusev's car. There was an atmosphere of euphoria, which was almost hysterical. Everyone congratulated Olga for her performance with the car. Nobody had stopped her and she had driven by the back roads to the Château. They toasted the absent Zepirov, by then on his way to the airport to establish his alibi in Lausanne. It had all gone through without a single mishap. Listening to Anton's account of their duel with the lorry made everyone laugh in retrospect. Only Nicholas was quiet, almost withdrawn.

'What's the matter, my darling?' Anna asked him. 'Has something really gone wrong and you didn't tell us . . .' She stood back from him in alarm. 'My God,' she said, 'is that what it is?'

'No,' he answered. 'It all happened exactly as Anton had planned. Except that Volkov murdered the Russian driver. He said it was an accident, but I don't think he even tried to stun him. It was a deliberate death blow. And Anton – give me a cigarette, darling, there's one on the table – ' He paused and lit it. She saw that his hand shook slightly. 'Anton,' he said at last, 'didn't tell the whole of it. There was another man with Gusev. Anton shot him through the head before we left.'

Anna stared at him in horror. 'Why?' she whispered. 'Why did he do that – Oh my God, Nicholas, this is different, this is murder!'

He sat down on the bed, looking ahead of him, turning the cigarette over in his fingers. 'I should have expected it,' he said. 'We couldn't leave a witness alive to tell how it was done. But I didn't think of it, Anna. I didn't see that killing anyone who went with Gusev was inevitable. I was just shaken, that's all. He took the gun and shot the man as if he was swatting a mosquito. He didn't lift an eyebrow over it.'

She came and sat beside him. He held her hand. 'It was the most terrible thing to see,' he said slowly. 'He was just lying there unconscious, helpless, and Anton killed him. I can't see it in perspective yet. If it had been Gusev himself, when the moment came, I couldn't have done that.'

'Thank God,' Anna said quietly. 'My darling, I don't know what to say . . .'

'I've been saying it all to myself ever since it happened,' he said. 'He had no choice, the success of our story depended on keeping the details a secret. He killed the enemy. . . . I've no right to judge him. He had to make the decision and do what had to be done. Think of my father and what people like the dead man did to him, and are doing to millions of people in Russia today. They don't have any scruples, do they?'

'No,' she said. 'But that's why we mustn't be like them. I'm worried about something else. I don't think Elise should be left to look after *him*. I'm afraid she'll ill-treat him.'

'She's dangerous, and she's full of hate,' Nicholas said. 'She and Volkov. He was coming round when I left the tower room. I'll go up and look in. And don't worry; she won't dare do anything.'

'When you carried him up,' Anna said. 'He looked so old. I'd never thought of him as an old man.'

'I think of him as my father's torturer,' Nicholas said. 'I think of the year they kept him in the Lubyanka, breaking him in mind and body until they hanged him. I don't see Gusev in terms of anything human. But I'll keep a watch on Elise. Do you want to come up with me?'

Anna hesitated. There was a repugnance about that sound-proofed room, with the bed and the handcuffs. And confined there, the perpetrator of a monstrous crime. She had a dread of seeing Gusev, of hearing him speak. Nicholas wanted her to come. The confrontation would be traumatic for him. He too had to face it, and she understood that he had chosen the moment when only she was with him.

'We'll go,' she said. 'We'd better see if he's all right.'

Gusev had a headache. The inside of his skull was full of hammers, pounding at the frail shell that housed his brain; his eyes stung and watered. He wiped them with his free hand. He felt less nauseated than when he first awoke; the initial shock of finding himself tethered to a bed in a strange room had given way to taut apprehension. Fear cleared his head; he sat up, awkwardly, and looked round him absorbing every detail of his surroundings. He recognized the insulation as soundproofing, and the sight of cloud passing the little window told him he was high up. From the circular shape of the walls he guessed himself to be imprisoned in a tower. And the preparations to receive him had been thorough. The sound-proofing, the double door, the glazing of the window. Whoever had got him was very efficient.

The first idea was the most obvious. He was being held to ransom and this was a terrorist coup, probably organized by the same group which had kidnapped the oil sheikhs and held them captive in a hotel, successfully escaping with a huge sum of money. In that case, he had no reason to fear. If he was the prisoner of the legendary Carlos, then no harm would come to him. His surroundings supported this. He was confined without undue discomfort. That alone indicated captors of sophisti-cation and confidence. He leaned back against the iron bedrail. He was thirsty, and there was a carafe of water and a glass on the table beside him. He tried to get to it, but it proved to be out of reach. He worked his tongue in his mouth, trying to produce saliva. He stretched again, trying to pull the table towards him, and only succeeded in half slipping down off the bed, suspended painfully by his tethered wrist. It took a few minutes of effort, while the pain in his head became unbearable, before he had regained his position. He forced his mind away from the water, closed his eyes and tried to prepare himself. They wouldn't be recognizable, of course; they would wear hoods or masks, to prevent identification when he was released. He imagined the world-wide furore his disappearance must be causing. It was entirely possible that the French would rescue him. He rather hoped they wouldn't try. His chance of safety lay in negotiation. He opened his eyes sharply, every nerve stretched at the sound of the inner door opening. He couldn't believe what he saw. Two people had come into the room and were walking towards him. A man and a woman. No disguise, no stocking masks or hoods, not even dark glasses. For a moment they stared at each other. Gusev croaked, his mouth and throat parched.

'Who are you? Where am I?' He spoke in Russian.

Nicholas looked at the dishevelled old man on the bed, his eyes narrowed in frightened anticipation, grey-faced and sickly, and found it difficult to speak. He felt physically nauseated with disgust and loathing. The little dark eyes probed at him, filled with visible terror and bright with cunning. 'Who are you?'

'Do you need anything?' Nicholas asked him. The old man started, hearing Russian spoken by a Russian.

'Water,' he rasped. 'I'm thirsty. I'm sick.'

'What's he saying?' Anna whispered. 'He looks dreadful.'

'He wants water,' Nicholas said to her. 'Give him some.'

She crossed over to the table, poured some water and handed him the glass. He drank it greedily, and held it out again. She refilled it.

'Move the table nearer,' Nicholas said. 'It's been put out of reach.' They glanced at each other quickly; the same thought was in their minds. Elise had arranged the room. If they hadn't come up Gusev would have been tortured with thirst for hours. Anna went back and stood beside Nicholas. She didn't want to look at Gusev; he spoke again and she couldn't understand, because he spoke in Russian.

'Tell me where I am,' he said to Nicholas. 'And who you are.'

'I can tell you nothing,' Nicholas answered. 'Except my name. Yurovsky.'

Gusev showed no reaction. 'Are you going to kill me?'

'No,' Nicholas said. 'Food will be brought to you later.' He turned and opened the door for Anna. They went out, and he shot the bolts on the heavy outer door. They climbed down the awkward stairs, and at the bottom Nicholas turned to her. 'We'd better go down and join Anton. We should watch the television news.'

'What was he saying?'

'Asking questions. I didn't answer them, but I told him my name. He can work out what that means for himself.'

'How did you feel, seeing him?' She asked the question anxiously.

'Sick,' Nicholas said. 'He made me feel sick to my stomach. I just wanted to get out of the room. I used to think of what I'd do and say when we were face to face. I thought I'd want to beat the life out of him. But it wasn't like that at all. I just felt disgusted.'

Anna put her arm through his. 'We'll be going back to Paris soon, my love,' she said gently. 'We'll have too much to do to think about him there. My mother is arriving on Monday.'

'I've got to talk to Anton alone,' Nicholas said. 'You were right about Elise. I don't want him hurt or tormented. We're not going to sink to his level.' They went into the library to find Anton and the other members of 'Return' grouped around the television set. The news was just beginning.

The first thing Jumeaux did, after the order for a general search was given, was to have the homes of every known member of 'Return' raided by the police. This was part of a massive swoop on all known anti-Soviet organizations, the Zionists heading the list. A number of people were arrested; Zepirov's wife and children were in their small flat in the suburbs of St Martin. A telephone call to the hotel in Lausanne established Zepirov's alibi. Natalie Maximova's flat-mate said she had telephoned and would be returning the next morning. Volkov was missing, and the *concierge* at Nicholas's apartment confirmed that Nicholas had not been seen since his wedding. The same information was given by the *concierge* in the house on the Avenue Gabriel. Madame Martin had left after her marriage and was in America. She was expected back with her husband on Monday.

Jumeaux put out a nationwide call for the arrest of Vladimir Volkov, but without any confidence in the result. The Russian would be found, drunk in some hole, as he had been before; Jumeaux didn't believe that he was connected with Gusev's disappearance.

The whole operation had been expertly planned. The disappearance of the car was inexplicable unless the Soviet driver was a party to the abduction. Except for the body of the secretary, Sashevsky, there were no signs of violence or a struggle where the Mercedes had been found. Someone had come forward and reported seeing the car standing by the roadside, with a man, presumably the chauffeur, looking in the boot. The driver of the family car concerned said that he had the impression of two people sitting in the back. There was no third person or other vehicle visible on that road for miles. Jumeaux sent an assistant round to his home for an overnight bag, and drove straight down to the police headquarters which had been set up in Chartres. By four o'clock he was standing on the road, looking at the exact spot where the Russian Embassy car had been found. The whole road had been cordoned off by police, and a white chalk mark enclosed the area where the Mercedes had stood. Police with dogs were searching the ditches and the roadway. There was a second chalked oblong about five yards away from the first. The inspector in charge showed Jumeaux a small patch of oil at the front of it.

'There was a second car, just behind the Russians,' he said. 'We found faint tyre marks and this oil patch. From the distance between the front and back wheels we've established a rough size for the vehicle. It seems to be substantial; big for a private car, not big enough for a commercial job. More like a limousine. This must have been where the transfer took place.'

'Footprints?' Jumeaux asked.

'Too many,' the inspector said. 'When the Mercedes was found there was a scramble to get here. But I had everything inside and outside fingerprinted.'

'I want to see Sashevsky's body,' Jumeaux said. 'And then an analysis of everything found in the car. Ashtrays, down between the seats, fibres, anything possible. And I'll get the fingerprints of Sashevsky, the driver and Malenkov checked out with the Embassy. If there's one print that doesn't tally, we may have something. Let's go.'

The mortuary smelled of damp and formaldehyde; it was a smell Jumeaux knew well. He and the inspector followed the mortuary attendant into a dismal room lined with refrigerated cabinets. It was mostly used for road accidents awaiting identification. The attendant told them there were only three bodies in the place.

He showed them Sashevsky lying naked and purpling, an identity tag attached to his wrist. There was a bullet hole in his left temple, surrounded by black powder burns. The expression on his face was peaceful, his eyes were closed. There was no rictus of fear about the open mouth. Jumeaux studied this.

'Point blank,' he said. 'Whoever killed him was right up close. Anything in his hands?'

'It's all in the office,' the inspector said. 'I think they found something.'

He told the attendant to put the corpse away. It slid out of sight, covered by a sheet. He spoke to Jumeaux as they turned away.

'The Russians want him delivered to them,' he said. 'They've been raising hell since we found the car.'

'They can't have him,' Jumeaux answered. 'Not till we've had that bullet out and seen what sort of gun it came from. I'll deal with the Embassy.'

The inspector had put his own office at Jumeaux's disposal. A team of men from SDECE were already installed in the police headquarters. Jumeaux went into the office, called for coffee, and settled behind the inspector's desk. Two telephone calls interrupted him. One from the Foreign Office, asking for the latest developments, and an angry exchange with the Political Secretary at the Soviet Embassy, demanding, on behalf of the Ambassador, that the body of Sashevsky be returned to Russian keeping. Jumeaux refused politely, and when the argument continued, excused himself and suggested that the Foreign Office should be contacted. He disliked his fellow civil servants in that department, and had no scruples in loading the problem on to them. The autopsy on the murdered Russian would take place that evening. He should have the ballistics report the same night. He turned to the sheaf of reports on his desk, and three envelopes, one of them large and heavy.

He opened that first. It contained a Smith and Wesson .38 automatic. He held it by the muzzle in a handkerchief; the ballistics boys would know in a very short time if it had been fired. He rang, and had the gun sent along to them. The second envelope was small. It contained fluff, an old cigarette end, crushed flat, a little ash in a tiny plastic triangle, and a woman's kirbygrip. It was marked 'found in car interior'. The third and last envelope was smaller than its fellows. He opened it carefully, and shook it over a piece of tissue paper. A single withered little object fluttered out. It was the head of a flower. A little yellow flower, crushed and bruised by the dead man's clenched hand. When the hand opened in death, it had been found stuck to the palm. Jumeaux picked it up with tweezers and looked at it. Then he replaced it in the envelope. The telephone rang on his desk and he picked it up. Paris on the line. He straightened instinctively in his chair when the caller announced himself. They had spoken before, just after the disappearance of Malenkov had been flashed through. The exchange had been furious, menacing. The military title of colonel covered the caller's true identity. It was a name that exercised real terror among his subordinates, a name that by-passed all normal channels of authority in France. The head of SDECE spoke down the telephone, and Jumeaux's jaw began to sag in disbelief.

'But it's not possible,' he said. 'It can't be . . .'

The brusque voice interrupted him. 'That's our information from the Americans,' it said. 'They got the call about an hour ago. It could be a hoax, but it's impossible to check. Certainly the caller was a Russian; their operator who was called to the line was definite about that. Let's just hope it's genuine. It'll get us all off the hook if it is. So go easy, Jumeaux. Don't rush anything. It'd be the biggest coup for our side since the war.'

Jumeaux replaced the receiver. He had forgotten about his precious pipe in the agitation of the past few hours. Now he searched for it, needing its solace.

It couldn't be. It wasn't possible. And yet already the pieces of the puzzle that seemed most ill-assorted were beginning to fit. There was a knock on the door. One of his men came in.

'The Soviet Embassy telexed these through, sir,' he said. 'And ballistics say the gun was fired. I've brought the finger-print record found on the Mercedes' interior and coachwork. And on the gun.'

Jumeaux took the papers from him. 'Good,' he said. He lit his pipe and sucked at it hard. The taste of the strong tobacco was comforting. He spread out the reports on the desk in front him. The ballistics boys had been quick. One bullet had been fired from the gun within the last twelve hours. He knew without waiting for the autopsy that it had been used to kill Sashevsky. He began checking the fingerprints. There were dozens of them, blurred and intermingled, the record of God knew how many people who had used that car. Passengers, drivers, mechanics; but all Russians whose prints could be checked. It would take time, but it was possible to match up everyone with a known Embassy official or employee. He glanced immediately at the prints found on the gun. There were two sets. He puffed at his pipe again to draw it, and studied the separate sheet bearing the fingerprints of the Soviet chauffeur and Sashevsky. As he had expected, Malenkov's were not recorded, or had not been made available. He checked them against those found on the gun, and Sashevsky's were clear. There was a clear impression of a thumb and middle finger which belonged to someone else. Jumeaux began to compare them very carefully with the multitude of fingerprints his men had exposed inside the car. He found one that matched. Then two more; a good impression on the inside door handle, on the opposite side from where Sashevsky had been found. The same hand had held the gun. Jumeaux placed the papers together, shuffling them into place. The pieces were fitting. The second set of prints on the gun did not belong to the vanished driver. Whoever had killed Sashevsky, it wasn't him. He used the inter-office phone, and was put through to the Soviet Embassy. He spoke to the same Second Secretary whom he had re-routed to the Foreign Office. He was extremely courteous and apologetic, and promised to have Sashevsky's body delivered later that night. He stressed the urgency of identifying the different fingerprints found in the car, and asked that tests be made of the rooms occupied by Comrade Malenkov, so that his could be identified. He was assured that this would be done. Then Jumeaux sat back. They hadn't heard at the Embassy yet. And for the moment it would be kept very quiet. It was being treated as a hoax, but he knew that his chief, the dreaded Colonel, was inclined to believe it.

He wanted to believe it himself. Only an hour ago, a call had come through to the American Embassy in Paris. The caller had announced himself as Grigor Malenkov, and asked for an assurance of political asylum from the United States. He had claimed to be in hiding and would telephone again.

'It's just as well,' Elise said, 'that you don't keep dogs, M. Kruger. We don't want anything digging him up.' She leaned on a spade, breathing heavily. Volkov stood beside her, his spade standing upright in a mound of soft earth. Anton looked at the woman and nodded. It had taken three of them to bury the Russian driver. The grave was in the woodland which surrounded the Château, where the earth was soft and friable with centuries of rotted leaf mould. They were sweating and dirty; they had dug very deep and it had taken two hours of sustained work to make the grave big enough and to fill it in afterwards.

'That German puppy should have helped,' Volkov grumbled. 'Him and his scruples – did you hear the fuss he made over the shooting of Sashevsky? I nearly punched his head for him!'

'That's why I didn't tell him about the driver,' Anton said. 'He's young and he doesn't like killing. It's a reaction to his past. A lot of Germans feel like he does. Don't be intolerant of the boy. He'll be brave enough when his turn comes.'

Elise looked at him, she wiped her sweating face with her sleeve. 'He keeps asking about Gusev,' she said. 'I caught him sneaking up there this morning. I sent him off pretty quick! I don't trust that one – he's a softhead – typical Germans, either they're crying their eyes out or they're stringing you up with piano wire!'

Kruger turned and they began to walk slowly back.

'Fritz didn't see it first hand,' he said slowly. 'Not like we did. It's different for us. It's a good thing the young generation values human life; people with that boy's attitude are needed in the world if it's ever going to improve. Better the Germany of Fritz von Bronsart, than the Baader–Meinhof!'

'I can't philosophize,' Elise said. 'I just know what I feel.

I know how they dragged my father away to his death, and how I cried and screamed while my bitch of a mother held me back. Killing one of them could never worry me.'

'We'll go in the back way,' Anton said. 'Wash very carefully, make sure there's no earth or dirt left anywhere. Leave the spades in the gardener's shed here, wipe the soil off them.'

He went up to the rear of the Château and slipped in through the back entrance along the stone passages leading to the kitchen quarters. He kicked off his shoes. There was mud and old leaves sticking to them. That didn't matter. He often went for walks through his woods. He heard the cook and the housekeeper talking, and paused, putting his head round the door.

'Ah, Louise, something smells good.'

'*Coq au vin, monsieur*,' the cook told him. The housekeeper, a widow in her forties, had been with them ten years. She lived with her thirteen-year-old son in a cottage on the estate. The cook had her house in the village; her husband and son worked in the gardens, and her daughter-in-law helped clean the Château with another woman from Grandcour.

They were quite accustomed to the influx of guests at the Château; the Krugers often had friends to stay. It was a jolly gathering this time; they spent a lot of time talking and watching television, and Madame Kruger was much relieved because the nephew who was going to be a pop musician and played the drums all day had decided not to visit them.

'Marie, our guests will be leaving by the end of the week,' he said. 'Madame and I are going to Paris for a few days. So you can close up the house and take a rest. It's been a busy time for you with so many people to look after.'

The housekeeper denied it quickly. She didn't mind having people, so long as they weren't too demanding, and she had grown accustomed to the Krugers' generosity and courtesy; equally she knew that the highest standards were expected in return.

'It's no trouble to any of us,' she said. 'Louise has made you a *bombe surprise* for tonight.'

'My favourite!' Anton exlaimed. 'Thank you. I've had a long

walk; Marie, would you be kind enough to bring tea to the library?'

He went out leaving them content. Gusev was fed twice a day. At six in the morning before the staff came in, and at ten at night, when they had gone. All traces were cleared away, and the food was kept to the basics so that nothing would be missed. Eggs, bread, cheese, a mug of soup at night. Everything disposable.

He had gone upstairs once since Gusev arrived, and looked at him through the seeing eye in the inner door. He had been sprawled on the bed asleep, his mouth gaping; Kruger stayed for some time, just watching him. He didn't go into the room. He wouldn't confront him until they all did. Elise reported that he never spoke to her. He kept completely silent, and seemed to be very much afraid.

Anton found Régine in the hall; she was arranging flowers on one of the tables, standing back to see the effect. A remarkable woman, cool-headed and calm, playing the hostess to their fellow conspirators as if they were no more than guests enjoying a week in the country. She saw him and smiled. Love had never cooled between them; it had scarcely fluctuated. He came and put his arm round her.

'Everything all right?' They had put the dead man in a wheelbarrow the night before and taken him into the woods. She had found the tarpaulin to cover him.

'Yes, sweetheart. All done.'

'Nicholas rang. Anna's mother is arriving on Monday; Rousselle's message will be waiting for her. He's seeing her that night. He'll ring and let us know what happens.'

'Good,' Anton said. 'I thought Jacques would find her interesting. It's so useful to have friends –' He squeezed her gently and they both laughed.

6

Sheila Campbell, accompanied by Ruth Paterson, arrived by
Concorde exactly on schedule at Charles de Gaulle airport. Sheila
enjoyed flying; she said it gave her time to work in peace and
was privately amused by Ruth's nervousness; the surreptitiously
swallowed tranquillizer was an unexpected sign of human
weakness. Sheila made no concessions to other people's
neuroses; Ruth had had to travel everywhere with her, in all
varieties of planes, including a four-seater where the secretary
had been literally sick with fright. Sheila's view was uncompromising. If she could do it, so could anybody else. She set out
on the trip after a well-publicized press conference and TV
coverage. The disappearance of the top Soviet diplomat during
his French visit was a godsend to her publicity men. She
answered questions about her own stay in Paris, emphasizing
that she was going on a fact-finding tour to inform the American
public of the climate of opinion regarding *détente* with the
Russians and whether this involved anti-American manoeuvring on the part of the French government. She gave the
impression that she expected to find that it did, without
actually saying so. Questioned about the sensational kidnapping
of Grigor Malenkov, Sheila felt she would be in the right place
at the right time if anything broke. Then, as she anticipated,
the woman reporter of a popular daily with States-wide
syndication asked if she would be staying with her daughter,
Countess Yurovskaya, and her new son-in-law. Sheila gave a
dazzling smile, and replied that she didn't believe in mothers-
in-law intruding on newly married couples, so she would be
going to the Ritz. Just before they landed she glanced at Ruth,
who was dozing beside her. She had fortified herself with a

drink, and the effect on top of the pill had anaesthetized her. She dug her sharply in the ribs.

'Wake up,' she said. 'We're landing in a minute.' She put her sheaf of papers together, and Ruth locked them away in her briefcase. Sheila examined herself quickly in a small mirror, used her lipstick and powder, and pulled a small silk beret at a smart angle on her head. There might be photographers at the airport so she got ready for them, but it was doubtful. The French papers, like the world's press, had been devoted to the disappearance of Grigor Malenkov.

Sheila watched the aircraft come down over the city; the announcement of imminent landing was made, the 'no smoking' and 'fasten seat belts' flashed above them.

The rumour had reached Washington the night before she left. Malenkov hadn't been kidnapped. He had engineered his own escape and was going to defect to the West. The American Embassy in Paris was on standby to receive him. She hadn't mentioned it to Ruth or to anyone else. The possibilities were huge, politically incalculable so far as Soviet–American relations were concerned. But at all costs if Malenkov wanted asylum, then he must be taken in by the United States; both France and Britain were on tiptoe in case he veered in their direction. But so far the second telephone call to the Embassy had emphasized his wish to take refuge with them. It begged for secrecy at all costs, because his only hope of reaching the shelter of the Embassy alive was to keep his own people in ignorance. He had promised to relay the plan for his appearance in a third call. But he dared not hurry. He was perfectly safe where he was, so long as the French security services modified their zeal in searching.

Sheila knew very well that once the news was whispered to her, it would be flying through Washington in a matter of hours. The press could be cajoled into keeping it secret for a time, but inevitably there would be a leak, and if Malenkov hadn't made his move by then, it would be too late. The massive intelligence forces of Soviet Russia would be mobilized to prevent any contact being made between him and the West. If he arrived unexpectedly, asking for asylum, there were enough moral issues to argue in favour of keeping him, for a time at least, while negotiations with his government went on. But America could not be seen to be conspiring with him. The Ambassador had given his views on that to Washington, and the United States President had confirmed them. First let Malenkov reach the Embassy; then discussions about the rights and wrongs could have free range. But on no account was the Embassy to be involved in bringing him in. If the French valued relations with their NATO ally, then they would stop trying to find him, and give him a chance to make his own way.

The landing was smooth, the disembarkation easy. An official from the Embassy was waiting to take Sheila through customs and escort her to a car. As she came out into the lounge she saw Anna waiting for her. Anna with a tall fair man beside her.

She felt a stab of irritation which for a second showed on her face. In the excitement gripping the diplomatic world, she had forgotten about her daughter.

Anna saw the quick little frown; for a moment as her mother walked towards her she froze. She felt Nicholas's hand on her arm, moving her forward. They came face to face, and Sheila bent and kissed her. There were no photographers, only the American Embassy official.

'Darling,' she said. 'How good to see you.'

'Hello, Mother. I want you to meet Nicholas.'

Sheila held out her hand to him, palm down; her experience of titled Russians in exile included having her hand kissed. She didn't smile at him. Nicholas stared her straight in the eyes, nodded politely and shook hands with a firmness that crushed her rings against her fingers.

'How do you do, Mrs Campbell,' he said. Sheila turned behind her.

'My secretary, Ruth Paterson.' She looked back to Anna again. 'How nice of you to come and meet me, dear. The Embassy sent a car for us; our luggage is just coming through. I'm going to have a couple of hours' sleep and catch up on my jet lag. Why don't you come to dinner tonight? I have a horrible schedule the rest of the week.'

It was Nicholas who answered.

'That's very kind of you,' he said. 'But we have planned a dinner for you. We will collect you about eight. Have a good rest.' He took Anna by the arm and walked her towards the door, with Sheila, Ruth and the American following.

Ruth raised her eyebrows high and let them drop again. It was the first time in her years with Sheila that she had ever been upstaged. Apart from the political three-ringed circus that Sheila organized wherever she went, her contest with her new son-in-law looked like being very interesting. Now that she was safely on the ground, and the aircraft hadn't crashed, been hijacked or blown up in mid-air, Ruth felt full of energy. She would meet a lot of influential people with Sheila, make an impression on her own account. At the moment she stood at the entrance to the arena, ushering in the acts, but one day she was going to be the ringmaster. Every move Sheila made was a lesson she learned. She slipped into the back of the big Embassy car beside her. Sheila looked at her sharply.

'What did you think?'

'Better looking than his pictures,' Ruth said. 'And no pushover; quite a tough proposition.'

'She's lost weight,' Sheila remarked. 'Looks tired too. I thought he was an uppity son of a bitch. I'm not going to dinner tonight. They can come to me. Call them when we get to the hotel.'

'I think you should go,' Ruth said. She was surprised at her advice; it might be nice to see the Russian win the first round. 'It puts you in the wrong if you duck out on their invitation. He wants to take you out, you'll have to go. You'll get a better line on him in his own playground. Your daughter looked nervous.'

'She always does,' Sheila said irritably. 'Nervous and faintly disapproving. If she wasn't my child, Ruth, I'd say she was just the least bit of a pain in the ass. All right, I'll go along. Jesus, hasn't the city changed – look at those awful buildings at the end of the Champs-Elysées! I thought we were the only people who did things like that!'

They went up to their suite on the first floor of the Ritz Hotel. There were flowers from the manager, telegrams from friends in the States and in Paris, a fruit basket from the American Ambassador with a personal letter, invitations to functions and private parties – Ruth ripped through them all, placing them on file. She went through to the bedroom, where Sheila was already undressing. A bath was running and there was a heady cloud of scent seeping through from the bathroom. 'What's the mail? Anything urgent?'

'I can deal with it,' Ruth said. 'But there's one I thought you'd better answer right away. Télévision Française wants to send a representative to see you tomorrow morning to discuss an appearance on their *Forum* programme.'

'*Forum*?' Sheila paused, peeling off her dress.

'It's the top political interview spot on the French networks,' Ruth said. 'Number one rating. It's like the Wanger programme back home. You must do it.'

'You can be sure I will,' Sheila laughed. 'I'm good in front of the cameras. That's just what I needed for this trip. Call them at once and make the appointment for tomorrow. Find out who'll be on it with me, who the interviewer is – do they have a team or is it always the same person?'

'It can vary,' Ruth answered. 'Usually it's a journalist, taking the opposite side to the guest, chaired by Jacques Rousselle. He's very good, a sort of French Frost.'

'Tell me.' Sheila sat on the bed in her underclothes. Her figure was as trim as a woman in her twenties. 'How the hell do you know everything about everything?'

Ruth smiled at her.

'Because you'd fire me if I didn't. I'll go and make that call. I'll see you're woken in a couple of hours.'

Gusev had been dreaming. He was fighting a crowd of people with one arm trapped behind him; they were clawing at his face, spitting and screaming; he felt the rip of nails near his eyes and with only one hand he couldn't protect himself.

He woke sweating and gasping for breath. The room was full of morning light; there was a fierce pain in his manacled right arm where he had been dragging and wrenching it in his sleep.

He heaved himself upright, awkwardly, his heart racing until he felt as if it would burst in his chest. He wiped the sweat out of his eyes, and his free hand shook. The people in his nightmare had real faces, and they wore German uniforms; the voices cursing and shrieking at him were Russian voices.

There was no water; the sadistic bitch had emptied the carafe, watching him as she did so, and left him to a night of thirst again. He made an effort to calm himself, asserting the willpower that finally regulated his rocketing heartbeat, checked his watch as he always did, to keep track of time and the date. He was hungry. She stood over him while he ate, snatching the tray away before he finished. He found himself gulping the sloppy food like an animal under her eye. She tortured him in small ways, by watching him use the chamber pot. If he refused to do so, she put the pot out of reach and left him for hours until he soaked his bed.

Gusev knew the technique; the woman acted on instinct but it was as sure as if she had been trained. He sensed the suppressed violence in her, the longing to inflict real physical injury, and he wisely never spoke or offered provocation.

It was his only safeguard. He lay back and collected his thoughts as he did every morning, forcing himself to concentrate instead of listening for the door to open and the woman to come in, bringing his breakfast. She terrified him; if she were late that frightened him even more. He had panics when he imagined being abandoned in the soundproofed room to starve to death. Only thinking of his predicament and making plans how to meet it saved him from doing what his tormentor wanted. Asking to know what was going to happen to him.

He wouldn't do that. He didn't need to ask who held him captive. In the long hours of that first night after his capture, he had remembered the name spoken by the young Russian who had come to see him. Yurovsky. Thirty years later, almost buried in his memory, the name was spoken again, and the face swam back into his consciousness as he had last seen it. The eyes closed, the lips moving in some silent prayer, just before the trap fell on the gallows. They had been hanged one after the other, and Yurovsky had been the first, as the least important of the criminals. The others watched until their turn came. Count Michael Yurovsky. The traitor, the Tsarist officer who had escaped just punishment in 1919, only to reappear in the ranks of the German enemy. Other names followed, coming at random, dredged up by the desperate need to remember, to see them in the context of his own danger.

No group of international terrorists, bargaining for massive stakes, but a band of Russians, renegades, connected with the repatriation of traitors and cowards. That first night he had expected death; when nothing happened to him he began to speculate and hope that his captors were indeed bargaining for him. The release of the dissidents being held in mental hospitals, the writers and intellectuals sentenced to labour camps. They could be the price of his freedom.

If they were, would the Soviet Union pay to save the life of one of their most powerful public figures? Would the ailing Chairman and the Party President persuade the Praesidium to submit to blackmail in order to rescue Grigor Malenkov? He had a lot of enemies. He could imagine the arguments they would use against acceptance of the kidnappers' terms. He could think of them himself. Better for a loyal, courageous Soviet leader to die, than permit the dignity and sovereignty of his country to be questioned by terrorist fascists, seeking the release of the mentally unbalanced and the politically subversive. Better to let Malenkov be martyred than set such a dangerous public precedent. When he rehearsed the arguments to himself he had a horrible feeling that they made more political sense than those in favour of releasing him. But still he hoped; the life force too powerful in him to admit despair for long. France must be convulsed by the political implications of his disappearance. He could imagine that, and it cheered him. He hadn't wanted the French to find him when he thought himself in responsible terrorist hands.

Now they were probably his only hope. He rehearsed the events leading up to his collapse in the car, thinking back on every detail to the moment when he saw the driver pulling on a gas mask, and the posy of flowers hurtled back on to the seat beside him. What had they done with Sashevsky, and his real driver. . . . or was it the real driver . . . he hadn't noticed the man's face.

Were they dead? Or held like him somewhere in the house? He didn't think so. They would have been killed, or Sashevsky at least. He wasn't part of the conspiracy, he had brought out his gun; but too late. It was some kind of instant gas. Niacyn probably. Very sophisticated. Perfect planning. How had they got away from his escort – somewhere on the road, he guessed. A military operation carried out by civilians. And he had only seen three of them. The man called Yurovsky and the blonde woman, whose accent he recognized was American, and the sinister female jailor. He kept wondering what her name was and the connection. His eyes had been closed, and he opened them suddenly with a start to find her standing by the bed, a tray in her hands.

'Food, you bastard,' she announced. 'I'll give you three minutes to eat it.' She went round the bed and kicked the metal chamber pot. She stood and looked down at him. 'One day I'll empty this over you,' Elise said. 'One day something will happen and I'll have you all to myself for a bit. Before I choke the life out of you. Know how I'll do it, eh? Dirty stinking murdering son of a bitch? With this!' She pulled a piece of cord out of her apron pocket. Gusev watched it and then looked quickly away. It was knotted at intervals.

'Like you did with our generals,' she said. 'Only slower. I'll throttle you and I'll take plenty of time about it. Give me that, you've had enough!'

She grabbed the tray away from him; he stuffed a piece of bread into his mouth and she stood and laughed at him.

'You look a right pig,' she said. 'A pig, with a crust in its dirty mouth! You stink, you know that? The whole room stinks of you! Like some fresh air, wouldn't you? Clean sheets? Water to wash? Maybe I'll give them to you – but not just yet. You can wait for a bit. You're not going anywhere, are you?'

He wouldn't answer. He swallowed the bread and looked away from her.

She went on, holding the tray. 'You want to be cleaned up, all you have to do is ask,' she said. 'Just say please to me, and

I'll make you comfortable and bring you a cup of tea with something in it, eh? Just talk to me. Just ask?'

Gusev looked up into the heavy face, the eyes bright with hatred, the mouth twisted back into a sneer. He did the only thing he could do, if she were not to sap his spirit.

'I want nothing from a great ugly cow like you,' he said. 'And I'll report everything you've done to whoever is in charge. Take that food away, it's pig swill; get out!' He turned his head away and shifted his body as far as he could.

He sensed how near she was to losing control; he could feel the vibrations coming from her and tensed himself for the attack. He had at the same time a wild feeling of relief. He had never really understood the sudden, suicidal defiance of state prisoners until that moment. He heard the door hiss on its swing hinge as she went out; he found himself trembling with relief, and new hope and strength flooded into him. He wouldn't be afraid of her again. Not even of the garrotte she carried in her pocket. And she had proved very effectively one thing. She was under orders not to injure him, and she had obeyed them when the test came. Someone was in command and that someone was his real opponent. Not the young man Yurovsky; he was certain of that. But a man of whom that monstrous woman was afraid. Soon, he must meet him face to face.

Sheila Campbell turned to Anna. 'Where is this place? – I've never heard of it.'

Mother and daughter were sitting uneasily side by side in the back of Nicholas's car. He had avoided having drinks in the suite and therefore passing the initiative to Sheila; he had left Anna downstairs and come up to collect her.

'It's not far,' Nicholas answered. 'You won't have been there. It's mostly Russians. We thought you'd like change from Maxim's and the usual places.' His reflection smiled at her in the driving mirror. Sheila could have killed him, but she decided to go along with his rules for the moment. She was going to make her own when they were in the restaurant. She murmured to her daughter, looking still very pale, but unusually beautiful – must be sex, Sheila supposed – 'You know I just hate borsch and all those pickled things.'

Anna answered calmly. 'You'll like this. It's beautiful food.'

'You look a little washed out,' Sheila said, again keeping her voice low. 'But I like that dress. Not your usual denim and jeans.'

'Nicholas chose it,' Anna answered. 'He didn't like my clothes much either. I think you'll have a lot in common.'

'My,' said Sheila to herself. 'I do believe she's growing claws.' She had caught a flash of diamonds by the neck of the simple grey silk dress when the car door opened and the lights came on. She wondered what it was. Not like Anna to buy herself jewellery. Maybe he was educating her in that too. Teaching her to spend her money was more like it. In the darkness her expression hardened. She could tell, even during their brief exchange that day, that Nicholas was going to be much more difficult to handle than his predecessor. Paul Martin had been comparatively easy. He wore his inferiority complex like a party membership badge. There was nothing self-conscious about this man. He had a habit of taking control in small things which irritated her, like making her sit in the back with Anna, instead of beside him, which she would have preferred. They had crossed to the Left Bank, and after ten minutes' winding their way through dark back streets, they stopped. The restaurant was brightly lit under a canopy. Chez Ludmilla. Sheila had never heard of it and couldn't imagine what it would be like. Balalaikas and phoney Russian. Cabbage soup and blinis. Stale, outrageously expensive caviar for the tourists. She smiled sweetly as Nicholas helped her out and swept in.

The smile was still there as they were shown to a banquette table, but it was a little forced. The décor was subdued nineteenth century; red plush seats and gilt mirrors, dazzling white tablecloths, fresh flowers and an enormous table at one end covered with every imaginable variety of cold *hors d'œuvres*. Waiters in black tailcoats and old-fashioned white ties came forward; the manager himself showed them to their table and bowed to her, hoping that she would find everything satisfactory.

He spoke Russian to Nicholas, which annoyed her. It was

one of the most elegant places she had ever been to, a step backwards into a world of style and manners of many years ago. She looked after the manager, splendid in black coat and red carnation in his buttonhole. 'Don't tell me,' she said to Nicholas, 'he's a prince?'

'No,' Nicholas said. 'As a matter of fact his grandfather was a chef to a prince – only the waiters have titles here. I've chosen our dinner. I hope you'll like it.'

'I hope so too,' Sheila said. She took out a Cartier cigarette case and fitted one of her personally made filter-tipped into a gold holder. Nicholas lit it for her. The diamonds on her daughter's dress were flashing.

'That's an unusual brooch,' she said. 'Where did you buy that, dear?'

'Nicholas gave it to me,' Anna said. 'It belonged to his grandmother. The Empress Alexandra gave it to her.'

'How very grand,' her mother said. 'You're lucky you didn't have to sell it,' she said to him. 'But then your grandfather, Etienne Druet, was quite rich, wasn't he?' If the attack surprised him, Nicholas didn't show it. He nodded, and she had the feeling that she hadn't scored.

'Not when the war ended,' he said. 'He lost everything.'

'Of course,' Sheila said. 'He was a collaborator. Like your father.'

'Mother!'

She turned to Anna and made a placating gesture as if she were suggesting patience to a child. 'Nicholas doesn't mind, do you, dear? I had to find out something about you. All I got after the news of your wedding was a long ecstatic letter from Anna, saying how wonderful you were. Nobody could be that perfect, so I just made a few inquiries. You don't mind, do you?' She addressed him directly, ignoring her daughter. But it was Anna who answered. Her voice was low but level.

'*I* mind,' she said. 'I mind very much that you probed into Nicholas's background and brought up things about his family, hoping to embarrass him. I know all about the Druets, Mother; I know his grandfather died in prison and that his father was sent back to Russia and hanged. Murdered, I should say, without trial. There's nothing you can tell me that I don't already know. We've come out to dinner to have a pleasant evening, and I hope we're going to have one. I want you to get to know Nicholas. If you're not prepared to try, then don't let's waste everybody's time.'

For a moment there was silence. Mother and daughter looked at each other, and the latent hostility of their whole lives together became almost tangible as Nicholas waited.

'Okay.' Sheila let out a deep breath. 'Let's drop the social niceties, since Anna's begun it. I have a duty to Anna and that's to see she doesn't make a fool of herself. She did once already. Martin was a disaster and I'd have told her so if she hadn't married him first. Exactly as she did with you. I found out about you, Nicholas, because my daughter is a very rich girl and she has to be protected. I'm a republican and I don't approve of titles and I don't approve of Russians marrying into my family. If you want me to accept you, then you've damn well got to prove yourself.'

Nicholas reached over and took Anna's hand; he squeezed it, telling her that it was his battle now.

He poured some wine into Sheila's glass, and immediately a waiter hurried over to attend to them. He let the pause continue until they were alone again.

'I see your point of view,' he said. 'In your place, with so much money and an only daughter, I'd do exactly what you did. But you're wrong about one thing. I don't have to prove myself to you, Madame Campbell. I don't want Anna's money, and I don't even want to know what she does with it. I have enough to support us both.'

'I know,' Sheila said contemptuously. 'You work for Wedermans and you earn peanuts.'

'By your standards the President of France earns peanuts,' Nicholas replied. 'For a very successful political figure, you're right out of touch with normal people. You see everything in terms of millions; you see your daughter's husband only in relation to yourself. I said I didn't have to prove myself to you. I hope we'll be friends, and I shall be sorry if we're not. But the only person who has to approve of me is my wife.'

Sheila's lips compressed tightly and then suddenly she shrugged. 'Then there's nothing else to say, is there? Anna has made her decision without consulting me, and I don't feel I have to pretend to be pleased about it. Some of the press comments in the States weren't exactly favourable, from my point of view.'

'You can always reply in your own magazine, Mother,' Anna said. 'After all, I haven't exactly featured in your life for some years. I don't see why I should be important now.'

'You're not,' her mother said. 'I'm the one who's important. I'm the one the Democrats are shooting at; you're just ammunition, that's all. But I don't expect you to care about that. You've never taken any interest in what I was doing. You've gone your own way and I haven't stopped you.'

'No,' Anna said slowly; she ignored Nicholas, who shook his head. Things were being said at last that had festered unspoken for too long. For the first time in her life she felt able to stand up to her mother and not back away, pretending that it wasn't worth a fight. 'No,' she said again, 'You never tried to stop me. You saw I wasn't your kind of a person and you just cut loose. You went after what you wanted and to hell with me, growing up. All you ever did was tell me I couldn't expect anyone to want me for myself because I was too rich and you were too important. That was it. When I married Paul you crucified him. I don't say the marriage would have worked, but you made sure it didn't. You're trying to do the same with Nicholas; make me distrust him, put him on the defensive. Just to prove that I've made a mistake, and I'm as big a fool as you've always said I was.'

Sheila turned and stared at her.

'Balls,' she said shortly. 'No, I'm wrong, that's what you didn't have. You couldn't cope with me or our way of life, so you ran off to Europe. Where you did exactly nothing. Lived off the money you were so ashamed of, married a guttersnipe who screwed everything that moved, and justified it all by telling yourself I was a rotten mother. Now you want me to go all hearts and flowers over another mess-up!'

'That isn't fair,' Nicholas said quietly. 'I'm sorry to interfere but neither of you are making much sense. All you're doing is blaming each other, and it seems to me that both of you are partly right. Anna told me about her letter; and she showed me your cable. She doesn't want hearts and flowers or silly nonsense that you don't mean. She just wants you to wish her well, that's all. Can't you at least do that?'

'Now I'm the bitch queen,' Sheila said. She gave a short laugh. 'You're a smart talker, Nicholas, I'll give you that. The trouble with me is I speak my mind and I don't suffer fools. If the cable was tough, I'm sorry, but it's how I saw it at the time. If Anna wants me to wish her well and hope it works out with you, then I do.'

'In that case,' he said, 'Let's drink to it; let's call a truce for this evening, and enjoy our dinner. I think it's rather good for you and Anna to fight, but I'd rather you did it when I wasn't here. Why don't you have lunch tomorrow and go on from there?'

He was watching Sheila as he spoke; hard as nails, selfish and ruthless and mercury-quick minded. But she had a sense of humour. And she could respect an opponent who stood up to her. He saw the beginning of a smile that deepened, and a look in her eyes that acknowledged him. He knew that she would come closer to liking her daughter after that night than she had ever done before. The waiter came to their table.

'Caviar blinis,' Nicholas said. 'They make them really well here. Anna, darling, I've ordered venison and chestnuts; you loved it the last time we came.'

She looked at him, and again their hands touched in communication. Sheila saw the glance that passed between them without seeming to do so, and wondered whether she wasn't actually seeing two people in love, the way it was supposed to be.

She felt oddly relieved and stimulated by the exchange with her daughter; while she resented being challenged and hated the criticism, her own tough spirit was glad to find an echo in the child she had thought of with contempt for so long. Anna was indeed developing. And it could only be due to the man sitting opposite, whose self-composure had never wavered under insult or innuendo. He was the victor in the first round fought that night. While Sheila didn't intend for a moment to let him end up winning, she almost liked him for having given her as good as she had given him.

'Just to change the subject,' she said, 'I've been asked to appear on *Forum*. I'm seeing the producer Rousselle to discuss it tomorrow morning. I gather it's a very top spot in French political television.'

'It's the best,' Anna said. She hadn't expected Kruger's hand to show so quickly. She made an effort to seem interested. Nicholas was looking very impressed.

'Politicians fight to get on that programme,' Anna went on. 'It's a great compliment to you, Mother. You'll have me feeling proud of you in a minute.'

They all laughed and suddenly the last of the tension vanished.

'Rousselle likes controversy,' Nicholas said. 'It won't be easy for you.'

'I don't scare easily,' Sheila answered. 'Anyone wants to have a go at me, I hit right back. I'm looking forward to it.'

'You'll be marvellous,' Nicholas said. 'Anna and I must be in the audience. You know it's done live?'

'All the better,' she said. 'I've got quite a few things I want to say to the French people. By the way there's a party for me at the American Embassy. Our dear Ambassador is diplomacy's number one bore, but I want to meet as many people as I can while I'm here. Lovely Embassy to have, though.' She glanced at Nicholas and smiled.

'I had myself lined up for the post,' she said. 'I even married a Frenchman to show what a francophile I was. Nothing came of it, and it was one hell of an expensive divorce. This food really is good.'

Nicholas looked at Anna, and this time Sheila didn't intercept it. 'It's going well,' the message said. 'For us personally and for what we have to do.'

It was past midnight when they drove Sheila back to the Ritz. She promised to call Anna when she saw a gap in her itinerary, but there didn't seem a spare moment for the next few days.

The television interview was scheduled for the end of that week.

Raoul Jumeaux made his headquarters at Chartres. He had commandeered the first floor of the Prefecture, brought his personal assistants down from Paris, and organized his investigations into the disappearance of Malenkov as close as he could to the place where it happened.

He ate lunch at his desk; a tray with cheese and salad, bread and a bottle of red wine was sent up and he worked through without interruption. The pressure being exerted upon him was *not* to find the Russian. There was an official hiatus in the investigations which was the result of American intervention from the highest level. If Malenkov were about to defect to the United States, then it was imperative that he should not be found before he was able to do so. Jumeaux's chief had made that factor plain; at the same time, Russian protests were growing and diplomatic niceties had to be observed. While not really looking for him, Jumeaux had to satisfy the Soviet Union that the whole of France's security resources were devoted to his recovery. So far there had been no other communication except the ultra-secret calls, which claimed they were from Malenkov himself, announcing his intention to defect. No ransom demands, no terrorist claims, beyond a spate of hoaxes and crank calls. Just silence. Jumeaux didn't like it. He didn't like the three calls which the Americans said they had received, and he didn't like the silence which went with them. He didn't believe the explanation which his chief, the Colonel, seemed ready to accept. Something in the theory didn't fit; he couldn't define it, but his instinct rejected the idea that Grigor Malenkov would engineer his own disappearance in order to seek asylum in the West. It just didn't happen like that. And yet he could see how his superiors and their allies were being duped by it; wishful thinking assumed the appearance of truth, when the figment itself was so desirable. It couldn't possibly be true, but if, by some miracle it were – so let's believe it, let's act upon it, and perhaps the miracle will take place.

He had made a long list in his own handwriting of every

event of the morning Malenkov had disappeared. He had read it and studied it until he knew it off by heart, and every time there was a factor that eluded him, a tiny piece missing from the pattern which should have been there.

He finished his lunch, filled up his wine glass and dumped the tray with its debris on the floor. He took up the list and studied it again.

9.37   Malenkov leaves the Russian Residence. His escorting security men follow him.

11.03   He arrives at Chartres. The people presented to him were listed. He had personally interviewed them all. Malenkov tours the cathedral. Jumeaux had talked to every gendarme and security man present in the building.

11.20   Malenkov's official car comes back to the west door.

11.30   Malenkov comes out of the cathedral.

Jumeaux gave a sudden exclamation. '11.20 Malenkov's car comes back to the west door.' Back from where? He riffled through the file, putting his own list aside. There it was. Russian security men had made their own report, and it tallied exactly with everything Jumeaux had collated. It was staring at him, perfectly clear and supported by two of his own men and a gendarme outside the cathedral. A senior French gendarme officer had driven away in Malenkov's car, and the car had been absent for approximately eight minutes before it returned again. The escorting Zim had not been moved on. But someone had told Malenkov's driver to drive round the cathedral. A senior French gendarme officer. There was another page, detailing all gendarmes and their rank. There was no one of the rank of colonel on the list.

Jumeaux sat back and swore at himself. Who had moved on Malenkov's car – who had appeared wearing gendarme uniform and bluffed the driver into leaving his post outside the church? Eight minutes. It didn't take eight minutes to go round the cathedral. Jesus Christ, he muttered, repeating the imprecation. A man impersonating a senior gendarme. He stretched out to reach for the telephone and then stopped. Wait. Was this the missing piece in the detailed pattern he had worked out? Yes, it was a missing piece, a huge glaring gap which he must have been blind not to see. But not the one he was looking for when he started. It wasn't the gendarme who turned out to be on no one's list of personnel that had been keeping him awake the night before. . . . He forced himself to go on, reading the timetable.

11.30   Malenkov leaves the cathedral. He shakes hands with the Prefect, and the few local officials, a child gives him a bouquet, he enters his car.

11.35   He drives away followed by his escort.

Raoul picked up the wine glass and emptied it. He poured what was left of the bottle and sipped it slowly.

Another list, also clipped in the big file. The contents of the Mercedes. The envelope containing dust and debris from the seats and the ashtrays, the withered flower found in the murdered secretary's hand. The gun, with Malenkov's fingerprints on it. He saw it now, the missing factor. Malenkov had been given a bouquet. It hadn't been found in the car. Only a flower crushed by a dead man. And that proved to Jumeaux that the bouquet hadn't been thrown out. Sashevsky had the single flower in his hand when he was killed. The child who had given the bouquet had disappeared, taken back into the crowd by a woman. The woman had not come forward. What had happened to the little posy? It hadn't been thrown by the roadside when Malenkov left the Mercedes, nor was it found in the car. The whole area of country had been searched. Why were the flowers missing, and why had the dead man clutched at them as he died? Jumeaux emptied the little envelope and the petals and the stamen fell out. Then he did pick up the telephone. 'Bertrand? I want something sent for analysis – at once.'

He didn't know why the flower should be tested or for what. He didn't know what worm of suspicion was uncoiling deep in his mind, he only knew that this should be done, and that something might be proved from it. If there was nothing to hide about that child's bouquet, then why hadn't it been found . . .?

He telephoned again. 'Bertrand – yes, listen, I want all theatrical costumiers in Paris contacted. Amateur theatrical societies locally. If anyone hired the uniform of a colonel of gendarmes in the last month, I want full details. No, never mind why – get on with it!'

He leaned back in his chair and sighed deeply. They were wrong. His chief was wrong, the American Embassy were wrong and they had misled the security forces and their own government. Malenkov hadn't defected. He had been taken by force and according to a perfectly timed plan. Whoever was making calls to the Embassy had been identified as certainly a Russian. But it wasn't Malenkov.

He had not engineered his own escape, as Jumeaux had insisted to himself from the beginning. He was either dead or being kept for a purpose, while time was bought by arousing the political greed of the West. He felt complete certainty that his was the true explanation, although the vital details were still missing. The fact that he knew of their existence was proof enough. But he could say and do nothing so far as his chief was concerned until he had at least one of the two questions answered. The gendarme and the bouquet. It was like the title of a musical comedy. There was a knock on the door. Bertrand appeared, a stolid man in his mid-thirties, painstaking and precise.

Jumeaux gave him the envelope with the flower.

'What sort of analysis do you want, sir?'

Jumeaux hesitated. 'Scent,' he said, and didn't know what made him say it.

Paul Martin was sitting in Jacques Rousselle's office, in the Rue Carrier. It was a big untidy room, with a large desk, armchairs, modern pictures and photographs of well-known personalities signed and inscribed to Rousselle; it smelt of Gauloise tobacco and the producer's aftershave, which had a sickly musk base said to arouse women's sexuality. Paul Martin always associated Rousselle with the smell. The number of his conquests seemed to justify it; Paul thought his ability to promote careers was a more likely explanation. He was a tall thin man, always nervously smoking, with a thatch of greying hair and tinted glasses which diguised poor eyesight. His dress was conservative; he had a brilliant mind and an acute political sense. He was much feared by politicians and had a massive public following for his programme. *Forum* had been the making of some with political ambitions and the ruin of others. Rousselle had perfected the art of seeming impartial, while at the same time mercilessly exposing the bogus or the hypocritical. He had been a friend of Paul's for some years. He had met Anna just before they were divorced, but remembered little about her. His meeting with Anton Kruger at a private party two years before had been the beginning of a friendship which expanded into regular visits to the Château in the summer, lunching together when Anton was in Paris, and a constant exchange of news and views about the world in which they were both so powerful. He had an immense respect for Kruger's intellect and grasp of events beyond the confines of industry; the financier never asked for anything, and Rousselle appreciated this. It was a friendship he valued, and occasionally he picked up information which was of use to him professionally. Like the visit of Congresswoman and right-wing millionairess Sheila Campbell. Kruger had suggested her to him for an interview on *Forum*, and Rousselle immediately saw what superb television could be made out of it. That was why he had telephoned her ex-son-in-law Paul Martin and asked him to come and see him.

Rousselle's own politics were liberal, with a slant to the left, but he personally detested extremism in any form. Sheila Campbell had once been described in an article as holding views which were to the right of Hitler on questions like race and Communism. Rousselle couldn't wait to get her comfortably seated against his well-known backcloth of a map of the world, with the cameras on her and the ammunition loaded.

He wanted Paul Martin, well known for his left-wing

Socialist views, to sit on the opposite side of the table, with himself to act as catalyst.

Paul was leaning back in the armchair and smiling.

'You know, Jacques, this is extraordinary – quite extraordinary! I was working on an article about her for the paper – I had a perfect line of attack, and I was going to make it my principal contribution for the month. The enemy of East–West *détente*, the archetypal American matriarch rich enough to stand in the way of progress and to lobby exclusively in the interests of big business. It was a bitch of an article. I was delighted with it!'

'This is much better,' Rousselle said. 'Face to face she can reply and you can counter-charge. She's a very tough proposition; it should be quite a battle.'

'She'd never have agreed to do it if you'd told her,' Paul said.

'I don't know –' Rousselle said. 'She was very eager indeed. We sketched out some questions for her, and she didn't object. I told her it was live and without a prepared script; all I could do was give her an indication of the line I would probably take, but I couldn't guarantee anything from my other guest. I told her it would be Xavier Denis from AP and she said that was perfectly acceptable. I had the feeling that she wasn't going to quibble about anything so long as she got on the programme and got the chance to throw a few bricks at us. She's certainly not frightened of exposure.'

'She wouldn't be,' Martin said acidly. 'She's about as retiring as a Sherman tank. My God, I can't wait to see her face when she finds it's me and not old Xavier in the other chair! What happens if she refuses to go on?'

'She won't,' Rousselle said. 'Not without making a perfect fool of herself. I'll introduce you as a replacement – Xavier owes me several favours, he won't mind backing out at the last minute – we'll be very careful to avoid any mention of a past relationship. If you can keep your temper, and get her to lose hers, it'll be the programme of the year!'

'I wonder how my ex-wife will like seeing us together,' Paul murmured. 'She's married again anyway, so I don't suppose she'll care. In a way I'll be paying off a few scores for her too. That woman should never have had a child. She gave Anna so many complexes she was impossible.' He lit a cigarette from the glowing end of the one he was still smoking, and drew on it hard. Rousselle watched him without saying anything. Martin had more than a political quarrel with Sheila Campbell. It might be all of three years since his marriage ended, but he still minded.

'One thing,' he said. 'One thing you've got to promise me. You won't let it become personal. If she falls into that trap, you mustn't join her. Your stand is purely against her beliefs, not her personally. That's the only thing that worries me, Paul. Can you stay objective, when you feel so strongly?'

'Yes,' Paul Martin said. 'I always could. However hard she tried, the old bitch never got a flicker out of me. I won't let you down on Friday.'

'Not a word to anyone,' Jacques said. He grinned, looking quite boyish. 'Be at the studios for make-up by seven.'

Martin stood up; he clapped Rousselle on the shoulder.

'I'm going home to work out some questions and get my facts and figures right. I'll have to shelve the article. But this is going to be just beautiful!'

His car was parked two streets away. He walked to it whistling, got in and began to drive through the traffic. It was a glorious June day, too warm for comfort in the city, but Martin had never liked the country. He had grown up in a town and worked in provincial towns until he came to Paris. It was his city and he loved it. He had never shared Anna's enthusiasm for spending the weekends away. He hated walking, and the country bored him. He wondered how she was. It was a marriage doomed to failure: she had nothing in common with a man like Yurovsky. The White Russians were all the same; introverted, ill adjusted, feckless. Not much of a man to give in to Anna so easily, and abandon his friends.

He stopped at a traffic light, switched on the radio and found some music. Malenkov had been missing for five days. The newspaper world was full of rumours. He'd been found dead, and the French were trying to cover it up. He was going to ask for political asylum and the whole kidnapping had been rigged by himself. A vast ransom had been asked in secret and the French government was desperately negotiating, with Soviet knowledge. All rumours, flying at random, but not a shred of real news, not a clue. But something was going on; everyone knew that. The Russian papers and official party spokesmen were screaming about the outrage and accusing the French of inefficiency. Speculation was continuous throughout the world. China had made a scathing reference. But nobody knew what the real situation was. There was even gossip that Malenkov had shot the secretary Sashevsky himself before disappearing with his driver.

Jumeaux had been unreachable, shut up in his HQ at Chartres. The lights changed, and Paul drove on. He turned into the Place Vendôme, passing the splendid façade of the Ritz. Sheila Campbell was staying there. Typical, when she could have gone to her Embassy. He remembered the evening he had met Anna in the bar and tried to stop her marrying Yurovsky. It seemed suddenly trivial and silly, all that anxiety about a few Russians with émigré backgrounds, writers of pamphlets and cheap books, demonstrators in a world which didn't even know they had a cause. How much more had Jumeaux really known, than he had ever told Paul? He thought back again, to the dinner they had together, and Anna's white face as she heard the story of Baratina and the repatriated Russians. Nicholas Yurovsky hadn't seemed the straw man that he later showed himself, marrying and trotting off obediently on his honeymoon and to America. Perhaps he had seen the futility of what he and his few friends were trying to do. Perhaps Anna, with her practical American approach, had convinced him that unfurling a few placards on the stage of the Comédie Française was not going to alter the direction of Soviet policy or awaken the sleeping conscience of the world.

How had Yurovsky enjoyed his, Paul's, experience of staying with his mother-in-law in America? His position must have been equally uncomfortable. They must have travelled back together. He knew exactly the date of Sheila's arrival because it had been a news item printed briefly by the Paris press. It was odd that nobody had thought it newsworthy to mention that her daughter and son-in-law were with her. The marriage itself had attracted a lot of publicity. The photographs and coverage had caused him ugly pangs of jealousy.

He parked his car behind the apartment block where he lived, went inside, made himself coffee, sat down at his desk to begin work on the *Forum* interview. He had his typewriter primed with paper, and the inevitable cigarette alight. He preferred to work on something so important at home. He dialled his office number. His secretary answered; they had been sleeping together but less regularly in the past few weeks. He had begun to tire of her, but it was difficult because she did her job so well and her personality was pleasing to him. He hoped to keep her after the affair was ended.

'Monique? Get on to Air France – get a list of passengers for their flight in from Washington on the 22nd, will you? No, I'm not sure which one, but Mrs Sheila Campbell came in that day. That's the one, yes. Yurovsky. I'll spell it. Y.U.R.O.V.S.K.Y. Count and Countess or Mr and Mrs Nicholas. Good. Call me back here, will you, when you've got it.'

He drank the coffee and went out to the kitchen to make more. He was framing questions in his mind. 'Why, Madame Campbell, are you such a strong opponent of American aid to the Third World, when you yourself have described these unfortunate countries and their underdeveloped peoples as a breeding ground for the virus of Communism?

'You are quoted as saying that right-wing military dictatorships in the Central Americas are a necessary bulwark against similar dictatorships from the left. In your view, is there any level at which tyranny becomes morally unacceptable?'

He sat down again and began to type. The telephone rang.

'Paul – I've checked through the passenger list for the Concorde flight. There was nobody of that name on it. Two more flights came in that day, and I checked them too. Nobody called Yurovsky flew in from Washington that day. Is that what you wanted?'

Paul Martin didn't answer immediately. He pushed the

typewriter carriage over with his free hand. They hadn't travelled back together. Maybe they arrived the day before. Or the day after.

'Monique – look up Wedermans' number for me, will you – I haven't got the directory at hand. Right. 773.24.57. Thanks. I shan't be in till tomorrow. I'll call you later. You can make me dinner tonight.'

He got through to Wedermans' publishing house himself. He asked for Nicholas. A girl answered. 'M. Yurovsky's office.' Paul gave his name. He was gripping the telephone very tightly without realizing it. Nicholas came on the line.

'Hallo,' Paul said. 'I think you know who I am, although we haven't met. I was going to telephone Anna and suggest we met for a drink, but I can't get a reply.'

He sensed the hesitation. 'I expect she's out with her mother,' Nicholas Yurovsky said in his ear. 'They were lunching together. It's nice of you to call; I'll tell her.' There was a finality about the way he spoke that warned Paul he was going to hang up.

'I'd like to meet you,' he said quickly. 'Wish you and Anna good luck. How did you like the States?'

'We had a wonderful time. Thanks for your good wishes. I'll tell –'

'When did you come back – I tried to call before?'

'On Monday. You must excuse me, I've got a caller on the other line. Thank you for ringing. Goodbye.'

Paul Martin put the telephone back. Monday. Monday the 22nd. The day on which Sheila Campbell had flown in. The day when no one called Yurovsky had come in on any flight from Washington. He sat quite still, smoking.

Yurovsky had lied. He reached for the phone again and put a call through to Jumeaux at police headquarters at Chartres.

Fritz von Bronsart hesitated at the foot of the tower stairs. It was mid-afternoon and the temperature had climbed into the high seventies. Anton and Régine had gone upstairs to rest after an excellent lunch; Elise had disappeared into the grounds.

In spite of the heat and her bulk, she spent most afternoons walking in the fresh air.

The Château was still, its reception rooms shaded against the sun by blinds; there was an air of peace which made Fritz walk on tiptoe through the hallway and round to the back. He hadn't been able to read, and he was too restless to try and replace the night's sleep he had lost by going to lie down upstairs. He hadn't slept properly for the same reason that he found it impossible to concentrate on a book. The thought of Malenkov imprisoned in the tower room wouldn't leave his mind. Ever since talking to Anna, he had been uneasy. More uneasy still when he saw the unconscious old man being carried up to the room with its soundproofed windows and sinister swinging handcuff. The idea of leaving a helpless human being in the hands of Elise worried him; this anxiety was forgotten in the shock of discovering that, contrary to Kruger's promise, there had been a killing. The news of Sashevsky's murder had horrified him. He had protested furiously to Kruger, and been told that there was no alternative to shooting the Russian, because he had recovered consciousness and seen them. Fritz had believed the explanation, but his conscience agonized over the killing, and his association with it. Kruger had been firm but convincing. He had taken Fritz to one side and told him earnestly how sorry he was, and how sickened that he had been forced to take a human life, but the safety of the plan and all connected with it were at stake. He had no choice but to put his friends' lives and safety above that of the Russian. Fritz had accepted the explanation because he couldn't do anything else. His first inclination had been to withdraw from the scheme in protest, but that didn't seem to be fair or loyal to the others. And nothing could alter the fact that Gusev was upstairs. His disquiet focused upon him once more. His encounter with Elise, when she found him going up to the room had been ugly and confirmed his inner fears. The thought that he was being ill-treated haunted Fritz – the fat woman filled him with increasing repugnance, and her aggressive attitude heightened his suspicions that she had something to conceal. That afternoon, when everyone was out or asleep, Fritz decided to go up to the tower and see Gusev's condition for himself.

He climbed the stairs, still moving very quietly, as if he could be heard, and stopped outside the outer door. It was bolted and he slid the bolt back. It had been oiled and made no sound. He peered through the seeing eye. The room was full of glaring light; the figure of Gusev, distorted through the tiny prism, lay on the bed. Fritz opened the inner door and then stood still, appalled.

The stench of human sweat, urine and faeces was overpowering. He almost retched. The heat was unbearable, not an inch of window admitted fresh air, and the old man lying on the bed watching him was scarlet and dripping with sweat. Fritz found his handkerchief and held it to his mouth and nose. Gusev came upright slowly, manoeuvring himself awkwardly. The young German hurried over to him, supported him and helped to lift him. They looked silently at each other.

'Oh, my God,' Fritz muttered, looking at the filthy bed and the distressed old man, panting for breath, suspended by his right hand. Deeply engrained into his consciousness was the guilt of Nazi mistreatment of the helpless. Torture, imprisonment, brutality and mass murder were the crimes which had besmirched the image of his people and his country and clouded his own childhood. His rejection of cruelty was also a rejection of the acts and standards of the Germany of Hitler. His decision to join 'Return' was to clear the infamy of being a war criminal from his grandfather's memory, but it had been contingent upon the immunity of Gusev himself from personal violence. Now that he saw him in conditions of suffering and degradation, the effect was shattering. He stumbled for words. He spoke German without thinking.

'My God, how could she do this –'

Gusev had been watching him, seeing the shame and distress on his face; the way he had helped him move on the bed showed sympathy. He answered in the same language, his voice hoarse.

'Who are you – are you one of them?'

'Yes,' Fritz von Bronsart said. 'Yes. Don't be afraid. I'm not going to hurt you. I'll try and let some air in.'

He wrestled unsuccessfully with the double glazing; the frames were screwed in tight. His shirt was sticking to his skin; the little room was like a bake-oven and the smell was so pungent and disgusting that at one moment he turned away and heaved.

'Give me some water,' Gusev croaked. He sounded worse than he felt, and he saw the young man hurry to the water carafe, pour a glass and bring it to him. He saw the unemptied chamber pot.

Gusev drank greedily, making his hand tremble. He sank back and gasped for breath. 'Thank you,' he said. 'Thank you. I've been so thirsty in this terrible heat. She leaves me without water.'

'I'll empty this,' Fritz said. He bore the stinking pot away, out of the room and down the stairs. He emptied it in the lavatory in the back passageway, flushing again and again to remove the stench. There was soap and a handtowel. He soaked the towel, and brought it back with him. He bent over and wiped Gusev's face with it.

'You need clean bedclothes, and a change of clothes,' he mumbled. 'Tell me, what else has she done to you?'

'She takes the food away before I can eat more than a mouthful,' the Russian said. 'She carries a knotted cord in her pocket. She says she's going to strangle me with it. You say you're one of them – why do you try and help me?'

'They told me you wouldn't be hurt,' Fritz said. 'In spite of what you'd done, they promised there wouldn't be any violence.' He said it more to himself than to Gusev. A knotted cord. Hunger and thirst and heat and filth. The dead secretary. This was not why he had become a member of Kruger's group, to be a party to the ill-treatment of a helpless old man. Whatever his past crimes.

'Who are you?' Gusev whispered. 'You're a German –'

'Von Bronsart,' he said. 'My grandfather was the General Klaus von Bronsart you hanged.'

'Ah,' Gusev sighed. 'I see why you are one of them. The fat woman – what's her name?'

'Rodzinskaya. Her father was sent back and shot. You picked him out.'

'I don't remember,' Gusev said feebly. 'It was such a long time ago. Thirty years. What are you going to do with me? When am I going to die?'

'You're not,' Fritz said fiercely. 'Whatever you are and whatever you did, killing you won't wipe it out. Listen: I'm going to put a stop to this. She won't look after you any more. I'll offer to do it. You needn't be afraid from now on. You'll get fair treatment. I promise you. My word of honour.'

'The word of a Prussian gentleman,' Gusev said slowly. 'I never thought I'd believe in it. Will you really help me? If you don't, she'll find a way to murder me, whatever you've been told –'

'I'll see to it. I'll go and see to it at once.'

He went out, remembering to bolt the outer door. The action filled him with distaste. He went down the winding stairway slowly, and paused at the bottom, feeling sick. The smell of the room was still with him. He felt anger stirring in him, overcoming his disgust, and not just anger with Elise Rodzinskaya. But a sense of rage and betrayal. Anton had made promises and broken them. First a murder, now the deliberate ill-treatment of their prisoner. She would never dare keep him in that condition unless Kruger had given her a free hand, knowing from the warnings given by himself and Countess Yurovskaya that the fat woman was mad with hatred and capable of anything.

She carried a knotted cord. Fritz made his way back to the main part of the house and into the cool shaded library. He went and poured himself a stiff whisky, splashed soda into it and drank it down. Then he filled it again and went to sit in one of the comfortable armchairs. His first impulse had been to bang upon the Krugers' bedroom door and drag them up to see Gusev. Now he was glad he had resisted it. He needed time to think.

7

'Do you realize,' Nicholas said, 'That the day after tomorrow it will all be over?'

They were in bed together, the curtains undrawn so that the street lights cast a soft reflection into the room. She lay in the crook of his arm, his hand cupped round her breast, sleepy after a long lovemaking. She looked at him, watching his profile. It seemed impossible to Anna that she could love him more, and yet with every day they lived together, it was happening. Since they married, their sexual relationship had deepened; his desire for her was stronger than when they started having an affair. It was as if he too needed the stability and continuity of marriage.

'I can't really believe it,' she said. 'Every time I think of it, my heart nearly stops. Mother was full of it at lunch – I keep thinking something must go wrong. There are dozens of people in the audience, all the camera crews, the technicians. How can you get away with it?'

'How could we kidnap him in the first place?' Nicholas reminded her. 'By planning – Anton and I have gone over it a hundred times. Everyone knows what they have to do. And he'll do as he's told. What alternative has he got?'

'I don't know,' Anna said. 'I just feel nervous, that's all. I wish you didn't have to take part in it.'

'Darling,' he said gently, 'You must stop worrying. The most difficult and dangerous part is over. Anton threw everyone off by pretending Gusev was going to defect. Nobody has any idea we are connected with his disappearance. Anton has got tickets for the show from Jacques Rousselle, and you'll get some through your mother. It's going to be very easy.'

She shifted closer to him. 'And you really think you'll be allowed to get away with it? That the French will just stand by and let it happen and let us all go afterwards?'

'Yes,' Nicholas said. 'That will be the deal.' He kissed her. 'Paul Martin rang me today. He wanted us all to meet and have a drink.'

'No, thank you,' she said promptly. 'I don't want to see him, and you'd have nothing in common. He's just curious, that's all. I wish he'd leave me alone. I hope you didn't encourage it.'

'I didn't,' he admitted. 'I cut him off as soon as I could. I don't think he'll try again. You ought to be flattered,' he teased her. 'Three years divorced and he's obviously still in love with you –'

'And you ought to be jealous,' Anna smiled at him. 'Which you're not. You know I'm going to be boringly faithful to you.'

'I know you'd better be,' Nicholas murmured. He turned to her and immediately she settled into his arms; he began to kiss her face, her eyes and lips and downwards to her throat. She clung to him, responding fiercely. It was all going to be over in two days. The danger, the tension, the lies . . . it was going to be easy, minutely planned, as successful as the incredibly daring seizure of the man himself. She had been frightened then, beset with premonitions of disaster which turned out to be unfounded.

It was just the same nervous reaction that filled her with dread when she thought of the day after tomorrow. Making love to Nicholas would calm her fears. Or at least make her forget them. When she fell asleep at last she dreamed in wild confusion, parodying the television studio so that it became a vast roofless cavern filled with whirling lights and monstrous cameras, and through it all she kept trying to find Nicholas. And when she finally caught up with him, he turned and she saw it was Paul Martin.

'Somebody's been up there,' Elise said. Kruger looked at her; she was standing in front of him, her hands resting on her big hips. She had caught him alone, just before dinner.

'You're certain?'

'Yes, positive. Things in the room had been moved. I tried the handcuff to make sure he hadn't slipped out of it, but it was tight. I tried to get it out of him who'd been there, but the swine wouldn't answer.'

'You didn't hit him I hope,' Anton said sharply. 'We can't have any bruises showing!'

'You won't see any marks,' Elise said. 'I have an idea who it is. It certainly isn't Volkov. It's that Fritz. I told you I caught him trying to sneak up the day before!'

'What was moved in the room?' Kruger asked her.

'The pot had been emptied. The water carafe was full. And *he* was cagey as a rat. I knew by his eyes he'd been up to something. I knew I hadn't emptied the pot. I left it to stink till tonight.'

'Elise,' Anton said slowly, 'If you've been playing rough up there –'

'I haven't,' she insisted. 'I haven't laid a finger on the bastard. Maybe I haven't worried too much about his comfort but I haven't hurt him. He needs a wash down and the bedding changed, that's all.'

'This could be very serious,' Kruger said. 'If Fritz went up there, why didn't he say so? It sounds as if he was upset by the conditions. If Gusev wouldn't tell you then it's even more suspicious. They must have talked. He must feel Fritz was sympathetic. Good Christ, this could be his opportunity! Don't you see that?'

She stared at him, sucking anxiously at her lower lip.

'You don't think that fool would listen to him, do you? You don't think he'd turn on us?'

'I don't know,' Kruger said. 'The killing upset him. If he started feeling sorry for Gusev . . . he's not really one of us, he never was. I'll talk to him tonight. I'll see if there's any change in him. Meantime, you get up there and clean the swine, take some clothes from my room, Régine will give them to you. Volkov can go with you, just to make sure he doesn't try anything when you unlock the handcuff. But don't let him touch him, understand? Make the place respectable. I may have to take Fritz up myself and pacify him. I'll see what he says first.'

Elise went out; she found Volkov and went to the Krugers' room, where she explained to Régine what was needed. Then together they went up to the room at the top of the tower.

'Fritz,' Anton said, 'I've been worried about you.' He had slipped his arm around the young man's shoulders. His expression was concerned.

'You've been upset by what's happened, haven't you? – I feel you're still not satisfied.'

'I don't understand,' Fritz von Bronsart said awkwardly. 'Upset about what?' Kruger moved away from him and stood before the fireplace, his pre-dinner glass of whisky in his right hand. 'About the killing of the Russian,' he said quietly. 'I know how much you value human life. You've always made your position clear and I gave you our promise as an organization that there wouldn't be any killing. I never anticipated any myself. I'm just worried that you're still upset. The day after tomorrow is our big day, remember. We've got to work in perfect harmony.'

'I've been thinking about that,' Fritz answered. His blue eyes were guarded in expression. 'Supposing Gusev won't cooperate. Supposing he tries to escape or the French authorities won't give us our guarantee – what happens then?'

Kruger paused and sipped his drink. Elise was right. The German had indeed been up to Gusev and had undoubtedly talked to him. During the preliminary conversation Kruger had asked him how he'd spent the afternoon, and the boy had said he spent it reading. He was a bad liar and Anton had not been deceived. In those few seconds, Anton took a gamble. Fritz von Bronsart was above all a candid, honest person in whom deceit was out of character. Concealing his visit to Gusev was a very bad sign. Anton had hoped he would admit it, explode with indignation, accuse Elise, do anything rather than pretend. If he wasn't to be trusted, then it was better they should know.

'Well,' Kruger said, 'We've got to face these possibilities. Things can go wrong. Just as that man Sashevsky opened his eyes at the wrong moment as we were taking Gusev, so something could wreck the whole plan. If Gusev tries to cheat on us, then we'll have to shoot him. And shoot our way out. People will get killed. Some of us will get killed. You've got to face that, Fritz.'

'And if nothing goes wrong and it all works out, he'll go free?'

'Of course. He has to; that's part of the deal we made. But I have to ask you a question,' Anton said carefully. 'If you are holding a gun and you have to fire it on Friday night, can you do it? Don't be afraid or ashamed to say no. But you must be honest with me.'

The young man stiffened. There was genuine dislike in his face as he turned to Kruger. 'Why should I be ashamed? And I'm certainly not afraid to say I won't shoot another human being. If you ask me to kill that old man, my answer will be no. If I have to shoot to defend myself, I'm not sure. I can't guarantee anything.'

'In that case,' Kruger suggested, 'would you rather not take part?'

'I have a right to be there,' Fritz said. 'I shall be speaking for my grandfather.'

'That's true,' Kruger nodded. He was calm, understanding. 'But you must agree to be armed.'

'I'll carry a gun,' Fritz said shortly. 'What I do with it is up to me. Good evening, Madame Kruger.'

Régine came towards them smiling; she linked her arm through Anton's.

'Dinner is ready,' she said. There were two spots of colour on the young man's otherwise pale face. He looked strained and angry. Her own husband appeared relaxed and genial. 'Let's go in,' she said. 'Elise and Vladimir are just coming.'

There were long silences during the meal; Elise and Volkov hardly spoke. Régine kept an intermittent conversation going between Anton and the young German, but there was a poor response from Fritz, and her husband was almost too much at ease. They didn't linger at the table. They gathered in the library, and Kruger put on a recording of Beethoven's Seventh

Symphony. The music filled the room, bold and lyrical, evocative; Kruger leaned back and listened with his eyes closed. Régine did needlework, Elise and Volkov slumped at opposite ends of the sofa, bored. Fritz let himself drift on the tide of the music. Serenity and grandeur, hope and spiritual exaltation – it was his favourite symphony, rather than the more popular Ninth or the Fifth, with its association with Allied broadcasts during the war. The best of the great German composers, personifying in his glorious music the purity of the German soul. Fritz had always hated Wagner.

He loved his country and his people; he was proud in spite of everything of being a German and a member of his family. He had held hard to that pride and to the belief that only a regeneration could expunge the guilt inherent in the past. He had made his own commitment to pacifism when he was very young; the girl he loved and intended to marry had done the same. He had joined 'Return' because he believed it was the means of righting the injustice done to his grandfather, and its great appeal had been that it would be a bloodless vindication. But not any more. Blood had been spilt already. Kruger had told him very clearly that violence and death could be the outcome of their planned dénouement. Including the murder of Gusev. That evil woman sitting near him carried a garrotte. He believed Gusev. He had spent that afternoon trying to think clearly, to see what he should do.

He didn't hate the old man imprisoned upstairs. It had been a shock to discover that. He had tried to equate his image of Gusev as he had seen it in the old newsreels at that fateful dinner given by Kruger. Young and upright, merciless. An old man, lying in his own dirt, helpless and afraid.

Nothing seemed the same to him now. His grandfather had been a man of honour who had been put to death for doing his duty to his own country. Seen in the context of that evening, listening to the music of Beethoven, Fritz's own duty had become equally clear. When the last movement ended, he excused himself and went up to his room.

Raoul Jumeaux arrived in Paris early the next morning; he drove himself at a high speed along the autoroute. He was on his way to the house in the Place de la Gravité, where his chief, the Colonel, had his office. It was a lovely hot day, the promise of a beautiful weekend, Friday, June 26th.

The Colonel received Jumeaux in his office on the first floor of the eighteenth-century house in its quiet residential street. It was not a luxurious room; it was oddly old-fashioned and untidy. The Colonel himself was a tall, heavily built man with bright blue eyes under bushy grey eyebrows. He was a veteran of the murderous Algerian campaign, where his ruthless methods brought him quick promotion. He was held in fear by his subordinates; he had a lashing tongue and he never excused mistakes.

Jumeaux had failed on occasions before; the Colonel had inflicted verbal wounds on his self-esteem that took a long time to heal. He had also punished him with tedious, dead-end jobs which dragged on for months. Jumeaux knew he was being given a chance to redeem himself when he was suddenly put in charge of an investigation into a spy ring operating through a Czech export company. His success had resulted in the closure of the company's Paris offices and the expulsion of its staff. A senior official in the French Trade Ministry committed suicide, but this was not publicly connected with Jumeaux's assignment. The Colonel had reinstated him and promoted him; he stared at him coldly that bright morning, and kept him some minutes before inviting him to sit down. Jumeaux didn't dare produce his pipe, because his chief disapproved of smoking. He longed for its comfort; he never felt at ease in that office under that fierce scrutiny. The Colonel didn't believe his officers should feel relaxed.

'Well,' he said sharply, 'What is all the panic?'

'Malenkov,' Jumeaux said. 'I'm afraid it isn't what we hoped. He isn't going to defect to anyone. We've been hoaxed.' He used the word 'we' deliberately. The Colonel was not going to be pleased with what he had discovered.

'Explain to me why. Our government and the Americans are convinced that those calls were genuine. You were told to stall the investigations. What have you been doing?'

Jumeaux opened his briefcase. He got up and handed the papers inside to the Colonel. The Colonel began to read them. The silence in the room was heavy.

He looked up suddenly at Jumeaux.

'Niacyn gas! That was found on this flower –'

Jumeaux nodded. 'The bouquet was fixed,' he said. 'If we'd done a post-mortem on Sashevsky, we'd have found the gas in his lungs. He and Malenkov were both knocked out by it, and that means the fingerprints on the gun were a plant. It also means the driver was part of the plot. My guess is' – he paused, coughed, then went on – 'the bogus gendarme officer took Malenkov's car somewhere, and the Embassy driver was substituted. He's probably buried somewhere. Otherwise there's no reason for the gendarme to get in and have the car driven away. I'm certain they put another man in. That makes the incident of the Citroën and the container lorry look like part of the whole kidnapping operation. That brings us to the telephone calls. They were made by a Russian.'

'Definitely; I've heard them on tape and they've been authenticated. It's a voice belonging to a native-born Russian speaker, of about Malenkov's age.'

'But it isn't him,' Jumeaux insisted. He looked at the floor for a moment, and then up and into the Colonel's eyes. His whole career was at stake at that moment, because he was about to admit that he had made the mistake which had allowed Malenkov to be abducted.

'It is a Russian who said he was Malenkov,' he said. 'And I believe he's in the hands of Russians. Émigré Russians, operating here in France.'

The Colonel leaned a little forward, both hands balanced on the flat of his desk.

'What émigré Russians?' he asked softly.

'A small group who call themselves "Return",' Jumeaux answered. 'I've kept an eye on them and, before Malenkov's visit, I was satisfied that they were harmless. The man I was concerned with is the son of a Tsarist officer who fought for the Germans, was repatriated and hanged. I believed I had broken up the organization and made sure this particular man was out

of the country. I learned yesterday that he did not go to the
States as he was supposed to, and that he pretended he had.
Other members of this anti-Soviet group all have alibis for the
time of the kidnapping, but his was fabricated. To me, that
means one thing. If we investigate those other alibis, we'll find
they're phoney too. I thought I was dealing with a little group
of fanatics who might simply be a nuisance to us. But if I'm
right, and Malenkov is in the hands of these people, then they
have a highly sophisticated and dangerous organization. The
fact that they could obtain Niacyn proves that.'

'What have you done about this man – what is his name?'

'Nicholas Yurovsky. Nothing, until I made this report. I
want to pick him up and his wife, but I couldn't do it without
your sanction. His wife is the daughter of Congresswoman
Sheila Campbell who's on an official visit here.'

'I see,' the Colonel said. 'An ugly diplomatic scandal, eh?
You haven't been very efficient, Jumeaux. Not exactly thorough. You have these people under suspicion and you let them
gull you. You let a highly dangerous organization flourish right
here in France, and you do nothing to annihilate them. I shall
want a full report from you. Right from the beginning. You'd
better begin now. Then we shall see if it's possible to rectify
your criminal stupidity and dereliction of your duty. I do hope,'
he said, lowering his voice to a hiss rather than a whisper, 'that
for your sake we get Grigor Malenkov back alive.'

Fritz von Bronsart woke very early; he had slept well, fortified
by the decision he had taken. He awoke just as the dawn was
breaking, dressed himself, packed his case, and opening the
bedroom door, he crept out into the passage. He didn't switch
on a light; he knew the house too well to need one. He nego-
tiated the stairs and came into the hall, which was filled with
greying light from the tall windows. He paused to listen for a
moment; there was no sound of movement, everyone slept. He
unlocked the heavy door, closed it behind him, and walked
down the steps to the courtyard.

The birds were clamouring in the trees and streaks of pink

were showing on the skyline. It was cool, and he shivered for a moment. The garages were to the left of the Château; he walked quickly round to them, and pulled up the swing door.

The Krugers' big Mercedes was inside, and the little green Citroën used by Olga Jellnik. Fritz tried the Citroën first. It was locked. So was the Mercedes. He searched the garage, looking for a bicycle. There was nothing. If the doors had been open, he could have started the Citroën's engine. If he forced the door, it would take time, and increase the risk of discovery. There was nothing he could do, except walk and hope to pick up a lift along the road. He closed the garage up and went along the drive and out into the country lane. The sun was coming up; it was going to be another beautiful day. If he had to walk to the main road it would take about three-quarters of an hour. Once on the route into Chartres, he should get a lift. And by the time the Krugers came down to breakfast and noticed his absence, he would be with the police.

Volkov woke that morning much earlier than usual. He drew back his bedroom curtains and stared out at the rosy morning, scowling, rubbing his chin, dark with stubble. He saw nothing peaceful or beautiful in the gardens; he lived inside himself, introverted, violent, unblessed with imagination. Anton Kruger had taken him aside the previous night, when the women had gone to bed, given him a drink and told him solemnly that he was the most valuable member of 'Return', a brave and dedicated fighter who had never hesitated in his duty. Volkov had glowed like a boy; praise from Anton Kruger was his accolade. He had mumbled and denied it, but the old man actually embraced him, and with tears in his eyes, had asked him for his help. And his advice. Nobody asked Volkov how to do anything; he had always been given the orders and carried them out.

Even the anti-Soviet pamphlets he had printed out of his own meagre pocket had to be rewritten by somebody else. He had promised to do anything for Kruger, and his own eyes filled with emotion. Then Kruger told him about the German.

'He's turned against us,' Kruger said. 'I don't trust him any more. I should never have brought him into our group.'

'But why?' Volkov asked. 'Why – how do you know – what's he done? –'

'Made friends with Gusev,' Kruger said softly. 'Behind our backs. My friend, he could betray us all. What am I to do?'

And Volkov had given the answer. 'Kill him,' he said. And then while Kruger hesitated, the idea took fire in him. 'You must,' he went on. 'If he's turned traitor, that settles it! Think of what's at stake – that murdering swine could escape us, you and Madame Kruger and all of us could go to jail – you and I to the guillotine! There's that driver buried out there, remember?'

'And he knows I shot Sashevsky,' Kruger said. 'You're right, Vladimir, my friend. It's just that for a while he was our comrade.'

'To hell with that,' Volkov snarled. 'We treated him like one of us – we took him to our hearts – I'll see to him, don't worry about that.'

'In the morning,' Kruger said. 'Early. We'll have to make it look like an accident.'

'I'll break his neck,' Volkov said, and laughed. 'Easy. While he's asleep. We can think of something later. Nobody else need know.'

'My son,' Kruger had said simply, putting both hands on the big man's shoulders. 'God will justify it. I leave it in your hands.'

Volkov turned back from the window. His watch said six o'clock. He pulled on his shabby dressing-gown. The dirty little traitor; lily-livered from the start, with his pacifism and his Prussian airs and graces, yapping on about the secretary being shot, holding himself better than the rest of them. Made friends with Gusev, had he, Gusev, who'd butchered Volkov's father and brother and been responsible for his mother's suicide.

Wanted to run to the police and get Gusev released . . . have his friends arrested, while he talked about his conscience and what he would and wouldn't do . . . the miserable little German cur. Volkov flexed his heavy hands. He didn't deserve a quick blow. A rat like that should be strangled and have time to know about it. He slipped out in his bare feet and crept along the corridor to Fritz von Bronsart's room.

As Volkov and the Krugers began to search the Château and the grounds for him, Fritz got a lift from a lorry on the main road.

The driver was taciturn; he and the inside of the cab smelt of sweat and stale tobacco. Fritz settled into the seat beside him and watched the countryside slip by, not seeing anything. The Château would be surrounded; if they manoeuvred properly with his knowledge of the tower and its entrances, they could storm up and rescue Gusev before the household was aware of what was happening. He had spent a long time imagining the scene, and by now it caused him no scruples. Kruger was a murderer; Volkov brooding and sullen – Fritz had hardly exchanged a word with him – Madame Kruger was charming, but he couldn't let her influence him. Elise Rodzinskaya was a monster. The others, Maximova whom he liked, little Olga Jellnik, the Yurovskys, Zepirov – he couldn't balance life for life. They had been duped as he had. Murder was not part of the oath they had all sworn. And murder had already been committed; he was certain that the murder of Feodor Gusev would inevitably follow. He could not and would not be an accessary to it. The lorry set him down on the outskirts of the city. He could see the great cathedral's spires pointing above the rooftops. It was still very early; there was little traffic and only a few people walking or cycling to work. One or two shops showed signs of opening.

Carrying his case, Fritz began to walk towards the centre of the city, to the gendarmerie.

Kruger first telephoned Nicholas. His voice was hoarse and strained.

'We've got a crisis! Von Bronsart has walked out – I think he's going to the police. . . . Yes, yes, I've sent Volkov after him. Ring Olga and Natalie. Tell them to go to the safe house till they hear from me. I'm moving our friend out now. Right away. Meet me at the Auberge St-Julien. Hurry!'

Nicholas sprang out of bed, Anna following. He explained it exactly as Kruger had done to him. 'He thinks the boy's gone to the police. He's taking Gusev to the Auberge and we're joining him there. Quickly, darling, just get some clothes on and we'll go straight away!'

'But it's hopeless,' Anna protested. 'Once they know Anton's got him, we'll all be picked up! You might as well let him go!'

'No!' Nicholas swung on her. 'I'm getting him to that studio if it's the last thing I do! Besides, Volkov may get to Fritz first. Come on.'

They jumped into the car and Nicholas swung out, driving with fierce concentration. By nine o'clock they turned into the little car park of the Auberge St-Julien.

When the Krugers and Elise burst into his room Gusev was asleep. His first reaction was panic; he crouched upright on the bed, expecting death. The woman Rodzinskaya, a heavy-set man with greying hair and the face of a Slav, a tall woman, very pale. They had come to kill him. Gusev was not a coward. The powerful will asserted itself, and with it the fatalism of his character. The grey-haired man held a gun. The fat woman advanced upon him, and Gusev stiffened. She had washed him and changed his clothes and bedding the night before. His ribs ached from where she had punched him, trying to make him betray the young German. He looked at her with hatred. She unlocked his handcuff, and his arm fell stiff at his side. He was going to be shot. So be it. He would know how to die properly. Better than some of *them* had died, screaming and struggling, cutting their throats with broken glass. He had had plenty of time to remember *them*. . . .

'Gusev,' Anton Kruger said, 'Feodor Gusev. We're moving you out of here. Either you cooperate or we take you out unconscious. Which will it be?'

He had spoken in Russian, and Gusev answered in the same way.

'Where are you taking me? And who are you?'

'My name,' Anton said, 'is Krosnevsky. It won't mean anything to you. By the grace of God I escaped you. We're taking you to a safer place.'

'To kill me?' Gusev sneered. 'Why not do it here? I'm not afraid.'

'We're not going to kill you,' Anton said. 'You'll only get hurt if you don't cooperate. You can travel laid out with a lump on your head, or you can go in comfort. We're leaving now.'

Gusev got up; he staggered a little, and then steadied himself. He looked at the gun pointing at his chest. 'Why haven't I seen you before? Are you the leader of these people?'

'There are no leaders,' Kruger told him. 'We are all comrades; each one of us does his part.' He moved the gun towards the door. 'Hurry. Elise, you go in front of him, I'll be at the back and Régine after me. Just follow Elise,' he told Gusev. 'And if you make one move, I'll shoot you through the spine.'

The doors were opened; the fat woman moved ahead of him; she gave him a malevolent glare over her shoulder. She started down the narrow stairs and Gusev slowly followed. Once, when he hesitated descending a steep step, the gun thudded into his back, and Kruger's voice behind him said, 'Go on!'

They walked in file through stone passages, and out through a heavy back door, which the fat woman held open for him. He stood in the back courtyard of the Château, breathing the warm fresh morning air, and saw the big Mercedes drawn up.

'Get in,' Kruger ordered, and Gusev climbed into the back. The gun muzzle sunk into the soft flesh of his side. Kruger closed the door, and the fat woman clambered in and sat on the other side of him. He felt her bulk pressing against him and inched away. His mind was seething with activity, racing in different directions, seeking some way out. He wasn't going to be killed. He shouldn't have believed the Russian when he said that, but instinctively he did. And his instinct was a well-tried counsellor. Not death, but something more important to them, to the émigrés and their puny battle against the Soviet Union. Cossacks, *kulaks* from the Ukraine, Latvians and Estonians, the dregs of the exiled, still trying to sting the Motherland, with fitful help from the CIA. His contempt for them overcame his anxiety for himself, he felt strength flooding into him. Their only true resort against him was the bullet, and if they weren't going to employ that, then surely he should come out best, whatever the finale they had planned. He glanced at the man beside him. About his own age, Russian-born, peasant stock; he emanated authority and power. He had lied when he denied being the leader.

'Will you tell me what you are going to do, if you're not going to kill me?' Kruger looked at him.

'You'll be told later,' he said. 'And you'll be given a choice. Which is more than you ever gave anyone else.'

'Your people made their choice,' Gusev said quietly. 'They chose to fight with the enemies of Russia.'

The fat woman drew her arm back and rammed the point of her elbow so hard into his stomach that he gasped, and groaned for breath.

'Shut up,' she said to him. 'Shut your dirty mouth!' She called him an obscene name in Russian.

Kruger looked ahead, unmoved. Gusev folded his arms across his middle; he felt as if he might be sick from the force of the blow. He sat still and didn't speak again. Instead he watched the roads and noted the signposts. Nobody seemed concerned that he could see where he was being taken. Rambouillet eight kilometres. He saw it clearly.

His doubts returned, clamouring against his earlier optimism. They must be going to kill him. He sagged a little in his seat. No attempt was made to hide their final destination. He was pulled out of the car, with the gun resting against his spinal column, and taken into the place that a sign proclaimed to be the Auberge St-Julien. He was hustled upstairs into a little room, his wrists handcuffed behind him, and left. The window was small and tightly shut; there was no one to hear him if he shouted. He sank down on the bed and waited for whatever was to come.

'Why did he do it?' Anna asked them. 'What made him

change?' She looked at each of them in turn. Kruger, his brow furrowed, less colour in his cheeks, Régine pale and anxious, and Elise Rodzinskaya, with a tiny half-smile on her lips, inscrutable as a Buddha. Nicholas and she had found them sitting in Elise's private parlour at the back of the Auberge. The little thin husband was there too, hunched in a chair, cowed. He looked bewildered and afraid. His wife had taken him aside when they arrived, and the Krugers heard her shouting at him. Then she came out and just said, 'He'll do as he's told. He knows he's going to get it in the neck if he doesn't.'

They had too much else of importance on their minds to worry about him. Nicholas had asked the question too, but with less interest in the answer, which was given by Kruger. 'He got frightened when the crunch came.' Anna, remembering the morning they had waited together at the Château while Gusev was being seized, didn't accept that as a reason. There was something ugly in the air, something beyond the tension which their circumstances made natural. Fritz von Bronsart was not a coward. Young, yes, and sensitive, with imagination and some naïvety, but never the kind of man who would turn on his friends to save himself. Anna knew enough about the Prussian character to reject that instantly. She waited for the answer, and Kruger, with his superior intelligence, recognized that she was speaking as herself and not as Nicholas Yurovsky's wife.

'I think it began with the death of Sashevsky,' he said. 'I think he was emotionally upset by it. If you think of him, he wasn't a very stable person; all that insistence upon his family honour, hand in hand with pacifism. I didn't recognize it; all my fault. I think he cracked when the time came for him to take an active part. I don't think he could face it.'

'But that wouldn't make him go to the police,' Anna said. 'He could have run off without doing that.'

'How do you know he's gone to the police?' Nicholas picked up the point. 'He could have just opted out, as Anna says —'

'I couldn't take the risk,' Kruger said. 'I sent Volkov to make sure.'

'While we sit here speculating —' Régine Kruger's voice was

cold, disapproving – 'gendarmes could be swarming all over the Château. They could be hunting for us. I don't see,' she looked at Anna, and there was a hardness in the beautiful eyes which made them look like glass, 'I just don't see why you should be worrying about Fritz. I am simply praying that Volkov found him.'

'I'll get some coffee for us,' Elise heaved herself up. 'We're all getting gloomy. Vladimir will get the little rat before he does any damage. He'll ring us here at any minute and say it's all right. You'll see.' She waddled out to the kitchen. Incongruously, they could hear her humming.

Anna turned to Nicholas. 'Let's go outside for a minute.'

They had spent so many spring mornings in exactly the spot where they sat now, in the early days when they fell in love, warmed by the sun reflected from the rich brick tiling, enclosed by the trees of Rambouillet forest which sheltered the little Auberge garden.

'Darling,' Anna said. 'It's going wrong. You know it is.'

Nicholas lit a cigarette; she saw that his hand wasn't quite steady. 'It can't go wrong,' he said. 'Not now, not when we're so close.'

'It has,' she insisted. 'Anton's lying; that boy wouldn't run away without saying anything. He just isn't the type. If he didn't want to go through with it, he'd have said so. He'd never, never betray us to the police. Unless there was a very good reason we haven't been told.'

'What reason?' Nicholas said angrily. 'What could there be –'

'I don't know,' she answered slowly. 'He wouldn't stand for killing, I'm sure of that. The way Anton shot that Russian upset you, didn't it – we know it was traumatic for Fritz. But he didn't run then. Something else happened that we don't know about. And what exactly is Volkov going to do to "stop" him? –'

He turned away from her, smoking his strong cigarette. His profile was stony. She reached out and put a hand on his arm.

'Please, darling,' she said, 'don't go on with this. It isn't turning out the way we meant. The way you meant. Two people dead, the chauffeur and the other man.'

'The chauffeur was an accident,' Nicholas said quickly. 'I

was there; Volkov hit him too hard – Anton *had* to kill the other man.'

'Volkov has been sent out to kill Fritz,' she said slowly. 'It was in all their faces in that room. For the last time, I beg of you, tell Kruger it's finished. If he wants to go on, then let him. But you should stop it. Let Gusev go.'

He had avoided looking at her until then, or responding to the hand on his sleeve. Now he covered it with his own. He shook his head.

'I can't,' he said. 'We're in too far to back out now. You said it yourself. Two dead men. The only hope we have is to go through with it and get immunity in exchange for Gusev. And when the truth is known, we'll get a lot of support. If we release him now, no matter what he promises, we'll all be arrested within a few hours. You too, my darling. You haven't thought of that, have you? You let yourself become involved in this and now there's no way out. We have to go ahead. Things *can* go wrong when you start on something like this. People get killed. Volkov hit the driver too hard . . . they sent a man in the car with Gusev; we didn't reckon on that . . . Fritz goes missing on the last morning.'

'And if he's murdered too?' she asked him. He didn't answer. The sun was high in the blue sky, its rays beating down upon them. He looked at his watch.

'We've been here two hours,' he said. 'Volkov hasn't rung; he didn't find him, so you needn't worry about that.' He got up and went inside. Anna didn't follow him.

Fritz found the suitcase heavy; he changed it from one hand to another but it slowed him down. He looked in vain for a taxi; it was too early, there were none on the streets.

He caught a bus, asked for the gendarmerie and, being rewarded with a suspicious look from his fellow passengers, mostly workmen and shop girls, was told that he was travelling in the opposite direction and had better get off at the next stop.

He started walking back the way he had come; it was becoming very warm, although it was still early. He felt hungry and hot; the suitcase grew leaden. Passers-by directed him to the gendarmerie, where Jumeaux had set up his headquarters, to the discomfort of its incumbents. It was a large, ugly nine-teenth-century building on the corner of the Boulevard Chasles. Seeing it, Fritz's steps quickened. He had no qualm of doubt about what he was going to do. He had accepted that he too would be punished. He didn't see the little green Citroën parked on the opposite side of the street, or the shadowy figure of Volkov behind the wheel.

Volkov had driven along the country lanes like a lunatic; there hadn't been a sign of anyone. When he reached the main road, he paused, trying to think what to do next. The German must have got a lift, or else started far earlier than they reckoned. Kruger said he would be on his way to the police at Chartres. Since there was no means of transport, he must have walked. Hitched, of course. Volkov cursed and swore to himself as he drove, keeping an eye on the kerbside, in case he should see him standing there, but his hopes of finding him were sinking. As they subsided, so his fury rose.

He had never liked the young man, calling him the German, to himself. The fate of one Prussian general more or less aroused no sympathy in Volkov. He abused Fritz vilely under his breath, as he twisted and turned through the narrow city streets, making for the Boulevard Chasles. He had a gun in his pocket, given to him by Kruger. He didn't need to be told that, at the cost of his own life if necessary, he had to stop von Bronsart from talking to the police. He parked the car and waited. He tortured himself imagining that the German was already inside. He smoked continuously the cheap French cigar-ettes which were all he could afford, and watched both sides of the street. And then he saw him. Walking quite briskly, with his case in his right hand, making for the gendarmerie. Volkov acted on instinct. He flung open the car door and leaped out.

Fritz was twenty yards away from the entrance when he heard him shout. He swung round, unbalanced by the weight of the suitcase, and saw Volkov bounding along the road towards him.

'Stop! Stop –' he heard him yelling; a woman on her way to

work was directly in Fritz's path. He dropped the case, barged into her so heavily that she almost fell, and ran for the entrance to the gendarmerie. Volkov raised his arm with the pistol in his right hand, and fired. The first bullet whanged into a wall and ricocheted, the second shattered a window, and the third hit Fritz von Bronsart in the back. Volkov fired a fourth time, and he saw the German crumple up and fall face downwards, a few feet from the entrance he had been trying to reach.

The woman was screaming shrilly, on and on; Volkov had an impression of others coming into the street. He turned and raced back to the Citroën, flinging himself inside. He set off with the door swinging wildly, until he grabbed it and pulled it shut. He drove flat out, tyres screeching, face set in a rictus of savage concentration, realizing too late that all he was doing was calling attention to himself. He slowed abruptly. He shouldn't have used the car; the woman in the street had seen it, others too; his wild progress through the city centre would be remembered. He was sweating so much that his hands slipped greasily on the wheel. He pulled into a side street and got out. He had the gun in his pocket. There was a second clip of ammunition.

He would leave the car; it would be safer. Make his way back to the Château. But how? He dared not stay in Chartres, in case witnesses had got a good look at him. A bus; if he could catch a bus, get away somewhere, where he could hide until it was dark. The railway station. Anything. He'd done the job. Von Bronsart had fallen like a dead man. Kruger would be pleased. He began to walk, and to his surprise a car with an elderly woman pulled up. She smiled kindly at him. 'Do you want a lift? Where are you going?'

He stared at her hesitating. 'Paris,' he said at last. It was the first thing that came into his head.

'Well, you're lucky,' she said, smiling. 'That's where I'm going. I'm visiting my sister. Get in.'

Volkov climbed into the seat beside her. She was a pleasant looking woman, with grey streaked brown hair, dressed in a cotton skirt and blouse. She reminded him of Olga Jellnik. He made a tremendous effort to relax.

'You're very kind,' he said. 'It's a hot day. This will save me the fare.'

'It's going to be very hot indeed,' the lady said. 'Much too hot to walk about. I hate this sort of weather. It tires me out. What are you going to Paris to do?'

Volkov swallowed. 'I've been promised a job.'

'I hope you get it,' she said kindly. The car turned out on to the main road and gathered speed. She drove sensibly, but not slowly.

'You're not French, are you?' she said.

'No,' Volkov answered. He felt as if he were moving through a dream. 'I'm Russian. But I've lived here all my life.'

'How interesting,' she said. 'I've always been fascinated by Russia.' She drove on, and from time to time, she gave him a little glance sideways, accompanied by the amiable smile.

It was cool in the hospital room, the windows were shaded by venetian blinds and the air conditioning hummed gently. The detective sitting beside Fritz von Bronsart was longing for a smoke. Four hours in the operating theatre, one bullet lodged in the lung and another within a centimetre of the left kidney. Deeply unconscious after the anaesthetic, and with little hope of pulling through. A nurse sat in a chair on the opposite side of the bed. A saline drip and a blood drip were suspended above the still figure, trailing their leads into his arms. His face was the colour of dirty clay. He looked already dead. The nurse didn't interest the detective; she was elderly and very thin, with a sharp, suspicious face. Every quarter of an hour she checked her patient. The detective had been there for an hour and a half; his relief should arrive soon. Shot outside the gendarmerie, with only one hysterical woman as a witness, and reports that the killer had got away in a green car. They had found the car abandoned that morning. It was being finger-printed and its registration checked. Obviously stolen. The victim had been identified by his passport, found along with other papers, in his suitcase. Fritz Heinrich von Bronsart, with an address in West Berlin. Occupation, student. His mother had already been notified. She was on her way, but without much hope of getting to him in time.

Real bastards, both bullets. Missing that kidney was a miracle. He looked at him again and then at the nurse.

'There's no way you can wake him, just for a minute or two –'

'None,' she said aggressively. 'He won't come round till this evening. That's if he lasts that long.'

'*Merde*,' the detective said, loud enough for her to hear, and wished his relief would hurry up.

'What do we do?' Régine Kruger asked her husband. He looked across at Nicholas.

'We go ahead,' he said. 'Agreed?'

'Agreed,' Nicholas answered. 'But first you should ring the Château. If Fritz has betrayed us, it'll be full of police. If all is normal, then whatever has happened, they don't know about you. But it doesn't look good. No call from Volkov – it doesn't look good.'

'I'll telephone,' Régine said. 'If anyone answers but the staff, I'll ring off. Come in with me.'

They gathered in the little office where Elise made up the bills and took the bookings. Régine sat in Elise's chair, and put through the call. It rang for some time. Suddenly she stiffened. 'Hallo? Marie – yes, it's me. We left very early this morning. Just to tell you we'll be away for the night. Lock everything up will you? No messages, everything all right?' Her voice was sweetly unconcerned.

'Good. Thank you.' She swung round to them, triumph on her face. 'Nothing! Nobody's been near the house – no messages. He can't have gone to the police – or Volkov stopped him!'

'He should have telephoned,' Nicholas said. Kruger showed his first sign of impatience.

'Well, he hasn't – what are we to do, sit here and wait all day? I'm not worried now. Maybe your wife was right, Fritz just ran away – I didn't think so,' he looked suddenly grim. 'I still don't. I think Volkov got to him. More likely he's under arrest. None of you thought of that. They won't get anything out of *him*.'

'He's a brave man, and a true patriot,' Régine said quietly. 'He won't betray us. If Anton's right, we owe it to him to succeed tonight.'

'What happens if that pig upstairs won't agree?' Elise asked the question.

'He will,' Nicholas answered it abruptly. He didn't like the expression of anticipation in her eyes. It was as if she hoped Gusev would refuse, with the inevitable consequences.

'He's too clever not to; he'll think he can get the better of us. He'll agree to anything to stay alive.'

'And if he doesn't?' Anna's voice came from the doorway. 'Who is going to kill him?' They all turned and looked at her.

Elise chuckled. 'I am,' she said. 'Don't worry, Countess. You can leave all that to me.'

'Give him a proper meal,' Anton said. 'It's time we all had something to eat; then we'll go up and put the proposition to him. Don't look so worried, Anna, my dear. Everything is going to work out perfectly; I know it is. Nicholas, will you go upstairs with Elise and watch him while he has his food?'

The fat woman opened her mouth as if to protest, and then closed it again. She went to the kitchen and after an interval came back, carrying a tray.

Nicholas got up and followed her out of the room.

Elise's husband prepared them lunch; Régine said they wanted something simple which could be eaten outside. The inside of the Auberge was stuffy and hot. Anna sat beside her; she felt unable to eat anything. Suddenly the Krugers, whom she had admired and liked so much, seemed almost sinister in their detachment, sipping wine and commenting upon the pâté, as if they were lunching out in the country in the most normal circumstances. Anton kept filling her glass.

'You need it,' he told her. 'All this is a great strain. Don't think I don't feel it too.'

But he didn't, and Anna knew it. He was inhumanly calm and self-confident. The gentle Régine was as nerveless as rock. Nicholas came back and she turned to him anxiously.

'What did he say?'

'Nothing,' he answered. 'Nor did we. Elise unlocked his hands and he ate like a wolf. He kept watching me, waiting for me to speak. I didn't.'

He shook his head when Régine offered him the pâté and salad. He drank some wine and the same unsteadiness of hand was there.

Anton looked at his watch. He pushed back his plate, and calmly finished his wine. He glanced at Nicholas first, then smiled reassuringly at Anna.

'I think we should go up and talk to him now,' he said.

Volkov fell asleep. The bedroom was very hot and he lay naked and sweating on the double bed, his face buried in the pillow. The middle-aged lady who had given him the lift in Chartres woke him with a gentle caress. He started up instantly, not knowing where he was. He saw her sitting beside him, smiling, and remembered.

She had suggested, very nicely, that he might like a cup of coffee and an omelette at her sister's apartment, when they arrived. He was hungry and in desperate need to telephone the Auberge. He'd agreed. When they went inside, she shook her head at his request, and said her sister didn't have a telephone. She had made him sit down, given him coffee, chattering to him from the tiny kitchen, with the door open.

Volkov had controlled his impatience. He was safe where he was, far away from Chartres. That was the main thing. When he left he could make a call from a public telephone, and then go to the railway station. He could get a taxi back to the Auberge St-Julien and join up with the Krugers there. . . .

When he had finished eating he got up to go. She came and put her arms around his neck, standing on tiptoe to reach him; she looked into his astonished face, and said pleadingly, 'Please, you're such a nice man, and I'm lonely. Don't go . . .' Volkov, whose mother had died so horribly, had an innate tenderness and respect for women, in contrast to the rest of his character. He had never married, or had a regular mistress. He treated even the common prostitutes he encountered, out of necessity, with a politeness that made them laugh at him. He couldn't bring himself to pull the frail arms away from his neck, or to refuse her when she kissed him.

He made love to her because she asked him to, and found a joy in it that drove everything else out of his mind. He hadn't meant to fall asleep, but he did, and it was dark when she woke him.

'You have to go now,' she said. 'My sister will be back soon from work.'

He looked at his watch and just stopped himself from savage swearing. It wasn't her fault. She looked sweet and motherly in her plain skirt and blouse. He had never known such passion and giving in a woman in the whole of his life.

He apologized hastily for having slept so long. It didn't matter, she told him. He needed it. Sleep was good for a man. She was sorry he had to go, but her sister. . . . Volkov dressed quickly. It was too late to go to the Auberge now. They would have left without him. He couldn't go to the studio, either without a ticket.

He took the little lady's hand and kissed it. She blushed.

'Thank you,' he said. 'You gave me a great happiness. I shan't forget you.'

'Loneliness is an awful thing,' she said softly. 'I don't want you to think I do this . . . I just found you such a charming man and such a gentleman . . . I live by myself since my husband died. If you are ever in Chartres again . . . my address.' She slipped a corner of paper into his pocket. She stood by the window and waved to him as he went down the street. He had decided to go back to the Château. Kruger had given him a key. Zepirov had returned from his business trip to Lausanne as scheduled and would be at the studio. He wondered which of them would speak for him and his dead father and mother when the time came. . . . He caught a train at the Gare Montparnasse.

Feodor Gusev pulled himself up straight. He was aware of

how ridiculous human beings looked with their hands fastened behind them; he had seen countless men and women rendered vulnerable both physically and mentally by removing the protective shield of hands and arms from the body. He was sitting on the bed, his back resting against the headboard, and he stiffened when the door opened and they began to file in. He knew every face now; the man who called himself Krosnevsky and his wife, the loathsome woman Rodzinskaya, Yurovsky and the blonde girl he had seen once before, just after he was captured. They came and formed themselves into a group. He watched them boldly, but with an inward qualm of horrible apprehension. Perhaps they had come to kill him, nullifying the old man's promise in the morning. But nobody carried a gun; he who had so much experience of death did not detect the human tension in them that presaged the ultimate violence man inflicted upon man.

'Nicholas,' Anton Kruger said, 'I think this should be done by you. You tell him what we want him to do. He knows the alternative, I'm sure.'

Anna watched her husband. The eyes of Gusev had considered her briefly, but they were studying Nicholas now, almost unblinking in their assessment of him and what he said. She heard the hatred in her husband's voice, saw the rigid stance and the clenched hands; and remembered with anguish the orphaned boy being given his dead father's watch . . . the watch she had found in another upstairs room in that same inn. It seemed so many years ago, yet it was hardly a month. She closed her eyes, listening to Nicholas. It was like a spider's web, sticky, enmeshing, impossible to escape. . . . She looked at Anton Kruger. He was holding hands with his wife. So much hatred to exist for so many years, to take such trouble pursuing the nightmares of the past until he had compiled the film record and traced the fate of Nicholas's father and the others into the recesses of Russia's secret police files. The dedication behind it had seemed heroic; now she felt it to be deeply frightening. Kruger had escaped. He had instituted a movement for revenge that spanned a lifetime. He had spent lives as carelessly as his own money. In order to reinstate the dead and punish the man responsible. An old man, hunched on the bed in front of them, listening and scheming to save his own life. He was going to agree to the terms Nicholas set out . . . he must, because if he refused and that woman Elise made a move towards him, she was going to have to stop her. . . .

'I see,' Gusev said at last. 'And if I won't do this?'

'Then you die,' she heard Nicholas say, and a great cold faintness threatened her.

'And you release me if I do this?' Gusev questioned.

'In return for guaranteed immunity for every one of us,' Nicholas answered, 'you walk out of there untouched.'

'I see,' the Russian said again. 'What if the French won't give this immunity? What happens to me then?'

'You'll just have to persuade them,' Nicholas said. 'They won't sacrifice you. You know they won't. We want an answer. Yes or no.'

'No time to think about it?' Gusev parried, concentrating. Of course the French would make any deal necessary to save his life. That didn't present a problem. But the price he personally had to pay – he thought of the full implications and saw clearly the chasm opening up in front of him. In those few seconds he debated whether a bullet wouldn't be the better solution.

'No,' Nicholas said harshly. 'Just answer. What's it going to be?'

The faintness came at Anna again as she saw him put his right hand in his pocket and draw out a gun. She stepped up to him and caught him by the arm.

'No! Nicholas, no –' He shook her off; he didn't seem to hear her. Gusev waited; he gave her a deliberate glance of appeal which she didn't see. Another ally. But what had happened to the other one, the German. . . . If he did what they wanted, everything would then depend upon his own wits. The wits of a man brilliant enough to rise to the Praesidium of the Supreme Soviet, pitted against people not even united amongst themselves . . . Anna's gesture had made his mind up. Weakness, scruples . . . he would win.

'I'll go with you,' he said. 'And I give you my word I won't try to escape.'

'That will be unnecessary,' Anton Kruger spoke for the first time. 'Count Yurovsky will have a gun trained on you the whole time. Right until the moment. We'll be leaving in two hours.'

Elise opened the door and Anna found herself pushing through it first. She heard Nicholas calling to her, but she didn't wait. He caught up with her outside, grabbing her arm, turning her to him against her will.

'Anna – stop! What's the matter with you – I shouldn't have let you go up there!'

'No,' she said, and her voice shook. 'No, you shouldn't. When you took that gun out and threatened that old man, something just snapped in me. Whatever he did in the past, we're in the wrong now! We've been in the wrong from the first moment someone got killed. I've known it inside and I think you have too.'

She pulled away from him. 'I can't stop you, Nicholas, and I won't do anything to try. But I won't be a part of it.'

'I never wanted you involved,' he said. 'Anton brought you into it, and you seemed to understand and feel the same as I did. I don't blame you, darling. You wanted a cause without knowing why.' He reached out and laid his hand against her cheek.

'You go back to the apartment; stay there and I'll come back to you when it's over. Don't stop loving me, will you?'

She shook her head; the tears were spilling over.

'Whatever happens,' she said. 'I could never do that.' She got into his car, started the engine and drove out of the court-yard.

Nicholas went back inside; they were all looking at him, questioning. He saw Elise's little husband watching round the kitchen door.

'She's gone?' Anton asked.

'Yes,' Nicholas said. 'I told her to go home. She'll wait for me there.'

'Ah,' Elise said, and her head wagged on her thick neck, 'another rat deserts us –' Nicholas stepped forward and slapped her across the face.

At five-thirty on the hot afternoon, with the sun slanting behind the roof of the Auberge, the big Mercedes glided out of its parking place. Gusev sat in the back, sandwiched between Elise and Nicholas. Anton Kruger drove with his wife beside him. They took the old road back to Paris.

Anna went by the autoroute; she didn't drive fast because she kept crying. As fast as she wiped them, fresh tears blurred her view of the road. She couldn't have stayed in that place another moment, or faced the little group who used to be her friends. Anton Kruger – how her image of him had changed, from the charming, dynamic father figure who had taken her into his confidence, won her trust and enlisted her help. A man able to kill in cold blood, and to talk of further killing. Poor Fritz von Bronsart – had he really taken flight and gone back home, or had the menacing Volkov reached him? – Régine, so elegant and feminine, a willing participant in everything that Anna found unacceptable. Ice cold, that woman, single-minded, fanatical. Elise Rodzinskaya had always made her shudder, even when she seemed no more than the proprietress of the secluded inn where she and Nicholas spent their weekends. And Nicholas, her husband; she couldn't forget that gesture with the gun, but it went with the shaking hand, the body rigid with tension. He had gone too far to turn back; he was living off his old hatred to keep going. She had seen that when he faced Gusev. And she had turned around and left him. Backing off once again from the crisis. Her mother used to accuse her of that; but as she drove Anna put that accusation against herself away.

This time it had taken greater courage to refuse to go on. The real moral challenge was in rejecting the methods and the standard which had made Gusev do what he had done.

The end never justified the means. She drove more steadily, coming through the early evening traffic, seeing the city at its most beautiful in the mellow light, with throngs of people idling their way along the broad boulevards, the pavement cafés full. She felt desperately tired, and terribly unhappy. Nicholas. Nicholas going on without her. Pleading with her not to stop loving him as she turned away. Her own promise that it was the last thing she could do. . . .

She parked her car, went into the elegant entrance to her apartment, and took the lift to the first floor. She felt too exhausted to walk up the stairs. The front door opened, and there was the familiar hall, and the indefinable comfort of being safe in her own home. As she shut the front door Jumeaux emerged from the drawing room.

'Good afternoon, Madame Yurovsky,' he said. There was another man behind him. 'We've been waiting for you.'

8

Sheila Campbell, accompanied by Ruth Paterson, arrived at the studios of Télévision Française exactly at seven o'clock. She had chosen her clothes with care; she wanted to present the image of the working Congresswoman rather than the millionairess owner of an extreme right-wing magazine. She dressed in a royal blue silk suit with a spotted blouse, neatly bowed at the neck, wore no jewellery but little gold studs in her ears, and insisted upon doing her own make-up for the cameras.

She waved the make-up girl away, speaking in her accented but impeccable French, watched by Ruth who knew the formula so well.

'No, thank you, Mademoiselle – I always do my own face. I like to look like Sheila Campbell, not somebody else!' Jacques Rousselle seemed anxious to hurry her to the cosmetic room. Sheila didn't mind, aimless chitchat bored her; she wanted to get on with the business. She looked at herself in the mirror critically. Hair well done, not too stiff, but dignified, the face garish in its exaggerated make-up with eye shadow and heavy brows and lashes, but essential if she were not to appear washed out on the screen. The blue she had chosen was a good television colour. She turned round to Ruth.

'I'm looking forward to this – everyone is watching tonight. It's going to be relayed on CBC networks with an over commentary tomorrow . . . Okay, I'm ready, let's go and meet my protagonist, Mr Denis. I gather he's a regular leftie – we should have some fun!'

On official occasions Sheila swept, rather than walked, into rooms; Ruth wondered whether it was a deliberate or subconscious change of pace. If she'd had a long cloak it would have flown out behind her . . . Jacques Rousselle was in the little ante-room where the drinks were, and there was a man standing with him. Sheila stopped dead. Rousselle came forward, smiling apologetically, taking her by the arm.

'My dear Madame Campbell. As you know we've had a last-minute change of plan because of Xavier Denis's illness. You know Paul Martin, of course?'

'I do indeed,' Sheila said. She hadn't taken a step forward. 'And what am I supposed to know about a change of plan?'

'My secretary telephoned you this afternoon. Surely you got the message?'

She turned round to Ruth. Ruth answered sharply. 'Nobody telephoned me, M. Rousselle. We had no message of any kind.' She stared at the man who had been introduced as Paul Martin. Dark, casually dressed, cigarette dangling, a Belmondo type; he was obviously enjoying the situation. She couldn't actually believe that this was Sheila's former son-in-law. But she knew from her employer's reaction that it was. He moved towards them, and held out his hand. His eyes were sleepy, but there was malice in his smile.

'Hallo,' he said. 'They asked me to step in for Xavier at the last moment. I hope you don't mind debating with me.'

For a moment longer Sheila hesitated. She had been set up and she knew it. This was going to be a hatchet job. Her anger flared, but no sign of it showed. If she refused to go on with Paul Martin, it would make the headlines, and also show her up as a temperamental prima-donna type. Which was the last thing she wanted to appear. Imperceptibly the jaw squared, and a fighting glint sparkled in her eyes.

'Mind?' she said to Paul. 'Not at all. I'm very pleased to see you after all this time.' She turned to Rousselle, who had a stiff grin on his face; he had just had an awful moment of panic when he thought she was going to walk out and his programme would be ruined.

'You know Paul was once married to my daughter? Ruth, darling, get me a glass of white wine, will you? – now, I'm perfectly happy to be on the programme with Paul, but I do think we should ignore the relationship.' She gave Paul Martin a contemptuous smile. 'We wouldn't want to be accused of nepotism, would we?'

'No, no,' Rousselle agreed. 'It certainly won't be mentioned. Paul, you're allowed one Scotch before the programme – you know the rules.' He chuckled, trying to make a joke of it, and hurried over to the table to get the drink.

Sheila walked over to one of the Swedish leather armchairs and sat down, crossing her slim legs. She looked at Paul.

'Was this your idea?'

'I didn't give Xavier Denis the flu.'

'Flu my foot!' Sheila said. 'You don't get flu in June. I'd like you to know that Anna is very happy. She's made a good choice this time; I thoroughly approve!'

'I'm glad to hear it,' Paul took the small Scotch from Rousselle, who moved away to talk to Ruth. 'What did he have to do, sprout wings?'

'No,' she answered. 'Just treat my daughter properly. Like a gentleman.'

'Ah,' Paul nodded. 'I see. I thought you might like the phoney title. Good luck to them. From my own experience of marrying into your family, my dear Sheila, they're going to need it.'

She looked up at him, her eyes narrowed a little.

'I have a gut feeling,' she said pleasantly, 'that you have fixed all this because you want to have a public go at me. Well, let me tell you this. When I first saw you, I damn nearly walked out. But now I'm rather glad. You want a fight – I'm going to give you one.'

'I'm sure you are,' Paul Martin answered. He finished the meagre drink in one swallow. 'It'll make marvellous television.'

Rousselle came up to them. 'I think we should go on stage and get ourselves settled,' he said.

It was an enormous sound stage, its cavernous roof disappearing overhead into the shadows. Cameras and lighting and sound equipment were suspended over the setpiece of Rousselle's *Forum*, a semi-circular table with Rousselle seated in the middle between his two guests, a map of the world as a backcloth. Papers containing his programme notes were in front of his place, three carafes of water sparkled in the brilliant light.

In the shadows, the invited audience of ticket holders was gathered behind the cameras. Three rows from the front Anton Kruger, Régine and Feodor Gusev were in their places. Nicholas sat beside Gusev, his coat covering his lap and the gun which just touched Gusev's side. Gusev wore a straw hat, dug out of Anton Kruger's cupboard. It gave him a funny, rakish appearance and made him unrecognizable at first glance. They had walked into the studio, Nicholas holding Gusev by the arm, presented their tickets and taken their places. Zepirov had joined them but sat further back. He kept glancing over his shoulder to the control room at the back of the studio, where the cameras were monitored.

Ruth Paterson was in the audience at the front. She had whispered to Sheila just before she took her place, 'Good luck. Give him hell,' and got the response she expected: 'Don't worry – I will!' She looked at her from the darkness outside the blinding lights. Sheila was cool and composed, chatting to Rousselle, waiting for the red light to show. Ruth had never admired her more than at that moment. The knives were out for her, and the whole world was watching. She sat in the glare of the lights, in her bright blue suit, her red hair shining, laughing at something Rousselle had said (he had a great gift for relaxing people just before the programme) and Ruth knew she was going to put up the fight of her life.

Anton Kruger got out of his seat; as he moved to the front one of the technicians hurried over to bar his way. 'Go back to your seat, you can't come on stage – we're going live in a minute!' Anton pushed a note at him.

'Give this to M. Rousselle – quickly, before the programme starts. It's terribly important.'

'I can't,' the man said, shaking his head. 'We're going on the air.'

'You give it,' Kruger said, 'or I will. Now!' The technician took it, ran across the stage and handed it to Rousselle, gesturing towards Kruger as he did so. Anton stood where he was, waiting. The man came back and caught him by the arm. 'Come on, back to your seat please –'

Rousselle opened the note, frowning, and Kruger turned and

went back to where Régine and the others were sitting. He had a good view of Rousselle's face and he saw the mouth drop wide in a gasp and then close as quickly. He half rose from his seat, and somebody called out, 'Quiet, please, everyone. Quiet! We're on the air!' The music of Vivaldi's Oboe Concerto was taped out, serene and cool; it was *Forum*'s signature tune. Kruger nudged Régine, leaned over to Nicholas and nodded. Jacques Rousselle nearly missed his cue. For the first time in his ten years as a top television political interviewer, he faltered in his introduction.

'Good evening, ladies and gentlemen. We have as our guests tonight – er, our guests – the distinguished American Congresswoman and proprietor of the well-known political monthly journal *Truth*, Madame Sheila Campbell.' He inclined his head and bowed to her; the cameras focused on her and Sheila smiled into them and said, 'Good evening.' 'And Paul Martin, the political commentator for *France Midi*.' Paul grinned into the camera and said nothing. Rousselle went on, ad-libbing, trying to decide what to do. The note was on the table in front of him. 'Grigor Malenkov is in the audience. He wants to appear on your programme. Make the announcement and he'll come forward.'

Zepirov had slipped out of his seat and gone to the back of the studio. The control room was up a flight of steps; he ran up them and silently opened the door. Three people, two men and a girl, were sitting at the control panel, with three monitoring sets, for each of the three cameras on stage. One turned round and saw him.

'Get out of here – there's a programme . . .' the man's voice tailed away as he saw the gun in Zepirov's hand.

'Don't move,' he said to three frightened faces staring at him. 'Just keep the programme going. Don't touch anything.' He leaned his back against the door and kept the gun levelled at the man in the centre. He watched the middle screen; Rousselle was speaking, looking deeply into the camera lens.

'I have to interrupt this programme, ladies and gentlemen, with what may be a very important, not to say historic, announcement. If the gentleman who sent me this note is in the audience, would he please come forward?' The cameras swung away from the stage and the lights followed them; suddenly the audience was fully lit, and on television screens all over France, Nicholas Yurovsky prodded Gusev to his feet, and followed by Anton Kruger they walked slowly towards the centre of the studio stage. Rousselle was on his feet, moving round the table; Paul had got up and Sheila Campbell sat rigid, completely taken by surprise.

Rousselle came towards them and Kruger reached up and removed the straw hat. There was a loud sustained gasp from the audience. In the control room above, the girl screamed. The face had been pictured on every front page and featured on every television screen for the past week. Rousselle was literally trembling with excitement.

'Ladies and gentlemen,' he shouted, 'the missing Soviet official, Grigor Malenkov! My God,' he went on to the cameras, beside himself, 'my God, this is just unbelievable! Quiet, quiet please!' He waved his arms at the audience.

Sheila Campbell had left her chair and was staring in amazement from the Russian to Nicholas.

'You are Grigor Malenkov?' Rousselle demanded.

'I am,' came the reply.

'Get a chair,' Rousselle called out, and one was brought forward. Nicholas dropped the covering coat away, and the gun in his hand was clearly visible. Rousselle shrank back; there were screams from some people in the audience. In the control room Zepirov stepped forward and held his gun to the back of the man in the centre's head.

'Touch nothing,' he said. A telephone in the control room began to shrill. 'Leave it alone.' Nobody moved.

'Sit down,' Kruger said, and Gusev did so. He stared impassively in front of him. Kruger spoke to Rousselle; the cameras followed him.

'This man, known as Malenkov, has another name. Feodor Gusev. That's why he has been brought here. To answer before the world for the crimes he has committed against humanity. The man guarding him is the son of Count Michael Yurovsky, who was murdered by Gusev. I myself escaped the same fate, a fate that condemned hundreds of thousands of Russians to execution and the slow death of the labour camps. This man, sitting in front of you, was the man primarily responsible for forcible repatriation after the war. For carrying out the terms of the Yalta agreement by which a million helpless souls were delivered back to Stalin's vengeance! We kidnapped Gusev to see that after all these years, justice should be done, and the world should know the truth. We haven't harmed him. But we are putting him on trial. Nicholas, I leave it with you, now.'

He turned and went back to his place in the audience.

Rousselle turned to Nicholas; his face was grey under the tan make-up.

'Please,' he said. 'Put that gun away.'

'I'm not afraid of it,' Gusev said. He looked at the interviewer. 'He won't kill me; this is a propaganda exercise. These people say they want the truth. They talk about a trial.' He crossed one leg over the other and folded his arms. 'In exchange for my life I've agreed. Please, for my sake, let them do what they want.'

'You bastard,' Paul Martin said loudly, glaring at Nicholas. 'Where's Anna –'

'Be quiet,' Sheila hissed at him. She had a native American respect for a man with a gun. 'Shut up, for Christ's sake!'

'Gusev,' Nicholas said. 'Tell them about the agreement at Yalta.'

'Now,' Jumeaux said, 'I've asked you the easy way; for the last time, where is your husband?'

She was sitting in his office, facing him; he had begun questioning her at his desk, offered her coffee, talked very politely about his regret at having to arrest her, and asked her where he could find Nicholas. She had given him the same answer.

'I don't know. He went out this morning and I don't know where he went.'

'You both went out,' Jumeaux corrected her. 'You were seen leaving together in the car. Where did you go to, Madame, and where is he now? Believe me I'm going to get the answer to this question!'

Anna didn't have a watch; they had taken it away and that alarmed her. Her request to telephone a lawyer was refused; she hadn't expected anything else, but above all she was playing for time. Jumeaux's face was no longer bland; his attitude towards her had soon become aggressive, threatening. He stopped squarely in front of her. For the last half hour he had been pacing up and down.

'I shall give up soon,' he said. 'I shall hand you over to a team of interrogators. You won't like it. You lied to me, didn't you? – you were part of this filthy conspiracy from the beginning!' He suddenly shouted at her.

'Where is he? Where's Malenkov?'

Anna looked up at him wearily. 'What time is it?'

'Half past seven. Not that it's going to matter to you, Madame. You won't care about whether it's night or day when my boys get started on you.'

Seven-thirty. She had bought Nicholas his time. There was nothing more she could do for him.

'If you have a television set, switch on to *Forum*. That'll answer all your questions.'

Jumeaux very nearly hit her; he swung his open hand back and then checked it just in time. She looked as if she were telling the truth.

'There's a set in the canteen,' he said. He reached down and pulled her roughly to her feet. 'I hope, for your sake, this isn't some kind of a joke,' he said.

'It isn't,' Anna said. 'I only wish to God it was.' They went down in the lift to the small office canteen. There was a set perched above the cafeteria bar.

Jumeaux switched it on; the canteen was empty; all but the night staff had gone home. They heard Nicholas's voice before the picture finally focused.

'Tell them about the agreement at Yalta.'

Gusev looked directly into the camera. He spoke slowly, distinctly, in his excellent French.

'My people were fighting a total war. The kind of war that

was not fought anywhere else in Europe. Our casualties were enormous, our country devastated. In order to stop the Germans we began the scorched-earth policy; we burned every grain of wheat, every building, every shed, we slaughtered the animals we couldn't take with us. We left nothing for the enemy but our dead. And nobody surrendered.' He paused. 'Nobody but traitors. And we had those. We had Russians who, to save themselves, turned against their own people and enlisted in the German army. Russians who fought against their own, who joined the SS divisions and the extermination squads. At Yalta Stalin asked for these criminals to be handed back.'

'Prisoners-of-war,' Nicholas corrected. 'Men who had surrendered and were in German camps. Isn't it true they were officially classed as dead, because you wouldn't admit they'd been captured?'

'So far as we were concerned,' Gusev said, 'there *was* no surrender to the Nazis. They bought their release from the camps by joining the German army.'

'They had no choice,' Nicholas said. 'They were tricked, told they wouldn't have to fight. The alternative was to starve to death.'

Gusev looked at him. The cameras zoomed in close.

'That's what the rest of their people were doing at home,' he said. 'Starving and dying to protect their country.'

From her seat in the audience, Elise Rodzinskaya began to mutter.

'Why is he letting him get away with this – why doesn't he make him tell about Baratina –'

'He will,' Anton said. 'He's letting Gusev have the rope to hang himself – sssh, listen –'

'Why were the Russian prisoners who *didn't* join the Germans so frightened to go home?' Nicholas asked the question quietly. 'What had they to fear?'

The whole studio was silent; Rousselle, Sheila and Paul Martin were leaning forward in their seats. Unknown to them, the building outside was being surrounded by armed police and troops.

'They were ashamed,' Gusev replied. 'Ashamed to face their

families and their neighbours. In Russia a soldier who gave up his arms to the enemy was looked on as a traitor. And there was Allied propaganda, of course.'

'Allied?' Nicholas asked. 'Propaganda from the Allies, who had promised to send them home? Don't you mean they'd had a taste of decent treatment from the Western forces – maybe they'd seen newspapers, read books – knew what freedom meant even when they were in a prisoner-of-war compound. Maybe that's what you mean by Allied propaganda?'

'They were told they would be punished when they got home,' Gusev retorted. 'That was the propaganda – to frighten Soviet citizens into renouncing their country!'

'As the agreement was kept secret, and the brutality needed to repatriate these poor people was hidden from the world, there doesn't seem much point in the propaganda exercise,' Nicholas said. 'And they were punished, weren't they? What happened to them, Gusev, the ordinary wretched soldiers who'd been captured, perhaps wounded, and spent their time as Nazi prisoners – weren't they right to be afraid of going home?'

Jacques Rousselle was stretching across his table, absorbed in what was the most incredible event on television ever likely to be screened. He saw Sheila Campbell staring transfixed at Nicholas Yurovsky. He only then remembered that the Russian was her son-in-law. Two sons-in-law . . . he could feel Paul Martin's restiveness. At any moment he was going to interrupt. Rousselle had lost control and didn't care what happened. So long as nobody burst into the studios and interrupted. But they wouldn't, not with that gun pointing at Malenkov's chest. Malenkov – Gusev – he lost himself listening to the duel taking place between the two men.

'Nothing happened to them,' Gusev answered. 'They came home and were reunited with their families. Only the guilty were punished. And they were very carefully screened to make sure. Everyone had a fair trial.' He paused and suddenly Paul Martin interrupted.

'What you're saying is you shot Russians who'd joined the German army, fought in German uniform against their own

243

people. Our side shot men for deserting; the people Yurovsky is calling innocent victims were traitors! I'll support you on this, Comrade Malenkov.'

Gusev looked round at the unexpected ally. Paul Martin was pale and tense; there was a sheen of sweat on his forehead under the hot lights. He glared at Nicholas.

'Your father,' he went on, 'Count Yurovsky as he liked to call himself, went round the prison camps recruiting Russian prisoners. That deserves the death penalty alone!'

'Thank you,' Nicholas said, 'for mentioning my father. My father left Russia in 1919. He was never a citizen of the Soviet Union. He had every legal right to join the German army in the special Russian division. He wasn't recruiting to fight for Nazism; he offered his fellow-Russians a chance to fight against the Soviet tyranny – most of his recruits came from the Western Ukraine, annexed in 1939. They'd lost their homes, seen their families murdered, *they* knew what Communist occupation really meant – certainly they joined my father, but it wasn't to fight for Germany, it was to fight for the liberation of their homeland!'

'In that case,' Sheila Campbell saw her opportunity, 'they were no different from the partisans and the *Maquis*, who are looked upon as heroes. These people were equally traitors to the governments that collaborated. It's a double standard, isn't it? – so long as you fight for Communism you're a hero, if you fight against it you're a traitor!' She flashed Nicholas a look of encouragement. Jacques Rousselle leaned forward.

'Your father was executed?' he asked Nicholas.

'My father was delivered to Gusev and the NKVD, in defiance of common humanity which forbids the repatriation of non-citizens against their will. He was kept alive in the Lubyanka prison for a year, with the other leaders of the Russian Freedom movement, and then hanged. One of the generals hanged with him was a German, Klaus von Bronsart, who had merely been attached to this division because he spoke fluent Russian. That in itself is a flagrant violation of human rights.'

'It makes a good story,' Gusev said. 'Except that you've

left some of the details out. Your father was a Tsarist officer in the White counter-revolution. He served under another White commander, Alexander Shuvalov. Known as the Butcher. This man, with officers like your father carrying out his orders, murdered some sixty thousand people during what we call the White Terror. He also joined the German army as a senior general. Yes, we did ask for him back. We wanted him for his crimes against the people. We hanged him for them.'

'After thirty years?' Sheila put in. 'There was a Red terror, if I remember rightly. How many innocent people did that kill?'

'It was a Civil War,' Gusev replied. 'The people won.'

'Gusev,' Nicholas said, 'How would you describe your personal role in this?'

'I carried out my orders and did my duty,' Gusev replied.

'And were those orders to proceed without mercy against your victims?'

Gusev looked at him sharply. The camera was focused on him in close-up.

'There were no victims, only war criminals.'

'Women and children?' Nicholas queried. 'Let me remind you of one incident. An incident that was typical of thousands at places like Baratina and in prisoner-of-war camps in Britain and Europe. There was a family called Zepirov. No grand aristocrats, but simple people from the Western Ukraine. A father, mother and two children, a boy and a girl. You interviewed that father, Gusev, and when he lied out of terror and pretended to be Polish, you trapped him into proving himself Russian. Then he admitted it, didn't he – told you he'd been taken back by force with the German army, along with his family, for slave labour in Germany. He begged you to have mercy, to understand. . . . He went on his knees to you, Gusev, and pleaded with you not to take his wife and children back to Russia; he accepted that he'd have to go himself. He wept and begged, didn't he – don't you remember?'

'No,' Gusev said flatly. 'The whole story is a lie. There were no incidents like that. British officers were present whenever I saw prisoners; they conducted the interviews, I kept a watching brief.' He shrugged contemptuously. 'You are just making up horror stories. There's not a word of truth in them.'

'Oh, but there is,' Nicholas said. 'Because the Zepirovs were very real. You did your duty, didn't you, Gusev, you carried out your orders? The whole family was to be sent back. No mercy, no human feelings, for the woman and her two little children. . . .

'The same day Zepirov and his wife killed their daughter and committed suicide. The boy ran away from them. He's here, Gusev, up in the control room, watching this programme.' There was a gasp from the audience. Nicholas shook his head. 'No, perhaps you wouldn't remember one particular case of human suffering. There were so many, weren't there? Just as terrible.'

For a moment there was silence. At his post in the control room Zepirov saw the three technicians turn and stare at him. He wiped his hand across his eyes and gestured with the gun. They turned back to the monitor sets.

The voice of Paul Martin ended the pause.

'May I ask you a question, Comrade Malenkov?' Gusev nodded towards Paul.

'Was there any opposition from the Western Allies to this agreement reached at Yalta?'

'None at all,' Gusev answered. 'These Russians were regarded as traitors by everyone. Except themselves, and the reactionaries who have made it fashionable to call them martyrs. The British and Americans were responsible for handing them over.'

'Yes,' Nicholas said, 'they were. Isn't it also true, Gusev, that the Soviet army had overrun prisoner-of-war camps with thousands of Allied prisoners in them, and these prisoners were held as a bargaining counter in the negotiations?'

'It's also true,' Sheila snapped in, 'that in the States alone there was mutiny among the troops who were ordered to get these poor people on the transport taking them back to their Soviet paradise. You say only the guilty were punished – how is it that men killed their wives and children and committed suicide themselves, if the innocent had nothing to fear – what had the women and children done except follow their men?'

'If they did,' Gusev said, 'it was because of Allied propaganda, as I said before. The responsibility lies with the Allies who told them lies and made them afraid to go home.'

'There was no Allied propaganda at places like Baratina,' Nicholas said. 'Quite the contrary. There were thirty thousand people there, with their officers. My father was there, so was General Shuvalov. They were all so terrified of what was going to happen to them that the British could only separate the officers from the men and their families by pretending they were going to be resettled in Germany. Mrs Campbell talked about mutiny among the American troops. The same thing happened with the British. They carried out their orders to send the Russians back to you, but they didn't like the way it had to be done. They didn't like the suicides, the women killing their children rather than go on the trains . . . they couldn't get regular troops to do the job, so in the end they used the Military Police. . . . Those transports used to arrive in your zone with the blood streaming under the doors. And you were there to meet them, Gusev, with your lists, given to you by the Allies, which our officers had given them in all good faith. The people on those lists were taken off the cattle trucks and shot. That was their fair trial. The rest of them went to the labour camps in Siberia. That was the price of being taken prisoner, never mind fighting for the Germans. Ten years of slave labour to rehabilitate them. Mothers and children separated, never to see each other again.'

'Where is the proof of all this?' Paul Martin said loudly. 'You have a man with a gun trained on him, and you call that a trial. How do you know that innocent prisoners-of-war were sent to labour camps – or was it the bloody Cossacks who butchered their own people the way they did for the Tsars, who really went there!'

'My source is Alexander Solzhenitsyn,' Nicholas said. 'The same system condemned him.'

'It seems to me,' Jacques Rousselle said. 'That the West isn't without blame. This is a very extraordinary situation, ladies and gentlemen, for which we in the studio were quite unprepared. But it seems to me that some kind of debate has developed about a subject which has remained a secret ever since the war. I knew something about it, but not very much. And only recently, since Solzhenitsyn exposed conditions in the labour camps to the Western world.

'Aside from the moral issues of the repatriation of these people and the way in which the Soviet Union dealt with them, there is the question of legality. Had the Allies the right to hand them back? Or was there, as M. Yurovsky maintains, a deal done in exchange for Allied prisoners –'

'There was certainly a deal,' Sheila answered. 'And not just because they were holding thousands of British and Americans and wouldn't give them up. It was dirtier than that.' She looked at the camera which was centred on her. 'It was a policy decision at the highest level in London and Washington that Stalin was to be placated and *nothing* was to be done to jeopardize Allied–Soviet relations. I have personal knowledge of this, because I have made the study of Anglo-American relations with the Soviet Union my particular province.

'Some of the official minutes would make you cry with shame if you could read them. We and the British gave way on every moral and legal and humane principle in order to satisfy Stalin's appetite for vengeance.' She paused for a second or two, and one hand gestured dramatically. 'This man, Grigor Malenkov, a senior member of the Praesidium, is said to be the Feodor Gusev who was in charge of this dreadful operation. But I say to everyone viewing us tonight that the real blame, both moral and political, lies in the attitude of appeasement taken by our governments towards the Soviet Russian tyranny. We *gave* Stalin these people – regardless of law or humane principles; we bartered men, women and children in exchange for the fallacy of Stalin's goodwill and what exactly did this dreadful surrender achieve? Nothing. It simply strengthened Stalin's opinion of the Western Allies as being too weak and scared to stand against him. The result was the Cold War.

'If we *had* stood up to him, not only about this issue, which is such an emotionally distressing one, but on questions as vital as the entry into Berlin and the spheres of Soviet and Allied influence, an awful lot of suffering would have been avoided, and an awful lot of Eastern Europe would be free today.'

And that was when Jacques Rousselle saw the police merging from the shadows into the camera lights.

In the control room, Zepirov saw them on the monitor, and stepped away towards the door. 'Don't move,' he said to the three who were watching him. He opened the door, slipped out closing it behind him, and started down the steps. Three armed gendarmes were waiting for him. He raised his hands above his head.

Jumeaux had taken Anna with him. He had raced upstairs to his office, dragging her after him. Pandemonium overtook the building; phones were ringing, doors banging, men running through the corridors. She waited, silent, while Jumeaux got his instructions. The room was filling with people; she was pushed into the background. It occurred to her that in the mêlée she could have walked out, but she did nothing.

'We're going to the studio,' he shouted. 'Jesus, the Russians are going mad! And you're coming with me!'

She was hustled downstairs and into a car; other cars were gathering; she could hear sirens shrieking in the distance. Jumeaux sat beside her, tense and grim.

'What a disaster,' he said. 'What a catastrophe – I'm ruined, you realize that? God alone knows what the repercussions will be.'

In the studio the cameras had ceased filming. Nicholas stood beside Gusev, facing the ring of police which had formed around the stage. He held the gun at his head, his left hand grasping Gusev's shoulder. Rousselle had grabbed Sheila and backed away from the set. Paul Martin followed, slowly. Jumeaux stepped forward into the bright lights. He held out his hands to show he was unarmed.

'Yurovsky,' he called out. 'It's all over. Let him go.' The atmosphere in the huge studio was febrile with tension; the camera crews hung forward watching the drama; in the audience the Krugers and Elise slowly rose to their feet. Everyone watched the two men in the glare of the lights, alone in front of the empty mock-up, with the map of the world spread out behind them. Gusev felt the cold metal of the gun muzzle on his temple. 'Don't come any closer,' he shouted in a hoarse voice, and Jumeaux froze.

'You're surrounded,' Jumeaux said. 'And I've got your wife here. She wants to talk to you.' He turned and pulled Anna forward.

Nicholas saw her as she came into the light. It was all over, exactly as Jumeaux had said. The incredible had been accomplished. The truth could never be hidden again. What they had begun that night would reverberate in discussion and condemnation round the world. There was no need for him to kill Feodor Gusev to pass sentence; he had done that upon himself.

'Nicholas,' Anna said clearly. 'Remember your promise. Let him go now.'

There was a shout from the audience; Elise was struggling forward, held back by Anton. 'Don't listen to her – kill the bastard! Kill him!'

Gusev spoke again.

'They want immunity,' he called out, and fear rattled in his voice. 'Give it to them! My life depends upon it!'

Nicholas spoke to Jumeaux. He could see a movement from the side, where police had inched towards him. 'If any of you takes another step,' he said, 'I'll shoot him. Let my wife come here to me.'

'Go on,' Jumeaux nudged Anna furiously. 'Go on!' She stepped forward and came to stand beside him.

'Anton, Régine and Elise, come over here. Where's Zepirov?' Nicholas demanded.

'Here,' Zepirov shouted. 'They've arrested me –'

'Let him go,' Jumeaux snapped, and the gendarmes unlocked the handcuffs securing Zepirov's wrists and gave him a shove forward. Paul Martin came close to Sheila Campbell. His face was grey.

'If anything happens to her for this, I'll personally kill that bastard! They'll never get away with this –'

'Oh, yes, they will,' Sheila retorted. 'They want Malenkov released unhurt. The French'll agree to anything they ask! I must say,' she turned and whispered to Ruth, 'I never knew she had the guts for anything like this –' There was a little smile of pride on her lips as she turned back to watch her daughter, ranged beside Nicholas.

'Any more?' Jumeaux called out. 'Any more of you in here?'

'No,' Nicholas answered. 'But there are others. I want an official guarantee that nobody will be prosecuted for any action taken. I want immunity for every member of "Return". And I want it made live, on television.'

Jumeaux paused. He had received instructions from the Elysée Palace to pay any ransom, release any terrorists, do anything demanded, in order to get Malenkov back alive. But to negotiate on every television screen in France was not within his mandate . . .

'Why television?' he asked. But he knew why.

'Because I want to be sure you keep your word,' Nicholas answered. 'If you're not going to keep it, I shall kill Gusev and then myself. We're all armed. You won't take one of us alive. Except my wife, who has nothing to do with this.' He spoke quietly to Anna. 'Go to your mother, my darling. And don't worry, it'll be all right.'

She shook her head; Paul Martin saw her do it, and guessed what she was refusing. 'No,' she said. 'I'm staying with you.'

Jumeaux had called Rousselle forward. There was a quick exchange between them. 'All right,' he called back to Nicholas. 'I agree; it goes out live.'

Rousselle was giving instructions; the big stage darkened again and the cameras turned. French television screens, already tuned to the scene outside the studio where commentators were giving the latest news on the siege inside, were suddenly transported back to the sound stage again. Nicholas said firmly, 'Come up here and give your assurances before the camera.' Jumeaux walked forward. He faced the cameras, seeing himself on a side monitor that showed the participants which angle was being broadcast.

'State your terms again,' he said to Nicholas.

'No prosecutions for the kidnapping of Grigor Malenkov,' he said. 'No prosecution for any of the acts committed, no arrests, no interrogations. We deliver him to you, and you give your promise on behalf of the French government that we walk out of here with immunity for life. Otherwise,' Nicholas looked directly into the facing camera, 'he dies and we kill ourselves.'

Jumeaux squared his shoulders; there was no future for him anyway, but he had the opportunity of saving Malenkov in front of fifty million viewers, before he gave in his resignation to the Colonel. It was a puny compensation.

'I have the authority to meet your terms,' he said. 'You have the guarantees you ask for. As soon as you release Grigor Malenkov, you are all free to go.'

There was a long gasp from the audience as Nicholas lowered the gun and, turning slightly, laid it on the table. Immediately Jumeaux seized Gusev protectively by the arm, and his men rushed forward to encircle him. He stopped and looked back at Nicholas, at Kruger and his wife, at Elise Rodzinskaya. He spoke to them in Russian, very quietly.

'You haven't got immunity from us,' he said. Then he was led away.

It was all over by the time Fritz von Bronsart recovered consciousness and mumbled his revelation about Malenkov and the Château Grandcour. His mother had flown in from Germany and was waiting by his bedside; she sat there after he had lapsed into a drugged sleep, until the dawn came and he woke again. His mind was surprisingly clear; he stared up at her out of a hollow, waxen face like a death mask. He felt no pain, only a great desire to slide away and sleep.

She held on to his hand and cried. They had expected him to die during the night. 'What happened?' he whispered to her. 'Malenkov . . .'

She told him briefly what the whole world was reading and talking about that morning. 'I was one of them,' he said, and she nodded, not really understanding. 'My grandfather – the truth –'

'Yes, darling,' she comforted. 'Yes, it's all right.' Her father, the executed war criminal, had been publicly exonerated. She had been told that, but she didn't care. She had never realized how much her son had minded.

'That's good,' Fritz murmured. 'Am I going to die, Mother? It feels like it.'

'No,' she wept, clasping his hand in both of hers, 'No, no, you're not – but you've got to try, darling . . . you've got to hold on. For my sake, and for Ilse – she's flying in today. Think of us, how much we love you – think of Ilse –'

He closed his eyes for a moment, and then willed himself to open them. He wanted to sleep; but if he did he mightn't wake, and then he wouldn't see her.

Ilse. He wanted to see Ilse very much. 'Don't worry, Mother,' he said. 'I'll try.'

Paul Martin watched them go. Malenkov had been escorted away, and now Jumeaux's men and the police stood back, leashed like hungry dogs while their prey walked across the stage and out of the studio door. Nicholas had his arm round Anna; the Krugers walked with dignity, arm in arm, the fat woman and the man called Zepirov a few paces behind them. He felt in his coat for a cigarette. Sheila Campbell was surrounded; reporters were pouring into the place, cameras flashed and popped, Rousselle was giving an interview and waving his arms. Martin kept in the background; Jumeaux had gone with Malenkov. He could imagine the scene outside. Huge crowds had gathered, the press of the world and the television cameras were trained upon the Soviet Embassy car which was waiting with the Ambassador to receive Malenkov into his country's bosom. Paul drew upon his cigarette. It had been brilliant. One of the most perfectly executed propaganda coups in modern history. And that was why he'd tried to stop it, tried to support Gusev's case. And failed hopelessly; the suicides, the women and children – and the ruthless skill of Sheila Campbell, making the final political summary. She hadn't known about it beforehand; her astonishment when the programme went haywire was genuine enough. But with the supreme opportunism of her type, she had seized the chance to press home the hard-line right-wing point of view. There wasn't a vestige of compassion or moral consciousness in her soul; she would have defended the savage South American dictatorships as fervently as she denounced Russia for punishing men who had fought beside the Nazi enemy. 'It makes a good story, but you've left out some details.' Gusev had been right; right in everything he said in his defence. Martin's cigarette was smoked down; he rubbed it out on the ground with his heel.

The gallant Tsarist officer Yurovsky, the Cossack generals, the volunteer Ukrainians, the romantic Cossack cavalry itself, a nation within a nation. They had killed themselves because they were guilty and afraid of punishment; they had been executed for treason, committed against their country and their own people during a war of pure survival. Now, because of a few émigré fanatics and a sharp American politician, they would go down in Western history as martyrs. He began to walk to the exit, slowly; the place had emptied, only a few technicians remained. The streets outside were empty too; the crowds, the police, the media, had all gone home. It was a warm June evening; he found his car and began to drive, with all the windows open. His head ached and he needed a drink.

Volkov had sat mesmerized in front of the television screen in the library of the Château Grandcour. He had drawn up one of the leather armchairs and hunched himself on top of the set; he found himself shaking, and rushed away guiltily to get a large vodka, which he drank very quickly. He didn't like taking Anton Kruger's drink without asking; he felt uncomfortable being alone in the Château while they were away, but he had nowhere else to go. There was no luxury like television in his own meagre room. He watched, still shaking spasmodically from nervous tension, and when the scene in the studio showed Nicholas and Gusev, he gave a choked cry and gripped himself tightly with both arms. Much of the subtlety of what was said passed over him; he heard only what he wished to hear, the long catalogue of his people's sufferings, epitomized in the deaths and suicide in his own family. He listened, and he wept, without noticing it, and his fists clenched until they ached. It was all coming out. The truth at last. He watched Gusev and gloated. When he described Volkov's father and his men as traitors, Volkov raged at his image on the screen. Volkov's father had been an officer in the White Ukrainian division. An émigré, like Michael Yurovsky. Elise Rodzinskaya's father had joined the SS and served in the extermination squads that operated against the Jews in Russia . . . that was nothing to do with him. . . . He didn't know who the other two who interrupted were. An American woman and a Frenchman; one seemed to side with Gusev, while the woman was speaking in *their* favour. . . . When the programme blacked out and switched to the streets outside, he swore at the sight of the police and the troops. He wished himself there with Yurovsky and the Krugers, sharing the danger with them. When the studio came into view again, and Gusev was released, he lost control of himself for a moment, and threw the empty vodka glass against the wall.

The commentaries still went on, the scene changed to the exterior of the building, and through the rage and disappointment, he heard words that calmed him.

A face well known as a news commentator appeared on the screen. 'So ends the most amazing sequel to a political kidnapping within living memory. Not just the man Grigor Malenkov, alias Feodor Gusev, was on trial tonight, but Soviet justice and Western morality! What some have called treason and others patriotism have had to be defined and defended. Whatever the verdict our world today delivers on the repatriation of those Russians to their homeland, the verdict on Grigor Malenkov cannot remain in doubt. The only doubt left is what will happen to him when he returns to Russia. Ironically, it is now his fate to be sent home.'

Volkov sat still, considering that. Slowly he smiled. Clever Anton Kruger. A man of genius. 'Ironically, it is now his fate to be sent home.'

A man who had allowed himself to be the subject of a public debate, to bring the Soviet Union into the witness box before the world – who had conceded a tremendous moral victory to the enemy in exchange for his own life. Volkov went down on hands and knees and cleaned up the broken glass. He went out, exhilarated, and poured another drink, bigger than the last, and drank it down. He pushed the armchair back into its place, and settled into it. He had forgotten about shooting Fritz von Bronsart; he fell asleep.

They were rushed out through a side entrance; two police cars raced up, back doors swinging, and the Krugers, Nicholas and Anna, Zepirov and Elise, were bundled inside and driven away. They had to pass the perimeter of the crowd outside the studio; there were television cameras and portable lights hastily erected, a mob of photographers and reporters, police cars and motorcyclists.

They proceeded in convoy until they had reached the centre of Paris; at the back of the Invalides the leading car, with the Krugers and Elise, pulled into the kerb. The second car stopped just behind them. The gendarme sitting in the front turned to Nicholas. 'We leave you here,' he said curtly.

'But I wouldn't advise any of you to go home. The media will have set up camp by now, waiting for you. And you're to give no interviews, and no photographs – understood?' He looked at his passengers with loathing; filthy terrorists, his expression said.

'We'll go to a hotel for tonight,' Nicholas said.

'Right,' the policeman turned away contemptuously. 'Get out, then.'

The Krugers were standing on the pavement, Elise beside them. Zepirov said anxiously to Nicholas, 'My wife – I can't just leave her to cope on her own – I've got to go home –'

'Go home then,' Nicholas said. 'You'll be all right. Take yourself off tomorrow – have you anywhere to go?'

'My wife's brother,' Zepirov said uncertainly. 'If he'll have us after this.'

Anton and Régine came close to them; Elise stood slightly in the background. Kruger looked suddenly very tired; for the first time Anna saw him as an old man. Régine was holding his arm protectively. They were alone in the quiet street, the six of them, standing in a little group under the lamplight. The police cars had gone. Nicholas came up to Anton and held out his hand. He clasped it and then they both embraced. 'We won,' Nicholas said. 'Thanks to you.'

'Everyone played their part,' Anton said slowly. 'Now thank God, our dead can rest in peace. But there won't be much peace for the rest of us for a long time.'

'I don't care,' Elise Rodzinskaya said. Under the lamplight her face was wet with tears. 'My father – I wish I'd had the gun . . .' She turned suddenly and hurried away into the shadows.

'I think I'll go too,' Zepirov said. 'I can get the Métro home –' He shook hands with Anton and Nicholas, bowed to Anna and Régine. For a moment he straightened as he looked at them.

'I'm proud of everything we did,' he said. 'My mother and father and my little sister – and all the friends we had who died rather than go back, they're proud of us too. God protect you all.' Then his shoulders drooped, and he became himself again as he too went on his way.

'We'll go back to the Château,' Régine said. 'They won't follow us there tonight; we're supposed to be staying in Paris. I want to get Anton home.'

Nicholas spoke to Anton. 'We'll get in touch tomorrow. After what Gusev said, we've got to decide what to do. Anna and I will spend tonight in a hotel; we'll probably have to stay away from the apartment for some days. Goodnight, Régine. Take care of him –'

Anna kissed them; for a moment she saw something sad in the older woman's eyes.

'Be careful, my dears,' she said. And then the Krugers too were gone. They found a taxi which took them to the Hôtel des Deux Mondes in the Avenue de l'Opéra. It was a modest, conservative hotel, much used by businessmen on trips to Paris.

Their room was clean and functional, brightly lit. Nicholas shut the door and held out his arms. For some time they didn't speak; they stood locked together, not even kissing. Anna held him close, her eyes shut, feeling the comfort of his body and the strength of his hold upon her. There was an extraordinary sense of loneliness in the impersonal hotel room.

'I want you to know something,' Nicholas said suddenly.

holding her a little away from him. 'And you've got to believe it. I wouldn't have shot him in cold blood.'

'I knew that,' Anna answered. 'I knew it was bluff; but no one else did, thank God. I can't believe it's really over – there's such a sense of anti-climax. Do you feel it?'

'We all did,' Nicholas said. He sat down on the bed, holding on to her hand. 'All the planning, the danger, the tension, and then suddenly it was all over – I feel terribly tired, that's all. But happy too, in a strange way.'

'Because of your father,' she said gently.

'Yes, and because of Zepirov's family and Maximova's and all the others. I can't think in millions, only in people. Now the world knows what really happened. That's more important than what they'll do to Gusev when he gets back to Russia – You haven't stopped loving me, have you?'

'You always ask that,' Anna whispered. 'When you know the answer.'

'It isn't over, my love,' he said, when they were side by side, waiting for sleep. 'You haven't got immunity from us.' Gusev's last words, and the death sentence in his eyes as he looked at them. She didn't know about that. He wasn't going to tell her, until he and Anton had worked out what was best for the members of 'Return'.

'I know it isn't,' Anna answered, not understanding.

'But the fuss will die down after a time. Go to sleep, darling.' He felt her slip away, but he lay looking at the reflection of the street lights through the gaps in the window curtains, unable to sleep. Elise, Zepirov, Natalie Maximova, little Olga Jellnik, Volkov – what had happened to him? – they would all have to be protected. The Krugers had the money and the means; so had he and Anna. All those on the outer perimeter who had helped in small ways, gathered bits of information, worked out routes – people without resources. Little by little they would be discovered. And pursued. The street lights were competing with the dawn before Nicholas finally slept.

Régine Kruger put her arms round her husband. 'You look so

tired, my darling. This has been a dreadful strain for you,' she said tenderly. 'Go straight to bed and I'll bring you a hot drink.' Anton shook his head. 'No, thank you, sweetheart; let's go into the library. I feel like a drink, then we'll go up together.'

Régine looked round the room. A single standard lamp was burning; the rest of the room was in deep shadow. There was no need for the housekeeper to leave lights on when the Château was unoccupied; it had been completely burglar-proofed. She must remember to mention that.

'What would you like?' she asked her husband.

'Whisky and soda,' he said. He eased himself on to the big leather sofa. His back ached and he felt very tired.

'I'll have the same,' Régine said. She came and sat beside him. They sipped their drinks in silence for a few moments.

'Well,' she said. 'You've done it for them.'

'Yes,' Anton nodded. 'I did my part. It was a perfect operation. He exposed himself as a murderer and a coward.'

'Getting Sheila Campbell on to that programme was pure genius,' his wife said.

'Yes,' Kruger smiled. 'That's where a professional politician scores over the amateur. I couldn't risk leaving it to Nicholas alone. She clinched the case against him. They ought to be well satisfied.'

'What will happen to him when he goes back?' she asked.

'Nothing spectacular,' Anton said. 'In the old days, of course, he'd have been given some kind of show trial so he could confess he'd been working for the West and the kidnapping was all part of it. Now – who knows? I actually brought this question up to them, and they said they weren't interested in making a public example of him at home. Politically, he's ruined, and that's what they wanted.'

'Zemenov –' Régine said. 'He could be another Beria –'

'Not if Gusev succeeded,' Anton disagreed. 'They've always been enemies. If Gusev became Chairman, Zemenov was finished; so the KGB got their blow in first.'

'But what a price to pay for ruining him,' Régine said slowly. 'It's one thing to have a few people know about Yalta, but now it's the whole world –'

'They wouldn't care about that,' Anton said. He cradled his glass of whisky in both hands. 'Stalin was the villain – but what about Britain and America? Allied soldiers sent them back, politicians like Eden delivered them . . . no, they won't care too much about the propaganda side of it. They'll sit back and watch the West tear itself to pieces over the moral issues and how guilty *they* were. We've destroyed Gusev for them and so far as anyone outside the service back home knows, it was all done by émigré Russians. It's been a very clever, cunning operation.'

'What about you?' she said. 'Surely to God they'll leave you alone now – you've done what they wanted –'

'I think there's a good chance,' Kruger said. 'I'm totally exposed after tonight. I think we can slip off somewhere like Switzerland, and they won't bother me again.'

'What about the others?' Régine said sadly. 'Nicholas and Anna – I grew so fond of them – poor Zepirov and his family –'

'Now, darling,' Anton said, 'don't get upset. They got what they wanted. They all knew the risks. They've buried their dead with honour. Maybe nothing will happen to them . . .'

'You don't believe that,' she said. 'They won't be allowed to get away with it. If the service is going to keep its part a secret from the Politburo, then it's got to deal with every one of them. . . . Isn't there anything you can do?'

'No,' he said. 'I can tell them to scatter and try to hide. But they'll be found. One after the other. And not only by us. Never mind that nonsense about immunity. SDECE will pick them off, just as a warning to anyone else with funny ideas. They're all as good as dead, my darling, and there's nothing we can do to help them.'

'Volkov,' Régine said. 'What happened to him?'

'It's not important,' Anton Kruger said. He finished his whisky, and heaved himself up. 'He was half crazy anyway – the sooner someone catches up with him the better. Come along, sweetheart; tonight we sleep and tomorrow we make our travel arrangements. I think Switzerland might be very peaceful . . .'

He stopped, seeing the expression on his wife's face; her eyes were wide and her mouth slowly opening to emit a scream.

Volkov stepped from the shadows into the light cast by the single lamp.

The headlines screamed at Sheila Campbell. KGB vengeance. Double murder at Château. Émigré Russians shot dead. . . . She read the newspapers, beginning with the sober statements from papers like *France-Jour*, and *Le Figaro*, and ending with the tabloids. Ruth was having breakfast with her, and she saw the colour fading from her employer's face. Sheila threw the papers down. 'Revenge killings,' she said. 'You realize what this means – get my daughter's apartment! She'd better come over here right away!' Ruth turned to her after a few moments. 'No answer,' she said. Sheila got up quickly. 'We'll go round,' she said. 'They're probably not taking calls. Maybe the press is camping all round them. Come on, hurry, ring down for the car.'

Ruth looked at her. 'You don't think they'd do anything to her?' she said slowly. Sheila pulled on her jacket, grabbed her handbag. 'If they've got to those other two that quickly, Nicholas will be the next. If they want to shoot him that's okay by me. But I want my daughter safe. Let's go.'

There were photographers and reporters and a TV van outside the house on the Avenue Gabriel. Sheila's car, with American Embassy plates, swept through them, and she pushed her way ruthlessly through the crowd. She pushed the entrance button and a voice crackled through the entryphone.

'It's Mrs Campbell. Open up!' The buzzer sounded; as the door came ajar there was a rush from the newsmen towards it. Sheila slid through it, and slammed it behind her, leaving Ruth outside. She ran up the stairs to the first floor, and rang the bell outside Anna's apartment. The door opened and she saw Paul Martin standing there.

'What the hell are you doing here? Where's my daughter?' He stepped aside and she brushed past him; she paused and looked round the hall.

'Anna? Anna –'

'They're not here,' he said. 'I came round as soon as I saw

the papers. They haven't been back all night.' She turned and looked at him.

'Why should you come?' she said. 'She's nothing to do with you any more.'

He walked into the drawing room ahead of her; he was smoking as always, and he looked more heavy-eyed and crumpled than usual.

'I came for the same reason as you did,' he said slowly. 'To get her to safety. Away from him. If they've hit the Krugers this quickly, you can bet they're waiting for Nicholas.'

'Where *are* they –' Sheila said. 'Where did they go last night?'

'I've called some of her friends,' Paul said. 'Not a word. But I don't know where *he'd* go – they probably took off somewhere to escape that mob outside.'

'Aren't you part of the mob?' Sheila said acidly. 'And how did you get in, by the way?'

'I used to live here,' he answered. 'I just kept a spare key.'

She threw her bag on a chair, and sat down, crossing her legs.

'I've got to find her,' she said. 'Jesus, what a mess she's got herself into this time –' She put a hand to her face and Paul saw to his surprise that she was crying.

'I tried to warn her,' he said. 'I told her what that bastard was mixed up in, but she wouldn't listen. I even got someone in SDECE to talk to her, but she lied to him and went along with the whole business – You realize, don't you, that her life isn't worth a sou, because of this? I never thought they'd strike so quickly – they must have followed the Krugers back from the studio last night.' He stopped and Sheila looked at him.

'You think they followed Anna and Nicholas? You think something could have already happened to them –'

'I don't know,' he said. 'What do you plan to do?'

'Call the Embassy,' she said, getting up. 'Get the Ambassador on to the top men in security. She's got to be found and protected. They can throw him to the fishes for all I care. I just want her back safe.'

'There's one thing you've overlooked,' he said. 'Supposing

she is found and they're both all right, what happens if she won't leave him?'

'We'll sort that out when we come to it,' Sheila snapped. She was beside Anna's desk, reaching for the telephone. 'There's no point in having muscle if you don't use it. And, thank God, I've got plenty of muscle!'

'I hope you didn't mind me coming here,' Volkov said. The lady looked at him across her coffee cup and smiled. He looked very tired, poor man, and nervous, as if he'd slept badly. When she opened her door to him that morning, he had just stood and stammered, until she gently ushered him inside. There was a large black neutered cat asleep on the armchair; she lifted him off and made Volkov sit down. She was certain that he hadn't had breakfast, so she made him some. It was such a long time since she had been able to look after a man.

'I'm very glad,' she said. 'I thought about you a lot, and I hoped to see you again. This is a really nice surprise.'

Volkov set his cup down; his hand was trembling. 'I have nowhere to go,' he said. 'I wondered if I could stay a day or two. I'd be happy to pay, of course.'

'I wouldn't dream of it,' she answered; the same pink blush had come into her cheeks as when he kissed her hand. 'You seem upset,' she ventured, very tactfully. 'Is there anything the matter? Can I help?'

He looked past her, focusing on the arrangement of potted plants which stood on a wire stand in the window, but seeing nothing of them. His eyes filled with tears and one slid down his cheek on to his chin, and fell.

'Last night,' he said. 'I lost a good friend. Someone I trusted; have you ever lost someone like that?'

'My husband,' she said quietly. 'I know how you feel. Was it a long illness?'

'No,' Volkov said slowly. He wiped his hand across his eyes. 'It was over very quickly. I feel quite dead myself.' She came and put her hand on his shoulder; it rested on him lightly as a bird. 'You mustn't fret,' she said. 'It doesn't do any good. I know – I used to cry and cry. And being on your own is the worst thing – you stay here with me for a few days till you feel better. I'd be very glad of the company.'

'I wouldn't be a nuisance,' Volkov said. He covered his face with his hands and she slipped her arm around him while he sobbed, and waited quietly. He couldn't have got the job in Paris, and then his friend had died . . . poor man, he really needed someone to look after him. And he was such a gentleman too. She had a spare bedroom where he could stay, and perhaps if she made him very comfortable . . .

'There,' she said, 'There – cry if you want to. It'll make you feel better. I understand just how you feel . . .'

'We found a long-range transmitter hidden in the stereo set,' Raoul Jumeaux said. 'And a lot of other stuff, including the latest Russian decoding machine, made up to look like a cassette. In my opinion, Kruger had been working for the Russians for years.'

Although it was light outside, the curtains in Sheila's sitting room at the Ritz were drawn and the artificial lights were on. Raoul Jumeaux sat and smoked his pipe, and sipped the drink Ruth had put by his elbow. Yurovsky and his wife were seated side by side on the uncomfortable little French sofa; his men had picked them up at noon, as they were leaving the Hôtel des Deux Mondes. Jumeaux had concealed his true feelings towards them. His Colonel's instructions were clear. Find them, and deliver them to the Ritz. The American Ambassador himself had intervened, and every precaution was to be taken to protect them. Until the girl could be put on a plane to New York and that pestilential female tycoon with her. . . .

Sheila, sipping a glass of white wine, stood by the fireplace, watching Jumeaux. She was immaculately groomed as usual, all traces of the morning's emotion soothed away by a hot bath and twenty minutes' relaxation on her bed. She had put her arms briefly round Anna when they first arrived, and then stepped quickly away, as if the display embarrassed her. She hadn't spoken to Nicholas at all. They were holding hands, and this disturbed her. It was going to make the arrangement she and the Embassy and Jumeaux had worked out that much more difficult.

Anna was obviously going to behave like a fool. As usual, when it came to men. She concentrated on the Frenchman. Very cool and pragmatic, with the pipe. She hadn't forbidden him to smoke it, though she objected to the smell, because he was so very necessary to the solution of the problem.

'Why?' she heard Nicholas ask, and his voice was hoarse and weary. 'Why did he do it – why did he work for them –?'

Jumeaux's broad shoulders lifted in a Gallic shrug. 'Probably blackmail. Kruger made a lot of money very quickly, and you don't do that without breaking a few rules. We'll find it out in time, but I'd say he was probably being blackmailed by the KGB and he went along with them. Your little group was a perfect cover for him; he used all of you to carry out a very intricate KGB manoeuvre.'

'I don't believe it,' Anna said slowly. Her hand gripped Nicholas's tightly. He looked grey and stunned. 'Anton Kruger hated the Communists – he'd never have done anything to help them!'

'My dear Madame Yurovsky,' Jumeaux hoped he sounded patient. 'One of the main reasons I discounted all you people was the extremely sophisticated and professional planning of Malenkov's kidnapping. That persuaded a lot of us that he had instigated the whole thing himself. When traces of Niacyn gas were found by our analysts, I *knew* that whoever had abducted him had access to materials which were quite beyond the resources of a group of Russian émigrés. But there was something else that bothered me.' He paused, applied his lighter to the pipe and puffed out smoke. 'If the kidnapping was efficient, the Soviet security was appallingly lax. Surely, it must have occurred to you, Yurovsky, that you got away with it all a little too easily? Didn't you ever have any doubts?'

'They let us take him,' Nicholas said. 'That's what you mean.'

'Of course they did,' Jumeaux said. 'They gave Kruger the gas, and they fluffed their own security to let you get away with it. The whole operation was masterminded by our old friend

Zemenov. I hope,' he added, allowing a little malice to show, 'that you realize exactly what fools you all made of yourselves.'

'Then why did they kill them both?' Anna demanded. The cold sick feeling couldn't be fought off; Jumeaux, Ruth the secretary, her mother – they were like figures in a play. Nicholas was holding her hand and that was real. The Krugers were murdered; her first reaction had been blind shock and horror. But the real horror was in that level, pedantic voice, explaining that it had all been a loathsome deception, an obscene hoax in which she and Nicholas and all the others of good faith had been manipulated.

'I don't know,' Jumeaux answered the question. 'Personally I don't think they did. I'm not very concerned, to be honest. Kruger got what he deserved. How far his wife was implicated' – again the shrug – 'she could have just been there at the wrong moment. But let us say that they disposed of their agent after he'd stopped being useful to them. What is absolutely certain is that every member of "Return" will be liquidated by the Russians.'

'Even though they cooked the whole thing up themselves?' Ruth stared at him. It was the first time she had spoken.

'They could hardly let the kidnapping of a member of the Praesidium go unpunished,' he reminded her. 'Especially if they want to escape suspicion at home. Whoever wanted to wreck Malenkov and it must be the KGB chief, Zemenov, at the back of it, they've got to keep everyone convinced it was these people. They'll get every one of them in the next few months. Which brings me to you, Yurovsky, and your wife. Frankly, you're an embarrassment to us. We're deporting you from France.'

Nicholas let go of Anna's hand. He brought out a cigarette case and took two cigarettes and lit them. He gave her one and gently smiled at her. There was an odd look about his eyes.

'Where are we going?'

'The States,' Sheila answered him. 'We can lose you there. It's been done with defectors, we can hide you and Anna – no problem.' She spoke curtly, dismissing his objections.

'I see,' Nicholas said. He looked at Anna and smiled once

more; she had a jolt of recognition. The face in the faded photograph in the little gold watch, with a curve to the mouth which was suddenly identical to his. . . .

'I don't want to go,' she said. Jumeaux considered her with blank eyes.

'You have no choice,' he said. 'You'll be put on the plane.'

'You don't know how damned lucky you are,' Sheila snapped, talking to Nicholas. 'You've had your heroics – you ought to know what's going to happen to you if you and Anna don't get out. Personally, I think the French authorities have been extremely helpful. I'm very grateful to them. The plane leaves in an hour and forty minutes. I'm going with you. But you and Anna travel separately. M. Jumeaux thinks it's safer.'

Nicholas stood up, Anna did the same. Again their fingers intertwined.

'I want to talk to Anna alone,' he said. 'Just for five minutes.'

Sheila hesitated, but Jumeaux showed no sign of disagreement.

'Why not?' he said. 'Go in there, into the bedroom. But only five minutes.'

Nicholas closed the door behind them. Sheila's bed, draped and majestic, stood in the centre; a big vàse of roses and stephanotis shed their scent.

He took her in his arms.

'We did the right thing,' he said suddenly. 'However it's been twisted and perverted, we told the truth. Three million people were sacrificed in secret; it can never be hidden again. We've got to hold on to that. It's all that matters. Kruger doesn't matter – the lies and the killing and the dirty intrigue – they haven't won, my darling. They don't see it, but it's our victory. Now I want you to be very sensible and brave.' He turned her face towards him. 'No tears, my love.'

'I know what you're going to say,' Anna said. 'And I won't do it. I won't . . .'

'You go back with your mother,' Nicholas said. 'I'll try and join you later. If they're looking for me they won't worry about you. And I've got to try and help the others. I can't walk off and leave them. . . . You're all I have in the world, my darling.

The best reason I know for saving myself because that way I'll come back to you. But I want you in safety. I'm going out to tell them now.'

She couldn't stop him. He pulled away from her, and her cry followed him as he went back into the room. She heard him say to Jumeaux, quite calmly, 'I refuse to go to the United States. I want my wife to go, but I refuse. She'll be in danger if I'm with her. And you can't deport me, or take any official action against me. You made a promise before fifty million people. You can't break it.' Anna stood frozen for those few moments, unaware of the tears pouring unchecked down her face. She heard her mother say, 'I think that's sensible.' And then the sound of a door closing.

They brought her downstairs in the lift, muffled in one of Sheila's coats; Jumeaux and Ruth Paterson, with her arm around Anna. She had been given the alternative to going freely: she would be given a sedative and taken out by ambulance. Jumeaux, listening to the hysterical pleading, was stony-faced and icy calm. She was going on the plane to New York. Her husband had elected to stay behind for her sake, which was very sensible and admirable, and that was the end of it. 'Come on,' Sheila said briskly. 'Pull yourself together. He did the right thing. He'll make his own way. Ruth, you go down with her, I'll see you on board.'

There was a moment in the hotel foyer when Anna hesitated; immediately Jumeaux caught her arm and Ruth closed in on the other side of her. They walked her out and on to the Place Vendôme. A car drew up, and the back door opened. Paul Martin put his head out of the window of the driver's seat.

'I'm taking you to the airport,' he said. 'Less conspicuous than going with Sheila. Get in.' He watched her in the driving mirror; the secretary was beside her. She looked tense and upset. It was difficult to see his ex-wife's face because her head drooped forward and a screen of hair concealed it. He saw Ruth Paterson put an arm round her. He moved the car away from the pavement.

'He'll be along,' Paul Martin said. 'Don't worry.'

'He isn't coming,' Ruth answered from the back. 'He's

staying behind. She's being put on the plane by force. They said they'd give her a shot if she gave any trouble.'

He could see Anna now; she'd brushed the hair away and leaned back.

'I'll come back,' she said. 'I'll just come back and look for him, that's all.' He winced, seeing the soundless weeping reflected. They were motionless at a traffic light.

'He wouldn't go because of her,' Ruth Paterson said. 'He didn't want to put her at risk. The goddamned irony of it is, they weren't going to take him anyway. Sheila and that Frenchman had it all fixed – you and I were to take her to the airport, and he was going to be left behind!'

'How very nice,' Paul Martin said. 'Very nice indeed.'

'He beat them to it,' Ruth said. 'He just walked out into the room and said he was staying. My Christ, that's what I call love –'

The car was moving forward; Martin had found himself a cigarette, and lit it, steering with one hand.

Anna leaned forward; 'If you ever loved me,' she said, 'stop this car and let me out.' He didn't answer; for a moment their eyes held in the reflection of the driving mirror. 'With my resources,' Anna said, 'we can get away. Alone, they'll get him. And when they do, I might as well be dead myself.'

He didn't answer. He eased the car into the pavement, to the fury of a Volkswagen behind, who hooted at him for not signalling.

'There's a cab over there,' Paul Martin said. 'Good luck, darling. Think of me sometimes.' The back door opened and slammed shut; he had a brief glimpse of her face as she bent towards him, and then she was running to the stationary taxi.

He looked round at Ruth Paterson.

'Sheila'll fire me for this,' she said.

'I won't be Jumeaux's best friend either.' He eased out into the traffic. 'We could say she just jumped out, if that'll help,' he suggested. 'I don't want to deprive an attractive girl of a good job.' There was a little grin on his mouth.

'I think,' Ruth Paterson said, 'I'm just about ready to quit anyway. Why don't we find somewhere and have a drink – I'll get a later plane.'

'Why not have dinner with me and get a plane tomorrow morning?'

'Why not?' She opened her handbag, slipped out the mirror and looked at herself. 'Tell me,' she said. 'Do you think they'll make it?'

Paul Martin shook his head. 'I don't know,' he said. 'But they'll be together. And that was what she wanted.' At the next intersection he swung left on the way back into the centre of Paris.

Bestselling Thriller/Suspense

☐ Voices on the Wind	Evelyn Anthony	£2.50
☐ See You Later, Alligator	William F. Buckley	£2.50
☐ Hell is Always Today	Jack Higgins	£1.75
☐ Brought in Dead	Harry Patterson	£1.95
☐ The Graveyard Shift	Harry Patterson	£1.95
☐ Maxwell's Train	Christopher Hyde	£2.50
☐ Russian Spring	Dennis Jones	£2.50
☐ Nightbloom	Herbert Lieberman	£2.50
☐ Basikasingo	John Matthews	£2.95
☐ The Secret Lovers	Charles McCarry	£2.50
☐ Fletch	Gregory Mcdonald	£1.95
☐ Green Monday	Michael M. Thomas	£2.95
☐ Someone Else's Money	Michael M. Thomas	£2.50
☐ Albatross	Evelyn Anthony	£2.50
☐ The Avenue of the Dead	Evelyn Anthony	£2.50

ARROW BOOKS, BOOKSERVICE BY POST, PO BOX 29, DOUGLAS, ISLE OF MAN, BRITISH ISLES

NAME ....

ADDRESS ....

....

....

Please enclose a cheque or postal order made out to Arrow Books Ltd. for the amount due and allow the following for postage and packing.

U.K. CUSTOMERS: Please allow 22p per book to a maximum of £3.00.

B.F.P.O. & EIRE: Please allow 22p per book to a maximum of £3.00.

OVERSEAS CUSTOMERS: Please allow 22p per book.

Whilst every effort is made to keep prices low it is sometimes necessary to increase cover prices at short notice. Arrow Books reserve the right to show new retail prices on covers which may differ from those previously advertised in the text or elsewhere.

A Selection of Arrow Bestsellers